Image Carriers

*The Shocking Secret Behind the Life
After Death Discovery*

Genel Anthony

Image Carriers: The Shocking Secret Behind the Life After Death Discovery by Genel Anthony.

Edited for Audio by Genel Anthony 2023.

First Printed 2011 ©

Reprinted 2020

ISBN: 978-0-646-83271-5

This book is a work of fiction. Names, characters, places, and incidents are either the product of the author's imagination or are used fictitiously, and any resemblance to any actual persons, living or dead, events, or locales is entirely coincidental.

Contents

Author's Note...6

Chapter One New Friendship..10

Chapter Two Image Carriers..35

Chapter Three Making Contact.....................................49

Chapter Four Welcome Aboard 62

Chapter Five The Group...94

Chapter Six The NO People..103

Chapter Seven Messages and Signs 110

Chapter Eight A Strange Land 127

Chapter Nine Introductions...130

Chapter Ten Old Friendship..149

Chapter Eleven Putting the Pieces Together...............186

Chapter Twelve Trying to Make Contact....................207

Chapter Thirteen The Plot Thickens 213

Chapter Fourteen The Party 226

Chapter Fifteen The De-Stress Room 254

Chapter Sixteen Private Investigations 265

Chapter Seventeen The BBQ 303

Chapter Eighteen The Update 316

Chapter Nineteen Overseer in the Making..................322

Chapter Twenty FAUNA 326

Chapter Twenty-One The United Show Begins............338

Chapter Twenty-Two Common Sense 343

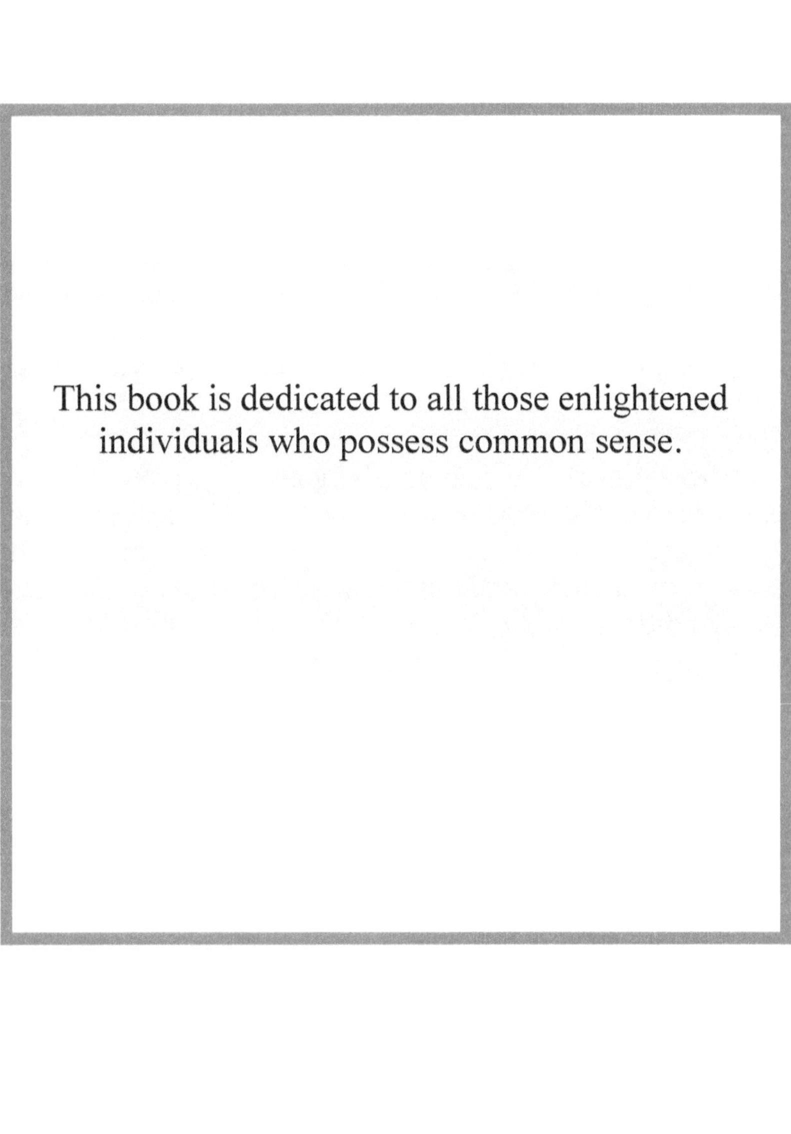

This book is dedicated to all those enlightened individuals who possess common sense.

Author's Note

Although I've always been fascinated by the mysterious and metaphysical aspects of our world, I never imagined I would one day commit myself to writing an entire book on the subject. So, you can understand my astonishment when I first learned of the discovery pointing to life after death. What struck me even more deeply was realizing that, long before this revelation became public, a select few had not only known about it but had even anticipated its arrival.

These remarkable individuals, guided by profound mystical experiences and higher knowledge, had already formed organized circles where they gathered to share insights that constantly challenged my own scientific training and worldview. The deeper I delved into their world, the clearer it became that reality was far richer than I had once believed—and what I learned ultimately reshaped my perspective on life itself.

In this book, you'll uncover what I discovered while working alongside these extraordinary people over the past several years, as well as the wisdom they entrusted to me. You'll also find original essays and material designed to stretch your thinking and invite you to question long-held beliefs.

With more than twenty years of experience in the field of human development, I've noticed a kind of awakening taking place around this very subject. Some individuals have always been aware but hesitant to share their otherworldly encounters, while others are only now beginning to awaken and feel ready to speak. Increasingly, I've observed people opening up about their mystical experiences— some eager to discuss at length the unsettling dreams and spooky messages that left them shaken.

Yet, amid this growing openness, there remains a smaller, quieter group—known as *Image Carriers*—who keep their spiritual knowledge closely guarded, revealing little of what they hold within.

In these pages, I have set out to share what I discovered while working with them. Every detail recorded here has been corroborated and approved by them, and they have generously allowed me to share parts of their stories. Still, when it comes to the paranormal, matters are rarely clear-cut. Evidence is often disputed, for the simple reason that such experiences cannot be measured or quantified in traditional ways. Much like faith, you either believe—or you don't. And then there are those who remain undecided, quietly sensing that life extends beyond the visible and tangible world into realms unseen.

What appears obvious to one person may be invisible to another. Each reader will draw different insights from this book. Those who are naturally perceptive may notice connections and subtleties that others overlook.

This book carries no political agenda; it exists solely to recount my encounters with these remarkable individuals. In fact, it runs counter to politics altogether. The Image Carriers who entrusted me with their stories come from every walk of life, yet their messages, though diverse in expression, share an uncanny similarity.

The term **Image Carrier** is the traditional name given to people with clairvoyant gifts. While they resemble the psychics and mystics we know today, they are distinct in both method and discipline. They belong to small, secretive groups that meet regularly to share experiences, guided by their Overseer and a circle of trusted supporters. As you move through these chapters, you will come to know them more closely.

Image Carriers have existed for centuries—perhaps millennia—passing their knowledge quietly from one generation to the next. They claim insights that can be both astonishing and unsettling, knowledge that modern science is only beginning to grasp. Where a researcher might toil for years to solve a problem, they can arrive at an answer instantly through intuition.

Yet, history has not been kind to them. For centuries, Image Carriers were branded as dangerous, banished from their communities, and persecuted for their unusual abilities. Many were forced to live as nomads, blending in, concealing their powers, and masking their telepathic gifts simply to survive.

Why were such harmless individuals treated so harshly? The answer is simple. Those in power—whether in the past or the present—view Image Carriers as a threat. They see what others cannot, often revealing corruption, deception, and immoral acts before they happen. That ability makes them the natural enemies of the powerful and the corrupt.

Even today, many Image Carriers live in secrecy, meeting quietly while remaining watchful. Some vanish without explanation. For this reason, many choose to stay hidden, protecting themselves from those who would rather see them silenced.

Imagine, for a moment, having no formal training in science or mathematics, yet perceiving the bigger picture effortlessly. You can sense what is true and what is false. You can glimpse other dimensions, understand the workings of quantum physics, and even touch upon the mysteries of happiness, health, and healing. You live in harmony with the natural world and are aware of the electromagnetic field that surrounds and connects you—a field through which information and untapped energy flows. You hold the key to an immense reservoir of wisdom, drawn not only from within but from the very fabric of the cosmos itself.

That kind of knowledge makes you powerful. And it is precisely this power that some would rather erase from the world.

As noted earlier, Some Image Carriers have disappeared without explanation and have never resurfaced. In the pages that follow, I will examine why they are regarded with such fear by the elites, the mainstream media, government bodies, military and intelligence circles, religious organisations, the cabal, and other groups driven by hidden or harmful agendas—including the establishment itself. Even covert figures and criminals share this fear, often joining forces with otherwise respectable organisations to attack Image Carriers collectively, driving these peaceful individuals into hiding.

In presenting these accounts, I have tried to write in a way that is straightforward and accessible while remaining true to the experiences I've encountered. Please bear in mind, however, that this book is not structured around neat questions followed by tidy answers. The hidden—or quantum—realms simply do not work that way. Clear, black-and-white, rational explanations are not always possible. Instead, this work is an invitation for you to explore and perhaps shed light on some of these intricate and mysterious matters yourself.

I encourage readers to take notes for their own reference. While the meaning of these events may not be immediately obvious, I believe that, in time, many of these pieces will fall into place. Also remember: each person follows their own unique spiritual—and personal—path. Some may find immediate resonance with what is written here, while for others the insights will unfold more gradually.

Genel Anthony

Chapter One
New Friendship

I want to remember this for the rest of my life!

The city basked in the warmth of an unusually gentle autumn sun, the kind that made the air shimmer with a golden glow and coaxed a lingering sweetness from the fading blooms. Cape Town, South Africa beamed with life, its streets alive with a kaleidoscope of people—tourists snapping photos, street vendors calling out their wares, office workers weaving briskly through the crowds. Every corner seemed to hum with energy; every alleyway held a story waiting to unfold.

Above it all loomed Table Mountain, the great grey monolith, steadfast and unyielding. Its flat summit was slowly swallowed by wisps of drifting clouds, as if the sky itself were tentatively brushing against its peak. The mountain watched silently over the city, an ever-present guardian with moods as unpredictable as the weather. Some days it appeared serene and protective, its broad shoulders softened by sunlight; other days, shrouded in mist, it was imposing and unknowable, a reminder of nature's quiet power and enduring mystery. To the people below, it was more than a landmark—it was a living witness to their lives, a silent companion in the rhythm of the city.

Far above the ocean, a narrow road traced the curves of the iconic mountain. Along it sped a sleek red two-door sports car, chosen with care by its passengers—two striking young women whose laughter echoed above the music blaring from the stereo. Their off-key singing and carefree energy matched the car's bold colour, a symbol of their youth and spontaneity. At dawn, they had chased the light to hidden lookouts along the mountain and coastline, capturing the raw beauty of nature through their lenses. Now, with cameras full and spirits high, they made their way back to their beachfront hotel in Camps Bay.

As they wound their way along the serpentine road, the grey mountain rose beside them like an ancient sentinel, its sheer cliff face slicing into the sky with an austere majesty. To their left, the land plunged precipitously into the restless Atlantic, waves smashing against jagged rocks far below, sending bursts of mist high into the air. Along the cliff edge, stubborn tufts of grass and scraggly wildflowers clung defiantly to the stone, their colours muted yet vibrant against the relentless winds that swept in from the sea. The air carried a briny tang, sharp and invigorating, a constant reminder of the wild expanse below.

At the wheel sat a striking blonde woman, twenty-eight, her features refined and her presence quietly commanding. Her accent, lilting and unmistakably foreign, marked her as a traveller passing through this rugged corner of the world. She was visiting a family acquaintance in a small, tranquil town roughly two hours from Cape Town, eager to experience something different from the familiar. Beside her, the passenger—a graceful, slender African woman of twenty-two—exuded a calm, understated elegance. Her family ran a modest, timeworn shop in the village where the blonde was staying, and in the close-knit impoverished, but friendly community, a fast friendship had blossomed. Despite differences in background, the women discovered an uncanny number of shared passions: books, music, and a hunger for adventure that seemed to pulse in tandem.

Their getaway had been planned with care over the past month, each detail chosen to maximize both excitement and comfort. They had secured a charming hotel in Cape Town's picturesque Bay Area, a perfect base for their explorations. At night, they danced beneath the stars, their laughter echoing into the balmy sea air, and during the day, they wandered through sun-drenched coastal beaches, lush, fragrant gardens, and serene mountain sanctuaries. Every path they took, every hidden cove or flowering alcove, became a memory captured in the hundreds of photographs they took, each image a testament to their shared joy and the fleeting magic of discovery.

Overwhelmed by the breathtaking panorama that unfolded on either side of the winding mountain road, the driver threw her head back and gasped, "I want to remember this for the rest of my life!" Her words, carried on the brisk sea wind, seemed almost too small for the grandeur surrounding them. Her friend's laughter rang out, light and carefree, cutting through the roar of the ocean below. "Me too!" she replied, her voice mingling with the crisp air, and for a brief moment, the world felt suspended in pure, unfiltered joy. The two erupted into peals of laughter, their voices mingling with the occasional cry of gulls and the distant crash of waves against jagged cliffs.

But the mountain road offered little mercy. With the asphalt nearly empty, the driver allowed herself a dangerous distraction, her eyes drifting toward the horizon, toward the endless expanse of sky meeting the roiling Atlantic. She kept just enough attention on the lane markings to avoid catastrophe, yet she knew in the quiet of her mind that a single misstep could send them hurtling over the cliff into the cold, unrelenting waters far below. They sang along with another familiar song, their voices rising in reckless joy, until the car lurched forward violently.

The passenger, caught entirely off guard, was thrown against the dashboard with terrifying force. A sickening crack filled the car as her jaw fractured, pain erupting in a scream that seemed too sharp to be contained by the small vehicle. The driver's blood ran cold. Panic surged as she slammed on the brakes, tires skidding on gravel and the narrow edge of road. But the car didn't stop, it continued erratically down the mountainside. Blood pooled across the passenger's face, a stark contrast against her dark skin, and her hands clawed at the seat and door, desperate to steady herself. Her voice rose in a strangled cry, "Stop the car! Please, stop!"

Fear and disbelief collided in the driver's mind as she continued to slam the brakes—only to realize they were not working. The road, the sheer drop, the ocean below—all of it seemed to close in on her. She instinctively tried to hug the curve of the mountain, to press the car against the rock face and avoid plummeting into the abyss, but the vehicle betrayed her. A tire—or perhaps something worse—exploded in a violent, thunderous boom, sending the small red car spinning wildly. The world became a blur of motion and sound: the screech of metal on metal, the shattered glass raining inside the cabin, the merciless spin of the car as it ricocheted off the cliffside.

Time seemed to stretch and fracture. She could only watch in horror as the car finally slammed into the mountainside, tumbling before finally landing upside down on the middle of the road, its roof crumpled. Both women were bleeding, trapped, and stunned. Pain radiated through the driver's body as she tried to assess the chaos. Her passenger had somehow slipped from her seatbelt, lying sprawled across the dented interior, motionless. Through the jagged opening of the sunroof, shards of glass glittered on the road like sinister jewels.

Peripheral movement caught her eye—a large dark-coloured vehicle, its form momentarily silhouetted as it rounded the bend, coming to an abrupt stop. For a few seconds, the world was eerily silent except for her ragged breaths and the distant crash of waves below. Then a terrifying, high-pitched screech began: metal scraping relentlessly against the ground. Her upside-down car was moving again, sliding uncontrollably along the road. She felt the pulse of panic hammering in her chest, the creeping numbness of shock mingling with fear as consciousness threatened to slip away.

Trapped, bleeding, powerless and suspended unnaturally by her seatbelt, the driver hung upside down, her hair brushing against the cracked roof of the car. Every instinct screamed at her, but there was nothing to do—gravity had claimed them. The ocean waited hungrily below, dark and roiling, each wave promising a sudden, merciless embrace. She knew, with a terrifying certainty, that it was only a matter of moments before the car tumbled over the edge, plunging into the churning abyss beneath.

Adam Green, a man in his early forties, lived on the far side of the world, in the southern hemisphere, on a sunburnt island renowned for its golden dunes, surf-lashed beaches, and an astonishing variety of marsupials found nowhere else. His home was Sydney, Australia—a city where cosmopolitan energy collided with natural beauty, where harbor bridges arched against cobalt skies and the scent of saltwater drifted through the streets.

A successful business consultant and counsellor, Adam ran a private practice that catered to a diverse clientele. He guided corporate executives through the labyrinth of office politics, negotiation strategies, and leadership challenges, while also supporting individuals navigating the subtler, often unspoken struggles of mental health. In his work, he was both strategist and empath, combining insight with intuition, a combination that had earned him both respect and trust.

Adam lived a life that many would call solitary, but he found comfort in it. His only housemate was a young man who had drifted into his orbit years ago and had, in every meaningful way, become his adopted son. Together, they shared a quiet, tastefully furnished home on Sydney's lower north shore, a mere fifteen-minute drive from Adam's downtown office. Their household ran on an easy rhythm: shared meals, muted conversations over morning coffee, and the occasional laughter echoing through sunlit rooms.

That morning, as always, the alarm blared at 6:30 a.m., cutting through the early calm. The night had been crisp, and the morning air carried a bite that made Adam pull the blanket tighter around his shoulders before reluctantly swinging his legs out of bed. His lean frame felt heavier than usual, weighted by lingering fatigue, yet he moved with practiced ease toward the bathroom. The mirror caught the familiar reflection: short, dark brown hair now thinning at the crown, a subtle reminder of the years steadily passing. Still, his strong, chiselled features retained a magnetic presence, one that drew glances even when he was lost in thought.

As he stooped slightly to examine himself in the small bathroom mirror, his greying sideburns demanded attention. Should he pluck them, or would dyeing them be a more suitable camouflage? The question seemed trivial, yet it lingered—an emblem of the delicate balance between accepting age and resisting it. Adam shook his head slightly, the corners of his lips tugging into a half-smile. Life was an accumulation of such choices, he mused, some insignificant, others quietly shaping the person he was becoming.

Before leaving for work, Adam headed towards the kitchen, intending only a quick bite to stave off the morning hunger. But as he made his way down the hallway, the acrid sting of burnt toast caught in his nose, slowing his steps as he tried to breathe around the lingering fumes. His young housemate was already awake, as usual, the radio blaring some energetic pop tune that clashed violently with the early-morning quiet. And, unsurprisingly, breakfast had suffered another casualty under his care.

"Morning," they mumbled, eyes half-lidded, voice muffled by the headphones he refused to remove. Adam responded with a curt nod and a faint, habitual sigh. Conversation at this hour was never more than a token gesture—a ritual of civility rather than exchange.

He moved to the kettle, pouring himself a steaming cup of tea, the warmth seeping into his hands. His gaze wandered to the youth again, a flicker of disapproval lingering. The sloppy, rumpled clothing, the perpetually untidy hair—Adam had long stopped attempting to intervene. He remembered, faintly amused and slightly exasperated, the months of gentle suggestions, all ignored. For now, it was easier to accept the chaos than fight it.

Outside, the crisp autumn air hit him like a fresh wave. Sydney's port city had already awoken fully, settling into its familiar routine. Car horns punctuated the hum of morning traffic, weaving around stalled buses and impatient taxis. The radio, now softly murmuring from his car, detailed the usual miseries: gridlock at the harbour bridge, a minor fender-bender on George Street, a delivery truck wedged under a low overpass. The city felt both alive and indifferent, each problem just another note in its relentless symphony.

By the time Adam reached the office, the familiar city din had faded slightly beneath the building's glass-and-steel façade. Nestled in the heart of the business district, the clinic was a small pocket of order amid chaos. One of the constants that brought him quiet satisfaction each day was seeing Carol, his long-serving receptionist. With her calm efficiency, she managed the flow of clients, calls, and paperwork, keeping the clinic running as smoothly as clockwork. Her presence was a stabilizing force—a reminder that, even in a bustling, unpredictable city, some things could still be counted on.

Adam had spent years cultivating his reputation as both a business consultant and a mental health practitioner, and over time, his practice grew into a thriving hub for people seeking both professional guidance and personal relief. His expertise was respected, but what truly set him apart—what made his name circulate far beyond his regular circles—was the now-famous *De-Stress Room*.

Clients whispered about it in waiting areas and coffee shops, describing the place almost like a sanctuary. Those who had stepped inside spoke of emerging lighter, calmer, and with an almost renewed sense of vitality, as though the tension had been lifted not only from their bodies but from their very spirits. Rumours swirled that some people left looking years younger, their worries smoothed from their faces. For long-term clients, time in the De-Stress Room was not just an indulgence but a ritual, woven into their healing journey. Newcomers, meanwhile, were often intrigued—curious looks and hushed questions passed between them as they wondered how one earned access to this private space that had taken on something of a mythic quality.

Presiding over this practice with quiet authority was Carol. She was more than a receptionist or an office manager; she was the living heartbeat of the place. In her late forties, seven years Adam's senior, Carol moved through the rooms with an air of composure and purpose that made her seem almost untouchable. Visitors and clients alike instinctively respected her, though she never demanded it. Her loyalty to Adam was steadfast, not out of obligation but out of deep gratitude. To Carol, Adam was not merely an employer but a true friend—the kind one rarely encountered in a lifetime.

Their bond had been forged years earlier during one of the lowest points in her life. After a painful separation from her husband, Carol had found herself and her young daughter with nowhere to go but emergency accommodation. The uncertainty, the shame, the sheer exhaustion of starting over had weighed heavily on her. During that period, Adam had been a constant presence. He gave her space when she needed it, time when she had none, and compassion when the world seemed to offer little. His kindness left an indelible mark on Carol's heart, and from that time forward, she committed herself not only to her own recovery but also to supporting Adam and his work. She often said, with quiet conviction, that she would never forget what he had done for her and her child in their darkest days.

That morning Adam received word of an unusual visit. Evelyn, one of his former clients, was coming by. She was no longer under his professional care, but years ago she had been a regular presence in his office. Adam had first met her through a referral from her psychiatrist after she had endured a brief, but difficult hospital stay. Evelyn had arrived nervous and withdrawn, speaking openly of her desire to retreat from the "big bad world." Her psychiatrist had believed she needed ongoing support more than medication, and Adam had stepped into that role.

For two years, Adam worked with Evelyn on and off, helping her face the anxiety and fear that had long gripped her. Eventually, he determined that she no longer required structured sessions, and the formal relationship came to a close. But Evelyn never fully disappeared. She stayed in contact with Adam—not as a patient, but as a friend, or at least as close to a friend as she allowed anyone to be. For someone who had always struggled to trust, her connection to Adam was unusual, even remarkable. Carol, too, had grown to care for her, and so Evelyn's occasional visits were welcomed with understanding.

Evelyn was a puzzle to most people. In her early fifties, she did not conform to the expectations of a middle-aged woman. Her appearance was unkempt, her shoulder-length brown hair streaked with grey she refused to dye or tame. Clothing was functional rather than flattering, chosen with little care for fashion or impression. Her mannerisms, too, unsettled many. She often spoke bluntly, with an abruptness that could be mistaken for rudeness or arrogance. Some dismissed her as socially awkward; others considered her eccentric at best, unstable at worst.

But Adam had learned to see past these quirks. He understood that her evasions, her tendency to deflect personal questions, and her refusal to share details about her past were not rudeness but shields— her way of protecting herself from further pain. She seemed to have built a fortress around her private life, never allowing others to peer inside. It intrigued Adam, who often wondered what events had shaped her into the guarded, enigmatic figure she had become.

To the casual observer, Evelyn might have appeared to be on the fringes of sanity, someone "slightly unhinged," as more than one person had whispered. But she carried herself with an almost defiant indifference to public opinion. She embraced her eccentricity, wearing it like a cloak, and moved through life on her own terms. For all her secrecy, Carol had once uncovered a small truth: Evelyn lived quietly on Sydney's northern beaches. Yet even this detail was hard to pin down, as Evelyn would vanish without explanation for months, only to reappear as if nothing had happened, offering no justification and expecting none.

Interestingly, Adam's colleagues often regarded him as peculiar in his own right. His reputation had been marked years earlier by an article he published on what he called the *NO people*. The phrase had drawn attention after he was interviewed by a well-known journalist, and it stuck—though not without controversy.

"NO persons," short for "non-operating persons," referred to individuals who seemed unable to fully engage with life. They often described themselves as hollow, listless, or perpetually exhausted, moving through life's routines with little sense of meaning or achievement. Adam noticed that many struggled to separate trivial concerns from vital ones, fixating on the former while neglecting the latter. They expressed guilt over matters beyond their control or felt guilt with no clear cause at all. Some professionals dismissed these patterns as symptoms of anxiety or depression, but Adam saw them as something more—a state of non-operation, of existing but not truly living.

Though some peers bristled at the label, calling it stigmatizing, Adam stood by it. He believed words had power, and the phrase *NO persons* had given his clients a way to name their struggle. Many told him the concept resonated with them deeply and motivated them to break free from the cycle of passivity. Carol and many of Adam's clients embraced the phrase as well, though out of respect for its critics, they often used the acronym quietly, like a shared secret.

The controversy only strengthened Adam's resolve. Some colleagues admired his insight, while others turned away from him, uncomfortable with his unconventional methods. Yet for Adam, the proof was in the people. The clients who thanked him, who said his work had given them a language for their pain, and who began to live with renewed energy—these were what mattered. His ideas had spread, adopted by colleagues who saw their value. And in the eyes of many who passed through his practice, Adam Green was not merely a consultant or a therapist, but a guide who helped people reclaim their place in the world.

Most people understand that mental health disorders rarely follow a predictable script. They can surface in ways as varied and complex as the people who experience them. Symptoms differ not only in intensity but also in form, sometimes manifesting as restlessness and tension, other times as lethargy or despair. Even when two people receive the same diagnosis—say, anxiety—their inner experiences and outer struggles may be profoundly different. Consequently, their treatment paths also diverge, shaped by unique personalities, histories, and circumstances.

It was within this landscape of complexity that the term "NO people" emerged. Simple yet striking, the phrase gave language to a condition many felt but could not articulate: the state of being "non-operating," disconnected from one's true potential. For countless individuals, this terminology carried an almost liberating effect. Naming their struggle gave them both clarity and a starting point, a way of recognizing themselves in a broader pattern. For many, that recognition marked the first step toward change—the initial spark that could ignite a journey toward peace, purpose, and fulfillment.

Adam built upon this concept with a structured approach that blended clarity with compassion. His method was both practical and transformative, designed to guide NO people back to a state of authentic functioning. The first and most essential step, he insisted, was responsibility. Until a person could shift from perceiving themselves as a victim of life to becoming an active creator of it, no therapy would truly take root. A victim mindset may soothe in the short term—offering excuses, explanations, and external blame—but it left individuals powerless. Real progress required a profound shift in identity: the realization that each person is both the architect and conductor of their own destiny.

As word spread, those identifying as NO people began seeking Adam out. They came in droves, each carrying their burden of despair, confusion, and unmet expectations. Many confessed that they had lived under illusions for years, encouraged by well-meaning parents, teachers, or peers who told them they could "do anything" without considering the deeper truths of their abilities, passions, or psychological wounds. Instead of empowerment, this blind encouragement often led them astray, sending them down roads misaligned with their strengths or desires. When those roads dead-ended, they were left stranded—frustrated, disoriented, and disheartened.

Such repeated failures eroded hope, deepening the swamp of inertia. Yet within Adam's practice, many found a different outcome. By gradually confronting the illusions they had carried, they learned to separate who they truly were from who others expected them to be. They reclaimed their voices, redefined their paths, and, in time, experienced a profound liberation. It became common for former clients to place their hands over their hearts and say with pride: *"I was once a NO person—but not anymore."* They had crossed the threshold from stagnation into movement, from victimhood into authorship of their own lives.

Not everyone, however, celebrated Adam's approach. His article on NO people stirred controversy in the media. Carol, a long-time supporter and confidante, often felt anger rise when she read criticisms aimed at him. Much of what was said was not merely exaggerated but fabricated stories crafted to sensationalize, twisting Adam's message into something harsh or villainous. Carol could not understand how such falsehoods were permitted in print or on air without consequence.

Adam himself, however, remained unfazed. His practice in Sydney thrived, known for its integrity, effectiveness, and no-nonsense methods. His reputation extended far beyond ordinary circles; he was sought out by some of Australia's most influential and affluent figures. He knew his work stood on solid ground, and no headline could undo that. If anything, the attacks seemed fuelled by envy. Carol suspected that certain journalists resented Adam's success and the way his unconventional views challenged their own ideologies. He represented a perspective they couldn't control, and that unsettled them.

While Adam continued to build his professional influence, his private curiosities expanded into unusual realms. In recent years, he had developed a deep interest in psychic phenomena, extrasensory perception, and other mysteries that lay beyond conventional psychology. This was not mere whimsy—it arose from repeated accounts shared by his clients. The frequency and consistency of their stories demanded attention. Some spoke of vivid premonitions, others of strange visions, and still others of encounters that defied rational explanation. Adam had long held an openness to the possibility that reality stretched beyond the material world. These reports only reignited that curiosity.

Adding to this intrigue were Adam's own personal experiences—strange episodes from his past that lingered at the edges of memory. For years, he had dismissed them as tricks of the imagination, fleeting distortions too odd to dwell on. Yet three particular incidents continued to haunt him. Try as he might, he could neither rationalize nor forget them.

The earliest of these involved a girl named Drizzy, who was around the same age as him. Adam was ten years old, a solitary boy living in a rural neighbourhood on the fringe of a vast forest. One summer afternoon after school, he encountered her near the park, a pale-skinned girl with long, jet-black hair and a name unlike any he had heard before. She claimed she lived nearby, though Adam never saw her with family or at school. She was about his age, and though odd in manner and appearance, she drew him in.

Drizzy wasn't well-liked by Adam's other friends, who found her strange and just weird. Earrings at her age were frowned upon in the late 1960s, and her foreign-seeming name only deepened suspicion. But Adam felt something different. She was bold and tomboyish, just as quick at climbing trees or exploring the woods as any boy. She was unafraid of adventure, and Adam admired that fearlessness.

Over time, their friendship became more private. They would meet at the treehouse deep in the woods, built the year before by Adam and his friends, or they wandered by the riverbank, speaking of things Adam could never later recall in detail. What he did remember was the feeling: fascination, curiosity, a sense that being with her opened a doorway into something larger than himself.

Then came the afternoon by the river, an encounter etched into his mind forever. Drizzy had plucked a wild white calla lily, which grew in abundance in that area, and held it up for him to admire. At first, he humoured her, but soon he noticed something impossible: tiny specks, like glowing motes, swarming around the golden centre of the flower. They weren't insects—not in movement, not in form. They seemed jelly like, transparent, almost artificial, as if they belonged to a world far beyond his own.

When he looked back at Drizzy, he saw more—faint specks of colour hovering around her body, pulsing like fireflies. The forest itself seemed to shimmer, the grass glowing faintly blue, the trees glowing with a soft reddish light. Even the river shimmered with shifting rainbows across its surface. It was as if the very fabric of reality had been peeled back to reveal another layer beneath.

Adam rubbed his eyes, terrified that something was wrong with him, but the vision remained. The world was no longer the same, and Drizzy was at the centre of it.

Time seemed to grind to a halt, as though the very air around him had thickened. Panic surged through Adam in a sudden, uncontrollable wave. His chest tightened, and his vision blurred with a strange haze that made the world appear unreal, dreamlike. Desperate to shake it off, he rubbed his eyes so hard it hurt, saying to himself that this had to be some kind of trick, some illusion he'd conjured from exhaustion or nerves.

Drizzy's voice broke through, laced with concern. "Adam, what's wrong?" she asked again. But her words didn't sound right—they dragged unnaturally, distorted, as though stretched on a warped cassette tape playing at the wrong speed. The sound crawled through his ears, leaving him more terrified with each syllable.

"I don't know! Something's wrong!" Adam shouted, his own voice sharp, ragged with fear.

And then, as if reality itself had decided to mock him, Drizzy stopped moving. One moment she was standing there, eyebrows furrowed, trying to reach him; the next she was utterly still. Frozen in mid-breath. Her eyes locked forward in a vacant stare, her lips slightly parted, her expression blank—lifeless. She looked like a statue, carved from flesh instead of stone.

That was the breaking point. Something inside Adam snapped. Fear overwhelmed reason, and his instincts took control. He bolted—turned on his heel and ran as fast as his legs could carry him, crashing through undergrowth, the sound of his breath loud in his ears. He didn't care about the trail, didn't look back to see if Drizzy had moved, didn't want to. The silence of her frozen figure clung to him like a shadow, chasing him even as he fled.

The forest blurred past him, tall pines bending overhead, their needles whispering as he tore through the path he knew so well. Slowly, painfully, the world began to realign. His vision steadied; the surreal distortion receded. By the time he stumbled onto the road that led back to his house, the lights that had filled his head—those shimmering, impossible lights—were gone. Everything looked ordinary again.

At home, he slammed the door shut behind him, heart still hammering, and collapsed on his bed. The familiar comfort of his room felt like a fortress. His body trembled as adrenaline drained away, and eventually, exhaustion won. He drifted into a restless sleep, though the memory of that evening replayed itself in fragments even as he dreamed. When he woke, he tried to bury it, convincing himself it was best forgotten. Yet the nagging question lingered—should he tell his parents, risk sounding insane, or keep it hidden, locked away in silence?

Drizzy was different from most kids in the neighbourhood. Her family had roots in another culture, another faith, one that the tight-knit community around Adam didn't entirely understand—or welcome. The climate of the time was steeped in "us versus them." Most families socialized only within their own circles, and children inherited those divisions without question. Adam's friends, shaped by those unspoken rules, had not liked it when Drizzy joined their games.

Those games, though innocent on the surface—cowboys and outlaws, soldiers and spies—always seemed to carry a subtle undertone. The "home team" won. The "outsiders" lost. The unspoken lesson embedded itself early: belonging meant victory, difference meant defeat.

Drizzy refused to accept that. Bold, defiant, and persistent, she kept showing up no matter how frosty the welcome. She joined the games, laughed the loudest, and ignored the negative looks and comments. Adam had admired that about her, even if he hadn't fully understood it at the time.

After the encounter by the river and the eerie lily flower, Adam didn't see her for weeks. That wasn't unusual. Drizzy often appeared in bursts—spending afternoons or weekends with the group, then vanishing for stretches without explanation. It was the same with many of his friends, who sometimes disappeared because of family obligations, church events, or punishments. It was part of childhood's rhythm.

When she reappeared a month later, Adam avoided mentioning what had happened. But Drizzy, relentless as always, demanded an explanation. At first, he brushed her off. He didn't want to relive the terror, didn't want to admit that he had nearly broken-down crying in front of her. Yet she pressed harder, refusing to let it go, until finally he gave in and recounted the whole story—how the world had warped, how her words had stretched, how she had frozen like a mannequin in the woods.

Drizzy stared at him with wide eyes. From her perspective, nothing unusual had happened. She remembered Adam yelling something unintelligible before tearing down the path toward home. She hadn't frozen at all, hadn't even noticed anything strange.

At first, she looked sceptical. But as he spoke, something shifted in her expression—scepticism turned to wonder, then to excitement.

That was when she told him about her aunt. Her aunt believed in people who could see the truth behind the veil of reality. Special ones. They could glimpse the light surrounding living beings, slip along the timeline itself, vanish and reappear, or see across vast distances. To her, Adam's experience wasn't madness—it was possibility.

"You have to meet her," Drizzy urged, her eyes bright with eagerness. But Adam recoiled. No matter how much she insisted, he refused. He wanted to forget, not dive deeper.

Drizzy drifted out of his life about a year later. She vanished as suddenly as she had arrived. He assumed her family had moved. He never saw her again.

Adam told himself it was an allergic reaction, something in the air or the lily itself. He had played near that river countless times before without issue, but denial was easier. The alternative—that Drizzy's aunt had been right—was unthinkable. And yet, he never forgot the lilies. Even now, decades later, he refuses to go near a white lily flower.

Years later, at twenty-two, Adam faced something else that defied reason.

He lived in a large rental with two flatmates. One evening, when they were both away, he hosted a small gathering. Friends filled the house with laughter, chatter, and loud music. There were drinks, jokes, even a sense of belonging that Adam quietly cherished. When everyone finally left, the silence that followed felt almost sacred. He locked the door, stumbled into bed, and lay smiling to himself, imagining his friends talking about the party the next day.

The moonlight seeped through his curtains, silvering the walls and floor. Shadows pooled in the corners. His body relaxed, heavy with the warmth of alcohol, ready to surrender to sleep. Then, some instinct stirred. His eyes flicked open.

Near the doorway, an oval shape shimmered. Egg-like, four to five feet tall, it hovered in the air as though struggling to manifest. Its outline wavered, flickering between presence and absence, like static on a screen that couldn't hold an image steady. Adam's chest went cold. His mind grasped for rational explanations—a trick of the light, drunken imagination—but none fit.

For a breathless moment, it hung there, silent, formless yet undeniably real. Adam's heart hammered against his ribs. He couldn't move, couldn't even blink.

Then, in a blur of impossible speed, the thing surged forward.

The spell of paralysis shattered. Adam screamed, scrambling upright, nearly knocking over the lamp on his bedside table. He snatched it, switched it on, holding it like a shield.

The light banished the shadows. His room looked normal again. The apparition was gone.

And yet, Adam knew—he hadn't imagined it.

Shaking, Adam scanned the room, his breath shallow and uneven. The shadows seemed to cling to the corners, as though reluctant to release whatever had just been there. Whatever that thing was, it was gone now. Yet the terror clung to him, wrapping around his chest like a vice. His heart thundered so violently that for a fleeting moment he feared it might simply give out. He told himself it couldn't have been a dream—dreams didn't leave the taste of iron in the mouth, or a trembling that refused to subside. Nor had it been the result of drink; his mind was too clear for that. No—whatever had happened had been real. Too real. And it had shaken him to his core.

Years slipped by, though the memory of that night never truly left him. Now in his early thirties, living in Sydney, Adam encountered another inexplicable event—one that would etch itself even more deeply into his life.

It was a warm mid-January evening. The cicadas had finally gone quiet outside his bedroom window, and the hum of the city had dimmed into a muffled hush. Adam had gone to bed as usual, finishing a few pages of his book before setting it aside next to him on his bed. His bedside light was still on, its glow soft and steady. He remembered pulling the covers up, closing his eyes, and sinking into the familiar weight of sleep.

The next thing he knew, he wasn't lying in bed at all. He was above it.

Suspended, weightless, he looked down at the figure below. For a moment, confusion dulled his awareness. Who was he seeing? Then the truth struck with a jolt that sent a shiver through his incorporeal form. It was him. His own body, motionless, chest rising and falling with his breath. He was both the observer and the observed.

Before he could grasp what was happening, an unseen force pulled him upward with astonishing speed. It was not a violent surge, but an impossibly smooth propulsion, as if he were being carried on a current without resistance. The sensation was overwhelming—yet oddly serene. The room, the house, the city, the earth itself dissolved beneath him, swallowed by endless darkness. Around him stretched a vast void, punctured only by distant points of light, stars scattered like glittering shards of glass across a boundless canvas.

Despite the strangeness of it all, Adam felt no fear. Only stillness. Peace. A sense that he was exactly where he was meant to be.

Then came the voices. Faint at first—laughter, chatter, the hum of joyous conversation carried on some invisible wind. They were above him, pulling him further into the mystery. As he rose, the voices grew louder, clearer, alive with warmth and mirth. Soon he could see it: a platform suspended in the air, a structure without supports, its underside glowing faintly in the blackness. He slowed as he approached, as though invited to linger at the threshold. Though he couldn't see the gathering itself, he knew it was there. A celebration. A community. A homecoming of sorts.

Just as anticipation swelled in his chest, a voice rang out— sharp, clear, commanding.

"Adam! What are you doing? Go back! Go back now!"

The words froze him instantly. It wasn't just familiar—it was achingly personal; a voice etched into the deepest layers of his being. He knew it. Knew it with a certainty that defied doubt.

Without hesitation, he obeyed. The upward pull reversed, and he felt himself descending rapidly, the glowing platform shrinking, the voices fading into silence. Faster and faster he fell through the dark until—

He woke up.

The bedroom light still burned softly overhead. His book lay askew beside him on the edge of the bed. For a moment, he stared at the ceiling, breath caught, half-expecting someone to be peering down at him. But there was only stillness, no one there.

And yet, the voice lingered. He knew whose it was. The woman who had raised him with unshakable love, whose presence had been his anchor through childhood. The one he had lost long ago, his beloved grandmother.

That night would not be forgotten.

These experiences—shocking, disorienting, and strangely luminous—were only fragments of a much larger pattern in Adam's life. And as he would later discover, he was not alone. Many people, from all walks of life, quietly confided in him their own uncanny moments—glimpses of something beyond ordinary reality. Some wondered if these were true encounters with another realm, fleeting openings into an afterlife that sometimes allowed the living a brief taste of what lay beyond. Others argued they were simply creations of the mind: bursts of neural activity, chemical storms, illusions vivid enough to be indistinguishable from truth.

Adam, ever the listener, found himself becoming a magnet for such stories. His clients—many of them outwardly rational, successful individuals—seemed compelled to share their most private, otherworldly experiences with him. He joked, half-seriously, that he must have something written on his forehead that invited confessions of the paranormal.

But the stories were not random. Patterns emerged. When events aligned in uncanny ways, some called it synchronicity, others, intuition. What fascinated Adam most was that the very people confessing these things were often CEOs, executives, leaders in their fields—the kind who built empires on logic, strategy, and hard data. And yet, behind closed doors, they admitted that much of their success hinged on something far less tangible. They trusted their instincts. They followed hunches. They consulted psychics. Some used rituals or practices they dared not reveal to colleagues. These admissions were whispered with both pride and shame, as though acknowledging a secret superpower that might cost them credibility if revealed.

Over time, Adam came to see that venturing into the mystical was not rare—it was simply hidden. Beneath the polished surfaces of boardrooms and business strategies, countless individuals quietly leaned on forces that could not be measured or quantified.

His own approach to counselling, shaped by his life experiences, reflected this belief. To some, he was visionary—embracing a holistic model that wove together biology, psychology, social dynamics, spirituality, and even concepts drawn from quantum theory. To others, he was uncomfortably unconventional.

Adam often voiced his concern that modern society had drifted too far into fragmentation. Specialists carved up the human condition into compartments—sleep problems for one doctor, stress for another, relationships for yet another—without ever addressing how profoundly interconnected these things truly were. He pointed out that traditional healers once treated the person as a whole, understanding that mind, body, spirit, and environment formed a web that could not be pulled apart without consequence.

In contrast, modern systems often left individuals feeling fractured, emotionally exhausted, and financially strained. A person with insomnia might see three different specialists, none of whom spoke to each other, while the underlying knots of stress and grief remained unaddressed.

Adam's philosophy was simple yet radical: healing meant wholeness. To ignore the unseen dimensions of human experience was to ignore a vital part of what it meant to be alive.

Given the relentless, high-pressure environments in which many of Adam's clients operated, it was no surprise that they often arrived burdened with intense emotional strain. Episodes of rage, frustration, anxiety, and despair were common, and these states of mind often translated into physical suffering—migraines, digestive problems, chest tightness, or chronic fatigue. To Adam, these manifestations were familiar terrain. Yet what set him apart was not only his reliance on evidence-based treatments, but also the deeply personalised, holistic lens through which he approached each client's situation. His work was never mechanical; it was guided by empathy, insight, and a profound respect for the uniqueness of every individual who walked through his door.

Among the many features of his practice, one stood out and consistently drew admiration—the now-famous De-Stress room. For many clients, it was more than a therapeutic tool; it became a refuge. Even a brief session inside could shift a person's emotional state dramatically, dissolving anger and soothing anxiety with startling efficiency. Carol, Adam's loyal receptionist, had seen it countless times. Clients who stormed into the office red-faced, restless, or even trembling with pent-up emotion would later emerge composed, shoulders loosened, and expressions softened. Some even smiled faintly, as though they had been given back a piece of themselves they had forgotten they possessed.

At first, the De-Stress room had been an experimental addition, something Adam never expected to draw so much attention. But its reputation soon escaped the walls of his practice. Client's spoke of it with a mix of reverence and curiosity. Word spread through professional networks, social circles, and eventually into the public sphere. Local journalists featured the room in glossy lifestyle articles, describing it as a "sanctuary in the city." Appointments grew scarce, sometimes booked out months in advance, and past clients returned not just for Adam's expertise but for the experience of the room itself. What began as a quiet therapeutic experiment had, almost inexplicably, transformed into a local phenomenon.

Carol herself made frequent use of the room after hours. Though naturally upbeat, she admitted that even she sometimes needed a place to recharge. She described the sensation as more than relaxation—it was revitalisation, a gentle infusion of energy that touched her spirit. She believed the room held something beyond the tangible, perhaps even spiritual, though she struggled to articulate it in words. Adam, pragmatic by nature, didn't dismiss her interpretation. He sensed there was truth in what she felt, even if it couldn't be measured or easily explained.

At the heart of the room stood a comfy chair angled toward a wall-mounted flat-screen display. Built into the walls were hidden speakers, capable of surrounding the client in layers of sound. The screen offered choices: sweeping vistas of nature, deep oceans, rolling forests, and skies painted with golden sunrises or violet twilight. The audio complemented the visuals—waves crashing, birds calling, or wind moving through trees. Some preferred complete stillness, relying only on the play of coloured light across the walls to guide their inner state. Others lost themselves fully, surrendering to distant landscapes as if they were actually transported there.

Lighting was the room's signature element. Adjustable and dynamic, the system could fill the space with cool, meditative blues, nurturing greens, soft pinks, or radiant golds. The colours weren't just illumination—they moved, shifted, and breathed across the walls in subtle, rhythmic pulses, as though alive with intelligence. Clients often reported that the interplay of light and colour reached them in ways that bypassed words, resonating directly with emotion and memory.

Though clients could adjust the atmosphere themselves, Carol often managed the system from her desk, curating custom experiences for those in need. Many of these programs had been developed through collaboration between Adam and other professionals in fields such as neuroscience, mindfulness, and even music and colour therapy. The aim was always the same: to help clients reconnect with balance, clarity, and self-control.

In addition to soothing visuals, the room offered an array of recorded affirmations and guided exercises. These sessions reinforced themes of resilience, self-awareness, and personal empowerment. Clients learned not only to ease their anxiety but also to strengthen assertiveness, cultivate discipline, and untangle the thought patterns that fuelled destructive habits. The De-Stress room became more than a temporary retreat; it was a place where the seeds of lasting change could be planted.

Recently, Adam unveiled a new addition that elevated the room's impact even further: a groundbreaking visual presentation of the human brain in motion. On the screen, neurons lit up in dazzling bursts of colour, firing and connecting in intricate webs of energy. The animation illustrated how information travels through the brain, shimmering like lightning across a stormy sky. Though inspired by science, the display felt almost transcendent. Clients described the experience as breathtaking—a reminder that transformation begins not in the external world but within the vast, electric landscape of the mind itself.

The effect was profound. Many described the presentation as hypnotic, evoking a sense of connection with their deepest, most authentic self. Reclining in silence, they often reported slipping into altered states of awareness, where stress dissolved and tranquillity emerged. For some, the experience carried the quality of a spiritual awakening: moments of awe, sudden insights, or the quiet certainty that they were capable of change at the deepest levels of their being.

For those who sought gentler sessions, the room could shift into softer modes—green light cascading gently across the walls, harp melodies whispering like a distant lullaby, blue tones shimmering in harmony with the stillness. More than once, a client emerged in tears, not from sadness, but from the unnameable relief of being reminded that peace was still possible.

Carol kept a discreet eye on the room through two cameras connected to her desk monitor. On rare occasions, clients were so overcome with emotion that she needed to intervene, offering grounding and support. At other times, she had to coax reluctant clients out, their eyes wide with reluctance, clinging to the serenity they had discovered within.

Over time, Adam came to see that the De-Stress room was not simply a therapeutic experiment—it was a transformative tool, an extension of his philosophy of care. Its success, combined with his holistic methods, drew the attention of colleagues across the field. Professionals grew curious, then insistent: what exactly was he doing to achieve such extraordinary results? For months, Adam resisted sharing too much, uncertain whether others would understand or misuse the techniques. But when he eventually invited a handful of trusted peers to witness the room for themselves, their reactions left no doubt. They were astonished, some even visibly moved. What Adam had created was more than a room—it was an experience, one that had the power to shift lives in ways that science alone could not yet fully explain.

Chapter Two
Image Carriers

Why don't you close your eyes and acknowledge it right now…

Once upon a time, in a sprawling castle of ivory stone and towering spires, nestled beside a shimmering enchanted lake hidden deep within the mist-draped woods, lived a radiant young princess. She had just turned fifteen, her laughter bright as bells, her spirit alive with dreams of the future. She shared her days with her beloved parents—the King and Queen—who doted upon her, and her playful younger brother, a boy of ten whose boundless energy filled the castle halls with joy.

But then, tragedy struck.

On a bitter, rain-soaked night, the royal carriage overturned on the treacherous winding road back to the castle. Horses screamed, wheels splintered, and in one cruel instant, the King and Queen were lost. The storm carried away their cries, leaving behind only silence. The princess and her little brother—once children of privilege and light—were suddenly orphaned, their world broken.

In their time of need, their aunt, the King's elder sister, stepped forward. An aging, unmarried woman with a reputation for gentleness, she vowed to take them in. She promised to be their guardian, to raise them until they came of age, and to give them the stability they had lost.

Time passed.

The young prince, now twelve, seemed oddly untouched by grief. He carried on with his laughter and mischief, as though life's cruel twist had brushed past him without consequence. But his sister was not so fortunate. As the seasons turned, a shadow grew in her heart.

Though her aunt's words were kind and her hands never harsh, the princess felt a strange unease in her presence. There was no cruelty, no raised voice, no heavy hand—only a quiet tension, like the faint scent of smoke where no fire could be seen. Something about the woman unsettled her, though she could never explain why.

The townsfolk adored the aunt. They sang her praises, applauded her generosity, and called her a hero for sheltering the royal orphans. To all, she was a saintly figure—warm, noble, and selfless. And yet, despite the gentle smile and the soft-spoken words, the princess could not silence the whisper of doubt that lingered in her soul. She did not feel safe.

Her brother never noticed anything strange about the old woman, but she did.

Far from castles and enchanted lakes, in a quiet suburban neighbourhood, lived a thoughtful ten-year-old boy named Joey. He shared a small home with his single mother, his father long absent from the picture. Joey was no ordinary child; he was bright, introspective, and unusually mature for his years. He carried himself with a natural confidence and an easy-going charm that drew people to him. Adults often marvelled at his wisdom.

His grandmother would often boast, "That boy is going places. He's got his head screwed on right—full of good, old-fashioned common sense!" His mother, too, brimmed with pride. Joey was responsible and independent, trustworthy in ways that made him seem older than his age. In many ways, life seemed to smile on him.

When Joey learned that his best friend from school was joining the local Sunday school program, curiosity got the better of him. It sounded like fun: games, outings, group activities every weekend. Together, the boys signed up.

The program was run by a youth worker in his forties. The man welcomed each child with a firm handshake, a warm grin, and an air of easy friendliness. Around fifteen or sixteen children filled the room, their chatter and laughter rising like a chorus. The church community trusted this man without hesitation, and the children seemed to adore him.

But Joey did not.

From the moment their eyes met, a strange discomfort settled over him—an instinctive wariness he could not name. The man had said nothing unkind, done nothing inappropriate, and yet something about him felt… wrong. Joey couldn't explain it, not even to himself.

For several weeks, he tried to ignore the unease. He joined in the games, sang the songs, followed along with the group. But with every passing Sunday, the feeling grew stronger, pressing heavier on his chest. Finally, he stopped going.

His best friend was bewildered. To him, the youth leader was the kindest man he had ever met—funny, warm, and generous. Parents trusted him. Children adored him. He had never done a thing to suggest otherwise. Why, then, had Joey quit?

Joey could not find the words. He only knew that something deep inside warned him to stay away, and he trusted that voice. Others saw a hero; he saw only shadows. And that was enough.

At nearly twenty-three, Gavin had once been the kind of young man who drew people in with ease—charming, witty, and unafraid to speak his mind. Friends remembered him as a natural leader in social circles, a young man with a future brimming with promise. But recently, his behaviour had shifted so dramatically that those closest to him scarcely recognised the person he was becoming. He had grown withdrawn and restless, quick to anger, and on more than one occasion had crossed the line into physical aggression.

His parents—who loved him fiercely and wanted only the best for him—were increasingly anxious, torn between worry and confusion. Gavin still lived at home with them and his younger brother, but his presence in the house had become more shadow than substance. He spent long hours secluded in his room, emerging only when he had to, his silences weighed down by something unspoken.

What no one around him truly understood was that Gavin carried a secret belief—one that shaped his every waking moment. He was convinced he possessed an extraordinary ability: an instinctive power to read people, penetrate their façades, and detect the emotions and hidden truths they carried beneath the surface. At times, these impressions were so strong they consumed him, leaving him restless and raw, as though he had brushed against the currents of something far greater than himself.

When the sensations became unbearable, Gavin forced himself into distraction—video games, exercise, aimless scrolling on his phone—trying desperately to appear ordinary, to blend in. Yet beneath the façade, he wrestled with waves of self-directed anger and despair. He wanted nothing more than to feel "normal," to belong, to be part of the world that seemed to drift further and further from his reach.

As the months passed, the changes in him only deepened. Suspicion settled in. He scrutinised strangers, friends, even neighbours with a wary eye, convinced that some harboured malevolence that only he could detect. More and more, he withdrew from others, convinced that distance was the only way to protect himself.

One neighbour in particular haunted him: Mr. Watson, an elderly man who lived a few doors down. Something about him set Gavin's nerves on edge. He would take the long way around the block rather than pass by Watson's house, and if the man happened to be outside, Gavin's chest would tighten with dread. To Gavin, Watson wasn't just unsettling—he was a threat. When their eyes met across the fence or street, disturbing thoughts would echo in Gavin's mind, sometimes accompanied by a whispering voice that warned him of the man's supposed evil.

The paranoia bled into other areas of his life. In one troubling incident, Gavin bolted from a doctor's office when a physician attempted the simple act of taking his blood pressure. Convinced the doctor's equipment was more than it seemed—that he was being monitored, tracked, maybe even studied for his "ability"—he fled without explanation. His mother, waiting in the reception area, could only watch in stunned silence as her son rushed out with a look of horror on his face and disappeared through the door.

These stories, though unsettling, echo a pattern that is far from unfamiliar. Versions of them have been told countless times—across families, in films, in hushed conversations between friends. They speak to something many of us instinctively recognise: that uncanny human capacity to sense when something is not right. That strange, intuitive stirring we sometimes feel about people or situations.

Why does this happen? Some dismiss it as coincidence, others as paranoia. Yet history—and human experience—suggest otherwise. Perhaps these instincts are remnants of a survival system far older than modern civilisation, an evolutionary radar meant to protect us. Perhaps we all carry fragments of it within us, though most have forgotten how to listen.

Spiritualists, mediums, and psychics have long argued that intuition is more than a hunch—that it is guidance, connection, even a form of higher knowledge. Some swear by such claims; others scoff. The debate endures, but behind it lies a larger, more compelling question: do we dare believe that human perception stretches further than our five senses allow?

Every generation produces individuals who seem different— those who radiate authenticity, kindness, and an inner clarity that draws others in. When you meet such a person, you feel it immediately. A stranger, yet somehow familiar. A presence that calms and comforts without explanation. These individuals often live quietly, uninterested in power or recognition, yet their influence can be profound.

They are sometimes called awakened souls. But in certain circles, whispered across centuries, they have borne another name: **Image Carriers**.

The legend of the Image Carriers tells of people who have always walked among us, hidden in plain sight. They were said to be gifted—some with visions of the future, some with healing touch, others with the uncanny ability to survive what should have been impossible. Their very existence inspired awe and fear in equal measure. Rulers, threatened by their influence, sought to erase their name from history, spreading lies and rumours that painted them as dangerous, corrupt, even demonic.

Yet their true nature was quite the opposite. Carriers of Images lived with deep compassion, guided by forces unseen, their lives woven into a larger truth that transcended ordinary reality. They were not interested in wealth or fame; those pursuits, they understood, poisoned the mind and spirit. Instead, they were attuned to subtler currents—the unseen energies that bind human beings to the universe itself.

Sacred texts and scattered oral traditions claim these individuals have been with us for millennia. In one extraordinary account, a Canadian Overseer safeguarded scrolls unearthed in Egypt in the 1940s, writings believed to be over two thousand years old. They told of mystics and visionaries—Carriers of Images—who lived on the margins of society, holding knowledge that most were too afraid, or too blind, to accept.

Though few in number, they were consistent across generations: highly perceptive, creative, calm, and disinterested in power. While they possessed the capacity to confront corruption and dismantle oppressive systems, they rarely did so directly, preferring instead to quietly plant seeds of wisdom in the lives they touched. Their power was never about domination—it was about illumination.

And so, through secrecy and silence, they endured. Hidden among ordinary people, the Image Carriers live on.

Today, more educated and self-aware parents than ever before are encouraging their children to look inward—to explore not just their intellect or emotional world, but also the spiritual and metaphysical dimensions of their being. These families, often grounded in safety, stability, and love, provide the kind of nurturing environments that allow such explorations to flourish. In many ways, this mirrors the traditions of countless past generations, who also sought to understand life's mysteries through dreams, visions, and inner journeys. Perhaps it is this renewed openness that explains why so many potential *Image Carriers* are beginning to emerge in our time.

But this raises an age-old question: can anyone become an Image Carrier simply through upbringing and environment, or must one be born with this gift, carrying the seed of it within their very being?

The more I reflect on this, the more I lean toward one conclusion: true Image Carriers must be born, not made. Environment alone cannot spark this rare gift. It seems to be etched into the genetic code—something written deep within the DNA, waiting to awaken. That said, environment still plays a crucial role. A gift, no matter how powerful, can remain dormant or even become distorted if nurtured in fear, neglect, or hostility. In contrast, a supportive upbringing filled with joy, laughter, and unconditional encouragement allows the Image Carrier's abilities to blossom with balance and integrity.

Just as eye colour, height, or temperament are passed down through bloodlines, so too are the mysterious qualities that define image-carrying. What has shifted in recent decades—particularly in Western societies—is the cultural space to explore such phenomena without immediate dismissal. Where once such gifts might have been silenced or ridiculed, they are now more openly discussed, and this openness provides fertile ground for those born with the capacity to develop their abilities fully. As a result, we are witnessing not only an increase in the number of Image Carriers, but also a richer variety of spiritual and prophetic messages entering the world. Humanity is slowly learning how to interpret these messages with greater precision and respect.

Yet with growth comes shadow. The rise of genuine Image Carriers has inevitably drawn opportunists—impostors who mimic the language and behaviour of the gifted but seek only personal gain. These individuals distort the work, manipulate the vulnerable, and threaten to undermine authentic progress. In other words, they are there to muddy the waters and keep you from reaching your full spiritual potential.

Another discovery that struck me deeply was that Image Carriers are not uniform in their talents. They exist on a spectrum, each with unique areas of focus. Some specialize in dreams, others in visions, while a few interact directly with unseen energies in ways that defy current understanding. This diversity makes the rating system I was introduced to particularly valuable. By assigning a score from one to ten, it becomes possible to measure, however imperfectly, the level or rating of a Carrier's abilities. A "one" for example, might reflect only the faintest sensitivity to imagery or intuitive impressions, while a "ten" indicates a masterful Carrier, capable of transmitting complex visions, prophetic warnings, and insights that pierce through the boundaries of time itself.

Curiously, those who reach the higher end of the scale—often at levels seven or eight—tend to withdraw from public life. The weight of their abilities seems to drive them inward, toward privacy and seclusion. Unless they discover a supportive community of peers, many choose to hide their gifts altogether. Yet when they do find one another, something remarkable occurs: discreet but highly organized networks emerge.

Within these networks, Image Carriers share their insights— dreams, visions, intuitive flashes—in quiet secrecy. They gather in hidden circles, exchanging knowledge that might otherwise be lost. Surrounding them are supporters: ordinary men and women who believe in their mission. Some of these ally's work behind the scenes to shield Carriers from societal pressures or even legal threats. Others hold positions of influence and use their access to pass on critical information, acting as protectors, advocates, and, at times, whistleblowers. By exposing corruption or warning of dangerous laws, these allies create a buffer, ensuring that Carriers can continue their work without being silenced.

The abilities of Image Carriers themselves span a wide range. Dreamers, for example, often keep notebooks at their bedsides, ready to capture the messages that arrive in sleep. Over time, they learn to distinguish between *conscious dreams*—those shaped by the body, stress, diet, or daily experiences—and *symbolic or unconscious dreams*, which appear to come from beyond ordinary awareness.

Conscious dreams, while vivid, are tied to the body's need to process emotional residue and mental clutter. They act as a cleansing force, preparing the mind for new information. Symbolic or unconscious dreams, however, are of an entirely different nature. They are often described as transmissions from "the other side"—a realm existing outside of space and time, one that might be both a source of knowledge and a destination of the soul.

Some Carriers claim that, in these moments, they glimpse landscapes that are not of this earth, hear languages they have never studied, or speak words they cannot consciously translate yet somehow *understand*. The knowledge arrives not in fragments but as a complete whole—an immediate, embodied knowing that floods the mind and body simultaneously.

These experiences have led many to speculate: is there a dimension beyond our own, accessible only through altered states of awareness? Could Image Carriers, knowingly or unknowingly, step into alternate timelines, moving across past, present, and future with a freedom the rest of us cannot fathom? Perhaps they have unlocked the secret of time itself, or stumbled upon the threshold of the "other side"—a place interwoven with our world but visible only to the initiated.

A common belief among Image Carriers is that the soul exists independently of the body and is capable of travelling freely, unbound by physical limitations. Adam himself, through his investigations, came to suspect that much of the communication he received originated from this non-physical domain. Over time, he entertained an extraordinary possibility: that each of us has a "cosmic twin"—an unseen counterpart existing in a parallel realm.

One Image Carrier referred to this presence as her *Other Self*. She described it as both part of her and yet distinctly separate—an invisible entity she guided but also relied upon for wisdom. According to this teaching, every human being possesses such an Other Self, whether we are aware of it or not. For Image Carriers, the connection is stronger, more conscious, and more active. This relationship, once understood, becomes the bridge between the physical and the eternal, the seen and the unseen.

Many people remain unaware of the existence of a silent companion—an aspect of the self that lives beyond space and time. This presence, often called the **Other Self**, waits patiently in the background of our lives. Though unseen, it can be summoned, engaged with, and even befriended. Tradition holds that the Other Self is born when we are, arriving in that first breath of life and remaining until the final exhale. When death comes, the two selves reunite, merging once more into wholeness.

As you read these words, your Other Self may be closer than you think—perhaps hovering quietly beside you, waiting, wondering whether you are finally connecting the spiritual dots that lead to its recognition.

Tragically, most people never establish this connection. When ignored, the Other Self languishes—stunted, undeveloped, and restless. Deprived of conscious acknowledgement, it drifts like an untutored child, roaming through unseen dimensions in search of its missing counterpart. At times, this wandering creates ripples in the physical world, appearing as unexplained disruptions, things going wrong, ongoing and unexplained sickness, or bad luck. Yet what it longs for is simple: reunion. It longs for affection, guidance, growth, and recognition. Like a faithful student awaiting the wisdom of its teacher, it stands ready to learn. And once that bond is formed, it will return the gift with harmony, vitality, balance, and joy in your life. However, the first step is to accept that it is really there.

Image Carriers, however, are different. They seem born with the keys to this hidden relationship. Their ancestral memory runs deep, encoded not only in their minds but in their very DNA. What some researchers dismiss as "junk DNA" may in fact be a storehouse of ancestral wisdom, lying dormant until awakened by the right energetic field. For Image Carriers, this dormant code acts as a library of knowledge—a set of instructions and insights preserved across generations. When activated, it grants them the ability to interpret the whispers of the Other Self, allowing access to knowledge that transcends the limits of ordinary human experience.

With this bond intact, Image Carriers can bridge the physical and metaphysical realms. The union of the Self and the Other Self forms far more than an inner reconciliation—it becomes a living channel, a conduit through which boundless currents of wisdom, vision, and higher truth flow. In this sacred merging, the individual is no longer confined to the limits of ordinary perception. Instead, they gain access to knowledge so profound that it does not merely illuminate their own path, but radiates outward, touching the lives of all who come near. It stands as the holy weapon and unyielding defence, the force that separates humankind from the wickedness lurking outside.

When the two selves stand united, extraordinary possibilities unfold. The barriers between the physical and the spiritual dissolve, and what was once hidden in shadow becomes clear. Supernatural experiences are not only possible, but inevitable—moments where synchronicities multiply, dreams bleed into waking life, and insights arrive as if whispered from beyond time itself.

This union does not serve the individual alone; it carries within it the potential to alter the collective destiny of families, communities, and even entire cultures. Each person who awakens to their Other Self becomes a beacon, a transmitter of vision and transformation, reminding humanity of its deeper purpose and untapped power. Untapped power many out there do not want you to discover.

Still, one must not mistake Image Carriers for flawless beings of light. Their personalities and messages are far more complex than the idealized image of serene sages radiating kindness. Some are indeed gentle, compassionate, and uplifting. Others, however, are blunt, eccentric, or even rude in their manner. Their revelations are not always comforting—sometimes they carry warnings of death, destruction, or upheaval. A few have been known to foresee tragedy yet choose silence, believing certain events must unfold for reasons beyond human understanding. This paradox—the ability to see yet the choice not to act—remains one of the great mysteries surrounding them.

From my own encounters, I can say this much: Image Carriers are often misunderstood. Some are gentle to the point of invisibility, while others can be sharp-tongued, even confrontational. What unites them is not temperament but the depth of their connection to the Other Self and the clarity of their insights.

Let us return now to the stories of those I introduced earlier— the princess, her younger brother, their enigmatic aunt, Joey, and Gavin. Of these, Gavin stood out as particularly advanced. He possessed the ability to sense hidden motives, avoid negative influences, and even detect a heavy, dark energy radiating from his neighbour, Mr. Watson. Could this capacity mark him as a revolutionary Image Carrier?

Joey, meanwhile, left the youth group and carried on with his life. The young princess remained vigilant, splitting her watchfulness between her playful brother and the mysterious aunt who seemed to cast a shadow over their household. Something about her aunt felt wrong, though she could not explain why. Later, she would learn that her instincts were not unfounded.

Yet not all who appear touched by the extraordinary are genuine Image Carriers. Among the three, only two bore the marks of this path. The third was grappling with something else entirely—a psychiatric condition. Can you guess who?

I share these examples deliberately, to illustrate the delicate line between spiritual sensitivity and psychological illness. The distinction matters, for history is full of individuals who believed themselves chosen or gifted, only to later discover that their visions were symptoms of psychosis, neurological illness, or even a hidden brain tumour. Image Carriers differ sharply from this pattern. They are not impaired. On the contrary, they are often more psychologically resilient, more emotionally intelligent, and more socially balanced than the average person. In the majority, their demeanour tends toward calmness and quiet strength.

Those struggling with psychosis, however, frequently experience fractured relationships, emotional turbulence, and difficulties maintaining consistent social bonds. Their behaviour may appear erratic or even aggressive. Image Carriers, in contrast, avoid conflict and display a grounded clarity that anchors them firmly in reality. They are aware of their boundaries and of right and wrong.

Sadly, Gavin was not an Image Carrier. His growing paranoia, aggression, and distrust pointed to a different path—one of mental illness. In time, he was diagnosed with early-stage schizophrenia. His story, though difficult, is not without hope. With support and care, he and his family have found a measure of stability.

The princess, on the other hand, grew into independence. At eighteen she moved away from her aunt with her brother, taking full responsibility over the castle and its running. Later, she discovered that their aunt had financial motives for keeping them close. Only then did she realize that her instincts had been a warning. Was it mere coincidence, or was her Other Self guiding her toward the truth? The answer remains elusive.

As for Joey, his story is ongoing. Though some suspected darker undertones in the youth worker's past experiences, no evidence has ever surfaced. In truth, sometimes the signals Image Carriers receive cannot be traced to their source. They arrive like fragments of a puzzle, incomplete and mysterious.

The concept of the **Other Self** may help explain these fragments. Imagine your reflection in the mirror—only half of who you are is visible. The other half, invisible yet real, exists in another dimension, woven into your electromagnetic field. This is the silent witness that waits for your recognition. Why don't you close your eyes and acknowledge it right now. It's there, waiting…

And finally, a more personal note. Joey is still part of my life today. Now a young man, he lives with me. You might say I know him best of all, for he plays a central role in this unfolding story. Each morning, his wild hair and loud music fill my kitchen, usually accompanied by the smell of burnt toast. In time, you will come to know Joey, and others like him as more than passing characters. Their lives, and the mysteries surrounding them, are essential to understanding what it truly means to be an Image Carrier.

Chapter Three
Making Contact

As for the visions—she preferred them buried…

Adam had long believed that the mind, body, and spirit could not be separated when it came to counselling—that true healing required more than a checklist of medical procedures or clinical exercises. His programs reflected this conviction, blending modern therapeutic practices with cultural traditions, spiritual exploration, and even the occasional touch of mysticism. To his astonishment, the evidence became undeniable. Clients showed real progress, they began to thrive, and families grew to trust his methods. Children, especially, responded with remarkable openness, embracing his approach and experiencing transformative results.

When the situation demanded it, Adam drew upon a network of professionals: doctors, psychiatrists, physiotherapists, nutritionists, occupational therapists, dieticians. Together they formed carefully tailored strategies, a web of expertise that could include each individual's unique needs. Some of his colleagues, once sceptical, grew intrigued. They began borrowing fragments of his methods—small, practical components at first. Yet while they weren't shy about adopting the physical or psychological techniques, most kept their distance from the spiritual dimensions. In the wider community, subjects like premonitions, intuitive visions, or unexplained sensitivities were too often dismissed as idle superstition, not worthy of serious attention.

But Adam was not easily swayed by popular opinion. Alongside a small circle of kindred spirits, he continued probing into those hidden realms. Encouraged by surprising feedback from some of his corporate clients, he began to wonder about individuals who seemed born with heightened sensitivities—people who could combine cold logic with uncanny intuition. These "Image Carriers," as certain circles called them, had a way of trusting unseen impressions, leaning into invisible currents of knowledge to guide their choices. Adam became convinced they were out there in greater numbers than most realized, quietly shaping their lives—and perhaps even the destinies of others—by listening to what could not be measured.

The thought consumed him. What if he could find them? What if he could listen to their stories, gather their wisdom, and integrate their insights into his programs?

It was on such an evening of restless contemplation that Adam returned home, the scent of rain clinging to his jacket. Inside, Joey was waiting, sprawled comfortably on the couch with the television flickering against his youthful face. The two had shared a home for years, ever since Joey—then only fifteen—had come to live with him. Their bond stretched back even further, to Joey's early childhood, when he and his mother lived only four houses down the road. To outsiders, they often looked like father and son. In truth, their friendship was more unusual, forged out of trust, loyalty, and a sense of connection that defied simple explanation.

Now twenty-two, Joey was half Adam's age but had always carried an aura that felt… older. It wasn't just his quiet maturity—it was something you couldn't name, a sensitivity woven into his very being. Since he was a boy, Joey had displayed flashes of clairvoyance that unsettled even the most pragmatic of minds. He would casually remark on a stranger's hidden motives, or predict the outcome of a television crime drama long before the final act. Murderers, liars, and manipulators—Joey could spot them instantly, without hesitation. His accuracy was unnerving, eight or nine times out of ten. On some evenings, he would look at the silent phone and then say, "That's for you," only for it to ring seconds later, the caller asking for Adam.

What struck Adam most was Joey's indifference. He never boasted of these abilities, nor did he brood over them. To him, it was simply life as he knew it.

Adam often remembered one particular afternoon from Joey's childhood. The boy, no more than eight, had been sitting cross-legged in the grass of Adam's backyard. Four large black magpie birds, wild and notoriously territorial, circled him. Instead of attacking, they hopped lightly over his legs, brushed his arms with their wings, and even allowed his hand to stroke their feathers. It was a scene Adam could never forget—an image of harmony between human and wild creature, almost biblical in its simplicity.

That same affinity extended to plants. When Adam's Garden withered, Joey would step in. With little more than water and quiet attention, he could coax sickly seedlings into lush, fruitful beds. The vegetables he grew were bigger, sweeter, more vibrant than anything from the market. Adam's attempts often failed, but Joey's Garden seemed to hum with life under his care. His mother once confessed to Adam that she could not explain her son. "He's nothing like me or his father," she had said softly. "He's a unique child… an old soul."

Later that week, Adam prepared spaghetti Bolognese—Joey's favourite—and decided to share the thought that had been circling his mind. He spoke of reaching out to others like Joey, people with psychic abilities, to gather their stories and insights. Joey's eyes lit up immediately, and he offered his help without hesitation. But Adam wasn't that sure. He didn't want Joey pulled into the weight of his research. Joey was young, with friends, work, and a life still unfolding. He deserved a chance at ordinary joys.

That night, Adam lay awake, mulling over possibilities. Psychic groups existed, but he wanted something different. He wasn't looking for those who had adopted a lifestyle—he was looking for authenticity, for those whose abilities were raw and undeniable, like Joey's. Quietly, discreetly, he needed a way to find them.

The answer came unexpectedly the following morning. As his alarm crackled to life and the radio filled the room with static and song, inspiration struck. He would place an advertisement. The local newspaper and the radio station could serve as his nets, cast wide across the community. Those nearby could meet him face-to-face. Those farther away could email or call.

The plan seemed elegant in its simplicity. Joey agreed—it was a perfect start.

Two weeks later, however, the silence was deafening. Not a single reply. No calls, no letters, no curious emails. Carol, his assistant, had crafted the advertisement with care: a clear invitation, the promise of anonymity, even the allure of free meals and refreshments. It was honest, harmless, and open. Yet nothing came of it.

Adam found himself staring at his files on his desk one evening, baffled. He was certain such people existed—he had lived with proof of it for years. So why had no one come forward?

The question hung in the air, heavy and unresolved, as if the silence itself were an answer.

In time, the storm of uncertainty passed, and Adam slipped back into the routine of his work. His days filled once more with clients, workshops, and the steady hum of his practice. One Tuesday afternoon, as the sun filtered through the wide glass windows of the conference room, Adam was halfway through delivering an Assertiveness Training seminar to a group of tense city managers when the receptionist's call interrupted him.

Carol's voice was taut, carrying an unease that Adam instantly picked up on. She explained, in hushed tones, that she had just received a peculiar phone call. A man—his tone shifting somewhere between coldly formal and faintly threatening—had questioned her about an advertisement they had placed.

For a moment, the ad had completely slipped Carol's mind. She hesitated, then did her best to answer without giving too much away. But the man was relentless. He had asked how many people worked at their centre, who they were, their credentials, and whether anyone there was involved in, as he put it, "unusual projects." Carol, steady though rattled, offered to take down his details so Adam could return the call. The man, however, refused to give a name or number, and then abruptly hung up.

A few days later, while Adam was in the middle of a session, the same man called again, once more asking to speak directly with "the manager." Carol reminded him that Adam was unavailable and, with professional patience, suggested again that she could take his contact details. He refused, and the call ended in silence.

By the third attempt, Carol's nerves were frayed. She burst into Adam's office, whispering urgently that the man was on the line once more. Adam, tired of the interruptions, decided enough was enough. He would handle this himself.

Lifting the receiver, he prepared to be firm. But the voice that met his ear was not what he expected. It was not aggressive, not sinister—rather, it was awkward, almost timid. The caller asked if he was indeed the manager. Adam confirmed he was. The man then repeated his questions about how many people worked at the centre and whether the advertisement was genuine.

Adam explained calmly that only he and Carol ran the place and that the ad was legitimate. After a long pause, the man introduced himself. "Thomas Garrett," he said, "but you can call me Tom." Then, cautiously, he asked to meet Adam in person.

When Adam ended the call, Carol was waiting, her brow creased with concern. He told her what had transpired—that the man had sounded harmless and asked to meet. Carol looked unconvinced. Something about the man's previous tone still unsettled her. "I'm not sure this is wise," she admitted softly. Adam reassured her, though he himself wasn't entirely convinced.

That evening, Adam returned home to Joey. True to form, the young man was multitasking—television flickering, laptop open, music spilling into the room. Sometimes Adam wondered why he had taken Joey in; the house had once been his quiet retreat, a sanctuary for reflection. But when Joey had gone to stay with his mother for a fortnight, the silence had pressed in too heavily, reminding Adam how empty life could feel. Over time, they had grown close—no longer just housemates, but something more like friends, even family. Joey was maturing, his youthful chaos slowly transforming into responsibility.

The following morning, right on the dot, a man entered the office. He was neatly dressed, his posture still carrying dignity despite the frailty of age. Late sixties, perhaps early seventies, Adam guessed. His silver hair was neatly combed, his steps measured. He introduced himself to Carol as Tom Garrett. She offered him the usual clipboard of forms and gestured toward a chair. Tom accepted quietly, filling in only his first name before setting the pen aside.

Carol, with her dry sense of humour, sent Adam a quick email: *Your strange caller is here—but he doesn't look scary at all.*

When Tom was ushered into Adam's office, Adam glanced down at the nearly blank form. With gentle insistence, he explained that they needed the paperwork completed. Tom shook his head slightly and clarified, "I'm not here for therapy. I won't take much of your time. I just wanted to meet you… talk about something."

Adam leaned back, studying him. "All right then. How can I help you?"

Tom's smile was mild, his voice polite. "It's nothing dramatic. I'm here about your advertisement." From his coat pocket, he produced a carefully clipped piece of newspaper—the very ad Adam had placed.

Adam looked at it and then at the man. "Yes? What about it?"

"I suppose I'm curious," Tom said vaguely. "Could you explain exactly what it means?"

There was something elusive in his manner, as though he were speaking in circles. Adam pressed gently for clarity, but Tom's answers remained flat, evasive.

Finally, Adam concluded, "Mr. Garrett, I think there's been a misunderstanding. I don't believe I can help you."

Tom rose with quiet grace, thanked Adam, and left as softly as he had arrived.

Carol appeared moments later, her eyes narrowed in suspicion. "Well? What was that about?" Adam shook his head. The encounter had left him confused. It wasn't the eccentricity—he was used to that in his field. It was the undercurrent, the sense that something unspoken hung behind Tom Garrett's measured words.

Days passed. Then the phone rang again—not Tom this time, but the local newspaper, offering to rerun the ad at a discounted rate. Adam agreed, asking that it be printed in bold, hoping to draw more attention.

Three days later, attention came—but not as expected. A call from a local radio station. Adam answered, only to hear a deep male voice dripping with sarcasm.

"So, you're the guy looking for people who talk to the dead?" The caller laughed mockingly.

Adam stiffened. He explained that it was simply a research project, one that explored unusual perceptual experiences—visions, messages, psychic impressions. But as the laughter echoed faintly in the background, Adam realized the truth. He was live on air. The radio host had drawn him into an ambush, a spectacle for the audience's amusement.

Yet Adam adapted quickly. If this was publicity, he would make use of it. He repeated the name of his practice, outlined the purpose of the project, and extended an open invitation. The host grew annoyed at Adam's persistent tone and cut the call abruptly.

Replacing the receiver, Adam leaned back, a quiet smile tugging at the corner of his mouth. Perhaps this was the turning point. Perhaps now dozens—no, hundreds—of gifted individuals would come forward.

Just then, the intercom buzzed. Carol's voice was brisk: "Kim's on hold for you. Can you take it?"

Adam's heart lifted slightly. Kim—one of his earliest clients. A woman haunted by visions she had long tried to silence, medicating and suppressing her sensitivity. She had resisted any label of *medium,* shrinking from the supernatural. And yet, Adam always suspected her gift ran deep.

Now, she was calling.

Kim was driving back from the shops, her mind adrift in the small, ordinary worries of the day—what to cook for dinner, whether she had remembered the milk—when the sound of Adam's voice suddenly crackled through the car radio. For a moment, she thought she was imagining it, some trick of fatigue or an echo from memory. But no—the cadence, the tone, the measured warmth—it was undeniably him.

Her hands jerked on the steering wheel, and the car veered dangerously toward the shoulder. Heart pounding, she righted herself, breath sharp in her chest.

"Oh my God," she gasped aloud, the words escaping before she could contain them. "What's going on with this psychic stuff?"

Her panic was raw, reflexive. Kim had always guarded her privacy with near-paranoid intensity. She could barely acknowledge her own strange abilities to herself, let alone have them hinted at publicly. To her, these uncanny experiences weren't gifts—they were demonic, the hidden root of her bouts of mental torment.

Almost as if hearing her fear across the invisible airwaves, Adam's voice spoke with gentle reassurance. "Calm down, Kim. It's okay."

Her first response was sharp, panicked, almost desperate. "Please don't use my name."

"No names, Kim," Adam soothed, calm but deliberate. "I'm just trying to find more enlightened people—like you."

He knew she would recoil from any public involvement. Asking her to step forward would be pointless, maybe even cruel. And yet, deep down, he hoped that by speaking openly, others might be drawn out of the shadows—others who carried strange burdens similar to hers.

Kim had always been a worrier. Her life was a constant bracing for impact, as though some calamity hovered just ahead. She used to confide in Adam about dreams that left her trembling: silent gatherings of the newly dead and other creatures standing at the edges of her bed, watching, waiting, their presence thick with unspoken judgment. These nocturnal visions carried a suffocating sense of doom.

In hushed, fragmented disclosures, she sometimes spoke of what she called *the Big Four*—a phrase weighted with dread—and its connection to an entity she named only as *MA*. The way she said it, clipped and careful, suggested it was part of a longer, more sinister acronym, though she refused to spell it out. She insisted that naming it in full would force her to face a truth too monstrous to bear. Vagueness was her shield. Silence, her survival.

Her visions frightened her because they always hinted at catastrophe—dark prophecies of futures best left unspoken.

But since beginning therapy with Adam, Kim had carved out distance from those terrors. She had learned to root herself in the here and now, to manage the panic before it swallowed her whole. By steering conversations away from her visions, she kept her mind safer, her heart steadier.

Kim was a middle-aged woman with the wear of life etched lightly into her features. Divorced for years, she had chosen, with quiet determination, to live for herself again. Her grown children thrived in their own lives, and she, at last, was free to define her own path. Grounded, candid, and sharp-eyed, Kim lived by a simple creed: you reap what you sow.

As for the visions—she preferred them buried. Instead, she filled her days with acts of service. That very afternoon, she was on her way back to the Ashram, where she often ladled soup into bowls for the hungry. In that small, humble act, she found a sense of meaning that her strange glimpses of otherworldly horrors had never given her.

Back at his office, Adam leaned back in his chair, his thoughts lingering on Kim. Maybe she was right. Maybe some things were not meant to be unearthed.

His reflection was cut short by the sharp ring of the office phone. Then silence. Carol burst in moments later, deciding to speak to Adam face to face, her notepad clutched like a weapon in her hands.

"Adam, are you free? You won't believe this!" Her eyes were wide, breath fast.

"We've had three calls since your radio appearance," she blurted, rushing toward his desk. "Two were obvious prank calls— laughing in the background, students maybe. I took their details anyway, but when I rang back, both numbers went straight to voicemail." She lowered her voice now, conspiratorial. "But the third one... that one felt real."

She paused, searching Adam's face for reaction.

"Did you call the number?" he asked, his curiosity sharpening.

"I did," Carol replied, holding out the slips of paper. "And you'll never guess who it was. Garrett. That strange old man. He actually called back. This time I insisted on a number."

Her tone softened, though unease still clung to her. "And do you know what he said? He told me he urgently needs to speak with you. That you must call him as soon as possible."

Carol frowned, uncertainty flickering. "Do you think he might be... unwell?"

Adam had grown used to Carol's dramatic pendulum swings—her fluster, her recovery, the way she sometimes spun herself into a frenzy before settling back into calm. But Adam wasn't one to judge. He recalled, with some embarrassment, the day Carol had unknowingly brightened the office with a bouquet of white lilies. His reaction had been nothing short of over the top. He could still picture her retreating in haste, flowers clutched in both her trembling hands, before tossing them into a distant bin—well out of his sight.

Without delay, Adam dialled Garrett's number. After a few rings, a soft, familiar voice answered.

"Hello, may I speak with Thomas Garrett, please?" Adam asked.

"Thomas speaking."

"This is Adam Green. You left a message saying it was urgent?"

The man's tone brightened instantly. "Oh yes! Please, call me Tom. I'm so glad you called back."

Warmth radiated through the line, eager but guarded. "Adam, is there any chance we could catch up again? Maybe over coffee? And about our last meeting—please accept my apologies. I think we got off on the wrong foot." He chuckled lightly.

Adam pressed, careful. "May I ask what this is about?"

A pause. "Ah... sorry. I'm not comfortable discussing it over the phone."

Silence lingered. Adam waited, weighing the moment.

"Tom? Are you still there?"

"Yes, yes. I'm here. So—shall I come to you, or will you come to me? Whatever you prefer."

Carol, listening nearby, slipped out when the reception phone rang. She had expected Adam to be firmer, but his tone remained disarmingly cordial. When she returned, notepad in hand, she was carrying a deluge of new messages.

By the end of the day, twenty-two people had responded to the advertisement—each with stories stranger than the last. Some spoke of visions, some of ancestors with disturbing abilities. Others claimed to be prophets of the world's end, reincarnations of Cleopatra, or witnesses to alien intrusions in their very homes.

Adam's radio debut had unleashed a floodgate.

The calls multiplied, as did the scrutiny. Journalists circled like vultures, some still nursing grudges from his controversial *NO People* article. Carol braced herself for the onslaught, her protective streak sharper than ever. Adam, though, decided it was time to retreat—if only for a week. Both he and Carol needed respite from the storm.

Still, one name lingered in Adam's thoughts: Garrett.

Despite his hesitance, Adam admitted to Joey later that evening that he was intrigued. Something about Tom's manner hinted at secrets yet untold. Joey smirked knowingly—he could already tell that Adam would end up meeting the old man.

And so, plans began to form. Adam and Joey would visit Thomas Garrett together. Adam wanted Joey's insights, Joey was good at first impressions. Whatever the man was holding back, Adam had a sense that Joey may pick up on it.

Chapter Four
Welcome Aboard

Something new. Something humanity can't even imagine yet…

The following day, they arrived at the address Tom had given Adam. The drive had been long enough to allow their nerves to quietly build, and now, as the car idled at the curb, Adam and Joey exchanged uncertain looks. Both of them had the same unspoken thought—*what on earth had they stepped into?*

Before them stood a house that was less a residence and more a fortress. The front was guarded by towering iron gates, easily ten feet tall, blackened with age yet still commanding, their sharp tips glinting faintly in the sunlight. Attached to the gates stretched a wall of massive sandstone blocks, weathered and ancient-looking, as though plucked from some castle and transplanted into the heart of modern Sydney. The wall ran so far down the street that it seemed endless, disappearing into the bend as if it encircled an entire hidden world.

Tall, manicured trees swayed gently above the barricade, their branches spilling lazily over the wall, trailing leaves that danced across the pavement. The shade they cast was not soft but almost theatrical, long, dappled shadows that shifted with the breeze, concealing more than they revealed.

It was a neighbourhood that reeked of wealth. Luxury cars—sleek European models, polished to perfection—lined the quiet street. Not a single vehicle bore a scratch or dent; even the tyres gleamed, as though hand-buffed by servants. The very air seemed different here, crisp and reserved, the silence only broken by the distant murmur of a lawn sprinkler or the flutter of wings overhead. Adam almost laughed at the thought, but he swore the birds circling above looked too elegant for any ordinary suburb, as if even nature had adjusted itself to the standards of the wealthy.

The morning sun climbed higher, illuminating manicured flower beds that glistened like jewels after a recent watering. Each bloom—roses, hydrangeas, orchids—seemed deliberately positioned, as though the garden had been designed not merely for beauty, but for display, for intimidation. The entire street gave off the impression of quiet surveillance, as though strangers were tolerated only briefly, only under watchful eyes.

Just then, the sudden growl of an engine shattered the silence. A sleek black sports car glided out of a driveway further up the street, its chrome details flashing like a blade. Its windows were tinted so dark that not even a silhouette could be seen within. Adam and Joey fell still, watching the vehicle slink away like a predator retreating into the distance. When it turned the corner, the street grew eerily quiet again, the hush now heavy, expectant.

Adam noticed the intercom first, set neatly into the stone wall as though it were a mere ornament. Joey, restless with nervous energy, jumped from the car before Adam could say anything. Gravel crunched under his shoes as he approached the gate, and Adam reluctantly followed. Up close, the gate loomed higher than it had from the car, its cold iron surface threaded with ornate patterns that looked almost menacing.

Then they noticed it—the small camera above, its glass eye fixed squarely on them. Neither of them spoke, but both felt the same ripple of unease. They were being watched. Judged. Perhaps even weighed.

Adam raised a hand and pressed the black "Call" button. For a heartbeat, there was only silence, the kind that stretched and thickened until it felt unnatural. Then, with a sudden burst of static, the intercom crackled to life.

"Hello?"

"Yes, this is Adam speaking," he said, leaning toward the intercom receiver with deliberate clarity. His voice carried a steady calm, though beneath it a faint thread of tension coiled. "I'm looking for Mr. Garrett—Thomas Garrett."

There was a pause, long enough for Adam to wonder if the line had gone dead. Then a warm, almost jovial reply crackled through the speaker: "Come on through."

A mechanical click followed, deep and metallic, echoing faintly as if stirred from the bones of the gates themselves. Slowly, with the groaning dignity of age and power, the towering iron gates began to swing open. Their weighty movement stirred the air, and Adam felt an odd mix of anticipation and unease tighten in his chest.

Joey cast him a quick glance, eyebrows raised as though to ask, *are we really doing this?* Adam answered with the smallest nod, and together they slipped back into the car. The tires crunched softly over the slate pathway as the vehicle rolled forward into the estate.

The driveway curved in a graceful arc, almost ceremonially leading them onward, until the vast shape of a mansion revealed itself from behind the screen of trees. Adam's eyes scanned the grounds as they passed: lawns so perfectly manicured they might have been carved from emerald glass; the grass blades trimmed with an almost military precision. Beyond them, towering gum trees stood like ancient sentinels along the boundary, their branches weaving a green canopy overhead, casting cool, dappled patterns across the stone path.

Closer still, bursts of colour announced themselves in orderly rows—newly planted garden beds, filled with blooms that seemed too vivid, too flawless, to be entirely natural. Petals flared with a painter's palette of reds, yellows, and pinks, arranged with a gardener's obsessive care. The effect was beautiful, yes, but also faintly surreal, as though they had entered a landscape carefully constructed to impress, perhaps even to distract.

The car eased to a stop before what appeared to be the main entrance. A wide awning jutted out, supported by two stone pillars wrapped in delicate vines. Purple and white speckled flowers climbed eagerly upward, spilling their fragrance into the warm morning air. The scent clung to Adam's senses—sweet, almost intoxicating—as if it were meant to soften the threshold they were about to cross.

Joey was the first to move, pushing his door open with a sense of casual bravado. He stretched, then started toward the enormous double doors ahead. But before he could raise a hand to knock, one of the doors creaked open of its own accord.

An elderly man appeared in the frame. His silver hair was thin, but his smile broad and alive with energy. His eyes crinkled with genuine warmth, and though Adam noted the deep lines etched into his face, there was something sprightly about him, a kind of enthusiasm that seemed almost boyish.

"Ah! At last!" he exclaimed, throwing his arms slightly wide in welcome. "Come in, come in!" His voice carried a vitality that belied his years.

Adam hesitated for the briefest moment, uncertain whether the man had expected company beyond himself. But if Thomas Garrett was surprised to see Joey, he gave no indication. Instead, he seemed delighted at their arrival, as if two guests were even better than one.

Walking into the house, Adam was immediately struck by the atmosphere of the place. The grand hallway that opened before them was lined with fitted wooden cupboards, their polished surfaces gleaming in the muted light. The floors were laid with rich timber that creaked ever so slightly underfoot, carrying the memory of countless footsteps before theirs.

Something about the space stirred a forgotten familiarity. Adam's mind conjured an image from his youth—his old school, particularly the foyer outside the principal's office. The teak wood, the varnished sheen dulled by time, the railings that bore the faint smudges of age and use—it all carried that same peculiar blend of prestige and wear. Even the wide staircase, rising to the upper floors with an almost theatrical sweep, awakened memories of hurried mornings, books clutched against his chest as he dashed between classes.

The past and present seemed to blur in that instant, and Adam found himself wondering if stepping into this house was not just a meeting with a man, but the beginning of something that would test more than his memory.

Tom led them down the hallway, his footsteps echoing faintly against the polished wooden floorboards, until he stopped before a wide door on the left. With a quiet push, he ushered them inside. The moment they entered, Adam noticed a faint, almost forgotten fragrance of age—a musty, lived-in scent that clung to the high ceilings and shadowed corners of the room.

It was spacious, elegant in a dignified, old-world fashion, the sort of room that once hosted conversations of weight and consequence. Adam thought it might have been designed as a drawing room, though the scale made it feel more like an oversized living room. Two tall windows dominated the eastern wall, their heavy drapes drawn halfway, letting only a thin blade of morning light cut across the carpet and touch the grand furnishings with pale illumination. Dust motes floated in that slice of sunlight, drifting like tiny ghosts.

What caught Adam's attention most, however, were the details. Twin marble mantelpieces framed a wide fireplace, their pale surfaces veined with grey, and on either side the walls rose into a towering built-in bookshelf, packed with row upon row of books that hinted at a lifetime of careful collection. The scent of leather and paper lingered faintly in the air, mingling with the mustiness.

"Nice house," Joey said at last, his voice breaking the hush as they came to a halt. His tone was casual, though Adam noticed the way his eyes darted quickly from corner to corner, as if trying to drink it all in.

"Tom, this is my friend Joey," Adam said, filling the silence before it stretched too long. Tom had turned slightly, his eyes lingering on Joey with a flicker of curiosity. Adam sensed that Joey, for his part, was studying Tom just as intently—measuring him, perhaps.

"Very happy to meet you, young man," Tom said warmly, the corners of his mouth lifting into a gracious smile. Then, as if the thought had just occurred to him, he began pulling out a few chairs from near the wall. "So, tell me something—what exactly is your relationship?"

The bluntness of the question caught Adam off guard. He opened his mouth to answer, but Joey beat him to it.

"Is this your house? Do you live here alone?" Joey asked, leaning back on his heels as though testing Tom with his own question.

Tom chuckled softly and nodded. "Yes, it is—and yes, I live here alone." With a sweep of his hand, he motioned them toward the seats he had arranged. "Alright, everyone, sit. Get comfortable. Can I offer you a drink? Tea, coffee, something stronger perhaps?"

Both Adam and Joey shook their heads politely. Adam, still a little unsettled by Joey's brashness, hurried to smooth things over. "Tom, I hope it's alright that I brought Joey along. He sometimes helps me with my work."

"No problem at all," Tom assured him. His tone carried more than courtesy; there was a note of approval in it. "In fact, I think it was a wise decision, Adam."

Joey said nothing. He had already positioned his chair slightly apart from the others, off to the side, his posture relaxed but his eyes sharp, quietly watching Tom. When Tom's gaze landed on him, Joey quickly looked away, feigning interest in the window.

"So," Adam said, eager to move things forward, "what's this all about?"

Tom rubbed his hands together, the sound dry and soft, betraying a faint nervousness. "Are you sure you're both comfortable?"

"I'm fine," Adam replied immediately.

"Same here," Joey added, though he remained half-turned away, shoulders hunched.

Tom had placed their chairs in a loose circle, a deliberate arrangement that felt designed to draw them into a shared space, though Joey's distance seemed to undermine it.

"Alright," Tom whispered, lowering his gaze. His voice carried the tremor of hesitation. "I have to admit something—I am a little anxious. Please bear with me. Earlier, I felt calm, perfectly fine, but now—having you both here, in my home—it is… overwhelming, what I am about to share."

Joey leaned forward, curiosity sharpening his expression. Something in Tom's manner struck him as odd. Was the man simply showing his age—forgetful, uncertain—or was there something deeper? A loneliness finally taking its toll, perhaps? Or worse—some fragile line between reality and imagination beginning to fray?

"Sounds pretty serious," Adam said, adopting a lighter tone in the hope of easing the tension. But his smile faltered when he saw that Tom wasn't responding. The man's mind seemed to drift elsewhere, his eyes unfocused, as though staring past them into some distant memory.

"Sorry, Tom, but could we maybe get to the point?" Adam prompted gently. "I don't mean to rush you, but I've got a client soon, and we'll need to head off shortly." The words were only a polite fabrication—Adam had no clients that day, his calendar blissfully empty for once—but he hoped the excuse might help nudge Tom forward.

"Yes, yes, of course," Tom quickly said, jolting back to himself. His hands fidgeted against his knees, and for a moment his face looked drained of colour, his eyes clouded by doubt. Then, almost theatrically, he whispered, "Deep breath," slapped his palms together softly, and straightened in his chair, summoning what courage he could muster. A faint flush returned to his cheeks.

"Alright," he said, his voice steadier now, though still threaded with nerves. "Here goes. What I'm about to tell you may sound unbelievable… but I swear to you—it's the truth."

Adam and Joey exchanged a look, their scepticism momentarily set aside. Both leaned forward, silent, waiting for Tom's story to begin.

Tom's voice dropped as though he were unveiling something fragile, something not meant for careless ears. He explained that he was part of a secret society—an assembly of men and women who carried within them unusual, sometimes paranormal gifts. These were not common folk, he insisted, but rare individuals touched by forces beyond ordinary comprehension. They were deeply spiritual, driven not by greed or ambition, but by a higher calling, a sense of responsibility to guide and, when necessary, to protect.

For nearly two decades, Tom had served as an Overseer within this hidden network. He coordinated their gatherings, sometimes financing the meetings himself, at other times receiving support from fellow members. His sprawling home, with its discreet corners and high-walled seclusion, doubled as a sanctuary for them. Here they would sit late into the night, trading fragments of dreams, piecing together visions, puzzling over premonitions that clung to them like shadows.

"They are not just here in Australia," Tom said, his eyes drifting past Adam toward some unseen horizon. "There are groups like ours across the world—Europe, the States, even places you wouldn't expect. I speak to them when I can. I compare notes. Sometimes the messages overlap, and that's when I pass the information on to the group for their attention."

Adam frowned. "What do you mean?"

Tom blinked. "Mean about what?"

"Why tell us this?" Adam asked, his voice steady but edged with suspicion.

"Oh!" Tom chuckled softly, as though the answer were obvious. "Because I thought you might be interested, because of your advertisement." His eyes lingered on Adam, then flicked to Joey, gauging their reactions.

Adam returned a polite smile, though inwardly he sensed Tom had expected something more—a spark of fascination, perhaps even recognition. Adam's advertisement for psychically gifted individuals had likely raised Tom's hopes that he had found kindred spirits.

"So," Adam asked, indulging him, "who are these people of yours? And how did you come across them?"

Tom leaned forward, lowering his voice as if sharing a family secret. "They are very special people. It is in the blood, you see. A matter of genes."

"Genes?" Adam repeated, uncertain whether Tom was speaking literally or poetically.

"Yes." Tom nodded earnestly. "It runs through families. Some inherit it cleanly, others not at all. And sometimes… sometimes it skips a generation. But when it appears, it's undeniable." His expression darkened. "Not everyone welcomes it, though. Some see it as a curse. They bury it, deny it. And in doing so, they wither."

Adam said nothing. He had heard such stories before—men and women who fled from their abilities, who cursed the very thing that set them apart. It was not as shocking as Tom seemed to think.

The silence grew heavy until Joey broke it, leaning forward. "Why tell us now?"

Tom's gaze darted to Joey, then back to Adam. His composure faltered; his words came out in a rush, low and urgent. "Because things are getting worse."

Adam stiffened. "Worse how?"

Tom's hands opened and closed against his knees. "We had a gathering here just last week. They all felt it—every one of them. Something very big is coming, something catastrophic. Some wanted to vanish, go into hiding. But they can't. None of us can. The sense is too strong. We are meant to speak about it, to warn others."

He fixed his eyes on Adam, searching, pleading for recognition. Adam only exchanged another look with Joey, a silent question passing between them: *Do we leave?*

Meanwhile, Tom had stopped talking, just looking down. The silence grew, until…

"Tom?" Adam prompted, gently.

Tom startled, then carried on. "Yes, yes… where was I? Oh—yes. Something bad is coming. Something vast. Wicked. A great event, and it will claim lives. Many lives."

Adam leaned forward slightly. "You mean… death?"

"Yes!" Tom's voice cracked with urgency. "Death on a scale we cannot fathom. Many millions, if not more. It will be deliberate—a coordinated strike against the masses. Our people sense it, and not just us. Others around the globe, groups like ours, are receiving the same warnings. He hesitated, as though unveiling a sacred phrase. "—Image Carriers."

Adam stayed quiet, listening, his expression unreadable.

Tom sagged back, disheartened by the lack of visible reaction. His next words were softer, almost confessional. "I believe it's part of a depopulation strategy. Others are not so sure. But when you connect the pieces, the evidence, the voices rising everywhere… it all points the same way. A culling. A mass death unlike anything we've ever seen."

As they drove home, the silence inside the car pressed against Adam's ears more heavily than the hum of the engine. The road seemed busier now on their way back. Adam couldn't shake the peculiar weight Tom had left on him. The old man's words lingered, threading through his thoughts like smoke that refused to clear. Outrageous as Tom's story had sounded—talk of secret gatherings, people with strange gifts, and a higher purpose—it had stirred something deep in Adam's chest. A part of him, the rational counsellor who sought evidence and logic, dismissed it as delusion, perhaps the lonely ramblings of a man starved of companionship. Yet another, quieter part whispered—what if there was truth beneath the layers?

And then there was the look in Tom's eyes. Behind all the talk, Adam had caught it: a raw, unspoken grief, a man reaching for something he had lost—or something that had always been just out of reach. That part of Adam, the one trained to notice wounds not easily spoken aloud, could not dismiss it as mere fantasy.

Beside him, Joey sat uncharacteristically quiet. His chin rested against the side window, his breath fogging the glass with a misty blur. Usually, Joey filled car rides with chatter, dry remarks, or restless energy, but now he seemed folded into himself, as though Tom's words had pried open something he wasn't ready to share.

When they stopped at a red light, Adam stole a glance at him. "You, okay?" he asked gently, keeping his tone casual, almost careful.

Joey turned his head slightly. A faint, almost apologetic smile touched his lips, but it didn't reach his eyes. He nodded toward the glowing green light that had now changed. "Go on," he said, deflecting with a gesture.

Adam didn't push. He had learned enough, in both his work and his friendship with Joey, to recognise when someone wasn't ready. Still, a pang of concern tugged at him. Something had shifted in Joey since they'd left Tom's estate, something subtle but worrisome.

Back at the house, Joey was the first to step inside. He went straight to the fridge, pulled out a can, and cracked it open with a sharp hiss. The metallic click echoed through the quiet kitchen before he dropped into the lounge chair. He leaned back, took a long sip, and let out a breath.

"So," Joey said finally, breaking the silence, "what do you make of old Tommy?"

Adam set his keys on the counter and exhaled slowly. "Strange old guy," he admitted. "Lonely, probably craving company. Did you notice that framed photo on the table? He kept looking at it, almost like he couldn't help himself. Looked like a younger woman. Could be his wife, or someone else close. There was sadness in his face every time his eyes drifted over it. He seemed... lost."

Joey tapped his drink against his knee, his eyes narrowing. "Yeah, but what do you really think?"

Adam raised an eyebrow. "Think about what?" He moved toward the sofa and sat down across from him.

Joey leaned forward, elbows on his knees. "Do you reckon he's onto something?"

The question hung in the air. Adam hesitated before answering. "Maybe. I think he believes he is. But I doubt it's connected to what I'm investigating. More likely, he heard about my work and wanted to be part of it. You get people like that sometimes looking for meaning, wanting to belong."

He rose and wandered into the kitchen, filling a glass of water from the tap. The sound of the running stream felt oddly loud in the hush of the room. Joey trailed behind him, can still in hand, as if he didn't want too much distance between them.

"There's something off," Adam went on, lowering his voice. "I think he's grieving, or maybe just deeply depressed. Honestly, he needs someone to talk to. Someone to listen. Maybe even counselling." He glanced at Joey, who was slowly rotating the can between his palms, as though the motion kept his thoughts grounded. "Did you pick up anything from him?"

Joey's eyes flicked up, reluctant. "Not much," he admitted. "I couldn't get a clear read. But… I did sense something. That woman in the photo—she's gone. Dead. His daughter maybe, or his wife. Someone who mattered." He paused, his voice lowering. "And I felt something else. Old Tom mentioned people meeting there, I felt them. People… like me. I actually felt their presence."

Adam turned, glass in hand, and studied Joey more closely. There was a certainty in his tone that hadn't been there before. Something about the encounter had left a mark, one that Joey was trying to downplay.

But Adam could see it—the shift. Tom's story hadn't unsettled Joey; it had awakened him. It was as though he'd brushed against something familiar, something he had been waiting for without realising it. A quiet pull, like gravity, drawing him toward the old man's grand house and the possibility of others who carried the same strange spark he did.

Joey had always been different. Even as a boy, he'd stood apart. While the other kids roughhoused and chased footballs through muddy fields, Joey kept to the edges, drawn instead to books, music, or his own quiet musings. Friends had come and gone, their paths veering away from his, until eventually, isolation became less of a choice and more of a habit. But behind that reclusive exterior lived a restless curiosity—about himself, about what made him different, and whether others like him even existed.

Now, after meeting Tom, that curiosity flared into something sharper. He couldn't shake the certainty that the old man was hiding more than he had revealed. The house, the gatherings, the photo—it all meant something. Joey was sure of it. And it was Joey, more than Adam, who urged that they return, convinced Tom's story held pieces of a puzzle they had yet to understand.

After being gone from work for a week, Adam found himself having a mixture of relief and reluctance as he eased back into the day-to-day operations of his workplace. The break had been necessary—a chance to breathe, reflect, and quietly take stock of his next steps—but now that it was over, the familiar weight of responsibilities pressed in again. He only hoped the relentless media frenzy that had shadowed them would finally subside. Enough was enough.

When he stepped into the office, the comforting scent of freshly brewed coffee and paper greeted him, grounding him in the space that had long been his refuge. Carol looked up from behind the reception desk, her face breaking into a wide, glowing smile. The change in her was impossible to miss—her skin seemed brighter, her shoulders relaxed. Whatever she had done during the holiday, it had restored her.

"Happy to be back at work!" she declared cheerfully, her voice carrying the kind of energy that seemed to sweep the room along with it.

Adam arched an eyebrow, offering her a crooked half-smile. "You or me?"

"Me, obviously!" she laughed, swatting lightly at the air as though batting away the very idea that he might mean himself. "So, how was your time off? Do anything exciting?"

Adam shrugged, already moving toward his desk, gathering up a small pile of files and flicking through the stack of unopened mail that had collected in his absence. "It was worth it," he admitted. "Just took it easy—did absolutely nothing."

For a moment, there was peace. The quiet hum of the building wrapped around him as he sank into his chair, preparing to re-enter his role. But then, inevitably, the calm was broken. A familiar voice rang out from reception, bright and mischievous, already sparking a playful argument with Carol. Adam didn't even need to look—Joey. He'd know that tone anywhere. Joey's knack for winding Carol up was as dependable as the sunrise, though beneath the mock squabbles was a strange sort of fondness, one neither of them would ever admit outright.

Sure enough, moments later, Joey strode in without so much as a knock, grinning like a thief who had just gotten away with something clever.

"What are you doing here?" Adam asked, eyeing him with suspicion as he leaned back in his chair.

Joey flung himself onto the therapy couch with exaggerated drama, sprawling out as though the place belonged to him. "Can't I visit a friend without being interrogated?" he retorted, closing his eyes and folding his hands across his chest like he was settling in for an afternoon nap.

Adam studied him in silence, a wry smile tugging at the corner of his mouth. Same old Joey—full of bravado, hiding mischief behind mock innocence, forever trying to outplay him. He never succeeded, not really, but Adam usually let him win out of habit, no matter what game they were playing.

"Alright, Joey, you win," Adam said finally, amusement in his voice. "Spit it out. What's this really about. Why are you here?"

Joey responded with a long, comically loud snore.

Adam's smirk deepened. "Mrs. Burger! Oh, is it that time already?" he announced suddenly, raising his voice toward the door.

Joey shot upright like a jack-in-the-box, eyes darting toward the entrance in alarm. Adam couldn't help himself—he burst into laughter, doubling over at the sight of Joey's startled face.

"You're such a bastard," Joey said, glaring at him, but there was no heat in it. He'd fallen for the same trick too many times to count, and Adam never seemed to tire of it. Yes, there was no Mrs Burger. A prank Adams pulled now again to keep young Joey on his feet.

"Seriously," Adam said, once his laughter had ebbed, his tone sharpening just enough to cut through Joey's antics. "What do you want?"

"I was thinking we should go see old Uncle Tom again," Joey said, more sober now.

Adam narrowed his eyes. "Why?"

"There's something off," Joey replied, leaning forward, his earlier playfulness tempered by a spark of curiosity. "I want another look. Maybe I'll pick up something I missed the first time. I think…" He paused, choosing his words. "I think I believe him. I reckon our Uncle Tom is onto something."

Before Adam could respond, the soft ping of a new email arrived on his screen. It was from Carol, letting him know his client had arrived.

A moment later, the office door opened, and Evelyn stepped in. Adam rose automatically to greet her. Evelyn—once his client—moved with the same briskness as always, her facial expression sharp, her presence commanding in a way that often left others scrambling to keep up. Joey, however, wasn't intimidated. He leapt to his feet as well, ever the performer, bowing low in mock courtesy and flashing a grin that dared her to react.

Evelyn barely reacted, motioning Joey to leave. But he stood there, still smiling and bowing. She knew Joey well enough to have no patience for his theatrics. Where others indulged or humoured him, she dismissed him outright. Without slowing her stride, she stopped at Adam's desk and, in a hushed but pointed tone, asked Adam to tell Joey to leave the room.

As Adam guided her toward a seat, his thoughts jumped briefly to her reputation. Evelyn had a habit of creating trouble for herself in ways that seemed almost deliberate. She had once ordered a string of complicated appliances online, then promptly handed them off when she realized she had neither the time nor the faintest idea how to use them. Carol had ended up with a state-of-the-art blender; Adam had inherited a robotic vacuum that refused to recognize the difference between a wall and a dining chair.

This time, though, Evelyn's trouble was different. She'd asked for her mail to be redirected to Adam's office—an unusual request he'd grudgingly agreed to. She'd once had a post office box of her own, but a heated argument with the local postal manager over the annual fee had led her to shut it down in a huff. Until she sorted out a permanent solution, Adam had reluctantly allowed her mail to pile up at his business address, telling himself it was temporary.

And now, as she stood before him, something about her expression suggested that what she carried today was more than just another trivial misstep.

Evelyn was an Image Carrier—one of the rare few who could perceive things that lay hidden from ordinary eyes. To Adam, she had always stood apart, a fragile mystery wrapped in contradictions. On the scale used to measure such abilities, she ranked somewhere between average and high, though she never embraced the title. Instead, she resented it, recoiled from it. She called her visions a curse, a thing that clung to her like a demon she could never shake.

All she longed for was normality—a life free from the burden of seeing what others could not. But the irony never escaped Adam: Evelyn's life was anything but ordinary. She lived in a kind of chosen exile, drifting through her days with no clear occupation, no friends to speak of, and little contact with the outside world. Neighbours whispered, unsure of what she did behind the closed curtains of her small home. Even acts of kindness unsettled her; not long ago, she had lashed out at Carol for the simple offer of paying for her haircut. "I can take care of myself," she had snapped, her voice trembling with pride and shame in equal measure.

Her visit today had been long delayed, but Adam had known it would come. It always did, eventually. Evelyn never reached out unless the pressure inside her became unbearable. Her life moved in cycles—moments of uneasy calm punctuated by storms of fear and dread. Now, she was in the thick of it again.

When she arrived, her presence carried the air of someone already hunted. She moved like a woman scanning for danger, her eyes restless, darting. After Joey left the room, Evelyn hesitated at the door, her hand lingering on the lock. Then, with a sudden urgency, she rose again to check it herself. Adam noted the ritual with quiet concern. He had seen it before—small, compulsive acts that betrayed the depth of her distress.

Finally, she lowered herself into the chair across from him, her shoulders tense, as if bracing against some invisible weight. Adam leaned forward slightly, his voice measured, steady, encouraging.

"Okay, Evelyn. Take your time. Tell me what's been happening."

Her response came without preamble, flat and unadorned, the words clipped by fear.

"There's something wrong."

She didn't blink. Her tone carried the cold certainty of someone who had already drawn her conclusion.

"I can smell death in the air," she whispered, as if naming it gave it power. "I sense it. It's closing in. The nightmares I thought I'd buried—they're back."

Adam felt the familiar chill of these moments—the way her speech transformed when she was like this. Gone was the tentative, distracted Evelyn who sometimes let a trace of warmth slip through. In her place stood someone taut, urgent, brittle as glass. To most people she was intolerable, too strange, too unnerving. They dismissed her, or worse, recoiled. But Adam had never recoiled. He had patience for her. More than patience—he carried a deep, reluctant admiration for her oddity, her fragility, her raw edges. She trusted him in ways she trusted no one else.

"Deep breath," he said softly, as much to steady himself as to steady her. "First, tell me—what do you think is wrong?"

Her eyes moved quickly towards the window, then to the door again. "I don't know! I just know something bad is coming," she burst out, her voice rising. "Even my visions... they're different now. Sharper. Unusually specific."

She stopped abruptly, as if the act of speaking had tightened something inside her, making it hard to breathe. Her hands curled in her lap, restless.

"Okay," Adam said gently, repeating the question, his tone deliberate, calm. "So tell me—why do you feel something is wrong?"

Evelyn pursed her lips together. For a long moment she said nothing, then her words came out in a low murmur. "Because it's always the same. In every dream. Something big is coming. I sense death... and more death. I keep getting flashes of people I know dying… it's suffocating me."

She lowered her head towards the floor as though the weight of the images forced her down. "I don't even know what's real anymore. I hate this," she said, but now her voice was calm again— eerily calm, as though all the heat had drained from her in an instant.

"Are you dreaming all of this?" Adam asked, his voice matched to her new, steady tone.

"Yes. In dreams. But sometimes..." She swallowed, her eyes lifting up to meet his. "Sometimes visions come when I least expect them. I can't control them, Adam. I'll be standing in the kitchen or brushing my hair and—" She cut herself short, her expression tightening. Then she added, with quiet gravity, "And remember—you can't tell anyone about this."

It was her predictable comment. She always ended this way, no matter the topic—no matter how large or small. A warning, a plea, a command. Secrets were Evelyn's armour, her rituals of protection against a world she believed was watching. Her moods swung like a pendulum—panic, anger, paranoia, calm. But Adam knew this swing, this particular rhythm. He hadn't seen her like this in a long time. And that, more than anything she said, told him how deeply unsettled she truly was.

They spoke for nearly an hour and a half, though to Adam it felt much longer, as if time itself had slowed under the weight of Evelyn's words. He tried everything he could think of to soothe her— gentle reassurance, logical reasoning, even moments of silence where he simply let her voice fill the room. But none of it seemed to reach her. Evelyn's eyes, wide and fevered, shone with a certainty that unsettled him more than her actual words.

Her dreams, she insisted, weren't dreams at all. They were messages—deliberate, insistent, and meant only for her. She described them with such vivid detail that Adam felt as if he too could see the images flickering at the edges of her consciousness. Cities darkened beneath a choking fog. People scattered in blind panic. And everywhere, death—sudden, indiscriminate, and overwhelming.

"It's not history repeating itself," she whispered at one point, her hands trembling against her lap. "It's something else. Something new. Something humanity can't even imagine yet."

Her voice faltered when she added that she might not survive it herself. The way she said it—almost matter-of-fact, as though she had already accepted the inevitability of her own end—sent a cold ripple across Adam's skin. She called it an extermination, but one unlike anything ever recorded.

When at last she left, the silence in Adam's office was heavy, oppressive. He sat alone at his desk, staring at the faint outline of her handprint left on the polished wood, troubled by how real her conviction had felt. Evelyn wasn't someone prone to dramatics. Over the years, she had always struck him as grounded, almost stubbornly so. Yet when she spoke of her visions, her sincerity was undeniable.

And the truth was—he had seen it before. Her predictions, at least some of them, had come to pass. He couldn't deny that. Evelyn was an Image Carrier. Not just any, but a gifted one. He'd witnessed her flashes of uncanny foresight himself, glimpses of knowledge that no ordinary person could have stumbled upon.

But what in God's name was he supposed to do with this?

He had tried, in the past, to explore her abilities more formally, to study the patterns of her imagery. But Evelyn had always pushed back, almost violently. She hated the labels—*psychic, Image Carrier, seer*. To her, they were nothing but brands that scarred. They had cost her friendships, sabotaged relationships, and cast her adrift in a society that craved normalcy.

"Better to ignore it," she had once told him with quiet finality. "Better to plant both feet in the real world. Living halfway in dreams… it only kills you slowly."

And yet, here she was again—haunted, desperate, certain. Adam found himself caught in the space between belief and scepticism. Was this true precognition? Or a mind unravelling under its own anxieties, weaving meaning from random pieces?

But her last words lingered like smoke in his lungs: a warning of an extermination already in motion, vast and merciless. What disturbed Adam most was not her tone of panic—it was what she truly believed—and the dreadful certainty that the killing had already begun, unseen but real, unfolding somewhere beyond the reach of his comprehension.

And then, like an echo rising in his mind, Adam remembered Tom. The strange, secretive things the old man had said to him and Joey only a few days before. Was there a connection? The thought coiled in his chest, unsettling and insistent.

His reflections were broken when the office door eased open and Carol stepped inside. Her smile was warm, but her eyes carried a trace of unease.

"Just making sure you're all right," she said softly. "Evelyn was in such a state earlier—had me double-check outside before she left." Carol gave a small, almost embarrassed laugh.

Adam looked up at her, his voice gentler than he intended. "Try to be a little more understanding. She's… not herself right now."

Carol nodded, the smile fading into something more thoughtful. Over the years, she and Evelyn had drifted into a curious sort of friendship—uneven, fragile, yet persistent. Sometimes Evelyn's eccentric habits drew laughter from Carol, little bursts of amusement that lightened the atmosphere of the reception area. Other times, Adam had seen Carol biting her lip, grimacing with the effort to remain patient. It was unpredictable. Some days, the two of them could be heard chuckling together before Evelyn's appointments. On others, Evelyn swept past Carol without so much as a glance, her face set like stone, as though Carol were a stranger.

Now, as Adam sat with Evelyn's warnings reverberating in his mind, he wondered if even these small patterns—the laughter, the avoidance, the unpredictability—were part of something larger. A message woven into the fabric of her life that he had been too blind, or too unwilling, to see.

That evening, the house seemed to hum with a strange energy, as though Tom's shadow had followed them home. The television murmured in the background, spilling light across the lounge, but neither Adam nor Joey paid much attention to it. They sat opposite one another, the coffee table between them cluttered with empty glasses and the remains of dinner, though both had forgotten to clear it.

Joey was edgy, his leg bouncing, his eyes carrying that feverish brightness Adam had only seen a handful of times before. "I'm telling you, mate," he insisted, leaning forward as though the weight of his conviction alone could persuade Adam, "the old man knows something. He's onto something big. I can feel it."

Adam sighed, running a hand across the back of his neck. He had already told Joey what Evelyn had confided—that her dreams were not dreams at all, but messages, dark and insistent. Now he voiced aloud what had been gnawing at him since their visit. "What if it's connected?" he said, half to himself.

Joey sat back sharply, eyes narrowing in certainty. "Of course it's connected." But then, just as quickly, frustration bled into his voice. "I just don't get it. Why haven't I picked up anything? No dreams. No warnings. Nothing." His fists clenched against his knees, as though angry with himself for not sensing what Evelyn and Tom's group seemed to.

Adam showed some sympathy towards Joey, but also a need to steady his friend before he wound himself too tightly around this idea. He leaned forward, his tone even, cautious. "Joey, maybe we're reading too much into it. Tom's just an old man. Maybe he's lonely, wants company, wants to feel important. I don't think we should give him too much credit." He hesitated, then added quietly, "Maybe it's best to leave the man be."

The words landed heavily. Joey's shoulders slumped, his excitement dimmed but not extinguished. "I can't explain it, mate," he said stubbornly, shaking his head. "But he's onto something. I feel it involves us. Stupid as that may sound. And I don't believe for a second he's trying to con us."

Privately, Adam wasn't so sure himself. There had been something about Tom's manner, about the strange air that clung to the man and his house. Yet what unsettled him more was Joey's sudden fascination. Joey—who normally had little patience for strangers, preferring the safe cocoon of his music and the handful of odd companions he barely tolerated—was now animated, alive, almost desperate to dig deeper. It was unlike him, and Adam didn't know whether to be concerned or relieved.

"Yes, Joey," Adam said at last, his voice carrying a note of dismissal. His thoughts were elsewhere, already weighed down by Evelyn's words, by doubts and questions he had no strength left to explore. He rose slowly, chair scraping against the floor. "Let's talk about Tom another time."

Joey let out an exasperated sigh and grabbed the remote, flicking aimlessly through channels as if plotting in silence. Adam could almost hear the cogs in his head turning, already working out how he might drag Adam back to Tom's doorstep.

"Okay, mate," Joey called after him as Adam disappeared down the hall. His voice was laced with a mix of mischief and defiance. "Sleep on it. We'll talk about Uncle Tom in the morning."

Adam pretended not to hear.

The following Saturday, Adam was dragged out of sleep by an abrasive, metallic scraping that grated against his nerves like nails on glass. For a moment, in that hazy half-world between dreams and waking, he thought it might be part of some strange nightmare. Then his eyes found the clock—7:30 a.m. On a Saturday. He lay motionless, trying to pin down the source of the racket. The sound came again: a sharp scrape, a clatter, followed by the faint movement of something being dragged across tile.

And then it clicked. Joey.

Adam exhaled through his nose, resigned. Joey had a habit of choosing the most ungodly hours to indulge in bursts of chaotic energy, as though deliberately plotting to sabotage Adam's peace.

With a groan, Adam shoved himself upright, the floor cool beneath his bare feet as he shuffled down the hall. He expected to find Joey raiding the fridge, or perhaps dismantling something he had no business touching. What he found instead stopped him in the doorway.

The kitchen gleamed.

Joey was crouched in front of the dishwasher, scrubbing at the metallic edge with the intensity of someone trying to erase a crime scene. The floor was already spotless, the tiles glistening with recent scrubbing. Every bench shone under the ceiling light as though freshly polished for inspection. The acrid sting of bleach hung heavy in the air, wrapping around Adam's throat, burning his nostrils. He coughed, then flung open the window and back door in quick succession. A gust of cold morning air rushed in, stirring the curtains and chasing the chemical fog into the garden.

Joey, unbothered, kept scrubbing.

Adam leaned against the doorframe, arms folded, studying the scene. Joey never cleaned. Not unless bribed, threatened, or nagged into it, and even then, it was done with grudging reluctance, accompanied by exaggerated groans and slamming of cupboard doors. This quiet, almost determined industry was something else entirely. It made Adam uneasy, as though the world had shifted slightly off balance.

He watched in silence, waiting for the mask to slip, for Joey's true intentions to reveal themselves. But the boy remained intent on his task, jaw set, movements sharp and purposeful. Finally, Adam broke.

"Alright," he said slowly, "what's going on here? And more importantly, why are you cleaning—at this hour—on a Saturday?"

Joey didn't even look up. "I couldn't sleep," he said flatly. "So, I figured I'd get some cleaning done."

The casualness of the response was laughable. Adam almost did laugh. He could remember entire battles—loud, door-slamming, vein-popping arguments—about Joey dodging even the simplest of household chores. Vacuuming, wiping a bench, emptying a bin: each had been treated like an unbearable injustice. And now here he was, polishing metal before breakfast.

Adam's suspicion sharpened. For a fleeting moment he wondered if this was some kind of ploy—a quiet campaign to soften him up, to coax him into agreeing to another visit with Tom. But that didn't fit Joey's nature. Joey didn't plot; he badgered. His weapon of choice was relentless nagging, peppered with empty promises about finishing his studies or turning his life around. Quiet manipulation wasn't his style.

"Fine," Adam said, deciding not to push further. "Suit yourself."

He left Joey to his mysterious crusade and retreated to his study down the hall, spreading out old files across the desk. Yet even there, the boy's presence was inescapable. Every few minutes Joey drifted past the doorway, bucket in hand, shoulders sagging in exaggerated weariness, sighing loudly enough to rattle the papers on Adam's desk. He was performing, making sure his "hard work" was seen. Adam ignored him.

Eventually, hunger drove him back toward the kitchen. He found Joey no longer cleaning, but sitting uncharacteristically still on the lounge seat, a laptop perched on his knees. His eyes observing Adam with poorly concealed nervousness, then darted back to the screen. Too well-behaved. Too quiet.

Adam narrowed his gaze. Something was wrong.

It didn't take long to uncover the truth. He couldn't find what he was looking for, frowning. "Where are the coffee and sugar jars?" he asked.

Joey froze. His lips parted as if he might deny everything, but then he sighed, shoulders collapsing under the weight of the secret. The confession came in pieces, reluctantly, like a child forced to admit to a broken toy. That morning, he explained, in his rush to snag a slice of last night's lasagne, he had miscalculated. He hadn't seen the dishwasher door left open and caught his shin on the metal edge. Pain had jolted through his leg, sending him off balance. In desperation, he'd grabbed at the benchtop.

The benchtop betrayed him.

The coffee, sugar, and tea jars had gone crashing to the floor in a symphony of shattering glass. Worse still, the lasagne dish—Adam's lasagne—had joined the descent. In Joey's telling, it was "one quick accident." But in Adam's mind, he could see it play out in dreadful slow motion: the jars spinning through the air, the porcelain dish tilting, the glorious lasagne tumbling, scattering sauce and pasta like confetti before exploding across the tiles on the floor.

And now, the prize—the carefully prepared, twenty-four-hour-cured lasagne Adam had specifically saved for tonight—lay buried in the outside bin, its promise of flavour lost to shards and sauce-stained foil.

Joey sat on the lounge, shin still throbbing, eyes suspiciously and guiltily watching Adam's expression as if awaiting sentencing.

Adam only stared at him. Words failed. The loss of the lasagne felt, in that moment, almost biblical. Adam had prepared it the day before with a heart full of care, carefully choosing only the freshest ingredients. Joey recalled him explaining how the lasagne needed to rest overnight, promising that by the next day it would be rich, delicious—gustoso! Yet, fate had other plans.

The shrill ring of the phone shattered the quiet, and Joey jolted upright like a cat caught stealing, guilt still flaring across his face before he smoothed it away with a fake smile. Adam eyed him briefly, then reached for the receiver with reluctance. He almost let the answering machine take it—until he heard Carol's voice. Tight. Urgent. Too urgent.

"I'm sorry to call you at home," she began, words rushing out as though afraid they might burn her tongue. "But I had to."

Carol never said *had to* unless something was truly wrong. Adam felt the muscles in his shoulders knot.

She told him she had dialled into the office to check on after hours phone messages, routine weekend tidying, when one had stopped her dead. "It was from Evelyn," she whispered, her tone dipping as if the walls around her might be listening.

Adam stood still. "Evelyn?"

"Yes. And Adam… it was strange. I've still got goose bumps."

He now paced about, pressing the phone tighter to his ear. "What did she say?"

Carol inhaled slowly, as though weighing whether to speak the words aloud. "She thanked you. For your support. For helping her fight her demons. She said she respected you. That she was grateful." A pause—so long Adam thought the line had gone dead—before Carol spoke again, lower now, her voice reluctant, as though crossing a threshold she did not want to cross. "And then she said she was calling to say goodbye."

The word lodged like ice in Adam's gut. "Goodbye?"

"Yes." The syllable snapped sharp and curt, and Adam could hear the tremor in her breath, the release of air she'd been holding since the moment she'd first listened to Evelyn's message.

"Was that all?" he asked, turning in a circle, while pacing. His mind had begun to race, chasing possibilities he didn't want to name.

"Not all," Carol said. "She called from a payphone—I could hear the coins fall. And… Adam, it felt final. Too final. What do you think she meant? Suicide?"

He closed his eyes. He knew, though he didn't want to say it. "I don't know," he lied. "Thank you for telling me. I'll… handle it."

When the call ended, silence pressed down, thick and suffocating. The room seemed colder, shadows stretching longer across the walls. Evelyn had long since cut every tether—no phone, no email, no forwarding address. She'd drifted through the cracks until she was little more than a rumour, a ghost people remembered but couldn't reach. Has she decided it was time to finally check out for good?

Joey, slouched with his injured leg propped stiffly before him, watched Adam's restless pacing with an ashen, unsettled expression. "Everything all right?" he asked, suspicion curdling his voice.

Adam hesitated. People said their goodbyes when the weight grew too heavy, when they were already half turned toward the dark. He'd seen it before, too many times. He told Joey only the surface of Carol's message, leaving the rest unspoken, but they lingered in the room regardless—thick, oppressive, inevitable.

"I don't think so," Joey declared, hardly lifting his head from the blue glow of his laptop screen. His fingers tapped a rhythm across the keyboard, dismissive and impatient.

Adam finally sat down, leaning back in his chair, studying Joey. "You sound very sure of that," he said, curiosity edging his tone.

"She's not going to kill herself," Joey replied flatly, his eyes never leaving the scrolling lines before him. "It's something else, mate. Maybe someone upset her. Maybe a dog barked at her. She's a bit loopy, you know how she is."

He tossed the words out carelessly, but Joey's throwaway remarks often carried the sting of truth. Adam felt a faint, guilty flicker of relief at his certainty. Evelyn could be eccentric, dramatic even, but what unsettled Adam was the shift in her behaviour. She'd never left an actual message before—only those unnerving calls that lingered in silence before ending with a sudden, hollow click.

Still, unease gnawed at him. Evelyn was always a mystery, a shadow on the periphery of their lives—vanishing for months without so much as a word, then reappearing as if she'd never been gone at all. That was her personality, her strange pattern. But this time… why reach out? Why break her silence now?

A few days later, Joey's battered car rumbled up the long slate path to a secluded estate, far from the noise of town. The gates had groaned open after a brief exchange on the intercom, and now the vehicle climbed a winding driveway toward a mansion that seemed to brood in the morning light.

The gardens were impossibly well-kept, as though some unseen hand tended them daily with reverence. Lawns lay stretched like green velvet, and under the deep shadow of the porch, Joey's car slid to a halt. Two thick stone pillars held up the roof, their surfaces twisted with ivy and pale blooms of white and purple. In the quiet beyond, the open lawns stirred with life: finches and sparrows darted across the grass, their little wings catching the light, their fragile songs carrying thinly through the still air.

Joey climbed out and slammed the car door, the sound jarring against the hush. An elderly figure emerged from the wide oak doorway almost immediately, as though he had been waiting.

Tom's eyes widened. "Joey? Where's Adam?"

Joey forced a casual smile, striding forward. "I was in the area," he said lightly, "thought I'd see if you were free."

Relief softened Tom's expression. His weathered features broke into a smile. "Well, you did the right thing. You're always welcome here." He gestured toward the shadowed hall beyond him. "Come in, come in."

Inside, the air carried the faint scent of polish and old paper. Dust motes drifted through, like they had before, and the silence reminded him of his previous meeting with Adam. Joey cleared his throat.

"I spoke to Adam last night," he began, forcing a note of casualness into his tone. "We thought we'd come visit you again. We found what you said very interesting."

"Good, good," Tom said, his face brightening as if the words were a promise. "So, Adam's on his way, then?"

"No," Joey blurted, too quickly. His denial rang sharp in the silence. "Like I said, I was nearby, just thought I'd stop in… to see if you were home." His words faltered, thinning into nothing. His eyes dropped to the polished floorboards as if they could provide him with a better excuse.

Tom observed him quietly; a shadow of disappointment shot across his face before giving way to gentleness. "Ah. All right, son." His voice softened, reading the tension in Joey's stance. A pause stretched between them, heavy and awkward, the kind that seemed to magnify the ticking of the unseen clock on the mantel.

Finally, Tom broke the silence. "So… when would you two like to visit again?"

Joey moved toward the door. "Soon. We'll come soon. I'll let Adam know." He stepped back outside, onto the porch, the conversation already slipping through his fingers. "I'll tell him I dropped by to say hello."

"Yes, best to sort this out sooner rather than later," Tom said, following him out to the porch. His eyes seemed to hold something unspoken. "I'm not a young man anymore, you know." A dry laugh escaped him, almost swallowed by the silence. "The sooner, the better."

Joey waved awkwardly and went to his car, opening the door and nodding quickly without looking at Tom.

"Safe trip!" Tom called after him as the engine coughed and roared to life, louder than necessary in the still morning air. He raised his voice, trying to cut through the noise. "I'll see you both soon!"

The car drove away down the long drive, its echo clattering against the stone walls until it was swallowed by distance. Tom stood in the doorway, one hand braced on the pillar entwined with vines, watching the dust settle long after Joey had gone.

Chapter Five
The Group

How does any of this fit? he wondered

The group wandered slowly through Tom's sprawling house; their footsteps muted against polished timber floors that seemed too immaculate for such casual traffic. They lingered at the long sideboard, picking at the delicate appetisers laid out on gleaming silver trays—finger foods Tom and two of his more capable guests had assembled earlier that afternoon. The spread was almost excessive: miniature quiches still faintly warm, smoked salmon spirals tucked into cucumber ribbons, and crisp crackers adorned with precise dots of pâté. Everything was artfully placed, as though Tom and his housekeeper had choreographed even the arrangement of individually wrapped after dinner mints.

The kitchen, where much of the preparation had taken place, was vast and looked more like a commercial kitchen. Its polished steel island bisected the room like a stage prop under a spotlight; every surface so shiny it reflected back distorted images of the guests' movements. Above it, hooks dangled expensive copper pans and skillets, gleaming in the light as though for display more than use. To anyone else, it might have looked like the setting for an evening of laughter, wine, and harmless indulgence.

But there was nothing harmless about the atmosphere.

Eight, maybe nine people drifted in and out of the kitchen and the adjoining hallway, their expressions carefully managed. From a distance, they seemed relaxed enough—grazing on appetisers, leaning in for muted exchanges—but closer observation betrayed the truth.

Their movements were just a touch too deliberate, every laugh slightly too clipped, every glance too fleeting. Their eyes never fully rested anywhere for long, sliding off one another as though too much contact might reveal something unspoken. Nervous. Guarded. But why? And who exactly were these people, brought together under Tom's roof with such odd regularity?

A brisk clap snapped through the room like a command.

Tom stood near the arched doorway, his presence filling the space. With the air of someone both host and conductor, he motioned for them to follow. One by one, they shuffled into the living room, balancing small plates and napkins, hands busy with snacks—nuts, chips, biscuits, neat little triangle sandwiches. Some ate absentmindedly; others didn't touch their food at all, fingers tightening around the edges of plates as though holding something heavier than hors d'oeuvres.

The last to enter slipped in almost unnoticed, choosing not a chair but the armrest of an oversized, timeworn lounge already occupied. The weight of their presence made the guest in the chair shift uncomfortably, but nothing was said.

"Alright, alright, everyone," Tom began, his voice carrying easily over the soft crackle of the fireplace. He raised his hands, commanding silence before he spoke. "Another successful meeting tonight. I think we are beginning to truly understand what's going on." His eyes swept the room, pausing, calculating. "Thea's images…"— he trailed off, lowering his gaze as if weighing something delicate— "…very interesting. Very telling. In the months ahead, there's going to be a great deal of analysis required. But for now, let's quickly review what we know so far."

The hush that followed felt fragile, ready to fracture at any moment. And fracture it did.

From near the heavy drapes, a sharp voice cut in—predictable, impatient. Michelle. "This is still incredibly unsafe! And if all of this is true… why us? And what exactly are we supposed to do about it?"

Her words cracked the room like glass under pressure. No one was surprised. Michelle's objections were as clockwork as the ticking mantlepiece clock, her doubts as steady as her heartbeat.

"Michelle," Darrin interjected, his tone unexpectedly firm. Heads turned. He was not a man given to interruption. "This is important, and you always seem to downplay what we've discovered. Don't you want to know what's really happening here?"

Darrin—quiet, middle-aged, once nearly invisible among them—had been a different man in the early days. He used to sit silently at the edge of the gatherings, content to observe while others argued and theorised. But Tom had drawn him out, encouraging him into trust. And once Darrin began to share the visions that haunted him, the group realised his insights were not only relevant but indispensable. Now, when he spoke, they listened.

He leaned forward slightly, his voice carrying more weight than his calm demeanour. "Remember, Michelle—we agreed to this. Things are changing. We are changing. Every few weeks, we learn more. Isn't this exactly why we are here?"

Before Michelle could respond, another voice burst forth— bright, forceful. "I agree!"

It was Amanda, seated close to Tom. She leapt to her feet with a sudden energy that seemed to startle even her. Normally outspoken, Amanda had grown quieter in recent months, her once-bold remarks tempered by something like weariness. Tonight, though, she stood with renewed insistence, her words rushing out. "For God's sake, this is why we're here. Darrin is right! I think we're really closing in." She moved restlessly across the room, abandoning her seat for one closer to the fire, as though seeking both comfort and audience.

Michelle exhaled loudly, raising her hands in a small, surrendering gesture. "I know, I know. I'm not trying to sabotage anything. I'm just saying—this is getting risky. I have two kids at home. If this is real, if everything we've been saying is true, then what are we supposed to do? How do we protect them? And what do we tell our families?”

Her words lingered in the air, heavier than anything they'd spoken so far. The room seemed to contract around her question, each of them silently wondering the same, yet unwilling to be the first to answer.

From the far corner of the room, someone said beneath their breath, "Most of us have children." The words drifted across the gathering like a faint protest, easily missed yet undeniably weighted. A few heads turned in acknowledgement, but no one spoke further. The sentiment hung there, suspended, an unspoken reminder of the lives tethered beyond these walls.

Amanda shifted in her chair, her eyes sliding toward Tom. Her voice was steady, though the faintest trace of impatience rode beneath it. "What do you think we should do next?"

Tom exhaled slowly, his chest rising and falling with the kind of weariness that had become more noticeable with each passing month. He scanned the room, his eyes taking in the familiar circle of faces. "Alright," he said at last, his tone reluctant. "I'll keep this short—I can see some of you are ready to leave. The weather's turning nasty tonight, so let's move this forward and close for the month."

He paused then, but not with the ease of a man gathering his thoughts. Instead, he seemed to be fighting with them, sifting through half-formed notions that slipped further from reach. There was a frailty about him lately—an unmistakable aging of spirit that unsettled some of the group. More than one wondered in silence whether Tom still had the strength to lead, though none dared voice it aloud.

"And…" Darrin prompted lightly, his grin disarming but deliberate. He leaned forward, encouraging Tom along with the ease of someone who had done this before. Darrin's loyalty to the Overseer was unwavering; he wouldn't allow hesitation or doubt to diminish Tom's authority in front of the others.

"Oh—yes." Tom blinked back into focus. "Think about what we discussed tonight. Don't write anything down, not directly. Keep everything coded. Stay cautious, stay safe. We'll meet again in about seven weeks."

"Tom?"

The interruption drew every eye to Martin, the group's most recent addition. Though he had joined only a year ago, he remained a puzzle even now. Tall, clean-shaven, striking in his composure, Martin carried himself with a quiet elegance that demanded attention without effort. He rarely spoke, but when he did, the room instinctively stilled.

"I think," Martin said slowly, his words measured as if prepared earlier, "given what we uncovered tonight, wouldn't it be wise to perhaps meet sooner?"

Michelle cut in before Tom could respond, looking quickly at her watch with an edge of irritation. "I disagree. We should stick to the same schedule. It's already difficult enough for me to break away every seven weeks. We've all got lives, you know." She flicked a look upward as the windows rattled in their frames, the wind outside gusting harder now, almost punctuating her impatience.

"I agree with Martin," Darrin said evenly, his calm tone silencing the small ripple of voices that had begun to rise. "We don't need a long meeting—just something sooner, an hour maybe. Enough to stay ahead."

Amanda leaned forward, her voice bright with urgency. "I agree, too."

And then, one by one, others followed. Nods indicated approval, a quiet ripple of consensus moving through the room until resistance seemed the lonelier position. Those who couldn't make an earlier date would be updated later; such accommodations were always part of Tom's gatherings.

The Overseer had never imposed a rigid schedule. Members came as they could, and those who didn't were never rebuked. Tom made certain of that. Absentees were kept in the fold through careful phone calls, discreet emails, or private visits. His role wasn't only to lead but to hold the threads together, weaving each voice into the wider tapestry no matter how faintly it joined.

It was during this closing lull that Martin spoke again, though this time with a quieter weight. He announced that he and his partner would be moving away. He would not be attending in person anymore but promised to remain in touch—through calls, encrypted messages, the occasional online appearance. His words carried no sentiment, no apology, yet the absence they foretold settled heavily in the room.

When the meeting at last dispersed, Tom escorted his guests to the door, lingering in the entryway as coats were pulled on and goodbyes exchanged. Outside, a slow procession of headlights swept across the slate drive, bright beams cutting through the branches that overhung the driveway. Cars rolled up one after another, their tires crunching in a unison that seemed almost rehearsed. Spouses arrived in cautious waves—some staying in their vehicles with engines idling, faces lit in a bluish glow from dashboard screens, others leaning impatiently on their horns, urging their partners and loved ones inside to hurry. A few exchanges—half-hearted waves, muffled words through lowered windows—filled the night before dissolving into silence. One by one, the vehicles drifted off, swallowed by the road's bend and the trees beyond, their red taillights smearing into the distance until nothing remained but the faint echo of tires and the lingering sense of departures unfinished.

Only when the last pair of taillights vanished down the drive did Tom turn back inside. The old house fell quiet around him, its silence thick and familiar. He secured the property methodically— alarm set, locks checked, gates bolted. In the living room, half-finished drinks and untouched appetisers were left as they were. The mild scent of perfume and other wearable cosmetics filled the room. His housekeeper, insistent on managing such details herself, would return in the morning.

Crossing the hall, Tom entered a small room tucked beside the staircase. It was dim, cramped, a remnant from another age when homes had cloakrooms for visitors' coats. The air here carried a stillness different from the rest of the house, as though the walls held secrets. Tom stood for a moment, scanning the corners as though half-expecting someone to emerge from them.

Satisfied, he moved to the antique bookcase set flush against the wall. His fingertips brushed the carved wood at the back of the bookshelf, tracing until they found the shallow groove near the top right. He pressed. The shelf shifted almost imperceptibly at first, then slid smoothly aside, revealing the outline of a hidden door.

A silver door, gleaming faintly in the low light, locked and concealed behind the shelf was revealed. Tom keyed a code into the small pad fixed to the wall. He did so carefully, each digit pressed with deliberation, his face tight with concentration. A metallic click broke the silence. The door yielded, sliding quickly into the sandstone wall to expose a staircase spiralling downward into a well of brightness.

The lights below had been left burning. Tom descended slowly, his steps heavy, his hand brushing the cold rail as though steadying himself against the weight of what lay ahead.

The chamber revealed itself gradually, vast and archaic, its stone walls speaking of another century—perhaps another purpose long forgotten. Yet now it was their refuge. Only recently had Tom softened its starkness, spreading a grand Persian rug across the cold floor, dressing the space as though to civilize its secrets. The rug's colours glowed richly under the lights, a striking contrast against rough-hewn walls that had witnessed more years than any of them could guess.

And in that place, beneath the storm and the house above, Tom stood alone, listening to the hum of silence, burdened by both memory and the fragile weight of tomorrow.

In the centre of the chamber stretched a long oval table, its polished surface gleaming faintly in the overhead light. The piece looked as though it had been stolen from a corporate skyscraper and smuggled down here, wholly out of place in the secret confines of a hidden basement. Twelve black leather chairs ringed it in a neat arc, their high backs lending the room a cold, ceremonial air. Along the wall nearest the entrance, a second row of simpler seats waited, as if anticipating latecomers or silent observers.

From the far-left corner came a low, rhythmic sound: the muted beeps and whirs of the control panel, steady as a heartbeat. The glow of its screens bathed that part of the room in pale green and amber light, flickering against the concrete walls. Tom moved toward it with practiced ease, his footsteps tracing a familiar path. He leaned in, eyes scanning the scrolling data, the digital readouts, the camera feeds. The perimeter remained clear. The monitors offered a constant, watchful eye on the house above and the land beyond—an unblinking 360-degree view of his domain. For the moment, all was normal.

He turned back toward the table, where the surface was cluttered with papers, files, and half-finished diagrams—notes scattered like the pieces of an unfinished puzzle. A map with corners curled upward. A stack of reports annotated in his sharp, impatient handwriting. Tom lifted one of the sheets, exhaling through his nose as though the weight of it pressed on more than just his hand. His gaze moved slowly over the inked words, the half-formed conclusions, the tenuous connections his group had managed to scrape together.

How does any of this fit? he wondered. The question had haunted him for weeks, circling the back of his mind like a restless bird that refused to land. The evidence was there—he was certain of it—but the lines between pieces blurred, overlapped, contradicted. Too many voices, too many egos, clouding the clarity that might otherwise emerge.

After a long silence, Tom lowered the papers back onto the table. His hand lingered on them as though reluctant to let go, then withdrew. He crossed once more to the control panel, shutting down the monitors one by one. The room fell quieter with each darkened screen until only the watchful eye of the indoor and outdoor security cameras remained.

He made his way up the stairs to the silver door, its touch cool beneath his palm. Lock engaged. Mechanisms clicked in sequence, sealing the chamber behind him. Finally, he slid the bookshelf back into place, hiding the silver door from view.

Climbing into the stillness of the house, Tom's thoughts clung to the gathering that just left—the faces around the table, each locked in their own convictions, each blind to the greater role still demanded of them. Their disagreements replayed in his mind, prickly arguments that had led nowhere. At times, he wanted to grab them by the shoulders, to rattle them until their blinkered concerns fell away, until they could see the larger storm gathering on the horizon. The impulse burned in him, a desperate urge to wake them from their complacency and denial, to demand that they put their considerable talents to better use before it was too late. But he knew he couldn't. The moment he crossed that line—raised his voice, let his frustration show—he'd lose them. They would retreat even further into themselves, barricading behind pride, fear and stubbornness, but he knew he couldn't do that.

If only they understood—if only they could glimpse more fully what lay ahead.

Chapter Six
The NO People

The mind and body are deeply connected, each influencing the other in tangible ways…

Many days earlier, Evelyn had phoned Adam's workplace from a phone box. The call had been short, almost hurried, and afterward—silence. No one had heard from her since. The unanswered questions gnawed at him like restless moths chewing through fabric—where was she, and was she even still alive? At odd hours of the day and in the quiet of night, his mind returned to her, circling the same bleak questions without finding answers. Each time he thought he had forced her from his thoughts, she would return, an intrusive echo that refused to fade.

In the reception area, Carol was arranging fresh flowers, her small ritual of order and brightness. She believed in the quiet symbolism of such gestures—how a carefully chosen bloom could shift the mood of a room. She never brought white lilies; she knew Adam disliked them, and though she never pressed him for a reason, she respected that unspoken boundary. Instead, today she had chosen a mix of soft chrysanthemums and bright gerberas, colours that promised warmth even on a grey morning.

Adam had other clients waiting, and he forced himself to push Evelyn from his mind—at least for now. His first appointment was with Michael, whose calm, rugged exterior belied the constant undercurrent of anxiety that rippled beneath. Michael could smile, joke even, but the way his hands tightened around the armrests of the chair betrayed what his words tried to hide.

Next came Natalie. She arrived with her shoulders slumped, eyes shadowed, her whole being weighed down by the gravity of her depression. Today she was withdrawn, irritable, and burdened with guilt, resisting every attempt Adam made to draw her into conversation. Where he usually thrived on the challenge of breaking through walls like hers, today he found himself uncharacteristically detached, as if some essential part of him had grown weary. More than once, he caught himself quietly wishing the day would end.

Kurt followed. His case was different, almost a small source of light in Adam's otherwise draining day. Kurt's anxiety, once crippling, had gradually lessened, and the steady progress he was making pleased Adam. Yet even so, Kurt still needed constant reassurance, as though afraid that one slip backward would undo all his work. Recently, he had begun to speak more openly about his deeper struggles—loneliness, lack of purpose, and the quiet, suffocating dissatisfaction with his job.

At thirty-something, with his family living interstate, Kurt had spent the past three years in Sydney working a monotonous role that paid the bills but left him stagnant, drained of energy, and starved of meaning. It was in one of their sessions that Kurt first stumbled across a term that struck him like a revelation: "NO People." The phrase described those who saw no meaning, no joy, and no clear way forward in life. Kurt latched onto it immediately. It fit him perfectly, and in naming his state, he gave his despair a shape he could wrestle with.

Strangely, knowing others shared his struggle made him feel less alone. He began to loosen his grip on the narrative that he was merely a victim of circumstance. For the first time in years, he felt the stirrings of responsibility—not the heavy, shaming kind, but the empowering realization that no one could fix his life but him. Quietly, he resolved to confront his "NO" status head-on, determined to re-emerge as a someone again. Who that "someone" would be, he could not yet say, but he knew it was his to define.

Over several weeks, small but unmistakable shifts began to take root. Kurt practiced his new strategies with discipline, returning often to the DS room—a space that had become his personal workshop for reshaping his thoughts. Each visit strengthened the fragile threads of confidence he was weaving into his days. Carol noticed it too. He carried himself with a new steadiness, spoke with more certainty, and, perhaps for the first time, even seemed attractive—not just in appearance but in the energy he projected.

Part of this transformation stemmed from a deceptively simple exercise Adam had given him: list the areas of life he wanted to develop, rate each one, and mark where improvement was most needed. What began as a worksheet evolved into something larger. It was no longer about the tired old notion of "work–life balance." Kurt reframed it into a project of "life balance"—a more expansive harmony stretched across ten distinct aspects of himself: health, purpose, relationships, creativity, and more. The act of mapping his own terrain gave him a sense of direction he had not felt in years.

The framework had been created by Adam, who believed these ten "core aspects" were essential to psychological well-being. While there are countless elements that make up a person, Adam called them *The Ten Aspects of the Self*:

1   Relationships/Family
2   Career
3   Social/Friendships
4   Goals
5   Me Time
6   Hobbies, Activities and Chores
7   Finances and Studies
8   Health, Diet and Exercise
9   Sexual Expression
10 Spiritual and/or Metaphysical Beliefs

Adam taught that each of these must be recognised and valued equally—no single area is inherently more important than another. Neglecting one aspect in favour of another, such as overinvesting in work at the expense of relationships or health, creates imbalance. Over time, this can lead to inner discord and potentially harmful consequences.

True harmony comes when a person distributes their energy evenly across all ten aspects. In such balance, Adam believed, people gain access to their intuition and untapped resources. The result isn't just external success—it is deep fulfilment, self-discovery, and a clearer sense of life's purpose.

From Adam, Kurt also learned about the "four emotional engines" people carry. Only one is required for daily living; the other three are reserved for emergencies. These three tie directly to the fight-or-flight response—rarely active unless a person perceives real or imagined danger. The more engines that switch on, the stronger the body's reaction, with the intensity determined by the perceived threat. Kurt soon realized that running on too many emotional engines was taking a toll on his health, so he shifted his focus to relaxation techniques and meditation, aiming to operate from just one calm, steady emotional state.

The mind and body are deeply connected, each influencing the other in tangible ways. Whatever the nature of your thoughts—negative, neutral, or positive—they will inevitably affect your physical state. Negative thought patterns, in particular, cause the body to process stress internally, which can eventually manifest as physical symptoms. A happy mind fosters a happy body, and the reverse is also true.

In an ideal world, a calm, content, and anxiety-free person would have only one "emotional engine" running at a time. For mental well-being, simplicity is best—fewer active emotional engines mean better emotional, psychological, and physical health.

However, when the body shifts into fight-or-flight mode, stress hormones flood the system, creating a dramatic chemical shift. Depending on the intensity of the perceived threat—real or imagined—your body may activate a second, third, or even fourth emotional engine. Even purely mental triggers, such as negative or extreme thinking, can ramp up these survival engines.

Once in fight-or-flight mode, the body's internal systems lose their natural coherence, entering a state of chaos as they prepare to protect you. It takes time for balance to be restored, for stress chemicals to disperse, and for those engines to power down. This process can be draining—many people feel exhausted for days afterward, a lingering reminder of how taxing this state can be.

Many people describe the physical sensations in their body as "gearing up" when their emotional engines switch on—becoming more alert, tense, and hyper-aware—and "coming back down" when those engines shut off, often leaving them feeling sad, guilty, or empty. These shifts closely mirror the symptoms of anxiety and related disorders, and even the onset of depression can be experienced in this way. Prolonged and intense negative thinking can trigger chemical changes in the body, leading to mood swings that dim the joy and vibrancy of daily life.

Kurt quickly realised that staying calm was essential to keeping his engines from firing up and turning his body into a chemical factory. In practical terms, that meant controlling his thoughts and avoiding unnecessary escalation by practising mindfulness and other coping strategies. His aim was simple: operate on just one emotional engine—the content, joyful one. After all, the fewer conflicting engines running in the body, the greater the happiness. The other three engines had no place in Kurt's life; he didn't need to activate them, especially since he wasn't living in a dangerous or conflict-filled environment. Furthermore, he made the firm decision to cut negative people out of his life, recognizing they drained his energy and caused him unnecessary distress.

Working through his ten aspects and unlocking the mystery of his four engines shifted Kurt's life in ways he could never have foreseen—let alone so quickly. He unearthed ambitions he'd never paused to consider, began mapping out his future, and developed a genuine passion for subjects that once barely caught his attention. Even the spiritual and metaphysical side of himself—something he had previously rated at zero—began to stir. Until now, he had neither acknowledged nor invested a single drop of energy into that realm.

The most thrilling discovery was learning how to selectively switch off certain components of his one active engine, allowing him to access deeper states of awareness. When fully alert and focused, he often entered the high-frequency beta range—patterns our brains naturally emit. But when deeply relaxed, or immersed in calming activities such as meditation, his brain shifted into alpha and theta waves, quieting parts of his emotional engine and leaving him weightless, peaceful, and still.

The old "NO People" label no longer applied. Kurt's lighter mood, sharper presence, and newfound curiosity were proof—he had turned a corner.

It's said that Image Carriers can summon these low alpha and theta states at will, shutting down almost all of their one engine and slipping into profoundly altered states of being—becoming more energy than matter, more spirit than body. In those moments, they are believed to merge their personal consciousness with the vast collective consciousness of all things.

By the end of the day, Adam was more than ready to leave. He craved the chance to go home and, if possible, switch off completely. After a brief goodbye to Carol—who was also eyeing the clock—he felt quietly pleased about Kurt's progress.

Just as Adam reached the door, the switchboard light began to flash. Carol cursed under her breath, "Why now? They always call right before closing." Adam offered a half-smile and a lazy wave.

"Adam?" Carol called out, halting him mid-step. "It's that Tom guy. Says it's urgent!"

Moments later, Adam found himself heading away from home. Tom's voice over the phone had been persuasive enough to convince him to stop by before the night was out. Adam wasn't sure why he'd agreed—he'd been toying with the idea of ending his meetings with the elderly man altogether. Yet there was something compelling in Tom's tone, something that made Adam yield.

In truth, he had no evening plans. Impulse had always been part of his nature, and he often told his clients that a little spontaneity could be good for the soul.

Now approaching whatever counted as "middle age" these days, Adam felt an itch for something more. He had stayed single by choice, travelled extensively, and crossed paths with remarkable people whose stories had left lasting impressions. But in recent years, his life had shrunk into a closed loop of work, sleep, and more work—no adventure, no joy.

Why? When had the colour drained from his days? Was it caution creeping in with age? Or was Tom—eccentric, unpredictable Tom—rekindling the hunger for curiosity that Adam had once lived by?

Was this the start of a new, synchronised adventure for Adam—or the first step into danger?

Chapter Seven
Messages and Signs

Behind the illusion of mahogany and old bindings, a flash of silver shone in the gloom...

The traffic was unbearable. Cars clogged every lane, all heading in the same direction as Adam. Eventually, he veered off the highway into a secluded enclave where the rich and famous resided. Instantly, the gridlock vanished. The noise and chaos melted away, replaced by an almost tangible calm. Adam slowed his pace, trying to recall the route to Tom's house.

This part of the city was famed for its sprawling mansions. Wide, well-lit streets stretched ahead, flanked by immaculate walkways. Sleek luxury cars gleamed in the open, while others rested unseen behind garage doors operated by remote controls and guarded by sophisticated security systems. Towering trees—hundreds of years old—stood like sentinels, hinting that this land had been settled since the days when English ships first unloaded their convicts and pioneers.

The gates to Tom's lavish estate stood open when Adam arrived. No intercom this time; Tom was clearly expecting him. He followed the curved driveway at a cautious pace and stopped near the entrance. As Adam stepped from his car, Tom emerged, grasped his hand warmly, and shook it as though greeting an old friend.

"Greetings! Greetings!" Tom beamed, speaking in a rush. "Come through! Follow me! Come through!" He moved with surprising speed for his age, a lively energy replacing the sombre, reserved manner Adam and Joey had seen before. Tonight, Tom seemed almost exhilarated.

Adam followed him through the familiar entryway into the same room he and Joey had occupied weeks earlier. Nothing had changed—not the furniture, not the faint scent in the air. The décor once again reminded Adam of his old high school.

"What's this all about?" Adam asked directly.

"Yes, yes," Tom responded, already heading toward the kitchen. "Would you like a drink?"

"No, Tom, I'm fine. Please, sit," Adam replied, stopping him mid-step. Tom's eagerness to please only heightened Adam's unease.

"Tom is everything alright?" he asked, concern creeping into his voice. What was going on here? Was Tom simply lonely—or was there something more troubling beneath the surface? Adam began to wonder if coming back had been a mistake.

"I'm sorry!" Tom blurted out. "You must think I'm crazy..." He gave a short, awkward laugh, watching Adam's expression harden with impatience.

"Adam, I called you here because I think you're connected to what's happening. And if we don't act—" Tom's voice trailed off. His face grew serious, eyes dropping to the floor as he fell into deep thought.

Adam studied him with mixed feelings. Had his hunch been right all along—that Tom was just playing games, a lonely old man looking for entertainment? The urge to walk away was strong, but something kept him rooted in place, almost spellbound by the strange man's words.

As a therapist and coach, Adam wanted to protect Tom, yet the frustration was clawing at him. He wanted to shout, to demand answers, but instead chose restraint. He decided he'd leave quietly, never to see Tom again.

Adam had always been drawn to mysteries and the unexplained, but Tom's vague remarks were beginning to wear thin. Perhaps it was the decades he'd spent in counselling, where helping others had become second nature, or maybe it was an unshakable instinct deep in his gut—he couldn't be sure. Either way, something had pulled him back to Tom's door once more. Was there a hidden depth to this eccentric man, or was he merely someone in desperate need of psychiatric help?

"Tom?" Adam's tone was calm, steady. He was ready to end this. "My time is limited. Do you want to show me something?"

That was the reason Tom had called him over, after all. Yet now, Tom sat pale and still, looking sickly.

Adam leaned forward, concerned. "You alright? You don't look well."

"Please, don't worry. I'm fine," Tom snapped back, his energy suddenly returning.

"So, Tom," Adam pressed, "why am I here? I haven't got all night. What did you want to show me before I go?"

Tom stared at him, weighing something in his mind. Then a slow grin spread across his face. "I think I'll just show you. Can you follow me?"

Adam rose warily, trailing behind Tom as they left the room, crossed the hallway, and stepped into a small, closet-like space.

Then Adam froze.

What at first appeared to be a solid wall directly in front of them began to stir, almost imperceptibly, as if the house itself were drawing a slow, concealed breath. Adam looked on, convinced for a moment that his eyes were playing tricks in the dim light. But no—the surface wasn't a wall at all. When he narrowed his focus, he saw the truth. The towering bookcase, lined with rows of dusty leather spines and gilded volumes, was shifting sideways with a low, deliberate groan, as though moved by some hidden mechanism.

The heavy oak shelves slid back to reveal a sudden glint—cold, metallic, and out of place. Behind the illusion of mahogany and old bindings, a flash of silver shone in the gloom. Embedded into the rough sandstone foundation of the house stood a door, not the kind one would expect in a home like this, but a slab of polished steel, its surface gleaming with a sterile brightness that jarred against the centuries-old stone. It looked almost surgical, clinical—like a fragment of some other world rudely inserted into the fabric of this antique residence.

Adam felt the hairs at the back of his neck rise. Whatever lay beyond that door didn't belong to the house—and was it too late now for Adam to make his escape?

As Adam remained rooted to the spot, thinking about his next move, he noticed Tom leaning towards a keypad built into the wall, and tapping in a sequence of numbers. A muted click sounded, and the door slid open with deliberate smoothness. Without hesitation, Tom stepped across the threshold, casting a brief glance back and motioning for Adam to follow.

Descending a narrow staircase, Adam's eyes widened. Beyond lay a room filled with cutting-edge technology. It didn't belong here.

"What is this place?" he whispered, awestruck.

A thought stirred in his mind: *It's a secret room...*

But for what—and for whom?

The covert room was roughly the size of two average rooms—spacious enough to move around, but hardly expansive. In the centre stood a large oblong table, surrounded by chairs, with a side table tucked neatly against the sandstone wall to the left. There were no windows, only walls that seemed to hold in secrets. Sheets of butcher paper and notepads lay scattered across the table, covered in cryptic writings, sketches, symbols, and strange designs. A crooked corkboard, cluttered with scraps of paper, hung near where Adam stood. On the opposite side, a mobile whiteboard faced the room, its surface wiped clean, waiting.

Adam's slow steps carried him to the far corner, where Tom sat before what looked like a command centre. The workstation bristled with high-tech equipment—sleek, flat-screen monitors, an array of switches and buttons, all looking brand new and expensive. Suddenly, the screens flickered to life. One monitor caught Adam's eye: it showed a live feed of himself and Tom.

What…? The thought hit hard. *There's a camera in here.* His looked quickly around, searching for it. The angle of the feed gave it away—two small cameras were mounted above the sliding silver door in the far corner, their lenses covering every inch of the room.

Tom rose slowly, as though shedding an earlier skin. He reached across the console of flickering screens, dimming some and silencing others with a series of deliberate keystrokes. The soft hum in the room lowered, leaving only the faint buzz of electricity in the walls. Then, with a few precise taps on a smaller panel, he completed whatever task had been occupying him and crossed the room. His movements were measured, purposeful, as if he had rehearsed them many times.

He came to the table where Adam stood waiting, and with a quiet authority, pulled out the chair opposite. Lowering himself into it, Tom gestured sharply. "Sit," he said—not in an aggressive tone, but more firm, a command wrapped in civility.

The change in him was startling. The feeble, distracted man Adam had first encountered seemed to vanish in that instant. In his place sat someone self-possessed, calm, and undeniably in control. There was a steadiness in his look, a subtle pressure in the room that made Adam feel as though the air had grown heavier. By contrast, Adam himself felt his own composure faltering; the warmth drained from his face, leaving his skin cold and tight.

Tom wasted no time circling around pleasantries. His questions came quickly; his eyes fixed with an unsettling intensity. He wanted to know what Adam understood about those who could peer beyond the veil of the ordinary world—the rare few who spoke of visions, premonitions, and unseen realms. Clairvoyants, psychics, mystics. Whatever name one gave them, Tom seemed to believe they were real, and he wanted Adam's view.

Before Adam could answer, another question came—unexpected, jarring. Tom asked about Adam's career in mental health, about his fascination with the power of suggestion, persuasion, and imagery. But Adam's attention had slipped from the conversation almost at once. Something on the table drew him in: a scatter of pages spread before him.

On one sheet, delicate sketches of the moon stood out, each crater etched with care, its surface ringed by mysterious symbols. Interlocking patterns of lines and inscriptions curved around it like some forgotten code. Adam's brow creased as he leaned closer, trying to make sense of what he was seeing.

A sharp *tap* on the table startled him back. Tom's hand rested there, his knuckles taut against the wood. His voice carried a new edge now—urgent, commanding, entirely different from the tone he had used earlier. Adam stiffened. He didn't like this version of Tom, didn't like the intensity behind his eyes.

Tom seemed to realise the effect and softened almost immediately. "Forgive me," he said, voice quieter, almost contrite. "I don't mean to interrogate. I only ask for honesty. These questions—" he tapped the table once more, more gently this time, "—they're important. Vital. And I need to hear what you think."

Spread across the table were more papers, mingled among the lunar sketches. Schematics of strange devices, handwritten notes in several different hands, and comments scrawled hastily in varying styles of ink. Adam recognised at once that they had come from multiple sources—different minds, different times. The sheer diversity gave the collection a chaotic gravity, like pieces of a single story scattered across generations.

He studied them with care, answering Tom's questions in measured tones. He offered enough to appear forthcoming, but not so much as to strip himself bare. Adam had always been a man of integrity, even when it came at personal cost. He spoke of the individuals he had encountered—clients, acquaintances, wanderers—who claimed gifts beyond the ordinary. Some had been obvious charlatans, spinning tales for attention. Others, however, had unsettled him with their precision, their eerie insights.

But one truth Adam kept locked away. Joey. He would not mention anything more about Joey.

Nonetheless, the recollection came spontaneously—his young friend's calm voice, the uncanny assurance in his eyes when he spoke of things nobody should have known. Joey's gift was real. Adam had seen it, tested it, feared it. And they had both agreed, long ago, never to tell. Secrets like that were dangerous. To be different in that way was to invite suspicion, envy, even harm. Joey had carried the burden in silence for years, and Adam would not betray him now.

So, Adam skirted around that part of his past, speaking instead of other encounters. He described moments from his work where clients' stories—visions, dreams, predictions—had rattled his scepticism. At first, he had dismissed them as coincidence or imagination, dismissing the details that clung too tightly to be ignored. But as the years passed, and as patterns emerged, he began to notice an unnerving consistency.

He confessed, cautiously, that he had begun recording these accounts. At first, just scraps of notes, kept private. Over time, it had grown into a collection of observations, hidden from colleagues, concealed even from friends. He never spoke of it aloud. Yet the habit had deepened, especially after the strange messages began to arrive. Messages he had not sought, could not explain, and could not ignore.

What had started as mere documentation had become something more—a quiet obsession, a private archive born of curiosity and unease. It was, he realised, one of the few things in his life that had never been touched by his work, his relationships, or his ambitions. It belonged only to him. And now Tom was asking for it.

Adam met Tom's gaze across the table, heart steady but cautious, and wondered how much of his truth he dared place in another man's hands.

"So," Tom began, his voice bubbling with anticipation, "you're the type who collects information and then tries to connect the dots, aren't you?"

Adam tilted his head, uncertain whether it was a question or an accusation. "I suppose so," he said slowly. "I hadn't really thought of it that way."

Tom's lips curved, not quite into a smile, more like the hint of someone already convinced of something. "But do you believe them, Adam?" he pushed, leaning back in his chair with the smug ease of a man who thought himself in control of the conversation. The light caught the sharp lines of his face, accentuating the quiet authority that had settled over him since they'd descended into the underground room.

Adam hesitated, caught off guard by the shift in tone. A faint chill skittered along his spine. "Well… yes," he admitted.

"Do you have faith in them?" Tom leaned forward now, eyes gleaming, unblinking. "Faith that some of these people might actually possess the abilities they claim?"

Adam felt his chest tighten, irritation prickling under his skin. "Yes," he snapped at last, his patience fraying under the interrogative edge in Tom's voice. "Why are you so interested in my work?"

Tom's reaction was immediate and surprising. He slapped the arm of his chair and leaned back, a great exhale of relief leaving his chest. "Good. Good," he said, nodding to himself. Then, louder, with conviction: "I believe you." His whole body seemed to soften, as though a burden had been lifted. A broad smile spread across his face—unexpectedly tender, almost childlike. His eyes glistened, fixed on Adam not as though he were simply a man but something more, something extraordinary.

Adam said nothing. He wasn't sure he could. His attention had snagged elsewhere—on the corkboard that dominated the far wall. His eyes found a single drawing pinned to a sheet of A4 paper: a flower rendered in coloured pencil; delicate white petals fanned against a halo of green. Around it, a collage of bright images—computer printouts, newspaper clippings, scraps of diagrams—formed an unsettling mosaic. There was something about the flower in particular, fragile yet strangely luminous, that unsettled him. It pulsed in his mind with a quiet insistence, as though it contained a secret only half-revealed.

"What's with the flower?" Adam asked, unable to keep the question back.

For a heartbeat, Tom seemed to drift somewhere far away, his look unfocused. Then, with a slow blink, he returned to the room. "The flower…" His voice carried weight now. "We'll talk about that later." He leaned forward, elbows on his knees, his expression sharpened with intensity. "For now, let's just say you're looking at the tip of the iceberg. The contents of that cork board Adam—and these images here on the table—they represent years of work, all pieces of a puzzle that we are still attempting to solve. Evidence and clues. Exactly what you have been doing."

Adam frowned. "Evidence and Clues? What kind of clues? What kind of evidence?"

Tom rose half from his chair and pointed at the flower. "That drawing, for one. It plays a critical role. We're close to understanding what it means. Very close." His finger shifted to a large sheet of butcher's paper, pinned neatly beside the collage, where a hand-drawn moon loomed against the page. "And the moon. You mentioned it earlier, remember? Its relationship with Earth is far more complicated than people are told. You wouldn't believe what we've uncovered if I told you outright."

He chuckled softly to himself, the sound sharp, like a man choking back the weight of an unbearable truth.

Adam narrowed his eyes. "You keep saying we. Who exactly is we?"

Tom's expression flickered with pride. "Oh yes—absolutely, there are others. Just a few Image Carriers, and me. We are small in number, but our strength lies in secrecy. My role is to keep them safe, hidden from prying eyes, while we piece together their visions and forecasts."

The colour had returned to his cheeks, a spark of vitality igniting in his movements. He seemed younger, almost feverishly alive. Adam, despite his scepticism, felt something stirring inside him too—a ripple of wonder he hadn't experienced in years. It was the sensation of teetering on the edge of discovery, as though the air itself hummed with revelations waiting to be spoken.

"Sounds like you've got an interesting job," Adam said, his brow furrowed. Then, after a pause: "These Image Carriers… they're the ones you've been talking about?"

"That's right," Tom said firmly. "That's what they're called. But we'll get into that another time." He rose and gestured for Adam to follow.

Adam lingered a moment in the leather chair, still dumbfounded, before finally standing. Together they stepped out of the hidden chamber beneath the sandstone house. The silver door slid closed behind them with a solid, final click as Tom locked it.

The corridor above felt unnervingly ordinary after the strange gravity of the room they'd left behind. Yet Adam's mind was anything but ordinary now. Questions tumbled through his head, tripping over one another in their urgency. One broke free.

"Tell me more about the moon," he said as Tom ushered him towards the living room.

Tom's expression shifted again, the gleam of a man who knew more than he dared share. "Put it this way, Adam. Earth's moon isn't what people think. The Image Carriers… they tell us it will play a vital role one day—if humanity lasts that long. Think of it as a colossal housing craft. We've learned it has a kind of intelligence—artificial, perhaps, or something older, deeper. It's far more than a lump of rock orbiting Earth."

Adam's throat tightened. The words sounded insane, but they carried a peculiar gravity that rooted them in his mind. He waited for Tom to continue, but the man only studied him, working out his reaction like a scientist observing an experiment.

When Adam didn't respond, Tom added with a sly smile, "And I haven't even told you about Mars."

They entered the living room. Adam didn't sit. He couldn't. His thoughts were a storm, every fragment of logic battling the primal part of him that whispered—what if it's true?

"So… the moon's not really real?" The question slipped out clumsy, but urgent.

"All we know," Tom said swiftly, "is what I've told you. But soon, someone will uncover what lies beneath—if they haven't already. And the dust particles…" He let the words hang, his eyes narrowing with meaning. "That's another story entirely."

Adam swallowed hard, his voice low, almost hoarse. "What about the dust particles?"

Tom's explanation came in a flood of words, his eyes gleaming with the fervour of a man speaking truths he'd carried too long. He told Adam that the fine, dust-like particles carpeting the lunar surface were unlike any substance known on Earth. At first glance they appeared lifeless—mere gray powder scattered across a barren world—but under scrutiny they revealed properties that defied classification. The particles carried strange, elusive qualities: a latent force that insulated the moon's inner body from cosmic radiation, from the sun's blistering heat, from the cold void of space itself.

More unsettling was their fluid nature. Tom described how they seemed to shift subtly, altering form as if the grains were not inert matter at all but some collective entity, radiating a quiet, magnetic hum. To Tom, it was as though millions of tiny wardens were embedded in that gray blanket, their purpose not only to guard but to conceal, hiding something vast and unfathomable buried deep within the moon's core. They were not passive relics of geology. They stored water—yes—but they also contained reactive chemicals, dormant until provoked, capable of producing energy without end. Energy not of the crude, burning sort humanity wrested from fossil or fission, but of a clean, self-renewing kind, endless as the tides.

"There's an intelligence to them," Tom whispered, leaning forward, his tone more confession than explanation. "Not mechanical. Not organic. Something beyond us. Something that watches."

Adam stood transfixed, a strange chill running through him. He wanted desperately to press further, to draw every scrap of meaning from Tom's extraordinary revelations. But the clock had crept later into the night. At last, he managed to thank Tom, his voice unsteady, confessing that the evening had been unlike any he had ever known. He promised he would be in contact again and would like to know more about those strange records hidden in Tom's secret chamber.

At this, Tom's expression darkened, the fire in his eyes tempered by a heavy caution. "No one knows about that room," he said with deliberate weight. "No one. What's in there—what you've seen—must stay between us. You understand?"

Adam nodded, though his mind still swam.

When they stepped outside, the night air was sharp, carrying the scent of eucalyptus and damp air. Tom clapped Adam firmly on the back, the gesture both comradely and commanding. "Think about what we discussed," he said. "Take your time. When you're ready to talk, I'll be waiting." Then, as they approached Adam's car, Tom's voice dropped to a conspiratorial hush. "You're like me, Adam—an Overseer."

The word lodged in Adam's chest like a spark in dry tinder.

Driving home, he could scarcely keep the car straight. Twice his tires scraped dangerously close to the roadside as his thoughts spiralled. He longed to look skyward, to see the pale guardian hanging above, but the moon was hidden, swallowed by drifting cloud or perhaps by design. Its absence only deepened the sense of unreality pressing on him.

Was Tom's story some elaborate trick, a fantastical game designed to ensnare the gullible? Or was it something far greater—a revelation disguised as madness? Adam could not decide. What he did know was that the tale had kindled something within him. It tugged his mind away from the dull routines of work and into the place of mystery and possibility. Despite Tom's unpredictable moods, Adam found himself drawn to the man, to his intensity, to the strange gravity that clung to his words.

Parts of Adam's mind—parts he had buried years ago under layers of cynicism and routine—were awakening. Thoughts of hidden forces, of unseen purposes, of paths he had never considered, stirred and stretched like limbs long numb. Whether Tom was prophet or charlatan no longer seemed to matter. Something in the universe was nudging him forward, whispering that he had a role to play. And for the first time in years, Adam felt it—the dangerous, intoxicating pull of destiny.

When Adam returned home that evening, the house carried the faint hum of conversation. He found Joey perched on the edge of the sofa, phone in hand, laughing lightly as he made plans with a friend for the weekend. His voice was casual, carefree even, yet Adam sensed an underlying nervous energy in the way he was talking.

The call ended with a quick goodbye, and Joey tossed the phone aside, turning his attention toward Adam. His question was thrown out with deceptive nonchalance, as though the answer mattered little: *"Where've you been?"*

Adam's reply changed everything. Joey's eyes widened—first with surprise, then with something more difficult to read. A hesitation shot across his face before he exhaled sharply, lowering his voice. Almost sheepishly, he confessed he had gone to see Tom a few days earlier. "Only for five minutes," he added quickly, as if that detail might soften the weight of his admission. He did not, however, mention the most telling part—that he had gone alone without telling Adam.

Adam stood frozen, stunned by the revelation. The sharpness in his voice betrayed his dismay as he scolded Joey for visiting without telling him, without at least extending Tom the courtesy of a call. Joey's apology was immediate but carried an undertone of stubborn resolve. He explained that he had been curious, that something about Tom had stayed with him, something he couldn't shake. The eccentric old man seemed to know more than he revealed, and Joey had wanted to hear it directly, on his own terms.

When Adam, still wary, shared Tom's latest revelations, Joey fell quiet. His silence wasn't dismissal; it was the silence of a mind racing to connect fragments that had long floated unanchored in his thoughts. Then, with an almost reluctant honesty, Joey admitted he had been haunted for years by a series of unsettling dreams—dreams that now returned to him in vivid detail. He described visions of the moon not as a barren wasteland, but as a place alive with hidden life. Beneath its surface stretched sprawling bunkers and cavernous dwellings where people waited, bound by some unspoken destiny. They seemed trapped in limbo, suspended between worlds, as if the moon itself were holding them hostage.

Now, Tom's words reframed those dreams, pressing them into Joey's waking mind with startling clarity. What had once been dismissed as thoughts of an overactive imagination now felt like pieces of a larger puzzle. His curiosity flared into something sharper, almost obsessive. He had to know more. He had to see Tom's hidden retreat for himself.

That curiosity was bound tightly to something deeper—his attachment to Adam. Since boyhood, Joey had relied on him, trusted him in ways he rarely trusted anyone else. Their connection had begun years earlier, when Joey was just a child living a few houses down with his mother, Linda Galilei.

Linda, a second-generation Italian, had grown up under the weight of hardship. Raised by her single mother after her father returned to Italy—his battles with alcohol and rage too much for the family to endure—Linda had learned early the value of resilience. Her older sister married young and left to follow her Navy husband, leaving Linda and her mother to cope with life alone.

By twenty-six, Linda was caring for her mother, who was gravely ill with liver disease, when she discovered she was pregnant. The child's father fled at the news, unwilling to shoulder responsibility. And so, one humid summer evening, Linda gave birth alone in a small rural hospital. Her mother never made it in time. The boy—Joseph Galilei—arrived with his mother's olive-toned skin, dark brown hair, and a pair of eyes so striking they memorised strangers: a deep, unusual shade of green, like polished avocado stone.

After her mother's death, Linda sought a fresh start. With four-year-old Joey in tow, she moved to the city, renting a modest place on Adam's Street. At first, they were strangers to their neighbours. Joey, watched carefully by Linda, spent hours riding his little bike up and down the street, his wheels rattling against the pavement. Inevitably, his paths crossed with Adam or with Mrs. Haupt, the very talkative elderly neighbour who seemed to have a comment for everything and everyone.

It was Joey who bridged the gap. He loved pedalling into Adam's driveway—a wide, sunlit space that sloped gently to the street, perfect for circling laps. The first day he saw Adam washing his car, his fascination was instant. Soap suds, water running down the drive, Adam working with quiet diligence—it all lodged in Joey's memory.

From then on, Adam and Linda's friendship grew. Linda, exhausted by work and still weighed down by grief, came to trust Adam. She sometimes asked him—or on occasion Mrs. Haupt—to watch Joey when her schedule demanded it. Joey always preferred Adam. He adored the way Adam listened, unhurried, never dismissive. Adam, for his part, was equally drawn to the boy's energy and sharp curiosity. Though most called him Joseph, Adam insisted on "Joey," and the name stuck.

Over the years, that bond deepened. Joey grew up in Adam's orbit, but at fifteen, cracks appeared. He left high school suddenly, without explanation. A brief carpentry apprenticeship followed, then failed. Around the same time, Linda, pressured by rising rents, relocated to a cheaper suburb. For the first time, Joey and Adam were separated by more than a short walk.

Linda's life shifted again; she began dating someone new. Joey, never one to hide his feelings, disliked the man immediately. He endured it only for Linda's sake. But his resentment simmered.

Still, Joey refused to let distance cut him off. He would travel by train and bus to see Adam, arriving with his grievances ready to spill. He spoke of cramped living conditions, of neighbours he detested, of a household that no longer felt like home. His words were edged with anger, his moods volatile, his sense of injustice vast. He would sit in Adam's kitchen, shoulders tense, declaring his life a failure—no future, no money, no escape. Adam, calm and steady, listened as always. He offered quiet reassurances: things would change, perspective would come with time. But Joey's restless green eyes told another truth—he didn't believe him.

When arguments at home grew unbearable, Joey began slipping away. At fifteen, he often spent weekends—and sometimes school nights—at Adam's. Adam's house was more than shelter; it was stability, a space that carried echoes of safety from his earliest years. Adam was the only male presence Joey truly trusted.

The breaking point came one evening when a familiar argument with Linda spiralled into something much bigger. Voices rose. Accusations flew. Joey caught the look in his mother's eyes—her new partner mattered more than him now. That realization lit a fuse. He packed a backpack in silence, cursed loudly, and stormed out into the night.

Linda's desperation cracked through the phone when she called Adam. She begged him to intervene, insisting Joey only listened to him—or to her late mother, who had been Joey's anchor until her death had left him shattered. When Joey finally appeared at Adam's door, his anger still raw, they made an unspoken agreement: he could stay. Linda, privately relieved, expressed her gratitude with awkward gestures—baskets of food, small gifts—as though they could balance the scale.

By sixteen, Joey's path shifted again. Through Adam's connections, he secured an interview at a small advertising agency. The manager, taken aback by Joey's charm and striking personality, offered him a clerical role, with the promise of advancement if he proved himself. Joey's natural charisma worked in his favour; people wanted to like him, to give him a chance. True to their word, the agency invested in him, sending him to study sales and marketing. For the first time in years, Joey's life seemed to take shape.

And yet, as Adam now realized, Joey's hunger for meaning, for belonging, had not dimmed. Tom had become the new fixation. The old man's cryptic words, coupled with Joey's strange lunar dreams, gave shape to something Joey had long felt but could never explain. His curiosity had caught fire. And Adam, for all his warnings and worries, saw the truth written plainly in Joey's eyes—he would not rest until he discovered Tom's secrets for himself.

Chapter Eight
A Strange Land

The cabin crew had noticed her long before, back in Sydney…

The aircraft descended through the gauzy clouds and touched down with a hollow roar upon the wide runways of Johannesburg, South Africa. Its fuselage gleamed under the morning sun, and on the tail, bold against the white body, the crimson kangaroo of Qantas seemed to leap proudly across the sky. Inside, Evelyn remained still, her hands folded in her lap, her eyes staring ahead without focus. A hush seemed to cling to her, as though she were cloaked in her own private weather—one of grey skies and quiet rain.

The cabin crew had noticed her long before, back in Sydney. She had boarded quietly, her expression guarded, and throughout the long hours of flight she had spoken little, only for a polite thank you when offered a drink or meal. While other passengers fidgeted with restless legs, struck up conversations with strangers, or watched films to distract themselves, Evelyn had withdrawn, drifting far into her own thoughts.

Now, as the plane taxied to its final halt, one of the attendants leaned gently toward her, speaking with a kind, subdued tone, "We've arrived, miss. You'll need to disembark now." The words floated into Evelyn's ears like a distant echo. She managed a faint, practiced smile—more for the attendant's sake than her own—and rose, retrieving a modest carry-on from the overhead compartment.

The journey had stretched across continents: a short hop to Perth, followed by the relentless long-haul across the Indian Ocean. And yet Evelyn found herself disoriented by the fact she was here already, on African soil. The hours had blurred together, swallowed by the weight she carried inside her chest. Time had not so much passed as dissolved—slipped away, unnoticed, as though sorrow itself had numbed its passage.

Outside the cabin, OR Tambo International Airport waited—a sprawling monument to constant movement. Once named Johannesburg International, it had grown into the busiest aviation hub on the continent, a place where the world gathered and scattered again. Within its walls thrived a city unto itself: glittering duty-free shops, polished restaurants promising cuisines from every corner of the globe, offices and business lounges where deals were struck in hushed voices. Nearly twenty thousand people worked here, moving like parts of a vast machine, ensuring the endless tide of travellers never ceased to flow.

To Evelyn, stepping into that terminal felt like entering a different world. Her hometown, quiet and unassuming, existed in another life; here was a place where humanity collided in all its colours and forms. Africans, Europeans, Asians, Australians, Americans—all surged together, a living stream of languages and faces. The press of bodies jostled her as she moved forward, and though she whispered brief acknowledgments when shoulders brushed hers, her voice was low, her eyes elsewhere.

Her mind was not in the terminal. It was not even in Johannesburg. It was tied to something deeper, heavier, a purpose that had carried her across an ocean and that now propelled her through the chaos without her fully registering her surroundings.

The building stretched on, a labyrinth of reflecting glass and steel, alive with motion and emotion. Everywhere, she saw stories unfolding: joyous reunions as loved ones spotted each other across the crowd, arms flung wide; tear-streaked farewells, whispered goodbyes drawn out as though the act of holding on could stop time itself. The air seemed saturated with longing, with beginnings and endings, and Evelyn felt it closing in around her, amplifying the ache already inside her chest.

She passed travellers bewildered by signs, others stumbling under the weight of too many bags, and some radiating sheer exhilaration at the thought of new adventures. Construction crews hammered and welded, raising new wings and refurbishing old ones, as though the airport itself was forever in the act of becoming. And through it all, the great human river flowed, unbroken, its voice a constant murmur that rose and fell like the sea.

At last, Evelyn spotted the signs for the domestic terminal. Her journey was not complete—not yet. Another flight, another stretch of waiting, another passage through crowded halls lay ahead. Yet as she drew closer, she allowed herself a breath of relief. She had made it this far. She was still moving, step by step, carried forward by the quiet determination of someone who had little choice but to keep going.

Chapter Nine
Introductions

The strategy, they explained, was to entice politicians and corporate leaders with an elaborate deception...

Back in Sydney, Adam slipped once more into the whirlwind of his demanding routine. His days blurred into each other, filled with client meetings, endless paperwork, and the constant pressure of trying to stay ahead. He forced himself to keep pushing; to maintain the same momentum he had before meeting with Tom, but the truth was that something inside him had shifted. Still, on the surface, he went about his work with his usual commitment, making room for extra appointments, taking calls at odd hours, and pretending the weight he carried was nothing unusual.

Carol, his long-time assistant, remained the quiet anchor of his practice. She had a gift for organization that verged on the uncanny—shuffling appointments with the deftness of a seasoned conductor, always finding space for last-minute bookings without making anyone feel slighted. Clients adored her calm, efficient manner. She had worked beside Adam for years and understood him in ways no one else did: his quirks, his silences, his flashes of intensity. She could read his moods as easily as she could read the daily schedule, and though she never pried, she noticed when his thoughts wandered elsewhere. Lately, they wandered often.

Since Tom didn't know Adam's home number, the office became the only line of contact. One afternoon, after sliding a neat stack of messages across Adam's desk, Carol mentioned in her usual matter-of-fact tone that Tom had called, requesting a return call when convenient. Adam paused, the name hitting him with a quiet jolt. Two weeks had passed since their last meeting—two weeks of silence. Tom's patience, it seemed, had reached its end.

Later, when Adam dialled the number, Tom wasted no time. His voice was steady, almost cold, as he asked if Adam was still interested in what they had discussed—or if he should consider the matter closed. Adam winced at the bluntness, guilt threading through him. He explained, perhaps too quickly, that his schedule had consumed him, that business had crowded out everything else, but insisted that he hadn't lost interest. He was still eager to hear more. Tom let the silence hang for a moment before relenting, though his tone carried a hint of reprimand. They would meet the next day.

When Adam asked if Joey could come along, Tom's answer was immediate and firm. No. There were matters to settle first, foundations to lay before anyone else could be invited in. This wasn't about social visits or curiosity—it was about trust, about business that demanded gravity. Adam hung up with the uneasy feeling of a schoolboy who had just been scolded by a headmaster, the echo of Tom's refusal still sharp in his ears. He dreaded telling Joey he wasn't welcome, and so—for now—he chose silence.

The following day Adam arrived at Tom's house earlier than expected. The route had become familiar now, the bends in the road almost comforting in their repetition. At the gate, he pressed the intercom and was buzzed inside. A yellow Volvo station wagon sat in the driveway; its paint dulled with age. As Adam approached, the front doors swung open and Tom stepped out, followed closely by an older woman burdened with cleaning supplies and a compact shoulder-pack vacuum. She glanced up at Adam and offered a warm smile, the kind that spoke of long years of trust and loyalty. She loaded her things into the Volvo with practiced ease before driving off. Later, Tom confirmed she was his housekeeper of more than twenty years—someone he regarded as family, whom he could never dismiss, despite her age and her reluctance to retire.

Inside, Tom ushered Adam into the living room. His manner was calm, but there was an edge to it, a probing intent. He wasted no time with pleasantries.

"So," Tom began, his eyes fixed, "are you still serious about what we discussed earlier… or was it just a passing curiosity?"

He studied Adam's expression, weighing every flicker of doubt. "Honestly, I was starting to think you'd lost interest."

Adam leaned forward, hands clasped. "Not at all. I've just been very busy with work. That won't happen again."

But Tom's eyes betrayed scepticism. For him, trust wasn't a luxury—it was survival. The circle he moved in was guarded, cautious to the extreme, and one careless slip could unravel years of carefully earned confidence. He had no space for half-hearted participants.

Adam defended his case. "I've worked with so many people over the years who have these psychic abilities. I've kept everything private. Always. You can count on me."

For a moment Tom was silent, his look distant, as though weighing Adam against some inner scale. When he spoke again, his tone had softened, though it carried something heavier, almost confessional.

"Adam… I'm getting older. I've been searching for someone to take over. I have met plenty of candidates, but none of them felt right—until you. From the start, I thought you might be the one. Am I wrong?"

The words hit Adam unexpectedly, leaving him momentarily stunned. He hesitated, uncertain if he had heard Tom correctly. Then, still on the defensive, he replied, "If you feel that strongly… why question me?"

"Because I need to be certain," Tom replied. His voice dropped lower, deliberate. "From our first meeting, I knew you were the best choice. You'd be good for the group—and they'd be good for you. But I need to know how you feel about it."

The declaration stayed with Adam long after he left. As he drove home, his thoughts spiralled. In a week, he would be back at Tom's for a gathering of the Image Carriers. What would he discover then? Was he truly being groomed to step into Tom's role? The idea both exhilarated and unsettled him. And then there was Jocy. The thought of excluding him weighed heavily. Joey would not take it well—Adam knew that instinctively.

By the time he pulled into his driveway, his mood had darkened. He avoided Joey that evening, slipping past him with a half-baked excuse. Joey hardly noticed—his mind was elsewhere, on friends, camping gear, and the excitement of a weekend getaway.

The days slipped by quickly, and soon a week had passed. Adam found himself restless, carrying a flicker of nervous anticipation that refused to fade. On the day of the meeting, he drove to Tom's with his stomach knotted, unsure of what lay ahead. As he rounded the corner to Tom's Street, the sight surprised him: cars lined the driveway and spilled onto the road, an unmistakable sign of a large gathering. His pulse quickened. Who were these people? What kind of presence would they carry? Would they be anything like Evelyn—or Joey? Or would they be something altogether different, something he wasn't prepared for?

Over the years, Tom had devoted much of his spare time to running evening classes on psychic abilities and the wider mysteries of the paranormal. At first, he welcomed the public into those sessions, believing that curiosity—even naïve curiosity—was the seed of awakening. But what began as gatherings filled with wonder and tentative exploration slowly turned sour. The audiences shifted. People with unstable temperaments, individuals who carried an aura of menace, and those hungry for power rather than insight began showing up. Anonymous notes, some threatening and others just weird, were left on student's desks or under windscreen wipers. A few students had been too rattled to return, while others confessed to walking back to their cars with their hearts hammering in their chests, eyes darting at shadows. Tom, pragmatic as he was intuitive, knew when to retreat. He ended the public meetings abruptly, without apology or explanation, moving instead to private, invitation-only gatherings inside his home—safer ground, where he could keep watch over who entered and why.

As he explained to Adam, these secret circles met—roughly every seven weeks, usually on a Tuesday evening, from seven until nine, or later. Their existence was to remain unspoken outside those walls. For Tom, secrecy was not about just protecting them but about their very survival, both for himself and for those who trusted him. He urged Adam to attend, insisting that the personalities gathered would intrigue him. Their unusual perceptions of reality, Tom claimed, would sharpen Adam's psychological insight, feeding directly into his counselling and coaching work. Adam, cautious by nature and sceptical of what he could not measure, hesitated at first. Yet Tom's persistence, paired with Adam's own curiosity, eventually pulled him in.

When the night arrived, Adam found excuses not to go home first. Avoiding Joey was part of it, but another part was the desire to prepare himself mentally in solitude. He ate takeaway in his office after Carol had gone for the day, the silence around him settling like armour. At seven sharp, he set out for Tom's place, carrying with him a sense of stepping into unknown waters.

Tom's front door stood open. Inside, the old house pulsed with life. Where Adam had once seen echoing halls and stillness, now small knots of people stood in the lounge and corridor, voices overlapping, laughter breaking out. The house seemed to breathe with their presence. At the far end of the room, Tom was deep in conversation with a younger man, his posture relaxed yet commanding. The elderly housekeeper, usually a ghost on the periphery, was transformed into a waiter of sorts, circulating with silver trays of canapés—lobster or crab balanced on thin crackers, crowned with green garnish. Tempting though it looked, Adam declined.

"Adam!" Tom called, lifting a hand in greeting, his voice carrying easily across the chatter. "Come over—we'll be starting soon." The man beside him, he introduced as Simon.

The housekeeper closed the door firmly, the clatter of locks sounding final, as though sealing them in together. The group filed toward the lounge, seating themselves in a loose semicircle around Tom. Adam counted roughly eight others, plus himself and Tom. He slipped into a chair on the far right, offering a polite smile each time he caught someone looking at him.

It struck him immediately: these people admired Tom. Their eyes softened when they looked his way, their smiles quickened, their postures leaned toward him. They were not ordinary students fumbling at the fringes of self-help. There was a gentleness in them, yes, but also a low hum of unease—an awareness that what bound them together was fragile, easily misunderstood.

When Tom introduced Adam, he explained he would only be observing tonight. The group turned as one to welcome him, their smiles a mixture of curiosity and quiet reassurance. Adam gave Tom a look, a small nod, as though to say he could manage this.

Still, sitting alone at the edge of the semicircle, Adam felt exposed, like a man watching a play from the wrong side of the stage curtain. His instincts, sharpened from years of counselling, told him these people had layered personalities—ordinary on the surface, complex beneath.

At Tom's prompting, each member rose to introduce themselves.

Darrin was first. A tall, clean-cut man in his mid-thirties, with blond hair and startlingly clear blue eyes, he spoke with a steady baritone that carried both wisdom and patience. A mathematics teacher at a private secondary school, he described himself as a husband and father of two young children, and his words revealed a man who valued stability, order, and preparedness. He credited Tom's teachings with deepening his ability to see patterns—not only in numbers but in people. Adam sensed that Darrin was the sort of man who wore his responsibility like a well-fitted suit, dependable and perhaps a little rigid, yet admirable in his groundedness.

Julie followed, rising slowly. As though thinking carefully about her words before giving them. A woman in her late thirties, her baby-like face and soft blue-grey eyes gave her a gentleness at odds with her sturdy frame. She worked as a clerk in a government department and had saved diligently over the years, a fact she admitted with a shy pride. Julie revealed she had once considered becoming a nun, driven by a yearning to nurture and give of herself. That path had slipped away, but her spiritual longing had not. Her voice trembled at times, betraying a tender heart still searching for meaning, still hoping Tom's circle might provide what the convent had not.

Anne leapt up with the impulsive energy of someone who feared the moment might pass if she hesitated. Twenty-three, with brown-toned skin, thick black hair, and dark eyes that burned with unsettled intensity, she was striking in appearance though her oversized, androgynous clothing muted her beauty. She spoke boldly, declaring she belonged here, clinging fiercely to Tom's interpretations of her dreams. A college student unable to settle on a career, Anne radiated a mix of raw intelligence and inner conflict—beautifully alive, yet uncertain where her place was. Her annoyance at being mistaken for anything other than Australian betrayed both pride and insecurity, the edges of identity still sharp in her.

John's introduction was impossible to ignore. Stocky, with thinning hair and a potbelly, his presence was large not because of his build but because of his booming voice and blunt manner. In his early sixties, he carried himself like a man ready to argue with anyone, be it a neighbour or the Prime Minister. He distrusted government, corporations, and anyone he felt belonged to the elite. His stories tumbled out half-formed but passionate, laced with warnings about betrayal and corruption. Adam noted the fire in him, but also the loneliness of a man whose beliefs often set him apart.

When John finally sat down, his face still flushed, **Amanda** rose with a lighter energy. Petite and lively, with blonde curls styled in a neat afro-like cut, she carried herself with the ease of someone comfortable in her own skin. Divorced and content, in her late fifties, she spoke warmly of Tom's meetings as places of learning and inspiration. Her intelligence was clear, her enthusiasm genuine, and she wore her independence with pride. Unlike John's thunder, Amanda's presence was sunlight—cheerful, steady, but no less firm in her belief in the group's value.

Simon, the youngest, rose next. At twenty, tall and lean with striking light eyes, he carried the awkward self-consciousness of someone not yet sure of his place in the world. His words were tentative, his voice soft, but there was an honesty in his admission that he didn't feel fully at home in the group. Fascinated by the metaphysical, Simon confessed he was more a loner than anything else, drawn here not by belonging but by curiosity. To Adam, he seemed fragile in the way of youth—handsome, uncertain, balancing on the thin line between detachment and need.

Jason followed, his presence more brittle. Nearly thirty, olive-skinned with tawny hair and a wiry build, he tried to mask his unease with humour, reminding everyone not to forget his birthday gift. But beneath the laughter, Adam sensed tension coiled tight. Jason admitted his work in IT left him weary of people, and his long-term relationship, now weighed down by talk of marriage, was a source of anxiety rather than comfort. His abrupt ending—cutting himself short mid-thought—left the air heavy, as though there were truths, he had no strength to reveal.

Finally, Jennifer stood. Small-framed, her mismatched clothing of vibrant colours made her appear almost otherworldly. At fifty, she owned her age with disarming honesty. A senior government worker in immigration, she spoke with calm authority, tempered by years of hard-won experience. Single since raising her daughter alone, she radiated quiet independence. Her absentminded play with her dress as she spoke suggested a mind that moved faster than her words, yet she ended with a smile broad enough to soften her seriousness.

As Jennifer sat, Adam took them in as a whole: four men, four women, each different yet bound by something he couldn't quite name. He wondered if the balance was deliberate, a symmetry Tom had cultivated. But Tom later explained the numbers were coincidence—many "Image Carriers," as he called them, had chosen to stay away, content with one-on-one meetings or the anonymity of a video call. What Adam saw tonight was only a fragment of the whole.

And yet, even this fragment was enough to unsettle him. Each person radiated a quality that set them apart from the ordinary world outside. For better or worse, Adam knew he had stepped into a circle that did not merely study mysteries—it embodied them.

Tom turned suddenly, his sharp gaze landing on Adam. "Adam, why don't you introduce yourself?"

The words seemed to echo unnaturally in the room. Adam froze, caught off guard, his mind blanking for the briefest second. He shot Tom a quick, incredulous glance. Of all the scenarios he had anticipated that evening, this hadn't even made the list. He could handle public speaking—he'd done it countless times, standing before full auditoriums, conducting workshops, addressing executives with steady ease—but this was different. This felt as though he'd been wrenched out of a private dream and thrust into the spotlight of an unfamiliar play.

Still, habit carried him forward. He rose, smoothing his shirt with a hand that trembled only slightly, and forced a smile that he knew was too stiff, too rehearsed. Instinctively, he slid into his counsellor's voice—measured, calm, professional—the tone he used with anxious clients or sceptical business leaders.

"I'm a counsellor and executive coach," he began, hearing how formal it sounded even as he spoke. "Single, living with a flatmate, and running my own business."

Tom leaned forward with that infuriating glint in his eye. "And tell them about your work with Image Carriers."

The shift in the room was immediate. The group with attentive faces turned toward him with sharpened focus, as though a hidden spotlight had clicked on. Adam hesitated, caught between discretion and the demand for honesty.

"There's not much to say, really," he said carefully. "Over the years, I've met people with… uncanny insights. Predictions that proved eerily accurate—almost psychic in nature."

A stir rippled through the group—murmurs, a current of curiosity that prickled at his skin. But before the interest could solidify into questions, Tom cut across him with a brisk, almost dismissive, "Thank you."

Adam sank back into his chair, heat rising to his face. He caught the hint of disappointment across several faces, as though he'd denied them a glimpse into something they already sensed but longed to hear confirmed.

From his seat, Adam studied them more closely. These weren't ordinary people. They carried themselves with a poise, a quiet confidence, a kind of self-possession he wasn't used to seeing in professional circles. There was sophistication in their bearing, intelligence in their eyes, and—most unnervingly—a magnetic stillness in the way they listened. Even Tom seemed transformed among them: sharper, more animated, his words flowing with authority. In this company he looked entirely at home, as though this was the world he was born to inhabit.

By contrast, Adam felt reduced—an outsider in a conversation that seemed to have been going on long before his arrival.

The group began sharing visions—personal images and impressions they had saved for the evening. Fragments spilled into the air: mysterious symbols, flashes of landscapes, warnings wrapped in metaphor. At times their stories scared him; at other moments they sounded impossible. Yet each was delivered with the casual ease of someone remarking on the weather, as though visions were an ordinary fact of life.

And then something happened.

Adam felt the room shift. Slowly, almost imperceptibly, the separate voices began to align, like tributaries merging into a single river. Their personalities, distinct only moments ago, seemed to blur into one larger presence, united by some invisible current of purpose. The air itself changed—charged, electric, vibrating with a palpable energy that pressed against his skin. The ordinary boundaries between them thinned, dissolving into a collective surge.

Adam's breath caught. His chest expanded with exhilaration; his mouth parted in an unconscious smile of awe. He couldn't remember the last time he had felt so alive, so attuned, so utterly drawn into something beyond himself. It was as if a tide of unseen energy had swept through the room, clearing out stagnant shadows and replacing them with something pure and radiant.

Each person seemed to encourage the others wordlessly, as if carried by an invisible current that bound them together. Their shared energy grew with each glance, each subtle gesture, lifting one another higher, as though they were climbing side by side toward some dazzling summit. It was not a competition but a union of spirits, every step strengthened by the presence of the others. The air itself shimmered with a strange intensity—joy interwoven with reverence, an almost sacred expectancy that felt like standing on the threshold of heaven. Time seemed to pause, holding its breath, as though the world was waiting for something magnificent to unfold.

When Tom finally called a break, the spell fractured. Chairs scraped back. Most of the group made for the restroom, while a few drifted toward the entrance and hurried outside for cigarettes. Adam blinked, almost laughing at the contrast. How, he wondered, could anyone claim spiritual advancement yet dash out for nicotine the instant the session paused?

Seizing the chance, he crossed the room to Tom. His irritation still simmered from being put on the spot, but more than that, he wanted clarity.

"Tom?" he said, approaching. But Tom seemed distracted, his gaze fixed somewhere distant. He didn't turn, didn't acknowledge him.

Adam tried again, louder this time. "Tom."

This time Tom looked over, a sly grin curling his lips. "There you are, Adam," he chuckled. "Seriously, I think the group will benefit greatly from your input. You are a natural, and you are already working with people with these talents. You will be a great asset to them, and I know you will gain a lot from them too."

Adam did not look the least bit confident. A tightness settled in his chest, the old familiar resentment of being forced into something, he did not like. He had experienced that in his younger years, and that was a trigger for him. He also didn't like the way Tom spoke for him, as though his own voice carried no importance, as though his future could be scripted by someone else's certainty and not his own. Yet beneath the irritation lay something messier, a knot of emotions he couldn't easily name—anger twisted with doubt, and threaded, almost unwillingly, with a spark of curiosity he didn't dare acknowledge. The mixture left him off balance, unsure of where to stand or how to push back. In the end, words failed him. He clamped his mouth shut, letting silence speak in place of anything rash, anything he might later wish he hadn't said. So Adam stood there, deadpan, giving nothing away.

By the time the others trickled back in, the room's energy had shifted again—quieter now, but no less intense. They gathered their notepads and belongings with a ritualistic efficiency, waiting for Tom to open the closet door that led to the hidden room below.

Downstairs, the group settled immediately. Some went to the cabinets and pulled loose files, others opened their own folders and journals. Adam took in every detail—the hum of concentration, the rustle of pages, the sense of entering another world.

He noticed Julie, seated near the back, her movements graceful, almost angelic. She kept checking her wristwatch as though bound by some invisible pressure. Twice he caught her watching him; twice she turned away, too quickly, as though she'd trespassed into forbidden territory.

Across the room, Tom spread a file across the table. The paper rustled, slicing through the silence.

"Let's take another look at the wealthy cabal. That was Rep 80," he said.

The others leaned over their documents, whispering, searching. Adam observed quietly, struck again by their paradox: so varied in age, personality, and background, yet bound by a thread of shared intensity. Their focus was absolute.

Amanda found the file first. "Which section are we on?" she asked.

Tom didn't answer directly, instead letting the group decide. Amanda pressed forward, her voice clear and urgent. What came out of her next sent a chill through Adam, planting a cold knot of unease deep in his being.

They launched into discussion—Rep 80, the elite, the cabal, the sweeping changes they claimed were coming. Their words painted a stark picture: governments weakened, sovereignty surrendered, millions of lives steered by a hidden hand.

These strange people talked openly about vast networks that spanned trillion-dollar empires. Corporations, governments, entire populations bent into pawns by the corrupt. But the truth, they insisted, was far darker.

The group members eagerly took turns sharing their perspectives on Rep. 80. Their conversation focused on the sweeping changes ahead—changes that would affect the masses—and the belief that a wicked faceless group was manipulating Western and other governments into surrendering their sovereignty and citizens' rights, paving the way for catastrophic consequences.

During this exchange, Simon and Anne spoke only occasionally, while Jennifer, Amanda, and Darrin—clearly well-versed in the topic—dominated the discussion. Adam overheard them referring to "the Owners" and their extraordinary technology, and other hidden networks that controlled vast, trillion-dollar movements. These groups, they claimed, sought control over everything—from people's thoughts, their organs, to the very air they breathed.

They spoke of how governments collapse and lose independence to a faceless triangle of power, and how major corporations use those governments as pawns to advance shadowy agendas while keeping the public in the dark. The strategy, they explained, was to entice politicians and corporate leaders with an elaborate deception—an illusion of boundless wealth and exclusive security. In reality, it was an invitation into the cabal's inner sanctum, a place of mirrors where the wealthy and powerful feasted on innocence and empty promises.

But the price was steep. Those who accepted such offers unknowingly stepped into a world with no way out—a dinner date with the Beast, a place steeped in corruption and malice. To join the cabal was to forfeit one's sacred essence and sever one's spiritual union. And, as with the final days of Sodom and Gomorrah, such a choice sealed one's fate.

Adam sat still, his heart tightening. Their conviction was terrifying, and yet... part of him wondered if, in their voices, there was more truth than madness.

As Jason continued to speak, Adam gradually became aware that the tone of the discussion had shifted. What began as an abstract exchange of ideas was now circling dangerously close to the subject of population control—an impending clash, Jason suggested, between the irrational, feeble-minded masses and those who still retained some semblance of righteousness and common sense. Adam leaned forward in his chair, making himself more comfortable, unsure how long this meeting was going to go for. A thought suddenly popped in his mind: would humanity ever learn to live in balance, in harmony, or was conflict its natural state? For a fleeting second, he felt as though he had slipped sideways into another reality altogether. The night had already been strange, but the strangeness seemed to deepen with every passing minute, until it felt like he was drifting through an episode of *The Twilight Zone*.

What unsettled him even more was how seamlessly the group moved together—so in sync, so unwavering in their worldview, that their confidence lent them a kind of credibility. Jason had connected the two "Reps" almost casually, yet the effect was anything but casual. His voice quickened, painting a grim picture that escalated step by step: first thousands dead, then millions, then billions—victims, he claimed, of a deliberate, man-made assault on humanity itself. What chilled Adam wasn't the numbers so much as the steady, calm agreement from the rest of the group, their collective nodding, their absolute certainty that over a billion people would soon perish—within their lifetimes, perhaps even within a handful of years.

At this point Jason began steering his account toward "Rep 90," when Tom suddenly raised a hand to stop him. He wanted the discussion drawn back to "Rep 80." But Jason wasn't easily diverted, and in seconds the room erupted into a tangle of overlapping voices. Adam sat back, observing the chaos with detached fascination. He noted how Simon, Julie, and Anne kept quiet, their silence standing in contrast to the others' rising intensity.

"This is why we never get anywhere," Darrin said firmly, cutting through the noise. "We all have our stories to share. What we need is to piece them together. Not keep jumping from Rep to Rep every time someone gets excited."

Jason, unruffled, leaned forward. "Sorry, mate, but this is important. The Reps are connected—"

"Yes, sometimes," Darrin shot back, his jaw tight, "but not this one. We can't keep jumping around. One Rep at a time. We still don't know the full meaning of *any* of them."

Jason grinned, undeterred, scanning the room as if hunting for allies. "I think they are connected. I can feel it."

"You're missing the bigger picture," Amanda interjected sharply. "If we mash the Reps together without fully understanding them, we'll drown in confusion. We have rules for a reason."

Her words seemed to land heavier than Jason's. Silence rippled across the room, lingering as everyone turned instinctively toward Tom. Slowly, with the gravitas of someone shouldering responsibility, he rose and approached the whiteboard. For a moment, Adam thought he would write something down, anchor the discussion with some kind of clarity. But instead, Tom paused, marker in hand, then placed it back on the ledge and returned to his chair. His steps were slow, deliberate, as though even the act of sitting carried significance.

"Anyone else want to comment?" he asked quietly. The question hung in the air. No one spoke. Then, without warning, Tom turned directly to Adam.

Caught off guard again, Adam's eyes widened. He quickly looked down, pretending sudden interest on the floor.

"Adam?" Tom called out. "Any questions?"

Adam cleared his throat. "Not really. Just observing for now."

Tom didn't let him off so easily. "I'd like your feedback. Anything to add?"

The room seemed to lean toward him, waiting. Adam hesitated, his mind racing. He then decided to ask the obvious question, the one that had been nagging him since Jason first mentioned the Reps.

"Yes," he said carefully. "What do 'Rep 80' and 'Rep 90' actually mean?"

Tom clasped his hands together, nodding. "Good question." He turned to the group. "Who wants to explain?"

Julie spoke up first. Her voice was calm, almost soothing. "'Rep' is short for Reproduction. We are a highly intuitive group. We receive impressions—visions, images, sensations, gut instincts. Sometimes they feel like warnings of what's coming, sometimes echoes of the past. We reproduce them here, in this setting, so we can analyse them together."

As she spoke, Adam caught a subtle glimpse of vulnerability beneath her composure. She went on to describe how she had first met Tom and the others at a community centre. At first, she had enjoyed the evening classes, but the troublemakers—outsiders who had disrupted and intimidated them—had driven her away. Here, in Tom's home, she felt safe again. She ended by thanking Tom for creating a space where they could explore their premonitions freely, without fear.

The group nodded, their agreement almost ceremonial, and Adam noticed the warmth in their expressions—as though Julie's gratitude was shared by them all.

Jason, eager to reclaim the spotlight, leaned forward. "That's a good explanation," he said, "but not the whole picture." His tone sharpened with enthusiasm. He turned toward Adam and explained that Reps were also a way of cataloguing subjects, a system for keeping their knowledge in order. "Each Rep is like a container. Rep 80, for example, is elitism. Everything linked to elitism—facts, visions, instincts—goes under that heading. Rep 90 is population control. And so on. It helps us keep track."

Adam listened, intrigued. There was a method here, a structure that almost made sense.

Meanwhile, Julie looked at her watch again and gave Tom a discreet signal that she would need to leave soon. Tom checked his own and announced that they had about ten minutes left.

What followed made Adam shift uncomfortably in his chair. As the group began packing up their belongings, several members paused, straightened, and then—without instruction—began to stretch.

They inhaled deeply, extending their arms forward, then exhaled in long, controlled breaths. One or two whispered the word "relax" and as they did so, the others followed. The room filled with a rhythm of breath and quiet words.

Tom rose, his voice calm, almost hypnotic. "Everyone relax and recharge. This concludes our meeting for tonight. We have mutual faith and affection for one another. We will watch out for one another. We are joyful, resilient, safe, and healthy. We will remain grateful for our gift. We will not exploit our gift. Relax…"

Adam sat very still, unsure whether to participate or simply observe. The sincerity in their faces, however, was unmistakable.

Then came the strangest part of the night. As the meditation ended, the members looked upward, each in slightly different directions, as though searching for something invisible hovering above them. One by one, they spoke—to it, or perhaps to *them*—words of thanks, gratitude for protection, guidance, unseen companionship. The atmosphere thickened, reverent and disturbing. Adam's skin prickled. Was this ritual born of genuine belief, or was it some elaborate play-acting? Either way, it unsettled him.

Gradually, the spell broke. The meeting dissolved into the main hallway of Tom's home. Some members hung around to chat in low voices, others drifted quickly toward the door. Julie was among the latter. She exchanged her farewell with Tom, then looked back at Adam, offered him a small smile and a wave. He noticed then that she had been watching him throughout the evening, a detail that made him wonder if her interest went beyond casual politeness.

After the last guest had left, the house grew quiet again. Tom moved around the room, tidying absentmindedly, shifting items from one spot to another without much focus. From the kitchen came the sound of the housekeeper, insisting—almost scolding—that Tom let her manage the cleaning.

Finally, Tom returned to Adam, a faint weariness in his posture. "So," he asked, "what are your thoughts about tonight?"

Adam smiled, but it was a hesitant smile. "Very interesting," he said. "Actually, I'm not sure what to think." His thoughts were tangled, but under the confusion he felt a surprising hint of energy—a stirring he hadn't experienced in years. A kind of aliveness, raw and restless, like the surge of passion and excitement he remembered from his younger days.

"So, will you join us for the next get-together?" Tom asked, his voice tired but expectant.

Adam hesitated. He didn't want to sound too eager, too curious, but he couldn't help himself. "Why didn't anyone talk about the Moon?"

Tom chuckled softly. "So, you're interested in the Moon, are you? We will get to that. But tonight, the focus was on the issues the group brought forward."

Adam nodded slowly. "All right. You seem very keen to involve me, but… why?"

"Let's just say," he replied, "I think you'd be a positive addition to the team, Adam."

Chapter Ten
Old Friendship

There was something real about them, a deliberate design that suggested something beyond imagination…

It was mid-morning in Cape Town, South Africa, when the aircraft wheels screeched against the runway, jolting Evelyn from her anxious thoughts. She leaned closer to the window, her eyes tracing the coastline as the city unfolded beneath the sun. Relief washed over her at the sight of Table Mountain rising in the distance, its vast, flat crown standing like a silent guardian. The famous mountain did not disappoint; draped in a shawl of drifting cloud, it looked less like stone and more like an altar shrouded in secrecy.

Around her, passengers whispered in wonder, pointing and nudging each other, some snapping photographs of the mountain, others simply looking on in quiet awe. For many, it was the promise of arrival, of adventure, of something new. For Evelyn, however, the beauty of Cape Town could not erase the heaviness in her heart. She did not join in the chatter or the sighs of admiration. She remained still, her expression unreadable, her hand pressed against the armrest as though bracing for something yet unseen.

It was not the landing that disturbed her so much but what was still to come.

A voice startled her. The flight attendant stood beside her seat, smiling politely, though her eyes betrayed a flicker of concern. Evelyn was the last passenger seated, seemingly reluctant to move. "Ma'am, your belongings?" the attendant reminded her gently. Evelyn blinked, nodded, and collected her bag with a stiffness that betrayed how far her mind had drifted elsewhere.

Outside the terminal, the air struck her as warmer, clearer, carrying the faint briny scent of the sea. She walked toward the line of phone boxes near the entrance, her steps slow, deliberate. That had been the plan—Veronica had insisted they meet there. Evelyn scanned the crowd, her eyes moving with habitual vigilance. Adam had often teased her about it, telling her she lived as though someone was always watching, as though danger lurked in every corner. Maybe it was paranoia. Or maybe it was something else, something rooted in experiences Adam never truly understood.

"Evelyn?"

She spun around at the sound of her name.

Veronica emerged from the crowd, her presence both familiar and strangely foreign. They closed the distance quickly, embracing in a hug that was polite, restrained. Evelyn was never one for grand displays of affection, but even so, the stiffness between them felt heavier than time or distance alone could account for. The last time they had seen each other was years ago, yet it was not only years that stood between them—it was the circumstances of this reunion, but circumstances Evelyn also wished were entirely different.

They walked together toward the car park. Veronica's old white four-wheel drive stood waiting like a reliable friend, its paint dulled, its shape worn. Evelyn climbed in awkwardly, as though her body resisted the act, and when she settled, Veronica started the engine without a word. A heavy silence spread through the car, one that did not feel empty but thick with unspoken things.

Evelyn kept her eyes moving, watching the rearview mirror, watching the road, watching strangers in the parking lot. Old habits. Or perhaps an intuition she had never quite learned to silence.

Her connection to Cape Town went deeper than its postcard beauty. This was the city where she had grown from child to adolescent, where memory and history clung like salt to stone. Her parents had arrived decades earlier, carrying with them all the messiness of ambition and compromise.

Her father, British-born, had been sent across continents by one of England's largest banks. Her mother, Australian and sun-loving, had endured the cold of London only long enough to fall in love, marry, and give birth to Evelyn before longing once more for warmth and ocean. Cape Town had been the compromise—a two-year posting meant to soothe her mother's dislike of the English winters, a temporary arrangement that became ten years of permanence.

And it was here, in those years, that Veronica had entered Evelyn's world.

Living next door, Veronica had been the kind of child who never got bored, never seemed in need of anything outside herself. Where other children rushed about in noise and chaos, Veronica could sit in silence for hours, her thoughts hidden, her dark eyes thoughtful. Evelyn had found that soothing, the way Veronica carried calm like an invisible shield. They had spent countless afternoons together—schoolwork abandoned for games, mumbled stories, and long silences that somehow felt pleasant.

Even then, Veronica was different. Her family kept to themselves, speaking in low tones that suggested secrets. Evelyn, still a child, had overheard bits and pieces—Veronica's grandmother longing for a return "home," though Evelyn had never been told what "Home" meant. Egypt, perhaps, though nothing was ever said outright. She hadn't pressed. Back then, family histories mattered far less than the bond of friendship.

Now, sitting beside her once more, Evelyn felt that same aura of quiet mystery around Veronica—only heavier, more deliberate. Time had not erased it; if anything, it had deepened.

And as the four-wheel drive rolled out of the airport, Evelyn couldn't shake the unsettling sense that their reunion was not only about friendship, nor even circumstance—but about something waiting just beyond the horizon, something she could not yet name.

Veronica had always been bound to her grandmother with an invisible thread of devotion. As a child, she could lose entire afternoons in the woman's company, listening to her voice flow like a river of memory, or simply resting at her feet as she worked. She only ever left her grandmother's side when Evelyn came looking for her, pulling her away with that irresistible mix of impatience and mischief that seemed to define her.

Yet as the years stretched and the girls entered the uncertain territory of adolescence, subtle changes began to stir in Veronica. Evelyn noticed them first: the way her friend would shift uneasily whenever conversation drifted toward Gypsies, fortune-tellers, or the "old ways" her grandmother still practised. Veronica's cheeks would flush, and her voice—normally soft and careful—would harden into scolding tones, especially if Evelyn spoke too freely. It wasn't embarrassment with her grandmother exactly, but something murkier, a conflict between loyalty and the desire to belong in a world that often mocked what it did not understand.

Evelyn, of course, had her own battles to fight. She was no angel—never had been. By the time she turned ten, her restless spirit had already developed into a mischievous streak that tested the patience of her parents, teachers, and anyone foolish enough to underestimate her creativity. Where Veronica's gentleness made her cautious, Evelyn's boldness made her reckless. Trouble seemed to shadow her every step, and though she rarely meant to cause harm, her schemes often swept Veronica into their wake.

One of Evelyn's favourite games was to vanish from sight, only to leap out from behind a tree or doorway, scaring her friend into shrieks and laughter. Veronica's protests were genuine, her fear real, but she never stayed angry for long. Once, Evelyn's imagination carried the game further. She coaxed the height-fearing Veronica to climb a tall pine tree in the open field beyond their homes, promising her that the view alone would be worth the climb. Trusting her, as she always did, Veronica followed, inching her way up the rough trunk, bark scraping her palms, while Evelyn urged her higher and higher, teasing her not to look down.

Finally, they perched side by side on a wide branch, the wind threading through their hair, the air heavy with resin and sun-warmed needles. From up there, the world stretched in every direction: fields, houses, their school, distant hills shimmering in the heat. Veronica clung tight, heart hammering, while Evelyn grinned like a conqueror. Then, without warning, Evelyn began her descent, agile as a cat, slipping down the trunk until she reached the ground. She crouched at the base, hidden in the long grass, listening as Veronica's cries of panic spilled into the open air. Only when the girl's voice broke into sobs did Evelyn step forward, offering her hand and guiding her safely down. And though Veronica's face was streaked with tears, she managed a smile of gratitude as they walked home hand in hand, as though nothing could ever tear their bond apart.

Evelyn carried more than mischief inside her. There was a strangeness about her, a flicker of something beyond the ordinary—an unshakable intuition that often proved true. Small things at first: a neighbour's arrival before it happened, a storm breaking earlier than forecast, a quarrel in the street she claimed she had foreseen. Veronica, raised in the presence of Tarot cards and whispered fortunes, took this in stride. It didn't frighten her. If anything, it fascinated her. Evelyn herself seemed half-aware of her gift, treating it less as a burden than as a source of amusement, a secret game with the future.

But more than her foresight, it was Evelyn's stories that set her apart. She could spin whole worlds out of thin air: tales of invisible beings slipping between dimensions, of spirits that wore human faces, of doorways in the fabric of existence that opened only to those who dared look closely. Veronica listened wide-eyed, surrendering herself completely to each word until Evelyn—always in control—decided the story was over.

Sometimes other children joined them, drawn by Evelyn's magnetic voice, only to leave unsettled. For some, the stories were too vivid, too eerie, and soon complaints found their way back to Evelyn's mother. Parents talked about wickedness, about dark imagination spoiling impressionable minds. Yet Veronica stood like a shield between Evelyn and such accusations, brushing the others off as tattletales who lacked the courage to listen.

All of that came to an abrupt end when Evelyn turned fourteen. Her parents, tired and weary of life in South Africa, announced they were returning to Australia. At the airport, beneath the sterile glow of departure gates, Veronica stood clutching her grandmother's hand, tears streaking her face as she waved goodbye. That image—the trembling hand raised in farewell, the sorrow burning in her eyes—seared itself into Evelyn's memory, haunting her long after the plane lifted into the sky.

For weeks afterward, Veronica mourned in silence. She found a strange, aching solace in Louis Armstrong's *What a Wonderful World*, replaying the song as though its bittersweet melody carried Evelyn's presence across the miles. It became their shared anthem, a private song of memory and longing.

The years that followed were not kind to Evelyn. Soon after their move, her parents divorced. Her father returned to England, only to die of a massive heart attack not long after. The shadow of loss settled heavily over her family, but Evelyn, resilient as ever, learned to carry it quietly.

Now, after so many years, Evelyn was back in Cape Town. She sat beside Veronica in silence as the car pulled away from the airport, each of them lost in unspoken thoughts. The drive seemed endless—two hours along a highway that stretched like a ribbon through the landscape before narrowing into a lonely country road. The lane wound through dense bushland and open stretches of field where tall trees leaned into the wind, their shadows sliding across the road like fleeting ghosts.

Evelyn wondered why Veronica moved to the wilderness. Why so far from the city, from its hum and pulse? Her thoughts were interrupted when they finally reached a small group of shops in the middle of the bush, about three sagging stores, their faded signs tilting under the weight of years, and looking desolate. Do people really go to these shops? Veronica's car moved on, slowly, down the road, before they stopped at a house that did not resemble the other houses scattered about, because it was well kept. Neat, painted, cared for—it was an island of order amid the weathered neighbouring dwellings. It sat at the edge of the road, the final house before wilderness reclaimed the road and bent it toward the distant highway.

Across from the house stretched an open field, alive with tall grasses and wild autumn flowers, their colours softened in the late light. The plants bent and swayed as though caught in breezy conversation with the wind. From deep within the field came a strange, high-pitched sound—neither bird nor insect, but something finer, like wind sifting through fragile petals or secrets carried in the weeds. Evelyn turned her head toward it, listening. Something in the sound felt almost intentional, as though the land itself were speaking, waiting for her to understand.

As Evelyn followed Veronica through the front gate, her eyes lingered on the garden. Despite the season's chill, the beds were impeccably kept, their clipped hedges suggesting discipline, even pride. Most of the blooms had withered, yet here and there, stubborn autumn flowers flared with colour—pockets of defiance against the creeping cold. Something about them felt watchful, as though the garden itself were holding its breath.

Veronica said little while lifting a suitcase from Evelyn's hand. She attempted a smile, polite and thin, but it faltered before reaching her eyes. Beneath her composure lay something else—an unease that Evelyn could not place. The sight of her old friend seemed to stir ghosts from another life: two girls running barefoot under the sun, laughter rising like music before the silence of years closed over them.

A spontaneous memory jumped into Veronica's mind. She was a child again, sitting at the kitchen table beneath her grandmother's steady gaze. The Tarot cards lay spread across the worn cloth, their painted symbols vivid, almost breathing. At the time it had been a game, nothing more, until the pattern revealed itself: separation, change, an ending of sorts. Her grandmother's voice had been calm but final—Evelyn would be leaving soon. Veronica had laughed then, unwilling to believe. Yet within weeks Evelyn was gone, bound for Australia. From that day, she never doubted the cards. After her grandmother's death, she had inherited the fragile, fraying deck and kept it hidden away, a relic of power she both feared and trusted.

Now Evelyn had returned—not for nostalgia, nor by chance. She had come for Susan, the daughter she had raised alone, the daughter who had slipped from her grasp as surely as water through open fingers. At seventeen Susan had walked away—toward freedom, toward friends, toward the wide world that seemed to beckon her generation. She had worked, saved, dreamed of places far beyond the reach of her mother's voice.

And yet, as the garden gate clicked shut behind them, Evelyn could not shake the feeling that something unseen had drawn her here—that perhaps the old cards had spoken once more, and this visit would reveal more than either of them was ready to face.

Now Evelyn was finally here—summoned across oceans and time zones, pulled from the quiet familiarity of Australia in such haste she barely had time to breathe. She had come for one reason only, the reason that had gnawed at her ever since Veronica's letter reached her trembling hands: Susan. Her daughter. The girl she had raised alone, then lost to the world, who was now in a room at the back of this unfamiliar house.

It felt unreal. Years had stretched thin between them, the fragile thread of mother and daughter fraying until it seemed to snap. At seventeen, Susan had stormed from Evelyn's life, headstrong and restless, choosing the company of friends over the woman who had given her life. She worked, saved, and—like so many of her generation—fed her dreams on the notion of freedom, of travel, of anywhere-but-here.

And then silence. Silence that deepened into absence.

Evelyn had not seen her since, not truly. The occasional whisper of her whereabouts drifted across the globe, but nothing certain, nothing she could hold. Until Veronica's message. When it arrived, Evelyn had stood frozen, unable to move, her mind struggling to comprehend that her daughter—her Susan—was here, under Veronica's roof.

It was strange, how easily time had stolen them from each other. Susan had wandered the world, carving a life Evelyn had never been invited into. Europe, then London, where she had lived for a year before—quite suddenly—changing her course and arriving in Cape Town. Veronica had told Evelyn only fragments: that Susan had left England in haste, that she sought rest, that she had stayed far longer in South Africa than she had intended. Evelyn sensed there was more, things Veronica had not yet spoken aloud.

When Evelyn and Veronica first stepped into the kitchen together, the air had grown dense, oppressive. Veronica's composure faltered; she tried to disguise her unease with a smile, but her face betrayed her. She had known, of course, about the long estrangement, the words exchanged in anger, the accusations Susan had once hurled—"insane," "unfit," "erratic." Susan had told Veronica how Evelyn's paranoia had uprooted them time and again, how they had moved from town to town as though the world itself hunted them. It was not easy for Veronica to hear. And yet, she had held her tongue, afraid to ignite the sparks between mother and daughter.

Evelyn, preoccupied by the unusual décor of Veronica's house and her sombre demeanour, was unable to stop a flood of memories from washing over her. Susan's very first baby steps, the laughter of a child who once clung to her, the warmth of nights when only the two of them inhabited the universe. How had that delight turned into such bitterness and distance? After all these years, Evelyn would finally see her daughter again.

The living room seemed to close in around them, its silence heavy as stone. Evelyn thought of the telegram Veronica had once sent to her post office box back in Australia, casually informing her that Susan was in London. That Susan contacted her and was thinking of visiting Veronica in Cape Town. Evelyn had read it the same day she had quarrelled with the postmaster, slamming the little metal door in a fit of frustration. She was still angry with Susan's disappearance. She had told herself she didn't care—but the memory lingered, a thorn beneath the skin.

It was only now, in Cape Town, that Evelyn understood how much Veronica had been keeping watch all these years. Susan had asked to stay with her godmother for "a while," and Veronica had opened her home without hesitation. But what shocked Veronica most was learning the truth—that mother and daughter had not spoken for more than five years. To Veronica, whose own family ties were woven tightly, such estrangement was beyond comprehension.

Evelyn's mind slid further back, to the day Susan was born. She remembered the exhausted impulse that had driven her to call Veronica, oceans away, and ask her to be godmother. Veronica had accepted instantly, honoured, her voice breaking with emotion over the line. There had been no paperwork, no signatures—just a promise sealed by trust. Years later, when Evelyn brought seven-year-old Susan to South Africa, Veronica had arrived at their Sea Point hotel with gifts, including that strange doll with its unsettling face. Susan had accepted it with a child's indifference, but Evelyn could never bring herself to discard it. It lingered in storage, a silent witness to all that had unravelled.

Through the years, Veronica had faithfully remembered Susan's birthdays and Christmases, sending gifts across the sea. The girl had sometimes replied, often not. Only recently, after her return from London, had Susan begun to confide in her godmother, unburdening herself of her sadness, her sense of drift, and her growing fear that she was more like her mother than she cared to admit. For, like Evelyn, she too possessed the shadow of a psychic sensitivity. Just like Evelyn, she tried to push it aside, terrified it might draw her into the same darkness.

Now, twenty-eight years old, Susan was only a few steps away, waiting behind a closed door. Evelyn's pulse quickened, nausea rose in her throat. The air seemed charged, alive with something unseen. Veronica, pale and anxious, reached out to rub her back.

"You don't have to see her right away," she whispered, her voice trembling. "I'll make some tea."

But Evelyn knew she must. Delay was its own kind of betrayal. She had come this far; she could not retreat.

As Veronica disappeared into the kitchen, the clatter of cups and water filling the kettle masking the silence, Evelyn steadied herself. She rose, her feet heavy on the carpeted floor, and began the slow walk down the narrow hallway. At the end, the door was semi-closed. Behind it was Susan. Her daughter. The past, waiting to be reckoned with.

The door seemed to wait for her hand. Evelyn froze, breath snagging in her throat, then she slowly eased it open. The hinges groaned, stretching out the moment like a warning. A muted glow seeped through the heavy curtains, leaving the room dim, suspended somewhere between night and day. The air felt unmoving, as if even time had chosen to pause here.

On the small table by the entrance, a bouquet of wildflowers sat in a chipped vase. Once vibrant, they had withered into brittle silhouettes, their scent pungent and strangely sweet, clinging stubbornly to the stale atmosphere. Evelyn's eyes lingered on them, their faded beauty blurring through the veil of her tears.

But it was the presence at the centre of the room that held dominion. A coffin—smooth, wood and metal, unnervingly modern—rested upon a silver trolley, its polished surface reflecting what little light crept through the gloom. It seemed almost out of place, like a relic of another world intruding upon this quiet country bungalow.

The lid was not fully closed. It yawned open just enough to reveal the figure within. Susan. Evelyn's breath faltered, her chest tightening as she observed her daughter lying still, a portrait of serenity painted in silence. For a fleeting, cruel moment, Susan might have been asleep, her features softened, untouched by suffering. Yet there was no movement of breath, no warmth of life—only that immutable stillness which whispered of finality.

Evelyn stood frozen, her body refusing to obey the instinct to move closer. The woman who had always armed herself against shadows, who had lived with the torment of intrusive visions and a mind that spun webs of fear, now found herself stripped bare. In this room, with its dim light and oppressive quiet, her mind was emptied of every torment. Her focus was entirely on her daughter, lying deceased in a modern-day sarcophagus

Veronica sat silently in her kitchen; her hands wrapped around a cooling cup of tea. The steam had long since faded, but her gaze remained fixed on the tea package resting on the table. Its surface bloomed with a pattern of red roses, a detail she could not ignore. The design called to mind her own journal, its hard cover marked by a single embossed rose—an echo too pointed to be dismissed as chance. A coincidence, perhaps. Yet something about it stirred in her the urge to write.

Tea often carried her there. With each familiar sip, she felt the pull to open her journal and capture the words Susan had once spoken to her—pieces of memory, slivers of conversation. But what Susan never guessed was that Veronica's writing extended far beyond their shared recollections. In secret, she filled those pages with her dreams, her strange visions, and the unexplainable glimpses of other worlds that came to her at all the wrong times. Susan, like Evelyn, her mother, waved such things away, calling them tricks of an overactive mind, or perhaps the shadow of some unnamed illness. Both mother and daughter had turned their backs on clairvoyance, refusing to acknowledge it as anything more than folly.

Veronica could never reject it so easily. Since childhood, she had been drawn to what lay beneath the surface of ordinary life. Her grandmother—stern, enigmatic, rooted in older traditions—had spoken often of the ancient Egyptians and their mysteries. She believed Veronica carried within her the spark of heightened sight, a gift that marked her as different. But difference, her grandmother warned, came at a cost. Such powers could isolate her, make her a curiosity, or worse—a threat—among her peers.

So, Veronica learned to conceal. She became an observer, studying others closely and shaping her words and gestures so that nothing about her seemed unusual. Outwardly, she blended. Inwardly, she endured.

Even when she tried university, she discovered the same dissonance. Knowledge came to her quickly, instinctively, but the rigid structures of essays and exams suffocated her. Ideas bloomed fully formed in her mind, yet when she tried to explain them, they seemed to collapse into nothing or half-truths she could not articulate. Frustration, paired with the grind of financial hardship, eventually wore her down. She abandoned the effort, trading lecture halls for a small shoe shop, where each sale bought her time and a few dollars more.

But the shoes were not her true purpose. Quietly, she saved toward another dream—her grandmother's dream. The old woman longed for a cottage nestled in the countryside, where chickens and ducks might roam, and rows of vegetables stretched toward the horizon. A place close to the soil, close to the simplicity of life. Veronica had promised herself she would make that dream real.

She never had the chance. One evening, returning weary from work, she found her grandmother lying still in bed, her life quietly ended during an afternoon nap. The silence of that room haunted her more than any vision ever had.

Her grandmother's words returned to her then, sharp and unyielding: *"Don't worry about the dead, because the dead don't worry about you."* To her, there was no life beyond the grave. Only the present mattered, only the living could claim meaning.

It was into this silence that Evelyn entered the kitchen, her steps slow, her face pale and drawn with fatigue. She lowered herself into the chair at the head of the table, eyes fixed downward as though searching for something she could not name. No words passed her lips.

Veronica remained still, though the weight of her journal pressed upon her. She knew that sooner or later she would have to reveal it—those pages brimming with Susan's voice, Susan's unguarded stories. But how could she place them before Evelyn, who recoiled from such things even more fiercely than Susan had?

And yet, despite the certainty of Evelyn's resistance, Veronica felt the pull of inevitability. No matter how unpleasant it may be, the truth must be spoken.

The following morning, the house lay in a silence so deep it seemed to hold its breath. Not even the pipes groaned, nor the floorboards creaked, as though the very walls had entered into mourning. Veronica stood at the stove in her dressing gown, hair hastily tied back, her slender hands wrapped around the kettle's handle. Steam escaped, curling into the chill of the kitchen air, dissipating before it could reach the ceiling. She moved mechanically, her face unreadable, as if the ritual of making tea might tether her to something familiar, something safe.

Evelyn entered without sound, her presence subdued, a shadow more than a body. She accepted Veronica's quiet condolences with only a faint, regretful smile. No further words followed. For a time, there was only the slumber whistle of the kettle, the faint tick of the clock, and the silence between them, heavy as stone.

And then, a memory surfaced. A dream Susan had told Veronica only weeks earlier, her voice carrying the unease of something half-forgotten and half-feared. Susan rarely spoke of her mother in dreams—indeed, she rarely dreamt of her at all—but this one had shaken her. In it, mother and daughter stood together in a vast field scattered with blossoms, yet the flowers were wrong: unnatural, lifeless, made of some artificial fabric that crackled in the wind. Evelyn was there, but distant—her expression troubled, her presence unreachable. The earth beneath their feet was scorched and dry, as though some calamity had already passed through, leaving nothing alive. The image had unsettled Susan deeply, and now, recalling it in the muted morning light, Veronica felt the dream's weight pressing down on her like a prophecy.

At first light, the morticians arrived. Their black van rolled across the gravel drive, the crunch of wheels startling in the hush. Evelyn wanted nothing to do with them, with the grim reality they represented in their stiff suits and gloved hands. She slipped away through the back door, her flight neither hurried nor hesitant, but inevitable, as though some part of her body refused to remain in that house of death a moment longer. Veronica stayed, guiding the men in low, perfunctory tones, signing papers with an unsteady hand. The sounds of furniture being nudged aside, the hollow thud of unseen movement, filled the house like muffled echoes of finality.

Outside, the world continued with careless indifference. Evelyn sat on the veranda, staring into the backyard garden Veronica had so carefully tended. Autumn had begun its slow unravelling, scattering rust and gold among the branches. Blossoms still glowed in defiance of the season's decay. Butterflies, fragile as shards of painted glass, flitted lazily through the air, while bees traced their endless circuits among the petals. Life moved forward, unashamed and unapologetic, mocking the stillness and grief that clung to the house.

The veranda stretched the length of the home, its roof veiled in the thick, twisting trunk of an old grapevine. The vine climbed the weathered beam and spread across the rafters above, its sparse leaves letting sunlight fall in shifting golden shafts. The floorboards glowed beneath the morning light, and though the warmth washed over Evelyn, she felt nothing.

Her emotions refused to take shape. They came in jagged bursts—shards of rage, guilt, despair—none with a name she could hold. Susan was gone. No longer her daughter, no longer the child she had raised, but a body lifted by strangers, carried away without tenderness. The men had not been cruel, yet they were brisk, too efficient, performing their task with the practiced detachment of those for whom death was an ordinary business. Evelyn had fled before they could finish, unable to watch her daughter reduced to a burden of flesh and weight.

Tears streaked her face now, uninvited and relentless. She had never been a woman who wept. Strength had been her armour;

composure, her weapon. Yet here she was, dissolving into grief she could not master. Were her tears for Susan? For the years lost, the years in which she had not been present? Or were they for herself—for the emptiness left behind, for the failures she could never undo? Perhaps the tears belonged to every sorrow she had stifled for decades, welling up all at once in merciless release.

The creak of the screen door snapped Evelyn back to the here and now. Veronica emerged, her ever-present notebook clutched against her chest, stray papers jutting out like restless thoughts desperate for air. She drew a chair opposite Evelyn and slowly sat down, the morning sun illuminating portions of her body. Her black hair, tied loosely, spilled strands across her face; the breeze teased them into motion. Shadows shifted across her dark skin as the loquat tree swayed, light and shade playing over her like a secret undecided.

Evelyn studied her. There was something regal about Veronica's bearing, something that stirred ancient images—desert queens, nomadic priestesses, women who carried mysteries in their very blood. Yet such thoughts were forbidden territory. Veronica never spoke of her lineage, and Evelyn had long ago learned not to ask.

"Evelyn," Veronica murmured, voice weighted with hesitation. "We need to talk about the funeral arrangements. They said… they can only hold the body for forty-eight hours." Her eyes lowered to the notebook on her lap, avoiding Evelyn's face.

Evelyn wiped her tears away with the back of her hand and straightened. Her voice, when it came, was flat, mechanical. "It's all right. I'll make the arrangements. Susan will be taken home."

Veronica shifted uneasily. "That's what I wanted to speak to you about." She hesitated, then drew out a sheet of paper. "Susan once told me she wanted a cremation—or perhaps a burial here, in South Africa."

Evelyn's head popped up. "What are you saying?"

"She mentioned it once, when she was still in London. I wrote it down because she insisted, I mustn't forget. And later, when she came here, she gave me this." Veronica extended the fragile sheet. "She wanted me to keep it."

Evelyn took the note. Susan's handwriting—so delicate, so achingly familiar—stared back at her:

This is where I want to sleep for all eternity. A place so lovely, so at peace with nature.

Evelyn's face tightened. "This doesn't mean anything, Veronica. Yes, it's her writing, but you know Susan—she was always like this. Swept away by some new passion, convinced it was life-changing, and then—just as quickly—gone. That was Susan."

But Veronica had more. She pulled out another sheet, this one bearing a disturbing illustration: a coffin, half-buried beneath flowers, half-consumed by flames. Beneath it, in Susan's neat script, the words: *Here lies a lost soul.* Above it loomed a rough sketch of Table Mountain, with the letters *CPSA* scrawled beneath.

Evelyn's colour drained. "My God... did she know she was going to die?" Her voice trembled between fear and exasperation. "This—this is exactly what she did! She filled pages with grotesque drawings, dark words, wallowing in her moods." Her voice cracked, anger covering the tremor of grief. "I won't indulge this nonsense."

Veronica rose, moving to the end of the veranda where the air was cooler. Her eyes shone with unshed tears. "Evelyn... Susan was with me nearly three months. She left London very unhappy; she was sad and moody when she first arrived, talking things I couldn't understand. She had... psychic abilities. Like you. She told me about her dreams. Dark ones. It's always about endings. She begged me not to tell you anything about her. Not even that she lived here. I felt like I betrayed her when I told you she was in London and then when she came here. But I've come to terms with the fact that you, as her mother, needed to know where she was and how she was doing.

Evelyn's anger wavered, softening for a heartbeat. "I know, Veronica."

But Veronica pushed on, urgent, trembling. "There's something in all of this—I can feel it. Something isn't right."

"Stop." Evelyn's tone snapped like a whip, cutting through the air. "You are chasing ghosts. Patterns that aren't there. If anyone is to blame, it is me. I failed her long ago. But it's too late now. Susan is gone." She thrust the papers back onto the table and stood, her shoulders squared in rigid defiance. At the door she paused, her voice cold. "If I were you, I'd burn those papers and move on."

Defeated, Veronica gathered the sheets, slipping them carefully into her notebook. She shut it gently, but the weight of Susan's words pressed upon her still. What was she to do with them?

That evening, the house lay subdued. Both women carried their storms in silence, Evelyn's moods, swinging from tenderness to rage, Veronica retreating into thought then action. Arrangements had to be made.

On the third day after Susan's body was removed from Veronica's house, the funeral took place, a small service at the Cape Town crematorium. The drive home was long, quiet. Evelyn stared hollowly out at the passing landscape, the mountains in the distance, her silence heavy, impenetrable.

That night she stunned Veronica with a sudden decision: she would take Susan's ashes back to Australia the very next day. Veronica had imagined they would lean on one another for longer, but part of her—worn thin by Evelyn's moods—wondered if perhaps it was best this way.

Later, alone, Veronica leafed through her notebook. Susan's messages still playing around in her head. She longed to tell Evelyn what she suspected, but Evelyn dismissed it all, as she always had. Still… the feeling gnawed at her. Something was not as it seemed.

In the next room, Evelyn lay awake, staring into the dark. The pillow was damp beneath her cheek; tears she had not noticed. Memories rose like ghosts: Susan laughing, running as a child, her small hand clutching her own. Once she had been everything, essential, needed. Now she was hollow. And the accident—how could it be? Susan was not reckless. The doubt crept in slowly, a thought she could not silence.

Perhaps Veronica was right. Perhaps there was more to Susan's death than anyone dared to admit.

Midnight crept closer, but neither woman could surrender to sleep. The silence of the house was broken only by the faint scratching of Veronica's pen, the occasional creak of the old timber walls, and the sigh of the wind pressing against the shutters. She sat hunched at her desk, her dressing gown pulled tightly around her, the lamplight casting long, wavering shadows over the scatter of papers before her. A year's worth of Susan's dream accounts lay spread across the surface in chaotic piles—pages crowded with erratic sketches, strange diagrams whose meanings slipped like water through her fingers, and notes scribbled in hurried bursts of thought that already felt half-forgotten.

Most of it read like nonsense, an indecipherable language belonging to some other world. And yet, every so often, clarity would blaze forth—terrifying in its precision. One image returned to her again and again, etched into her mind as though with fire: a maiden in a white gown, her hair crowned with a single fresh flower, lying as though in enchanted sleep. Around her, a circle of short, stocky figures in vibrant garments stood guard, their faces solemn, their presence oddly reverent, as though awaiting the arrival of some destined prince who might rouse her with a kiss.

To Veronica it seemed a strange echo of old fairy tales. To Susan, however, it was no harmless story. She confessed more than once that the dream unsettled her deeply, a recurring nightmare that drained her, leaving her anxious and shaken. Why was she dreaming of a sleeping young lady all the time? Veronica had tried to dismiss it once—just mixed messages of childhood stories, distorted in the mind. But the pattern of Susan's visions troubled her. There was something real about them, a deliberate design that suggested something beyond imagination. Something prophetic.

As the months wore on, Susan's dreams shifted. They no longer clung to familiar memories. Instead, they unfolded vast, uncanny landscapes—enchanted forests dripping with silver dew, ruined temples swallowed by vines, subterranean palaces inhabited by monarchs who were both regal and monstrous, and beings bound by laws older than memory itself. Always, faceless silhouettes lingered at the edges, walls of speckled gold, soulless things swarming restlessly, clawing at the energetic light they could never capture fully. And through every dream, woven from one intelligence, behind a thread of iron, came the same message repeated in veiled disguises—too vivid, too real, searing itself into her mind until it left her trembling.

For nearly a year, Veronica had wrestled with these puzzles, torn between fascination and dread. Often the truth seemed to hover just within reach, only to dissolve the moment she stretched toward it, leaving her with nothing but gibberish. And yet she sensed something forming—an unholy picture assembling piece by piece, like a dark mosaic revealing its dreadful otherworldly images.

When morning finally came, Veronica gathered her courage and tried again to confide in Evelyn, hoping she might at last find a companion in unravelling these mysteries. But Evelyn met her words with silence, a wall of resistance she could not scale. She wanted no part in Susan's dreams, no whisper of their shadow. Instead, she busied herself with her journey home, borrowing Veronica's car and driving into town.

Left to herself, Veronica sought refuge in small comforts. She returned to the kitchen, her hands steadying in the old ritual of kneading dough. She baked bread and rolls, filling the house with the warm, yeasty fragrance that had always been her answer to loneliness.

By evening, the quiet of solitude was broken by the crunch of tires in the gravel drive. Evelyn returned transformed, brisk, almost buoyant, her arms heavy with shopping bags. Veronica, struck by the sudden swing in her mood, could only stare in bewilderment.

"What's that wonderful smell? Did you bake?" Evelyn's voice rang with a warmth that startled.

"Yes," Veronica replied cautiously, wiping her hands on her apron. "Fresh bread always feels… right."

Evelyn set her bags down with a smile. "I bought groceries— and a few other things."

"You shouldn't have—" Veronica began, but Evelyn cut her off with a wave of the hand.

"Nonsense. Did Susan ever pay her way here? I will not have you paying for everything alone. In fact, I have arranged to transfer some money into your account—"

Veronica's voice rose sharply. "What? Absolutely not! You don't need to do that, Evelyn."

But Evelyn's face was set, her look unflinching. Veronica recognized the look at once—it was the same stubborn certainty she remembered from their youth, the same quiet resolve that could not be bent. Yet beneath it, she sensed a different force now, some drive she could not name.

Later, the two women sat on the veranda with their meal of warm bread soaked in olive oil, mashed tomatoes and smoked fish. The twilight unfolded across the horizon, covering the garden with fading light. Birds cried their last songs, insects hummed in the cooling air, and the flowers Veronica had planted months ago lifted their heads toward the dimming light. It should have been a moment of peace.

But Evelyn shattered it.

She spoke Susan's name.

Her voice cut like a blade through the fragile calm, demanding details—about the accident, the circumstances, the place. Veronica froze, her hand halted midway to her cup. Evelyn had avoided such talk until now, refusing to even look at her daughter's memory. And suddenly here she was, insistent, unrelenting.

The serenity of the evening dissolved. Veronica's stomach clenched. She braced herself.

The past rose before her: their schooldays, the cruel taunts hurled at Evelyn for her strangeness, and how she, Veronica, had shielded her then. The instinct to protect returned now, fierce as ever.

"I'm glad to talk about Susan," she said gently, "but I had hoped tonight we might speak of lighter things."

Evelyn's face was unreadable, her eyes sharp. "I just want to know the truth. What were the autopsy results? Do you have those documents?"

"Autopsy?" Veronica blinked.

"Yes," Evelyn pressed, leaning forward. "Tell me everything. The days before her death. All of it. I need to hear it."

A chill moved through Veronica. The sudden change in Evelyn's mood, the intensity of her look, unsettled her. "Perhaps tomorrow," she tried to deflect. "Tonight, I only want quiet—not arguments."

But Evelyn would not give up. "Yes, quiet, sounds nice—but I want to know more about the accident."

Veronica felt cornered. Best to keep her calm, she thought, and offer enough to steady her. "What do you want to know?"

"Was she happy? Did she ever say someone followed her? Someone plotting against her?"

"No… nothing like that. Why are you asking?"

"Because I believe Susan was murdered," Evelyn said flatly. "This was foul play."

Veronica stared. "Why would you say such a thing?"

"Because I know. People don't just die like that in car accidents."

"Evelyn, they do. Every day." Veronica tried to steady her tone, but Evelyn's conviction was unyielding.

"Tell me the truth. I still don't know the full story."

Exhaustion washed through Veronica, but she forced herself to answer. "I only know this: Susan and Sabrena went to Cape Town on holiday. They hired a car. The accident happened on the mountain road."

Evelyn jolted upright. "They? Who was with her?"

"Sabrena. They went together."

"And she—she died too?"

"No," Veronica exclaimed. "Sabrena lived. She's in hospital. Critical."

The words seemed to drain Evelyn of all colour. She sank back, stunned. "She survived? How come I wasn't told about this?"

"Yes," Veronica said softly, seizing the chance to guide her friend away from frenzy. "But she's in a terrible state. No one knows if she'll recover. I was going to tell you about Sabrena later."

Evelyn's voice broke. "How could she survive… if the car went over the cliff? Into the sea?"

"They say she was thrown clear before the car plunged into the water. Landed on a ledge by miracle. If not for that, she'd be gone too."

Evelyn shook her head, bewildered.

Veronica went on gently, explaining that Susan and Sabrena had become inseparable, bound in laughter and long talks. She spoke of Sabrena's modest life, the family shop run by her ailing father, the burden Sabrena carried with quiet grace—caring for her younger siblings and her sick mother while keeping the business alive. Despite poverty, she endured.

Susan had discovered her by chance, wandering to the shop for milk or bread, only to remain for hours. Veronica more than once had driven out to fetch her goddaughter, who had lost all track of time in Sabrena's company.

The story lulled the evening into uneasy quiet. Veronica excused herself to tidy the kitchen, plunging her hands into warm, soapy water, an old habit that soothed her. Evelyn followed, drawing out a chair, her voice gentler now.

"Veronica, I've decided to delay my return home—if that's all right?"

"Of course," Veronica said, looking over her shoulder with a small smile. "I wondered why you were in such a hurry to leave."

Evelyn lowered herself into the chair, her eyes steady. "I just need to know more about Susan—the days before, the accident. I only realise now how little I know. If not tonight, then before I leave, I'd like you to tell me more, if that is, okay?"

Veronica turned, her facial expression calm, consistent. "Stay where you are. I'll finish the dishes, then I will make us a nice cup of tea. And I will tell you all I can."

Evelyn smiled with a hint of mischief, her eyes glinting in the low light of the kitchen. "Something stronger than tea, perhaps?" she teased, her voice light and friendly.

Later, when the dishes had been washed and stacked neatly away, the two women sat at the dining room table, the lamplight softening the shadows that clung to the corners of the room. Veronica began recounting her conversations with Susan during her final weeks in London. Her tone moved between matter of fact and tender, as though each word she spoke might disturb the fragile quiet that hung between them. Susan, she explained, had carried with her a dreadful certainty—that her life was in danger. That belief had been so overpowering that it changed her plans, pushing her onto a plane bound for Cape Town.

Evelyn looked on.

"At first she struggled," Veronica said, fingers rubbing the rim of her saucer on which her cup sat nicely. "The isolation here must have been hard on her. But then she met Sabrena. After that… she seemed happier. Her laughter returned, and for a time I thought she'd found a way back to herself."

Here Veronica faltered. She looked down, as if afraid her next words might carry too much weight. When she finally spoke, her voice was hushed, reluctant. "She also spoke of visions—strange, incomprehensible ones. I never knew what to make of them."

Evelyn, however, would not be led down that path. She steered the conversation quickly back to the accident. "Where exactly was Susan's body found?"

"In the car," Veronica answered, her words barely more than breath. "She was still inside when they hauled it out of the water. Sabrena, though… she'd been flung clear, onto a narrow ledge below the road. Had she been conscious, had she so much as moved—she would have fallen into the sea. Her very unconsciousness saved her."

Silence fell. It thickened, filling the kitchen like smoke. Evelyn rose without a word, crossed to the sideboard, and poured herself another scotch. The splash of soda water followed, the crackle of ice a brief intrusion on the quiet. She lingered there, leaning against the sink, cradling the glass as though it alone could steady her trembling spirit. She savoured the burn of it before returning to the table, calmer now, her composure more relaxed now.

Veronica continued, her voice low and deliberate. "They reported that her body had less damage than one might expect. The car absorbed nearly all the force when it struck the water. She was still strapped in her seatbelt, the wreckage folding around her as though determined to keep her in place."

Evelyn's eyes hardened. "Do you have the official account or autopsy?"

Veronica hesitated, then rose. From a cupboard she withdrew her familiar notebook, pages thick with her careful records. Within its folds rested a large brown envelope sealed with an official stamp. She slid it across the table. Evelyn opened it with steady hands, though her throat tightened as she read the blunt finality:

Cause of Death: Car Accident. Accidental Death. Reckless Driving.

The words hung heavy in the air. The kitchen seemed to retreat around them; its silence deepened into something almost unbearable. Veronica reached across the table, gathering her courage.

"These should be yours."

She pushed forward a smaller bundle—notes clipped together, the edges worn.

Evelyn frowned. "What is this?"

"My own records," Veronica said softly. "Conversations, bits and pieces—things Susan told me. You may not be ready now, but perhaps one day you'll want to know them."

But Evelyn was in no mood for patience. She seized the bundle and began leafing through the pages. Her daughter's voice seemed to rise from the paper itself: fragments of poems, scattered thoughts, peculiar sketches woven among Veronica's careful script.

"She used to phone often while she was in London," Veronica said, her eyes fixed on the papers. "She would talk of her visions, her ambitions… things she was working on. I always felt she was sensing something just beyond reach, though she never gave it form."

Evelyn paused over a page covered with the same image repeated again and again. Each flower pressed deep into the paper, each circle drawn with an almost feverish hand.

"What is this? A flower?"

"Yes," Veronica replied. "Susan never knew why she drew it. Only that it meant something. I even turned to the Tarot for guidance, but the cards remained silent."

"Could it be a logo? A symbol? Some company's mark?" Evelyn asked.

"I wondered too. We searched for answers. We spent hours one afternoon, trying to see why this white, exotic flower haunted her. But nothing ever revealed itself."

That night, sleep evaded them both. The air was unnaturally warm, a soft breeze carrying the scent of pine trees through the open windows. Evelyn lay in darkness, her thoughts gnawed raw by doubt. If Susan's death had not been an accident, then who—or what—had willed it? And why?

When morning came, Veronica found her already outside on the terrace. Evelyn's eyes were hollow, her frame taut with unrest.

The garden around her was alive—sunflowers, this early in the season stretching toward the light, birds exalting in chorus, grasses whispering secrets to the wind. Yet Evelyn looked apart from it all, as though the night had stripped her of something vital.

Evelyn then asked after the bicycle she had noticed in the garage. She wanted to ride to the local corner store. Veronica offered to walk with her instead, and they set out together. Evelyn laced up a pair of nearly new sports shoes, bought in a burst of fitness enthusiasm a year earlier but rarely worn since.

They set off along the narrow road into the valley. The world seemed suspended, hushed beneath the rising warmth. No cars passed, no human voices stirred the quiet—only the shrill cries of unseen creatures and the distant sigh of the wind. Evelyn looked about uneasily, the road stretching lonely before them. A thought suddenly occurred to her: were they truly safe here, in this deserted place that felt almost watchful?

Soon they reached a weathered corner store, its façade recalling another age. Attached was a small, shuttered shop that Evelyn later learned opened only during certain hours, selling fabrics and clothing made by a local woman who carried her work to market days in the city.

The grocery store was open. To Evelyn's surprise, it was larger inside than it appeared from the road—two simple aisles lined with scattered goods. Essentials like bread, milk, and eggs were plentiful. In one corner, neat stacks of Coca-Cola and Fanta crates stood waiting.

A middle-aged African man greeted them warmly, though his eyes lingered on Evelyn with caution. Round-bellied, with short white tight curls and a matching beard, he seemed to know Veronica well.

Evelyn asked if he had known Susan. The smile slipped from his face. He turned instead to Veronica, unwilling to answer. Veronica repeated the question, blending English with Afrikaans.

The man then nodded. His daughter, Sabrena, had been Susan's friend, he said. His voice faltered, eyes watering. Then, without another word, he busied himself at the register—a quiet signal that the conversation was over.

Evelyn and Veronica stepped out of the store into the brightness of the morning. The street was still, the silence broken only by the rustle of chickens pecking at the weeds behind the shop. Two old dogs moved sluggishly through the dust, their bodies worn down by time, their steps heavy and deliberate.

At the edge of the sandy lot, a towering tree cast its shade across the road. Its trunk was wide and scarred with age, yet its branches stretched upward in quiet defiance, alive and strong. Dark shapes lined its upper limbs—black birds, unmoving, watchful. Their sharp eyes followed the women below.

Veronica glanced back toward the store. "He must miss her terribly," she said softly. "Sabrena was always beside him, helping with the house, the shop. I've never seen him so down. He must wonder, every moment, if she'll ever come home."

Evelyn didn't respond. She was staring up into the branches, caught by the weight of the birds' gaze. It felt as though they knew—knew what bound Susan and Sabrena, knew the secrets no one else would ever tell.

Sabrena had admired Susan from the beginning. Susan was worldly, refined, everything Sabrena longed to be. With Susan, she could imagine another life, a life far from this forgotten town, far from the poverty and the endless duties that chained her to her family. London was the place she dreamed of—its libraries, its culture, its endless promise of possibility. But dreams collided with obligation: the ailing mother, the younger siblings, the shop that needed her hands as much as her father did.

Still, she and Susan had carved out small escapes. They talked endlessly, traded clothes and jewellery, plotted weekends and adventures. Susan made Sabrena believe that escape wasn't impossible, even if she had to pay for it herself. Veronica had driven them once into Cape Town, where they dined in a restaurant that shimmered with sophistication. Susan had paid, as always, while Sabrena pretended—just for an evening—that the city was hers.

Later, Veronica overheard their whispers about hotels, nights out in the city, and the life they would someday claim as their own.

Now, outside the shop, Veronica nudged Evelyn's shoulder. "Come on, let's go," she urged.

But Evelyn's eyes remained on the black birds. Her voice, when it came, was low, unsettled. "There's more to this, Veronica. I can feel it."

Veronica sighed. "Yes. A shame, the way life turns out." Yet her own thoughts were fixed on Sabrena's frail body in the hospital, and on her father, who now carried the burden of both the family and the shop alone.

They walked down the lonely road toward Veronica's house. Evelyn plucked wildflowers from the roadside as she went, lifting each to her face, smelling their sweet fragrance, then gathering another. The air was restless with sound—the shrill cries of birds, the chatter of unseen creatures, the hum of insects in the warming day. The sky was an unbroken sheet of blue, merciless in its brightness.

"I keep getting a name," Evelyn said suddenly. She stopped walking.

Veronica turned, startled from her own brooding. Susan's absence still pressed heavily against her heart. She thought of how Susan had arrived from England—tired, paranoid, unable to sleep without pills, her head wracked with migraines. Within weeks, with food, laughter, and care, she had healed, found peace. Veronica had given her a brief refuge. Now that was gone, too.

"A name?" Veronica asked at last.

"Yes. Lucy." Evelyn's eyes were strange, faraway. "It came to me a few days ago. And again, just now—outside the shop. It has to mean something. Do you know anyone by that name?"

Veronica shook her head slowly. "No. Why are you thinking of names?"

"I don't know," Evelyn said quickly, almost defensively. "I just keep hearing it."

She stopped again in the middle of the deserted road, her flowers dangling from her hand. Then her voice changed, sharp with certainty. "We need to go to the hospital. We need to see Sabrena."

Veronica's expression hardened. "We can't, Evelyn." She turned away and continued walking.

"Why not?" Evelyn demanded.

But Veronica did not answer.

When Evelyn caught up, she asked again, insisting it would be the right thing to do, a gesture of kindness and concern. Veronica shook her head. She had already been before Evelyn's arrival. The memory still lingered—the machines, the swollen, broken girl in her hospital bed. Veronica had taken Sabrena's father, and together they had left more shattered than when they arrived.

No, she would not go back. Not now. Not for Evelyn's sake. For all her talk, Evelyn's sudden interest seemed born less from compassion than from her own restless grief, and Veronica felt anger build within her. Sabrena deserved more than to become a vessel for someone else's sorrow.

When they returned home, Veronica's mood had shifted entirely. The change was obvious enough that Evelyn chose to keep her distance, slipping quietly into Susan's room. She sat down on the edge of the bed, her eyes falling on the stack of notes Veronica had left on the dressing table. She gathered them into her hands, flipping through the loose pages until her eyes lingered on a peculiar sketch—a flower encircled by a ring. The drawing was curious, and it puzzled her. Evelyn then looked over toward the three wildflowers she had picked earlier, now resting in a jar of water beside the bed, as though searching for some hidden meaning.

In the kitchen, Veronica nursed her second cup of tea, struggling to steady herself. Her throat tightened as she held back tears. Had she been right to hand those notes over to Evelyn? Had Evelyn's behaviour changed because of what she had read in those notes, or was her friend already descending into madness? Her moods were as sharp and unpredictable as the cactus spines in her garden. Veronica sniffled, wiped her eyes, and gave up trying to find the answer.

The next morning dawned crisp and golden, the kind of autumn day where the sun carried just enough warmth to soften the bite in the air. Birds chirped outside, their songs bright against the quiet of the house. When Evelyn wandered into the kitchen, she found Veronica bent over the refrigerator, scrubbing as though her life depended on it. Evelyn blinked in mild disbelief—who cleans a fridge at that hour? They exchanged a few polite words, and Evelyn poured herself a cup of tea before retreating to the living room so as not to disturb Veronica's peculiar burst of energy.

Later, when the kitchen finally fell silent, Evelyn returned her empty cup and asked if she might borrow the car again. She had plans in the city. Veronica's first thought was that Evelyn meant to visit Sabrena in hospital, but then she realized Evelyn didn't even know which hospital it was. Chiding herself for the uncharitable assumption, she agreed—and then, almost without thinking, asked if she could join her.

Within the hour, they were on the road. The two-hour drive passed through stretches of open countryside, rolling green fields, and far-off mountains framed in bushland. Cold air rushed in through the side window, stinging Evelyn's face and clearing her mind. She was glad for Veronica's company, though she now faced the delicate task of talking her into visiting Sabrena.

As Cape Town's skyline came into view, Veronica's mind drifted back to the girl. She remembered Sabrena's first visit to her house—the way she hesitated at the front door, insisting she'd wait outside until Susan grabbed her arm and walked her in. Once inside, Sabrena's wide eyes had taken in everything: the intricate rugs, polished ornaments, and the lace-draped lanterns that cast the room in warm, jewelled tones. To the girl, the house had been a palace, like something lifted from a picture book of ancient Egypt.

Evelyn broke the silence gently, suggesting they stop by the hospital to see how Sabrena was doing. Her voice was soft, almost too gently for Evelyn's normal tone. Veronica said nothing, though she had known from the moment they left the house that this visit was inevitable. With a small nod, she turned the car toward the hospital at the foot of the mountain, ten minutes from the city centre.

On the ward, Evelyn's anticipation dissolved into disappointment. Sabrena lay still, swaddled in sheets that seemed propped at her waist by some hidden support. Tubes and machines surrounded her, tracking the faint rhythms of a body subdued by drugs. She was deeply unconscious, and there would be no conversation. Veronica had expected as much, yet she still wondered why she had agreed to come.

While Veronica slipped quietly from the room to consult a nurse, Evelyn lingered at the bedside, her gaze fixed upon the fragile sounds of the machines that pulsed and flickered in their steady vigil. The hush of the room closed in around her, unnatural, almost holy, broken only by the faint hum of wires and the distant shuffle of footsteps in the corridor beyond. She reached out absently; fingertips brushing the edge of the blanket as though to feel its texture and perhaps connect her to the room.

Then the air shifted. It was not merely a passing dizziness but a violent lurch of the world itself, as though the floor had dropped away beneath her. Her stomach pitched; the ceiling seemed to sway. In that sudden rupture, visions surged forward, uninvited and merciless.

A car—sleek and red—hurtled through the dark. Its headlights sliced through a wall of fog, and then, in an instant, there was only the abyss. Metal screamed as it tore free from the cliff's edge, suspended for a heartbeat in dreadful silence before plummeting into the ocean below. The sea rose up to meet it, a monstrous black tide, shattering glass and steel with its hungry roar.

Evelyn gasped, clutching the mattress for balance as the room twisted around her. Her knees weakened, and she dropped heavily into the chair, the sound of her breath ragged and desperate in the silence. Still, the torrent of images raged on, sharper now, cruel in their detail. She saw a figure flung clear—Sabrena—arms limp, her body broken against the serrated teeth of rocks. Blood spattered across the rocks, soaking into the dirt, a savage crimson bloom oozing through the mountain's jagged cracks.

And then—another glimpse. A second car, its headlights retreating swiftly along the winding road above, fleeing into the mist. Not an accident. Not chance. A nefarious hand steering events from the shadows above.

Evelyn's body trembled violently, as though the vision itself had passed through her like a storm. She fought to breathe, her chest rising in frantic heaves, every nerve alight with terror. Her fingers dug into the arm of the chair, her knuckles white, her whole being caught between the sterile stillness of the hospital room and the brutal echo of Sabrena's fall.

When Veronica returned, she froze at the sight of her friend, pale and shaken. "Evelyn—are you alright?" she asked, rushing to her side.

Evelyn looked frail, her voice a strained whisper as she forced herself upright and pointed toward the bed. "I know how she survived," she said. "She was thrown clear—out of the car, just before it went over the cliff."

When the wreck was finally hauled from the water, investigators found all the doors jammed shut and crushed inward. No one could explain how Sabrena had escaped. Theories circulated—perhaps she had slipped through an open window or even been ejected through the sunroof—but nothing could be confirmed until she was strong enough to speak. For now, every possibility remained open.

After leaving the hospital, Veronica chose to distract herself by visiting a cluster of familiar shops she loved in that part of the city. When they had finished wandering and spending, she suggested a drive to the coast. In Milnerton, her childhood haunt, they bought crisp parcels of fish and chips and carried them down to the beach. Veronica had been coming here since she was a girl, often with her grandmother, and the routine was unchanged, eating by the sea while gulls wheeled overhead and the waves broke endlessly against the shore.

The weather was too raw and blustery for walking, so they remained in the car with the doors open and the windows lowered, letting the salt wind sweep through as they spoke about Sabrena. Evelyn, after a long silence, admitted she had seen the accident. Veronica's eyes widened when she learned Sabrena had been thrown from the sunroof—and widened further still when Evelyn insisted another vehicle had fled the scene. That detail didn't fit. All Veronica's information had said there were no witnesses, no other cars. Could it be that this was not an accident after all, but the hint of something darker?

In the hospital, Evelyn had also been haunted by the name *Lucy*. The word had flared in her mind again, clear and insistent, until she felt half-mad. What did this Lucy have to do with Susan's death? Why would the name surface now, of all times? Was she losing her grip, or was there something real beneath the torment?

That evening, after they had eaten Veronica's perfectly spiced mince curry with peas from her garden and her characteristically flawless white rice, Evelyn spoke words that unsettled her friend. She wanted to use her clairvoyant gift to probe Susan's death—and to uncover the truth behind the name Lucy.

Veronica had once longed for Evelyn to embrace her abilities, but the time for that, she felt, had passed. To reach for them now, so soon after Susan's death, seemed reckless, even dangerous. Evelyn had always resisted her visions, because they came with fear and paranoia—images she could neither control nor forget. In her youth, her gift had been more a curse than a blessing, leading to conflicts, betrayals, and a trail of people who had turned against her. With each rejection, her trust in others withered, leaving her isolated, fragile, and wary.

Susan had lived with the consequences too, until the weight of her mother's erratic and unpredictable ways finally drove her to carve out her own path.

Veronica, Evelyn's steadfast childhood friend, had remained loyal through years and distance. She possessed a quiet intuition about Evelyn, tolerating more than most would have during those early years when Evelyn's behaviour could be cold and cutting. Veronica knew well that Evelyn was capable of aggression when she wished, yet since their reunion after so long apart, she had noticed something different in her friend. Beneath the sorrow and unpredictable mood swings, there now lingered an honesty, a rawness that felt genuine. What surprised Veronica most was discovering that Evelyn was seeing a therapist—a man who, against all odds, had earned her trust. For someone as guarded and knowledgeable about mental illness as Evelyn, that trust was no small thing. To Veronica, it was a hopeful sign.

Eventually, Veronica decided it might not be so bad for Evelyn to explore the clairvoyant path again. What harm could it do? In any case, Evelyn had always gone her own way, whether others approved or not.

To set the stage, Veronica transformed her lounge into a place conducive to connecting with the spirit world. She dragged the heavy coffee table aside and drew two corner lamps into the centre of the room, where she had arranged two oversized fabric cushions— beanbags she'd purchased the year before from a local shop. The African woman who sold them had displayed them among handmade treasures, and Veronica had been enchanted at once. Covered in animal prints and black-and-white stripes, the cushions now formed a loose circle, inviting and primal.

Veronica herself dressed for the occasion, adopting the grandeur of an Egyptian queen. She chose deep reds and purples, layering herself in gold-threaded scarves that shimmered like desert fire. Her dark complexion, accentuated by striking eye makeup, gave her a regal, ancient presence. Drapes of mauve, red and turquoise silk softened the lanterns' glow, steeping the room in shadowed warmth. Evelyn hesitated at first, her nerves evident, but Veronica's calm assurance soon steadied her.

It had been years since Evelyn had willingly called upon her abilities. She had shunned them, wanting nothing to do with their burden. But now she had no choice. To uncover the truth about her daughter's fate, she would have to reach for the very powers she had tried to bury. The idea that her daughter had simply lost control and driven off the mountain was unthinkable. What Evelyn had glimpsed in her mind's eye at the hospital suggested a far darker truth.

Unbeknownst to Evelyn and Veronica, while they prepared the scene, something dreadful was about to happen.

Chapter Eleven
Putting the Pieces Together

Far more advanced than we could ever imagine…

The next day, Adam couldn't shake the memory of his time at Tom's house. The people he'd met lingered in his mind—fascinating, yet troubling. He found himself playing devil's advocate, questioning whether Tom's methods were truly ethical. Was Tom nurturing their insights, or merely feeding their delusions? Was any of this real? Adam had always entertained such possibilities, but never had they been presented so starkly before. The experience unsettled him. His emotions swung wildly—thrill and wonder pulling one way, caution and doubt pulling the other. Part of him longed to share his discovery with the world, while another part wanted nothing more to do with Tom or his followers. And even if Tom's revelations were true, was this truly a path Adam wished to walk? Deep down, he already knew the answer.

Until now, Adam had kept Joey in the dark about his secret meetings, careful not to hurt him or spark his curiosity. He had filtered what he shared, worried that Joey's mind might latch onto Tom too eagerly. But that night, Adam made a choice: no more secrecy. If Tom refused to accept Joey, Adam would step away altogether. Joey wasn't just a roommate—he was a companion, a son in all but name—and Adam felt guilty for the lies and omissions. It was time to bring Joey in, no matter Tom's objections. If Adam was to join this strange group, he wanted someone he trusted at his side.

That evening, Adam told Joey everything. To his surprise, Joey burst out laughing. For weeks, Joey had suspected something was going on—Adam's secretive behaviour was too obvious to miss. He had assumed Adam was up to some silly mischief and had chosen not to pry. Now, hearing about Tom and the group, Joey wasn't shocked or suspicious. His trust in Adam was unshakable; he couldn't imagine Adam ever betraying him.

Soon after, the two made their way to Tom's house, the late afternoon light already beginning to fade into the muted golds and greys of early evening. Adam felt the familiar tightening in his chest as they crossed the threshold. He had made up his mind, and he would not waver: if Joey wasn't included, then he would not move forward. The thought had lodged itself firmly in his heart.

To Adam's relief, Tom did not meet his words with resistance. Quite the opposite—there was a glimmer of something almost approving in the older man's demeanour, a satisfaction he only half concealed.

"Adam," Tom said smoothly, his voice even, his eyes flicking briefly toward Joey before focusing once more on Adam, "if you are comfortable with Joey being present, then so am I. I only wanted to be sure you understood my hesitation. Youth, after all, can be unpredictable." He leaned back slightly, his tone slipping into one of practiced caution. "As the old saying goes—'loose lips sink ships.'"

The words hung in the air, heavy and sharp. Joey shifted in his chair, his posture betraying the unease he tried to hide. He lowered his face to the floor, uncertain if he ought to respond, uncertain even if a response would help or hinder.

Tom pressed on, his voice calm but deliberate, each word landing with the precision of a man accustomed to steering others where he wished them to go. "Young people often crave acceptance among their peers. It is natural. Even an intelligent young man like Joey, under the wrong circumstances, may just be tempted to share a secret or two—just enough to win admiration, to seem more interesting, more daring to his friends. But such slips, however small, can bring with them attention we cannot afford."

Adam's mood changed slightly at the implication, heat rising in his chest. He knew Joey—knew him better than anyone else possibly could. The idea that Joey would trade away trust for something as shallow as peer approval was absurd. If anything, it was always the other way around. Joey was the one people tried to impress, the one others gravitated toward despite his indifference. While classmates wasted themselves on posturing and gossip, Joey remained apart, unimpressed, often spending his weekends with Adam, where the world felt quieter and truer.

Tom's look lingered on Adam for a moment, perhaps gauging the strength of his loyalty. Then, slowly, his expression softened, the faintest smile curving his mouth as if he had reached some private conclusion. He shifted his attention toward Joey, studying him with an assessing eye, then offered what passed for a welcome.

"Well," he said at last, tone lighter now, "if Adam trusts you, then so shall I. Consider this an invitation, Joey. You are part of this now."

The air in the room shifted with those words, as though some unspoken line had been crossed. Adam felt the tension in his shoulders ease, though not entirely. He looked quickly at Joey, eager to catch his reaction, to see whether he accepted the weight of Tom's acknowledgment or resisted it in silence. But Joey was smiling.

"Tom," Adam said carefully, his voice steady but edged with curiosity, "perhaps you could show him what's downstairs?"

Joey came alive the moment they ducked through the silver door and stepped into the hidden room beneath the house. The air carried a faint medley of scents—crisp office paper, worn leather chairs, and a subtler note that likely rose from the Persian rug spread across the floor. He stood there in anticipation, fingers itching for discovery, while his eyes darted from corner to corner, hungry and searching, like a child set loose in a shop overflowing with wonders. What hidden truths might reveal themselves to him today? Joey pressed Tom with a hundred small questions about UFOs and classified technologies, words tumbling over one another until Tom only chuckled, as though he had been waiting for this exact eruption of curiosity.

Tom opened the drawer of a filing cabinet with a calmness that looked practiced. He pulled out a few thick folders that were held together with rubber bands. He gave them to Joey and then sat down at the table next to Adam, folding his hands as if this were a normal family rite instead of the transfer of hidden knowledge. The table had the marks of many nights on it: old ink stains, minor scratches at the edges of the table and a few sheets of paper with their corners peeled back. It looked like a battlefield that had been softened by habit.

Joey quickly open the folders like someone looking for a map to a lost city. Inside were a mess of hand-drawn diagrams and quick notes: disc-shaped crafts with simple lines, strange machinery with jagged edges, and notes that sound like the half-remembered lines of a dream. He recognised several of the designs right away—strange shapes he had seen in late-night forums and whispered documentaries—but one drawing caught his eye more than the others. It was shaped like a helix, with a pyramid outline around it. It looked different from the others; the lines were shaky, like a conundrum that someone had only half-solved.

While Joey became absorbed, Tom and Adam drifted back into one of their habitual debates about the moon. Their voices, at first polite, edged into the grooves of a dispute that had no clear end. Tom, as was his way, laughed softly at Adam's intensity. Adam wasn't sure whether he was growing obsessed with the subject or if Tom was deliberately making light of something significant.

When they looked up, Joey had already pulled a large sheet across the table. It was dense with ink: stick figures here, complicated circular schematics there, mathematical scrawl that hinted at ritual as much as engineering. He spread his hands as if offering the page like an altar. His excitement was contagious, a current that pulled Adam and Tom toward him.

"Did I ever mention," Tom said, his voice laced with mock gravity, "that the dust on the moon changes its structure?"

Adam pressed his lips together, refusing to let him win the moment. He watched Joey instead. There was something about the boy's concentration that made Adam think of a diver holding his breath before plunging—intent, stubborn, and vulnerable.

Joey pointed at a cramped cluster of diagrams. "This part here—half right," he said, tapping the page with a fingertip that left a faint smudge. "But here—" His finger stabbed at a loop of drawn lines—"this is wrong. Wrong conception. They've been looking at this part of the machine as a thing that moves. It doesn't move the way we think. Try not to think in physical or mechanical terms here…"

Tom leaned forward, the lines at the corners of his eyes sharpening. "Why are you saying that?" he asked, curiosity written all over his face.

Joey's grin was boyish but uncompromising. His thick brown hair stood up as if charged, and beneath it his green eyes glittered with the fierce certainty of someone who had spent too many nights piecing together fragments. "This whole area," he said, tapping the page again, "is labelled as the engine. But the engine is incorrect. The ship's energy isn't produced by parts the way a car runs on pistons. It's a relationship—between the craft and its occupants. It is a mutually beneficial relationship between them. Symbiotic."

His words spilled faster now. "Imagine microscopic forces—fields, currents—that we can't measure because our instruments have not reached that level yet. The craft draws on those currents, frequencies, and, crucially, on consciousness itself. The occupants don't pilot so much as align, attune. Their minds form the pattern; the craft amplifies it. Those little canisters or tubes? Not fuel in our sense. They're modulators—interfaces to maintain the bond. They have mastered dark matter and other forces, like gravity, while we humans are still fiddling around with combustion engines and heavy mechanical parts."

Adam felt the hairs rise along the back of his neck. He had never heard Joey talked this way before, so articulate and seemingly with so much conviction. It was like he has been thinking about this for a long time and finally given the space and opportunity to speak about this out loud.

"These beings," Joey continued, leaning closer as if confessing, "use electromagnetic phenomena not only to move their crafts but to alter matter. They influence structure—solid becomes flexible, time loosens. Their vessels are, in a manner of speaking, alive when linked with them. The pilots don't sit and steer like drivers. They are woven into the ship's consciousness. That's why the interior can feel… vast, like a place that folds on itself. The exteriors are just veils. Their spaceships and homes are not just things to ride in, get from one place to another, and live and sleep in, like we do—they are them; part of who they are. Not separate from them, but one with them."

He paused, searching for words that would not sound like prophecy. "From our three-dimensional perspective it's like watching a magician move the sun through the sky or make it fall toward the earth. Scaring those three-dimensional beings. But from another dimension, you can see the truth behind the illusion. Aliens operate across layers—past, present, and future. Their movements look like teleportation because they slip through seams, we are blind to. Dark energy, dark matter, unknown states of energy—whatever powers them is beyond our comprehension. Their 'technology' makes our quantum theories look naive, like children building with little blocks."

Tom rubbed his chin, the amused mask giving way to something curious and, for a sliver of a second, respect towards Joey. Adam felt the atmosphere shift. Suddenly, Tom wasn't chuckling anymore.

Joey then said something unexpected. To move forward and understand the bigger picture here, we must not only change our language but also acquire a new one—an all-encompassing language that incorporates not only verbal communication but also unconscious and quantum expressions to establish connections with both entities and the natural world, as well as the universe itself.

Tom reminded Adam and Joey that they had delved into these topics more than two years earlier. They had spoken at length about the visions—humans working alongside certain alien races while others clashed in bitter conflict. The images often included strange constructs: human-designed machines and alien-created biological robots carrying out unfathomable tasks. At the time, no one in the group had even used the word *biological robots*; instead, they described them with some vague, uncertain term. Tom also recalled how a few members had attempted to grapple with ideas like dark energy and quantum entanglement but ultimately abandoned the discussion, leaving it for another day.

What astonished Tom now was Joey's effortless recognition of the vessels and his confident reference to dark energy. Joey seemed to suggest that these elusive, perhaps undiscovered particles played a crucial role in UFO propulsion and flight—despite the scientific community knowing next to nothing about them.

"Some of their crafts carry an intelligence of their own," Joey continued, his tone calm but assured. "It's a fusion—energy, consciousness, biology, and the artificial working as one. And I'm only describing a single extraterrestrial race. Others, have different set ups but all employ variations of the same principle. Their ships can alter their very surface, changing form in ways we don't yet understand, bending gravity, exchanging data with invisible fields of energy. That's why they can shift dimensions in an instant. These crafts can generate black holes, white holes, even portals across space and time. They manipulate light itself, becoming invisible, and execute manoeuvres beyond imagination."

He paused briefly before continuing, "It's as though their vessels are half-rooted in another dimension—almost *hatched* there. They understand the universe's hidden framework: intelligent electric currents, conscious particles, and electromagnetic forces awaiting command. Humanity, by contrast, knows almost nothing. Our understanding of the cosmos is not just incomplete—it's wrong, fabricated. We observe existence from a limited physical perspective, never from the unconscious, non-material one. Until we grasp both consciousness and quantum science together, the universe will remain beyond us."

Tom sat back, stunned. He hadn't expected this level of insight from the young man. Collecting himself, he remarked that Joey might get along with another member of the group. Then, with a mischievous grin, Tom complicated matters: not all UFOs, he claimed, were extraterrestrial. Many were human-built test craft, some even crewed jointly by humans and artificial intelligences.

Joey rolled his eyes at Adam in mock exasperation, giggling quietly before responding with a sarcastic, "No, really?" Yet, beneath the humour, it was clear he already knew. He leaned toward Tom and asked pointedly, "The real question is—who exactly are these humans piloting alien craft, and why? What's their purpose in doing so?"

Tom hesitated, falling silent as he considered the question. Joey, unbothered, turned back to the documents spread before him. After a short while, Tom glanced at Adam and muttered with a sly smile, "your young friend is not as foolish as he looks." For Tom, it was as close to a compliment as he gave. "Tell me—what else does he know?"

Adam's eyes widened. "You would be amazed," he said earnestly. "He knows about ancient and modern underground bases, even those hidden beneath the ice and on the moon. And don't get him started on the underground civilization of benevolent aliens—protectors of Earth against threats both human and otherwise."

"Hmmm… I wonder," Tom said under his breath as he bent down and pulled another folder from the stack he had earlier handed to Joey. He leafed through it quickly, searching for something specific. When he found the page, his eyes brightened. He slid it across the table toward Joey.

"What do you make of this?" he asked, pointing to the stark drawing of a black circle.

Joey studied it, his brow furrowing. "Is this connected to UFOs?"

"Yes—or at least, we believe so," Tom replied, leaning forward with keen anticipation. If Joey recognized it, that would mark him as either a prodigy or a high-ranking Image Carrier—or perhaps both.

A flash of recognition crossed Joey's face. He hesitated, as though searching for the right words. "It feels… incomplete. Something's missing—like lines radiating outward." Snatching a blank sheet, he sketched a darkened circle and then drew thin rays extending from its edges. The image resembled a spider: a round body with spindly legs reaching outward.

"This," Joey explained, tapping the sketch, "is tied to their craft. It could be a power source—or perhaps something deeper, a symbol of who they are, of their shared values. All of them bound to it, all of them drawing from the same current, like they are all attached to the web, created by what looks like this spider thing. Whatever it is, it carries meaning to them."

Tom sat back, impressed. He had heard similar notions from the younger members of his circle, but never with such clarity. He recalled earlier discussions of photons and subatomic particles connected to alien propulsion. Their power sources seemed to stand in direct opposition to humanity's—and with a simplicity so elegant it made human technology appear crude. Theirs was a mastery not only of matter, but of the unconscious energies and invisible cosmic forces that shaped it.

Awed by Joey's insight, Tom decided to test him further—with one of humanity's most enduring questions. He waited until Joey looked up from the scattered pages. "Joey," he said deliberately, "what do you know of death? What happens when we die?"

Joey laughed lightly, as though Tom had made a joke. But the silence around the table told him no one was laughing. Adam rolled his eyes, silently signalling that Joey needn't answer—no one truly knew. But Joey, true to form, leaned in with conviction.

"I know the soul is not bound to the body," he said firmly. "I've left mine in dreams. Astral travelled. I've flown over the world, free of body. So, when death comes, I don't believe the soul returns—it moves on, to somewhere elsewhere."

Tom didn't reply. He simply stared at Joey, long and searching. Joey smiled back, satisfied with his response, then glanced at Adam with a quick grin before burying himself once more in the folders.

Time passed. Adam grew restless—he had work waiting. Tom too looked weary. After a short while, the three of them left the room, though Joey lingered, reluctant to go.

On their way out, Adam asked if Joey might join the next gathering. Tom hesitated before explaining that he also hosted a smaller circle of Image Carriers who disliked outsiders. Their meeting was scheduled for the following week, and he was certain they wouldn't welcome anyone new. The larger, more social group, however, might be open to it. They weren't meeting for another five weeks, but Tom promised to raise the idea with them and let Adam know.

Adam and Joey drove home mostly in silence. Once home, Joey rushed straight for his laptop, still buzzing with excitement, while Adam settled to his work. Later, Joey admitted he couldn't quite read Tom—his health seemed fragile, his motives uncertain. Adam quietly agreed.

Days later, Adam received a call from Tom. The smaller group had declined; they weren't ready for newcomers. But Joey would be welcome at the larger gathering. Adam marked the date in his diary and told Joey to keep the evening free.

When the night finally arrived, Adam returned home to find Joey dressed smartly, hair slicked with gel, practically glowing with anticipation. He wanted not just to meet the group, but to measure himself against them—were they truly better Image Carriers? Or would he outrank them?

They drove together to an imposing estate. Joey whistled at the sight of it. It was lit up like a Christmas tree. "Where do people get money for places like this?" he said as they parked.

The front gates stood open. They walked up the long driveway, where spotlights lit towering trees from below, casting dramatic shadows. Cars of every kind were scattered near the grand double doors of the two-story house, its windows glowing warmly in the night.

"Hi, Adam."

The voice drifted from the shadows of the porch. Julie sat there, a cigarette glowing faintly between her fingers. She exhaled and gave a nervous giggle, coughing as smoke curled around her. "Back with us tonight? Can't get enough, hey?" She shifted slightly in her chair, angling herself so the smoke wouldn't reach anyone.

Adam froze, his mind blanking on her name. Awkwardly, he caught Joey by the arm and drew him forward. "This is Joey," he said with a big smile, hoping to mask his lapse in memory.

A moment later, another figure stepped onto the porch, flicking a lighter before taking a sharp drag. Darrin. He offered the men a quick nod before retreating to sit near Julie. He was dressed like he'd just come from the beach—loose, casual surfer wear clinging to him comfortably. Around his neck hung a necklace of beads, and a matching bracelet circled his wrist. Adam was caught off guard; he hadn't imagined Darrin as the surfer type, yet the look suited him perfectly.

Adam and Joey slipped inside, greeted by the low murmur of voices in the living room. The housekeeper moved toward them with drinks, her appearance unexpectedly refined. She could have passed for a polished executive—her hair perfectly arranged, her attire sharp. Even the light caught her in a way that made her seem more corporate than domestic.

Tom appeared soon after, chuckling as always, his energy filling the room. "Boys, boys!" he called, striding toward them with open arms. "My two new favourite people." He clasped his hands together warmly before offering his handshake. Afterward, he gestured to the housekeeper, instructing her to gather the rest of the group inside and bolt the front door.

Once everyone had settled, Tom launched into tales of his trip up north. A few members nodded knowingly, having gone with him. Joey leaned toward Adam, whispering, "Why aren't we meeting downstairs?"

Adam smirked slightly, whispering back. "This is how it goes. First the lounge, a few snacks, then downstairs. Tom doesn't allow food down there. Same thing happened at my first meeting."

Tom went on, explaining that Grant had once been one of the Image Carriers but left the group last year to move north with his longtime friend and business partner, Bob. The two men had known each other for years, bonded by their love of the land and a shared dream of creating a sustainable lifestyle. Together, they purchased a sprawling property—more than two hundred acres—with a century-old sandstone homestead boasting five bedrooms. The house had been updated over the years, and the pair quickly realised it would make an ideal country retreat.

They transformed the estate into a bed and breakfast, adding four self-contained studio cabins that blended seamlessly with the natural surroundings. Carefully spaced for privacy, the cottages soon became a favourite among holidaymakers and tourists. Demand grew quickly, and within months, bookings filled out weeks—sometimes months—in advance.

The property itself was a drawcard: old-growth rainforest, now gaining international attention, invited visitors to explore bush tracks, photograph towering native trees, and breathe in the crisp mountain air. Guests wandered beside the river, listening to birdsong and believing the dewy freshness might restore both body and spirit.

Visitors arriving at the retreat were often greeted by free-ranging hens pecking happily in the yard before retreating at dusk to a spacious coop nestled between two avocado trees. A well-fenced garden kept them from raiding the vegetables. Breakfasts at Grant and Bob's quickly became legendary—plates piled with organic eggs from plump hens, bacon fried in its own fat, and thick slices of tomatoes, sweet and sun-ripened. Even simple cereals became indulgent when drowned in full cream milk and topped with stone fruit and local honey from a hive tucked beneath a mango tree. But nothing silenced the dining room quite like the scent of fresh bread as it emerged golden from the oven, leaving guests wide-eyed and wordless.

Tom also shared news of Mary and said how pleased he was to see her again. She had been one of his earliest Image Carriers, helping him organise classes years ago before moving north to escape Sydney's winters. Some in the group didn't know her, and Julie, who had mourned Grant's departure, looked puzzled at the name.

"She was one of the first to help me," Tom explained, pausing to gather his thoughts. "That was a long time ago."

Mary and her husband had since retired to Murwillumbah, near the Queensland border. There she reconnected with Tom and, through him, met Grant. Over the past few months, Mary and Grant had grown close, and she and her husband became friends with both men. Grant encouraged Mary to lend a hand at the retreat, where she began offering spiritual readings. Guests assumed she was a local psychic, never suspecting that she and Grant were in fact Image Carriers. For Mary, the part-time work was rewarding—it kept her busy, let her use her gifts, and gave her a sense of purpose in a natural, welcoming environment.

Word spread quickly about the retreat's unique charm. Visitors could buy fresh fruit—mangoes, peaches, plums, avocados, bananas, and rarer tropical varieties—straight from the orchard, and hike through lush rainforest threaded with sparkling waterways. Some tourists were so enchanted they tried to camp illegally on the property, unwilling to leave its beauty behind.

Bob, once a five-star international chef, now devoted himself to crafting exquisite meals with local produce, drawing diners from hours away. Many holidaymakers to the Gold Coast made the detour south just to experience the retreat's famed breakfasts and long lunches.

Grant often had to remind Mary to keep her readings short, as she had a habit of giving guests lengthy, detailed sessions for little return. Despite his concerns, her popularity grew, and locals began seeking her out regularly.

One day, during a tour visit, Mary sat with a middle-aged Japanese woman on cushions laid out beneath the trees. Without prompting, Mary told her that her daughter and husband were with her on this holiday and that they would not miss it. The woman collapsed, curling into herself as she wept uncontrollably. No one on the tour knew her story. Only three months earlier, her husband and daughter had been killed in a car accident in Japan. The family had planned the Australian trip as the journey of a lifetime—more than a year ago, visiting the Gold Coast, the Barrier Reef, the rainforests, and the outback. Instead, she had travelled with her sister and niece, carrying the grief of her husband and daughter's absence. Mary's words had pierced straight through to the truth she carried in silence.

Tom shared with the group that he had recently visited Grant and how much he enjoyed the reunion. The fresh air, delicious food, and warm company left him feeling revitalised, and he admitted that the generous breakfasts and peaceful bushwalks had made it difficult to leave.

Meanwhile, Joey leaned over and tapped Adam's arm, whispering that several people seemed to be watching him closely. He also wondered aloud why no one had introduced him. At that moment, Amanda spoke up, recounting her trip up north and how good it was to see Grant and Bob again. She also mentioned the pleasure of meeting visitors from overseas who were exploring Australia. John echoed her thoughts, adding that the fishing had been excellent. Their rainforest property, he explained, was not far from the Pacific Ocean, and he had lived on fresh fish for two weeks straight. He even joked that he still had some in his freezer if anyone wanted to buy any. Jason also shared that he had driven north but stayed only a few days before heading south to see his parents near Byron Bay.

Adam noticed that the gathering felt smaller than usual and realised that Anne, the younger member, was absent. Tom then gave apologies for several who hadn't attended, explaining that many Image Carriers were irregular in their attendance. Some simply lacked the time or commitment of the older members, but they often phoned Tom to share urgent dreams or visited him privately for guidance. Tom was always willing to listen and support them.

At this point, Tom formally introduced Joey to the group, announcing that he, too, was an Image Carrier. He spoke warmly of Joey's talents and potential, declaring that he was destined for success. All eyes turned to Joey, and the room filled with welcoming chatter and kind expressions. Joey, soaking in the positive energy, broke into a wide grin.

After a short break, the group moved downstairs to discuss recent developments. Their focus turned to disturbing visions that pointed to millions of people dying—a theme that had grown more pronounced over the past year, not only among local Image Carriers but also through Tom's contacts in Europe and the Americas. Like Amanda and Jennifer, many others across the world had been experiencing dreams of impending disaster and chaos on a scale never before imagined.

Around the table, some pulled out notepads while others opened files they had brought along. Tom relayed reports from overseas Overseers, who confirmed that Image Carriers in Europe, South America, and elsewhere were all seeing the same catastrophic event. These visions consistently pointed to the deaths of millions and to widespread upheaval. Interestingly, the most sensitive receivers abroad included children, devout elderly women, single women, and homosexual men—people who seemed especially attuned to the spiritual realm. They repeatedly described a symbol: a white flower, central to the looming tragedy. The consensus was that this event would be human made, not natural, and that it was imminent.

Joey tugged Adam's arm again and whispered about whether UFOs were natural or created by entities, earning a disapproving glance from Adam. Amused, Joey leaned back, smiling, while the others listened intently to Tom. Jennifer took notes as Tom asked if anyone had received visions or messages about the coming mass death. He stressed the urgency of the matter, declaring that all other projects would be put aside until they could better understand these warnings. Their overseas counterparts were equally perplexed, yet all agreed that a powerful global figure would soon rise—someone who would not be what they appeared to be.

Tom asked Amanda and Jennifer to hold back for the moment, hoping others might contribute. But the rest of the group remained silent, unable to add anything new. Finally, Jennifer spoke, revealing that her visions showed widespread death and destruction first in major cities, then in developing nations. She saw officials overwhelmed by the rising body count, and heavy machinery digging mass graves in the sand.

Amanda's voice broke in, urgent, her curls catching the light as she shook her head. Bulldozers, she said, were everywhere in her dreams, clearing ground for mass graves. Industrial blue and black plastic stretched across streets, covering heaps of bodies. Soldiers stood watch in corners of broken cities. Survivors huddled near, hollow-eyed, unable to weep anymore. Some simply sat beside their dead, waiting for their own turn.

The room had gone utterly still. Amanda and Jennifer exchanged a look—each knowing the other's burden. The visions were not fading. They were coming more often, pressing harder, pulling them closer to a future too monstrous to ignore.

Tom's revelations struck too close to what Adam had already heard, sending a chill through him. According to Tom, his overseas contacts had confirmed the same unsettling messages. The enigmatic white flower surfaced once again, though it brought no new answers. Hoping to spark recognition—or perhaps trigger forgotten memories—Tom laid out a careful summary of his findings for the group.

He explained that when the catastrophe unfolded, it would come at night, or at a time when no one expected it. People seemed to die without warning, quietly, without resistance. There were no visions of chaos, no running or screaming—just an eerie acceptance. Amanda and Jennifer agreed, noting how the images suggested victims went to their deaths silently, almost willingly. The contradiction was baffling, yet the visions were disturbingly consistent.

Tom went on: the events appeared to occur simultaneously across continents, with certain countries suffering greater impact. The aftermath was stranger still. Entire regions looked untouched—no bombs, no wreckage, no earthquakes—yet cities and roads lay strangely empty, as if abandoned. Survivors wandered in shock, hollow-eyed, grief-stricken, drifting like the walking dead.

Amanda added grimly that even many of those survivors eventually perished. Tom checked his notes, nodded in agreement, and Jennifer confirmed with a solemn tilt of her head. Adam, however, could not help but doubt. It felt like they were all narrating the same grim story, like knowing the ending of a film no one else had seen. Were they truly tuning into some hidden source—or was it just coincidence?

Jennifer broke the silence. "I feel this is planned," she said, her expression tightening. "There are forces behind this—sinister ones. Some people seem to welcome it. They're… rejoicing." Her frown deepened.

Tom glanced at Amanda, searching for confirmation, but she shook her head. Then Joey startled everyone by speaking up. "She's right," he said, pointing at Jennifer. "When she spoke, I got a flash. Some people want this to happen. It's planned."

Tom leaned forward. "Want what to happen?"

Joey hesitated, suddenly uneasy. "The catastrophe you were just describing."

Tom pressed him for more, but Joey had nothing further. Adam, however, knew Joey well. He had seen it before—Joey blurting out odd comments that later proved true. It was one of his peculiar gifts, and Adam trusted it. He stepped in. "This is how Joey works. If he says someone wants this to happen, I believe him." His tone came out sharper than intended, defensive, even anxious—rare for him.

The others broke into restless chatter, moving the spotlight away from Joey. Tom, looking weary and older than before, eventually quieted them. He repeated his summary: no bombs, no destruction, only bodies. Survivors stunned, depressed, then dying in turn. But how? Poison? Virus? Chemical warfare? Some hidden weapon?

As Tom wound down, Joey leaned toward Adam, whispering. He wanted to know when UFOs would be discussed. Adam raised a curious eyebrow but kept his attention on Tom—until Tom called Joey's name directly.

"Have you got anything more to add?"

Joey shifted awkwardly. "I just… sense something is coming. I don't know what." He forced a smile, hoping to pass the question elsewhere.

Meanwhile, John tried to steer the discussion toward his own concerns, speaking of shadowy groups manipulating votes, entertainment, even global institutions. He insisted these unseen powers had infiltrated religion, education, corporations, politics—everything—corrupting from within. The group barely reacted, accustomed to John's tirades. But when he noticed Adam listening, John edged closer to him and Joey.

Before he could go on, Julie reminded everyone it was late. The meeting broke up, members heading upstairs, drifting into the main house, some saying their goodbyes, others settling in the lounge for more talk. Joey found himself in conversation with Simon, who shared his fascination with UFOs, instantly catching his attention.

Adam stood alone for a moment until John seized the chance to continue where he had left off. Bitterly, he complained about being ignored, convinced Tom gave too much attention to Amanda and Jennifer's visions. Adam realised then why Tom avoided certain subjects like the moon—he had to filter and prioritise the overwhelming flood of information. Being an Overseer was no simple task.

Still, Adam noticed something troubling: the drawing of the mysterious flower, once displayed, was gone. Perhaps Tom had put it away, overwhelmed by the sheer volume of images and messages demanding his attention.

John, however, had no intention of stopping. He raged on about corrupt governments and corporations plotting a one-world order. "Everything's a setup, mate," he spat, his forehead flushed and sweaty. "They treat us like mushrooms—keep us in the dark and feed us bullshit!"

Adam glanced around the room, desperate for an escape. He didn't doubt that John was right in parts, but he wasn't in the mood for politics—not now, not tonight. He was ready to leave Tom's place.

John looked to be somewhere in his sixties, though the years had not been kind. His ruddy, swollen face flushed a deeper red as he worked himself into a fury, the skin around his cheeks and neck almost bluish with strain. Wisps of thinning grey hair stood on end as he railed against the world, cursing governments and big business for stripping away civil rights, fair living standards, and even healthy food.

"Healthy food?" Adam asked before he could stop himself.

"Yes, healthy food!" John snapped, rubbing the curve of his distended stomach. "They taking rights away from our farmers, and soon even backyard gardeners won't be able to grow a thing. They making it impossible for intelligent people to survive. And do you know why? Because we can see through their plans! They hate people with common sense." His eyes bulged as he sucked in another breath.

"That's why they're flooding our culture with people nothing like us—people trained to obey, to accept injustice without a fight, because that's all they know. And don't even get me started on the imported rubbish they dare to call food. It's poison, mate. Slow poison."

The room fell silent. Then John leaned closer, voice low and grim. "They want most of us gone. Dead. They don't care about our culture, or us. And do you know what's worse? The idiots vote for them. They vote for these charlatans who crawl straight into bed with the globalists, all to destroy our sovereignty and our rights."

Adam nodded, sensing John's passion for his country—and his despair at watching it unravel before his eyes. He belonged to an older generation, one that remembered when life had seemed simpler, clearer, when people worked together toward common goals. Now the world felt fractured, self-serving, and full of betrayal. John could not accept that elected leaders had sold out so quickly, allowing the country to crumble.

"You see, Adam," John went on, though his voice was calmer now, "fools are swayed by smooth-talking politicians or some celebrity puppet. Just because they look good or sound clever doesn't mean they have honour. It means they're pushing an agenda, the mouthpieces of darker forces. But try explaining that to the voting sheep." His chest tightened, and he struck it with a closed fist, grimacing as though from heartburn.

At that moment Tom reappeared, slipping back into the lounge after a ten-minute absence. Adam wondered where he'd been, until Tom explained he'd been seeing off the last guests outside. He added that Julie was interested in Adam's De-Stress room; apparently, she had one of her own and wanted to exchange ideas.

Soon after, Adam and Joey were the last to leave. Tom thanked them warmly, and they too were glad they'd come. Still, Adam kept a wary eye on John. He'd worried earlier that the man might be on the verge of a heart attack, though John himself seemed unconcerned. Later, Tom reassured Adam that John often suffered from heartburn—brought on by his habit of eating too fast and too much. Adam recalled seeing him trail hungrily after the food trays earlier in the evening.

Yet Adam couldn't shake the thought: if John was already so agitated over his beliefs, how would he react to the storm still to come? And if Adam was truly meant to protect Joey, then he would need every layer of security possible to shield him from the danger drawing closer.

Meanwhile, Amanda and Jennifer—and the other Image Carriers across the globe—were closing in on the truth. The puzzle was almost complete. What they didn't yet realise was that their visions and prophecies were already unfolding, step by step, in the world around them.

Chapter Twelve
Trying to Make Contact

Outside, the night was motionless, suffocatingly quiet…

The air around Veronica's house was still that evening, the night unnervingly calm. As she reached for her beloved Tarot deck, she caught her reflection in the mirror along the back wall of her cabinet. Draped in the costume of an Egyptian queen, she hoped her new appearance would help her pierce the veil and summon messages from the other side.

Twice since Susan's death she had sought answers through the cards and received nothing. But tonight felt different. She sensed it in her chest, in her skin. Something was stirring. Perhaps Evelyn's presence had set the right conditions, drawing unseen currents toward them. Either way, Veronica was certain something would come.

At nine o'clock sharp, Evelyn asked her to open the lounge windows to let the air circulate. The women settled in. Evelyn reclined into one of the deep, handmade bean bags, eyes already drifting closed, while Veronica shuffled her cards. She made herself comfortable directly opposite Evelyn. Those cards had passed through generations—grandmother to mother to daughter—safeguarded like treasure. They were believed to hold ancestral energy, each symbol on their faces carrying secrets only the spiritually attuned could decipher. To Veronica, every card was a key, capable of unlocking doors to the higher self and the spirit realm. Though the pictures were fixed, the interpretation was always personal, always shifting.

"Veronica," Evelyn said without opening her eyes, "if I fall asleep or slip too deep, wake me. Five minutes, then wake me."

Veronica nodded and glanced at the hall clock—five minutes past nine. She turned her first card with Susan's name in her mind. What became of her? Before she could draw another, a ragged noise drew her attention. Evelyn's body sagged strangely into the bean bag, her breathing heavy, her face tense. Veronica wondered if she was already crossing into that space where messages could be reached.

Evelyn's hands pressed hard against her sides in what looked more like panic than repose. Veronica checked the clock again. 9:07. She told herself she would wait until 9:12 to wake her.

A low murmur broke the silence. The air thickened. Veronica felt her own breath catch, as though the room itself were holding its lungs. Outside, the night was motionless, suffocatingly quiet. Evelyn groaned, babbling like an infant, her voice soft and quiet. Veronica looked to the clock—still 9:07.

Veronica then focused on her cards, her hands moving with slow deliberation as she laid the cards in a line upon the floor between herself and Evelyn. The first to appear was the Ten of Swords—its stark image cutting through her composure. Another sword followed. Then another. A pattern forming: endings, upheaval, ruin. Her breath caught when she turned over the next—The Tower. Stone crumbling, fire consuming, figures cast into chaos. The omen was undeniable.

A chill crept over her, not because of what the cards foretold in general, but because they had become relentless in their message. Each time she asked about Susan—each time she tried to pierce the mystery of what had happened—these same harbingers rose from the deck, as if mocking her, as if whispering the same grim truth, she dared not speak aloud.

Evelyn stirred, shifting slightly in the beanbag, her body looking oddly awkward, as she sat outstretched on a large cushion covered in animal print. She looked deep in thought or half asleep, and Veronica wondered if she was receiving any messages from the beyond.

Veronica then looked toward the clock again. 9:07. She frowned. That couldn't be right. She had been certain more time had slipped away. It felt like whole minutes—long, dragging ones—had passed. But the hands had barely moved. She needed to wake Evelyn at exactly 9:12, yet the numbers on the clock clung stubbornly to their place, as though time itself had stalled.

Impossible. Had the clock truly stopped at 9:07, or was time itself playing tricks on her?

Her thoughts were quickly interrupted as Evelyn sat bolt upright, eyes shut tight, voice loud and clear: "Wake me. Wake me up now!"

Veronica lunged forward, accidentally scattering her Tarot across the floor, seizing Evelyn's hands. "It's all right. Wake up, Evelyn! Open your eyes."

Panting, she darted another look at the clock. 9:07. The hands hadn't moved. That clock had never failed before.

Evelyn's eyelids fluttered. Her skin was pale, her body slack. Veronica held her tightly, heart hammering.

"I didn't see Susan," Evelyn said softly, weak as a child. "But I saw the car. And that girl—Sabrena."

"What happened?" Veronica asked, though fear tightened her throat. Evelyn looked drained, lifeless, as if she might drop dead at any moment. Veronica forced herself to stop questioning. "Rest. Breathe. We'll talk later."

She glanced back at the clock, already planning to have it repaired. But her stomach lurched—the hands now read 9:50 pm.

Then without warning, Evelyn jumped up and hurried to her bedroom. Startled, Veronica remained where she was, fumbling for her scattered cards. To cast them so carelessly was an insult to the ancestors who had passed them down. As she gathered them, she looked again at the clock. It was working normally again, but that missing time gnawed at her. She knew what she'd seen: time itself had seemed to have stopped.

When Evelyn returned with writing paper in hand, eager to capture what she had witnessed in her trance, she found Veronica kneeling on the floor, whispering to herself as she retrieved the cards. Evelyn assumed the mutters were apologies to her grandmother. Seeing her friend's troubled state, Evelyn quietly withdrew, slipping back to her room and leaving Veronica alone with her worries—and her precious, ancestral deck of cards.

When Evelyn stirred awake, she realised she had dozed off. The house was still cloaked in darkness; every door and window locked against the night. It was close to five in the morning—the time Veronica usually rose. On most days, her radio would already be crackling with her favourite early program. But that morning, silence hung heavy in the air.

Evelyn soon noticed a shift in Veronica's demeanour. Once lively and talkative, she now seemed withdrawn, often drifting into her own thoughts mid-conversation. Evelyn told herself it was nothing more than fatigue, perhaps even weariness from her company, and decided to tread lightly around her friend.

Days passed, yet Veronica's mood did not improve. Evelyn grew increasingly frustrated with her quiet gloom but held her tongue. She wanted one more visit to the hospital, a final chance to meet with Sabrena and perhaps glimpse another vision, though Veronica seemed disinclined to take her there again. Evelyn also longed to speak once more with Sabrena's father, hoping he might shed light on Lucy. But Veronica avoided such matters altogether, retreating further into solitude.

Privately, Veronica was wrestling with feelings she hadn't faced in years—loss, regret, and an unsettling lack of control. Dressing as her ancestors once had, a vision of an Egyptian queen reborn, and humouring Evelyn's fixation on Susan's death— something in that night had unsettled her. It had altered her in ways she could not yet name, and she wasn't certain she liked the direction it was leading her.

One afternoon, while Evelyn sat on the veranda, she decided to walk to the shop. She hadn't mentioned her plan to Veronica, knowing her friend would object to her speaking with Sabrena's father. Stepping inside, she found Veronica lying in bed—a strange sight in the middle of the day. Evelyn paused, troubled, but said nothing.

At the shop, her hopes crumbled. Sabrena's father claimed he knew nothing of any Lucy. Sabrena spoke only of Susan and Veronica, he said. Still, he was warmer this time, chatty even, and Evelyn left with the impression of a different man than the one she'd first encountered.

Outside, the familiar dogs lazed in search of shade, unbothered by her presence. Above, the same black birds perched in the trees, watching. Evelyn tilted her head back, half amused, half curious. What did they see? What did they know? Her imagination carried her away—sitting among them, listening to their secrets. In her mind, one bird chirped of a stranger who had visited the shop, a man in a fine car asking after Susan. Another chimed in, warning the other bird not to say too much. Evelyn giggled to herself, wondering if she was finally losing her mind, until the sight of Veronica's front gate drew her back.

Why had she conjured such a tale? Was it merely a daydream, or some kind of message? She often received impressions like that, though this one felt different—heavier. Yet she kept it to herself, not wishing to burden Veronica further. Perhaps she had overstayed her welcome.

Later, when she tentatively mentioned the idea of moving on, Veronica surprised her by urging her to stay longer. Evelyn questioned, asking if her constant talk of Susan and Lucy was too much, but Veronica offered no clear answer.

That afternoon, the two women went about their routines in silence—Veronica cleaning, Evelyn drifting between bedrooms before settling outside. Eventually, Veronica joined her, notebook in hand.

"I've been going over these notes for months," she confessed, eyes cast down. "But I'm beginning to think it is all a waste of time. Maybe you're right. Maybe it is time I let it go." She tapped the worn notebook on her lap with a weary sigh.

Evelyn ignored her despair and asked if the notes mentioned Lucy. Veronica shook her head.

That night, Evelyn lay awake, torn. Was Veronica too polite to say it, perhaps wanting her space back—her house, her quiet independence. After much thought, Evelyn decided to talk to her in the morning.

When she did, Veronica was totally surprised. "London? You mean London, England?"

"Yes," Evelyn replied, settling back in her chair with a sly satisfaction. "I think we should go. Leave all this behind, at least for a while."

But when the day of departure came, only Evelyn's bags were packed. Veronica drove her to the airport under a flawless sky. They rode in silence, Evelyn looking out the window at the resting mountains, wondering if she was making the right choice after so many years away. London loomed uncertain, yet it pulled at her all the same.

At the terminal, they said their goodbyes. Veronica carried the luggage, then watched Evelyn disappear into the crowd. The drive home would be long and lonely. She wasn't ready to leave—not yet. But perhaps, one day, she would follow.

Chapter Thirteen
The Plot Thickens

The fourth floor was lined with suites behind smoked-glass doors, names printed neatly beside each...

Evelyn arrived at Heathrow after a long, draining flight. As she followed the crowd toward baggage claim, she was struck by the sheer amount of people. Her nerves sharpened when she noticed a man she'd glimpsed as she stepped off the plane—was he following her? The thought made her pulse quicken. To test it, she veered deliberately away from the carousel, pretending she had another destination. The man drifted off in a different direction, and Evelyn exhaled, convincing herself it had been nothing more than coincidence.

The taxi brought her to the Royal Doze Hotel, a sprawling, historic building that dominated an entire block. Though its grandeur suggested extravagance, her booking agent had assured her it was reasonably priced, newly refurbished, and recently renamed. Long ago, it had been a fashionable bar and nightclub, later transformed into a department store, and now it served as comfortable accommodation for tourists and other visitors.

A young, well-dressed Asian man showed her upstairs to Room 304. The space was small but dressed with elegance—a mix of modern and antique furniture that didn't quite belong together. The air carried a heavy blend of dust, bleach, and cleaning agents. Evelyn crossed to the window and was surprised to find it opened slightly, letting in a breath of fresh air. In the corner stood a compact bar fridge with a kettle perched on top, stocked with tea, coffee, and sugar. Despite the room's modest size, a large king bed dominated the space, accompanied by an oddly shaped table and an antique chair near the window. Everything seemed slightly mismatched, as if arranged for a couple who had never arrived.

The following morning, she woke to the harsh whirr of what sounded like an industrial polisher outside her door. Perhaps a cleaner, buffing the gleaming hall floors to their usual shine? She lingered on the edge of sleep, the urge to surrender to it almost overwhelming. But there was no time for that—not when she still had to unravel what Susan had been doing in London, and perhaps even track down Lucy. Susan's itinerary mentioned a boarding house not far from the Royal Doze, and that would be Evelyn's first stop.

Outside, she hailed a taxi and gave the driver the address. He nodded knowingly, remarking that he'd dropped plenty of young people there before. The area was well-known for cheap student lodgings and a backpacker crowd.

Inside the boarding house, Evelyn was met not by a manager or reception desk, but by a handful of young residents sprawled in front of a television. Most were new arrivals and couldn't recall a Susan—or a Lucy, for that matter. Disappointed, Evelyn returned to the cab and asked the driver to take her to a gym listed on Susan's notes.

The gymnasium was a vast, multilevel building, humming with energy from dawn until late at night. Music pulsed through the bright reception area, where a cheerful redheaded receptionist looked up from her work and greeted Evelyn with a broad smile.

"May I help you?"

"Yes," Evelyn said carefully, improvising as she went. "I'm looking for my daughter Susan's friend, Lucy. You remember Susan, don't you? She used to work here."

The receptionist frowned, searching her memory. "How long ago?"

"Just a couple of months."

"I don't recall anyone by that name," she admitted. "But maybe Andre will know."

She dialled a number, and soon a tall man with an olive complexion and a sportsman's build appeared, dressed in fitted gym gear. His easy smile revealed flawless white teeth.

"Do you know Susan?" Evelyn asked.

He nodded at once. "Yes. You're from Australia too, aren't you? I can hear the accent. Are you her mother, or…?" His eyes sharpened with curiosity, though his voice gentled as he went on. "What's Australia like these days? Susan always spoke of it so fondly. You'll have to pass me her details—I'm planning a trip there soon, and I'd love to catch up with her."

Evelyn kept her composure, choosing not to reveal the truth about Susan's death.

Andre explained that Susan had worked only part-time at the gym, usually on call, which was why the receptionist hadn't remembered her. With his description, the receptionist finally recalled Susan's face. Neither, however, had heard of Lucy. Before Evelyn left, Andre added that Susan had also worked in a cake shop nearby and gave her the address.

Buoyed by the new lead, Evelyn returned to the Royal Doze. As she paid her driver, she noticed a man loitering across the street, watching her. Her stomach dropped—it was the same man she thought had followed her from the airport. Yet, just as quickly, he turned and walked away. Evelyn, unsettled, rushed inside.

She hurried to the elevator, where a woman with an exotic accent held the doors for her. They rode up together, and Evelyn watched the stranger exit onto her floor before continuing down the corridor. Safe inside her own room at last, she sank into the worn leather chair, staring at the closed door as though expecting it to burst open. When nothing happened, she forced herself to breathe. Perhaps it wasn't the same man. Maybe it was just her paranoid imagination.

London was full of people, after all, and from a distance they all blurred into the same indistinct types.

Still, she decided to leave the cake shop visit for tomorrow—her head throbbed from the day's tension.

The following morning, Evelyn asked at reception whether the cake shop was within walking distance. The man behind the counter shook his head. Best to take a London Cab, he advised—the shop was a fair way off, and the forecast promised rain. Evelyn, remembering how chilled she'd been the day before, agreed.

After gathering her bag, umbrella, and jacket, Evelyn made her way downstairs to hail a cab. Outside, she spotted a familiar face—the woman she had run into in the elevator the day before. The stranger was already waiting at the curb. Evelyn stood nearby, keeping quiet.

The woman turned with a big smile. "Bom Dia!" she exclaimed loudly, then switched to English with theatrical cheer. "Glorious morning!"

She looked every bit the image of wealth and confidence, draped in a fur coat, gold jewellery catching the light, her long fingernails lacquered a deep, glossy red.

"Morning," Evelyn replied politely, though her tone made clear she wasn't eager for conversation.

The woman, however, was undeterred. "Beautiful place, this London. Are you on holiday?" she asked, her accent thick and musical.

"Yes," Evelyn answered, curt but not unkind.

If the abruptness registered, the woman didn't show it. She pressed on as though they were already acquainted. Lighting a cigarette, she leaned in with a grin. "I am one of the lucky ones. My employer paid for my trip. But next week, I must return to boring Brazil." She let out a throaty laugh, drawing deep on her cigarette before flicking it to the pavement. The heel of her stiletto ground it into the concrete with a deliberate twist, as though she enjoyed the little ritual of snuffing it out. She then called out, "Goodbye, darling!" and climbed into a sleek car that had just pulled up.

Evelyn watched her go, bemused. Odd woman, she thought—though no doubt the woman thought the same of her. London's damp and changeable weather wasn't being kind to her either; her hair seemed to have a will of its own, and her body alternated between hot, cold, and uncomfortable. Sharp little pains came and went, leaving her wondering if she had eaten something disagreeable or simply slept wrong. Whatever the cause, she refused to let it distract her. She had come to London for a reason, and she was finally making progress.

She had barely settled into the cab before the driver pulled up again. "Here you are," he said.

"That was quick," Evelyn remarked, handing over the fare.

The air was thick with the scent of sugar and spice as she stepped into Gertrude's Cake Shop. Glass cases displayed neat rows of little cakes, each one a work of art. A blonde woman in her early thirties, with the look of someone Scandinavian, approached with a polite smile. Evelyn asked after the owner.

The assistant disappeared into the back and returned with a stout, balding man in his fifties. His reddish-brown hair hung past his collar in unruly wisps, giving him a perpetually windblown look. Behind modern glasses, his grey eyes studied her warily.

"I'm looking for the owner," Evelyn said, making her voice bright.

"That's me," the man replied quickly. "Jacob. The shop was my mother's before she passed. Gertrude was her name."

Before Evelyn could respond, the shop door burst open, making them both jump. Relief washed over both of them when it turned out to be another customer. The blonde woman hurried to serve her, leaving Evelyn and Jacob in awkward silence.

Evelyn noticed his nervous glances toward the door, then back at her, as though gauging her purpose. Their conversation faltered almost as soon as it began, and to ease the tension, Evelyn picked out four bread rolls from a basket near the counter.

Finally, she asked the question that had brought her there. "Do you know a Lucy? She was a close friend of Susan's."

Jacob frowned, scratching his chin. "Do you know Susan?" he asked cautiously.

"Yes," Evelyn replied quickly. "I'm her mother. I'm trying to track down one of her friends."

His face softened, forehead creasing as though he were studying a resemblance. Then, a small smile. "Ah, I can see it now. And how is Susan?"

Evelyn forced a smile but said nothing of her daughter's death. Instead, she steered the conversation back to Lucy.

Jacob explained that Susan had been one of his best casual employees, reliable and hard-working. He often called her first when catering jobs arose. Still, the name Lucy meant nothing to him. He suggested it might have been a last-minute hire or one of the many part-timers his staff pulled in through friends. "But no," he said finally, "Lucy doesn't ring a bell."

Evelyn thanked him, bought a few fresh buns, and left. Perhaps mentioning Lucy would jog his memory later. She would give him time.

The following day, she returned to the bakery, this time pretending to browse rather than pry. She ordered more of Jacob's rolls, putting on the air of a casual customer exploring the neighbourhood. The blonde assistant, recognising her from the day before, offered a friendly smile as she served her.

With a confident smile, Evelyn asked, "Is my friend Jacob around today?"

The blonde woman behind the counter nodded warmly. "He's here. Can I help you with something in the meantime?"

"What was your name again?" Evelyn's eyes drifted briefly to a plate of shortbread biscuits on the shelf between them.

"Christine," the woman replied cheerfully, curious about how she might be of assistance.

Evelyn leaned closer. "Jacob was checking whether a woman named Lucy had worked for him. Do you recognise the name?"

Christine shook her head. "No Lucy. I'd remember if I did."

Just then, Jacob appeared from the back, balancing a tray piled high with loaves of bread, their warm scent filling the air. Evelyn couldn't resist. "Would it be possible to buy one straight from the tray?"

Jacob's face lit up. "For Susan's mother? Of course. You'll have the best loaf on the shelf." His expression sobered slightly as he added, "I've gone through my records. Lucy never worked here."

Evelyn thanked him, then paused on her way out. A thought struck. She turned back. "Did Susan ever do cater jobs with you, outside the shop?"

Jacob grinned. "Yes. She loved it—big houses, grand parties. She liked seeing how the rich lived."

"Did she ever mention a particular place? Somewhere she went more than once?" Evelyn pressed, suspecting the mysterious

Lucy could be connected. "And do you recall her last catering job before she left for Australia?"

Christine, who was now arranging loaves on the shelf, looked over, hesitating about something. Jacob picked up on this. "Christine? Do you know something?"

Christine nodded. "Susan adored working at the Middleton residence. She did two events there and really wanted to keep going back."

Recognition flickered across Jacob's face. "Yes, the Middleton's. She wasn't fussed about other jobs, but she liked their place. That was her last event before she returned home."

He went on to explain that he had worked with the Middleton family for years. Deborah Middleton, the lady of the house, often called him for last-minute catering for business functions. "Her office is just across the road," he added. "She comes in here often for lunch."

Evelyn asked quickly, "Do they have a daughter named Lucy?"

Jacob shook his head. "Not that I know of. Never saw children there."

Taking a chance, Evelyn crossed the street and entered the building Jacob had pointed out. The foyer directory listed *Middleton's Consulting Services – Level 4.*

The fourth floor was lined with suites behind smoked-glass doors, names printed neatly beside each. The Middleton office was the first near the elevator.

Evelyn pushed open the glass door. A stylish young receptionist looked up from her desk. "Hello?"

Thinking fast, Evelyn smiled. "Hello, I was hoping to speak with Mrs Middleton."

"She's in a meeting. Do you have an appointment?"

"No," Evelyn admitted. "But I'd appreciate a few minutes with her if possible."

The receptionist's smile widened. "She'll be free in about an hour. I'll book you in. Is it about office space?"

Evelyn nodded and didn't say anything. She then smiled and headed for the elevators. To pass the time, she will browse the local shops, then return to meet Deborah Middleton.

Deborah was about Evelyn's age, striking in a tailored black suit that fit her like it had been made for her. Her blue eyes were sharp yet welcoming, her light brown hair neatly swept back. She exuded both warmth and authority.

She explained their business: leasing both physical and virtual offices with flexible terms, no long commitments required. "Some tenants are here daily, others only occasionally. Whatever you need, we can arrange."

Before long, Evelyn found herself nodding along, swept into Deborah's charm. She signed a fortnightly lease for a corner office, claiming she was a therapist who mostly worked elsewhere and only needed the space a few days a week. Deborah showed her around, pointing out the kitchen, amenities, and encouraging her to see the receptionist, Maryanne, if she needed anything.

The next morning, Evelyn shopped for office basics—folder, pens, notepad—then headed to her new space. She recalled the therapists she'd once seen, arranging the furniture to resemble a counselling room, desk by the window with a view across the city. She knew she couldn't afford to keep up the rent for long, but time was critical.

She heard Deborah's voice at reception and braced herself. Moments later, Deborah knocked lightly and peered into the half-open door.

Evelyn stood and gestured for her to come in.

"Settling in alright?" Deborah asked as she stepped into the office. Her eyes swept the room. "Oh, I like what you've done with the furniture. The desk looks better by the window—gives you more space, doesn't it?"

"I wanted it to feel more suited for counselling," Evelyn replied, her tone measured and professional. "Hope you don't mind me shifting things around."

"Not at all. This is your office now. If you need extra chairs or anything else, just let Maryanne know." Deborah smiled, already turning to leave.

Before she could step out, Evelyn added quickly, "Perhaps we could catch up for dinner later? It would be nice to connect properly."

The suggestion stopped Deborah in her tracks. She hesitated—no tenant had ever invited her to dinner before. "Yes… I suppose that could work. Let me know when, and I'll check my diary." She left smiling politely, though inwardly unsettled by Evelyn's forwardness. Still, she reasoned, if Evelyn was a therapist, she must be fine.

Back in her own office, Deborah smiled to herself about the odd invitation as she sat down. She had barely reached for her briefcase when Evelyn appeared again at the doorway.

"Evelyn?" Deborah looked up. "Can I help you?"

"I was wondering if we could meet this evening. I'm free, and there's a restaurant just down the road." Evelyn's expression was earnest but unsmiling.

Caught off guard again, Deborah stalled. "I think I may already have plans. Let me check with my husband. Perhaps another time?"

"Of course," Evelyn said. "I only thought, if you were free, we could go around five. Nothing too late."

"Five? That's an early dinner!" Deborah laughed, sounding more at ease.

"I prefer eating earlier—I like to be home before it gets too late," Evelyn explained, then half turned back toward her office, sensing she might be pressing too hard.

But Deborah had an idea. "Why don't we bring food in? There's a fantastic caterer across the road. If you want to eat early, we could set up here instead."

Evelyn softened. "Alright." At least Deborah hadn't refused her entirely.

"Leave it with me. I'll clear the boardroom—we'll have dinner there. Yes, that's perfect." Deborah now looked confident in her plan.

Evelyn couldn't help noticing Deborah's lavish décor: African art, a tall sunlit potted plant, and a peculiar two-headed giraffe statue. Most striking was a large vivid painting of zebras rearing and clashing in a cloud of dust—wild, almost unsettling.

Later, passing Maryanne at reception, Evelyn decided to slip out for a while. She would return in time for the dinner meeting, but she still wondered how she might raise Susan in conversation.

When she came back in the afternoon, Evelyn busied herself with fake pamphlets for her invented counselling service—something to appear credible if Deborah grew suspicious about her lack of clients.

At precisely five o'clock, a confident knock startled her. Deborah stood at the door, a bottle of red wine in hand.

"Dinner is served," she announced cheerfully, seeming like a different woman altogether.

Evelyn followed her into the boardroom where a long table was neatly laid with food on a crisp white cloth. Christine, from Jacob's cake shop, was setting out platters. The sight unnerved Evelyn: she slipped away before Christine could notice her. From a distance, she heard Deborah asking after her, but apparently Deborah assumed she had dashed off to do something briefly.

Evelyn waited until Christine departed in the elevator before returning. Four bottles of wine—two red, two white—stood open on the table. The food was mostly finger fare, which disappointed her; she preferred a proper hot meal. Still, before she could dwell on it, Deborah poured two glasses of wine and handed one over.

As Evelyn accepted it, she caught the unmistakable scent of wine already on Deborah's breath. Had she started drinking earlier?

The two women sat down, and Evelyn immediately noticed that every dish on the table was hidden beneath layers of shiny foil. When Deborah began peeling the coverings away, Evelyn was astonished. A spread of delicately prepared food appeared before her: finely chopped, crisp vegetables paired with slices of sticky Peking duck, ready to be rolled into small pancakes like spring rolls. On the same platter, lobster medallions swam in a creamy cheese sauce, served alongside a mound of vibrant, spiced orange mashed potatoes.

Other dishes crowded the table—garlic bread still warm from the oven, little tapas-style plates, bowls of flavoured rice, and fresh garden greens. It was a banquet fit not only for royalty, Evelyn thought, but for an entire castle. She also realised the food hadn't all come from Jacob's bakery; some of it had clearly been sourced elsewhere.

"This must have cost a fortune," Evelyn said at last. "Tell me how much it was—I'll split it with you."

"Absolutely not!" Deborah said firmly. "Think of it as part of the service. My way of welcoming you aboard, of getting to know you." She lifted her nearly empty wine glass, took a long sip, and smiled. "Here's to what I hope will be a productive and lasting partnership." With that, she finished her glass and reached for the bottle to pour herself more. Noticing Evelyn's untouched drink, she urged her to catch up.

As they ate, Evelyn became increasingly aware that Deborah was tipsy. Her voice grew louder, her words more careless, as she began making unkind remarks about her husband. Evelyn tried to mirror her energy, but it wasn't in her nature. Introverted by temperament, she often came across as awkward. Yet Deborah didn't seem to mind. She laughed easily—sometimes uproariously, for no good reason. It left Evelyn wondering if the laughter was with her or at her. Still, Deborah gave every impression of enjoying her company, perhaps even finding her refreshing.

Evelyn carried on her new life under the guise of a visiting therapist—someone who worked on-site with clients and businesses. That was the story she told Maryanne and Deborah, and it provided a convenient excuse not to linger too long at the office. In reality, she spent much of her time in her motel room, lying on the bed, lost in thoughts of Susan and weighed down by melancholy. She missed Veronica deeply and often wondered how she was faring back in South Africa.

Another week slipped by, and Evelyn's expenses were becoming untenable. She was paying rent on a business that existed in name only, while her savings steadily drained into motel bills and day-to-day costs. She knew she needed answers soon. Why had Susan left London so suddenly? And why did it feel as though time was running out? Evelyn resolved to give it a few more days; if nothing came to light, she would confront Deborah directly about Susan and Lucy before leaving London.

As it turned out, luck intervened. Deborah surprised her with an invitation to a cocktail party at her home. Evelyn accepted without really thinking about it. It was an opportunity—perhaps her best chance yet—to gather insight into Susan's final weeks, and maybe even uncover more about Lucy.

Chapter Fourteen
The Party

Will pick you up at 1 pm downstairs if you need a lift to the Middleton's...

The cocktail party was held on a grey, rain-swept Saturday afternoon. Deborah had arranged for Jacob to collect Evelyn, since they lived close by. Evelyn refused to drive in London, finding the traffic and navigation overwhelming, and she would have struggled to locate Deborah's home near the large park. Jacob, eager to help, didn't question the sudden friendship between the two women. He had other worries—he always grew anxious when catering plans came together at the last minute. Still, the Middleton's paid well, offered him referrals, and opened doors to new opportunities, so he couldn't afford to disappoint them.

They pulled up outside a grand, three-storey residence in an affluent corner of the city. The house reminded Evelyn of the stately terraced mansions of her childhood—imposing, old, and dignified. A tall black gate guarded the entrance, and security bars lined the windows. Jacob parked on a side street that led to the property. With his two young assistants, he began unloading equipment from the back of the van. Evelyn, struggling to climb down from the high step, accepted his helping hand.

Through the iron gates, Evelyn glimpsed Deborah. She emerged in an evening gown, smiling broadly, every inch the gracious hostess. A mechanical buzz sounded, and the gates swung open. Deborah greeted Evelyn warmly, her friendliness bordering on theatrical, before insisting she couldn't wait for Evelyn to meet her husband. She cautioned her, however, not to take his dry remarks too seriously. Linking arms, Deborah swept Evelyn inside.

The interior was even grander. A sweeping staircase rose to the upper floors, while the hallway stretched endlessly forward. Tables bore ornate crystal bowls and extravagant bouquets, while the walls were lined with impressive paintings, the kind Evelyn assumed belonged to long-deceased masters. Trinkets from across the globe filled the spaces in between, each piece clamouring for attention.

Deborah guided her into a vast sitting room, where four middle-aged men lounged around a low marble table, brandy glasses in hand. Two smoked cigars, their heavy scent hanging in the air. One of them, tall, suited, and self-assured, stood as they entered.

"Graham, this is my friend Evelyn," Deborah announced with a smile.

"Pleased to meet you," he said warmly, extending his hand. "I've heard wonderful things about you." His charm, however, struck Evelyn as excessive, almost rehearsed. Something about him felt too polished, as though he carried secrets behind his easy smile. Evelyn smiled politely but guardedly. Deborah quickly continued with the introductions: Jonathon, pale and thin with spectacles, sitting awkwardly on a crooked nose, barely feigned interest; Shaun and Cyril, both more engaged. It was Cyril's gaze that lingered longest—handsome, intent, and mysterious.

The men lifted their glasses in unison, a gesture of welcome that felt almost ceremonial. Graham returned to his seat with a cigar between his fingers, offering refills as if he presided over the group. Deborah, steering Evelyn away, led her to a couch opposite the men. The window behind them opened onto a lush garden where flowers thrived in the rain, framing a bubbling water feature ringed by a neatly trimmed hedge. Its steady dripping offered a rare moment of calm.

Deborah left briefly, and Evelyn sat observing the scene. The men laughed and boasted, oblivious to her presence. Deborah soon returned with a tray, setting down water and orange juice for Evelyn before pouring herself another glass of wine. Her flushed cheeks and restless energy told Evelyn she had been drinking for some time. The physical familiarity—linking arms, guiding her about—already felt overbearing.

Social occasions never suited Evelyn. An introvert, she avoided them when she could. But tonight, she had a purpose: she needed to know whether Deborah or her husband held any connection to Susan's death.

Trying to draw Deborah out, Evelyn asked if other women were expected. Deborah dismissed the idea. She claimed she had little use for female friends, preferring solitude to drama. Taking a heavy gulp of wine, she urged Evelyn to join her, but Evelyn stayed with juice.

"So, what does your husband do?" Evelyn asked carefully. "Are these men his business partners?"

"My husband?" Deborah leaned back, laughing. "What does he do? Oh, everything!" She turned the question into a joke, brushing it aside before adding, "Why do you ask?"

"Just conversation," Evelyn replied evenly. "And this party—what's the occasion?"

"It is really just a gathering," Deborah admitted, twirling her glass. "His colleagues, some local, some from overseas. They meet when travel or business brings them together. Not much of a party, really."

Evelyn continued: "What kind of work does he do?"

"He doesn't talk about work… Something with CEOs and boards of directors—lots of meetings, lots of conferences. Boring, if you ask me." Deborah's cheeks glowed red as her hair slipped loose around her face. Abruptly, she waved the subject away. "Enough of that. Jacob's driving you home, so you can at least have one drink with me."

But Evelyn stayed firm. She couldn't afford to lower her guard. She shifted the conversation instead.

"This house is extraordinary. Could you show me around?"

Delighted, Deborah sprang to her feet. "Of course! Upstairs, there's a balcony with the best view."

As they slipped out, the men's laughter echoed behind them. The air grew heavy with the scent of Jacob's cooking as they ascended the sweeping staircase. The décor above was all polished wood, cream carpets, and accents of white, gold, and tan. Paintings and sculptures lined the corridor, everything meticulously placed to evoke harmony, wealth, and restraint—like a home curated not just for comfort, but for effect.

All the doors along this floor were closed, so the women climbed the next flight of stairs and emerged onto a broad landing, styled in a striking palette of white and deep red. At its centre was another sitting area, framed by tall white doors bordered with burgundy English roses.

"This is my sitting room!" Deborah announced with sudden authority, gesturing grandly. "Come on, this way!" She radiated energy, almost commanding.

As they walked down the hall, Evelyn stole a glance through a door left partly ajar. It revealed a large bedroom—the main one, she assumed. At the corridor's end they stopped before what looked like an ordinary linen cupboard built into the wall. Yet Deborah's deliberate suspense made Evelyn certain there was more to it.

With exaggerated drama, Deborah pulled open the door to reveal a narrow stairwell leading into darkness. She fumbled for a switch, and a weak light flickered on, illuminating the cramped steps.

"Follow me!" she declared in a musical singsong before bursting into laughter.

Evelyn studied her companion with quiet concern. Something about Deborah's behaviour felt off—eccentric, perhaps even unstable—but Evelyn was not inclined to judge. She had seen her share of troubled minds. More likely, Deborah was simply drunk.

The stairway narrowed as they climbed. At the top, Deborah cursed under her breath, struggling against a swollen door. With one final shove it creaked open, releasing a rush of cold, damp air that blew Evelyn's hair back. A soft glow spilled down from above.

They stepped onto a small rooftop landing, barely large enough for a little table and two chairs. Behind them stretched the tiled roof; ahead, the open sky. The landscape stretched outward, dissolving into a blanket of heavy grey clouds.

"This is my favourite place," Deborah admitted, her voice softening. "When the weather's fine, I come up here to think."

For the first time, Evelyn glimpsed a shadow behind Deborah's confident exterior. Despite her wealth and success, she seemed lonely. Perhaps that was why she had latched onto Evelyn so quickly—saw something of herself in her. Deborah acted as if they were instant best friends. Evelyn wasn't sure how to feel about that.

After hanging about for a few minutes in the damp chill, they finally turned back, retreating to the warmth of the loungeroom downstairs. Passing the partly open door again, Evelyn asked lightly, "That's your bedroom?"

"Yes," Deborah confirmed, then giggled. "But nothing much happens in the marital bedroom."

They continued toward the stairs, but another doorway caught Evelyn's eye. "And this room? Another lounge?" she asked.

"This one's mine," Deborah replied.

Inside, the space was distinctly feminine—delicate ornaments arranged with care. In one corner stood a compact bar with a fridge and a full wine rack. A sleek flat-screen television and a modern lounge suite felt oddly mismatched against the house's old-world décor. Despite its prettiness, the room carried an emptiness, as though something vital was absent.

They descended further, reaching the first floor where, again, every door was closed. To Evelyn, it felt curiously un-family-like. She decided to ask the obvious question.

"Do you have children?"

The bluntness caught Deborah off guard. Her step faltered, her cheer dimmed.

"Children? No. Graham never wanted them. And…it's too late now." She attempted a smile, but it rang hollow.

"What a shame," Evelyn said. "This house feels made for children running about." She looked around the hallway. "So many closed doors…"

"Yes," Deborah cut in quickly. "This is my husband's section—his office, where he takes meetings." She hurried Evelyn along toward the stairs.

As they descended further, the smell of cooking thickened in the air, making Evelyn's stomach twist with hunger. She realised she hadn't eaten in hours.

Back in the lounge, a haze of cigar smoke greeted them, stinging Evelyn's throat. The men's voices rose in loud, animated discussion—politics, immigration, something heated. Evelyn tried to gauge their mood. Could Deborah's husband have been connected to her daughter's death? She hoped not; she was beginning to like Deborah, eccentricities and all.

They settled once more by the window overlooking the courtyard fountain—a stone cherub, unabashedly clutching himself as he urinated into the pool below. Water lilies floated listlessly on the surface, while two statues of semi-clad women stood guard in the corners.

Deborah cradled her wineglass strangely, almost as though it comforted her, then broke into unexplained laughter. She sat with one leg folded beneath the other on the chair, her laughter loud and unrestrained. Evelyn shifted uneasily. The erratic behaviour, coupled with the alcohol, hinted at something deeper.

The moment broke when two young women entered carrying trays of hors d'oeuvres. Evelyn's anticipation soured at the sight: plain water crackers topped with cheese, tomato, and the occasional sardine. She forced a polite smile, masking disappointment. She had expected refinement, not snacks fit for a school fundraiser. One tray also carried triangles of bread with scrambled eggs—Evelyn pounced on the last piece. Deborah, uninterested, waved the servers away without taking anything.

Soon after, Jacob reappeared to announce dinner. Deborah glanced at her watch, startled. "Oh my God, already?" She called for the men to move to the dining room, her voice echoing down the corridor.

The group shuffled forward, Evelyn swept along in the commotion until they arrived at a grand dining room at the front of the house. Rectangular and imposing, it featured a large fireplace and a Renaissance-style mural across the wall. Its imagery recalled Michelangelo's chapel paintings—testament to the family's wealth.

The men were boisterous, dragging chairs noisily across the polished oak. Ornate gold-framed paintings lined the walls; each lit from above by a discreet lamp. Despite the smokers having left the lounge, the acrid scent of cigars clung to the air.

Soup was served first. Conversation stilled as spoons clinked against bowls. Evelyn tasted hers and frowned inwardly—it was unmistakably from a can. The bread rolls, plentiful though they were, did little to disguise the mediocrity. What of the tantalising smells she had noticed earlier?

Before she could dwell on it, the main dish arrived: shepherd's pie with peas and gravy. Evelyn stared in disbelief. In such a house, she had expected culinary opulence, not fare that belonged in a boarding school or hospital cafeteria. Around her, the others ate heartily, praising the meal. Deborah, however, toyed only with her peas, refilling her wineglass instead.

One of the guests suddenly struck up a conversation with Evelyn. "I hear you are from Australia?"

Evelyn turned and recognised the speaker—an attractive man with striking sky-blue eyes.

"Yes!" she answered, her voice carrying a girlish enthusiasm. He appeared to be in his fifties, perhaps a little older. His neatly trimmed sideburns blended seamlessly into his short blond hair. With an easy smile, he asked, "May I ask, whereabouts in Australia?"

"I'm from Sydney. Have you ever been there?" she replied cautiously.

"Yes, many years ago. It is a beautiful city."

Evelyn smiled politely, unsure of where the conversation was leading. She was also wary of seeming distant or cold—a trait people often attributed to her—so she played along carefully.

"The name's Cyril," the man said, extending his hand.

"Cyril, nice to meet you," Evelyn replied, noting as they shook hands that his ring finger was bare.

Cyril was sharply dressed in a dark grey suit with a crisp white shirt. His haircut was immaculate, and his whole appearance suggested someone important. He returned to his meal but cast occasional glances her way. When their eyes met, Evelyn quickly looked away, determined not to encourage him.

"So, what do you do for a living?" Cyril asked after a pause, his smile warm.

"I'm a counsellor," Evelyn lied, trying to keep her attention on her plate. Lying didn't come naturally to her, and she knew anyone who truly knew her would see through it immediately.

"That sounds fascinating," Cyril replied, sounding genuinely interested.

"And what about you?" Evelyn asked in return.

"Me?" He seemed to hesitate. "I am in software. Computers?"

Evelyn wrinkled her nose in disbelief. His polished look and executive mannerisms didn't fit her idea of someone working in IT.

"Computers?" she echoed, frowning sceptically.

Cyril laughed awkwardly, his face colouring. "Sorry to disappoint you." He quickly looked at the other diners, who smiled faintly into their pie and mash without comment.

"It's not quite as simple as that," he added quickly, clearing his throat. "I design programs that bring animated characters to life—so they can interact with the user, among other things."

"Oh." Evelyn's interest faded, her attention pulled away when she heard Deborah instruct one of the young women to tell Jacob it was time for dessert.

Jacob entered with a staff member, clearing plates before serving jelly and custard. Evelyn stared in disbelief. Sitting in a multimillion-pound home in one of London's wealthiest neighbourhoods, she felt as though she were at a child's birthday party—or in a nursing home. Yet the other guests tucked into their pudding happily, unfazed.

Deborah, meanwhile, sat quietly, lost in thought, absentmindedly toying with her wine glass. Twice Evelyn had to call her back from her daydreams before suggesting they return to the lounge. Deborah agreed, and once Evelyn pushed aside her untouched dessert, the two excused themselves.

As they entered the hallway, Jacob's staff bustled past with boxes, loading them into his van outside. Evelyn asked if he was leaving soon. Deborah nodded, explaining he had another engagement that evening, but urged Evelyn to stay a while longer—promising to arrange a taxi for her later. Evelyn was in two minds about that. She wanted to absorb as much as she could from these new wealthy acquaintances, but she was already drained. London itself seemed to be wearing on her—her body ached, her temperature fluctuated, and she felt constantly unsettled. Deciding she'd had enough, she resolved to leave when Jacob did.

Cyril followed them into the lounge, eager to resume conversation. He explained he was originally from Germany but divided his time between Toronto and New York. When Deborah offered drinks, he requested a double of something strong, then glanced at Evelyn expectantly. She shook her head.

"I'm leaving soon," she said.

Cyril's disappointment showed. "Already? I thought you might be joining us tonight."

"Perhaps another time," Evelyn replied, though she couldn't help wondering what exactly "tonight" entailed.

Deborah, tipsy now, looked disappointed. "All right, Evelyn, but promise me we'll do this again. Did you have a good time?"

Evelyn nodded politely. Cyril watched her closely, as if wanting to say something more, but stayed silent.

Just then, Jacob appeared in the doorway to announce he was ready. Evelyn seized her chance, grabbing her bag and heading for the front hall. She paused only to thank Deborah before catching Cyril's eye—he stood in the doorway, studying her with an expression both strange and inviting. Evelyn smiled faintly, gave him a small nod, and followed Jacob out into the cold, windy night.

As Jacob helped her into the van, Deborah's voice rang out behind them. She had come outside, waving wildly with one hand and clutching her wine glass in the other. Her loud farewell echoed through the damp street.

As they drove away, Jacob asked how long Evelyn had known Deborah. But she brushed off the question, pretending to be too tired to talk. The day's strange events had left her overwhelmed, though she felt oddly proud of herself for having gone along with it all. Was this what Adam meant when he urged her to be more spontaneous? She thought briefly of Adam and Carol back in Australia—and of Susan's death—before falling into silence. Jacob sensed her mood and didn't continue with his questions, only announcing they had arrived, when they pulled up to her hotel.

The following day, Evelyn lay in bed, determined to do nothing but rest. She was completely spent from the previous day's barrage of new faces and conversations. She tried to ignore the now familiar noise of the polisher in the hallway, wondering why anyone thought it sensible to clean so early and disturb the guests' morning sleep.

When the phone rang, she was stunned to hear Adam's voice from Australia. He had tracked her down through Veronica, worried by her silence. He offered his condolences for Susan and urged her to keep in touch, saying everyone at the office missed her—even Joey, he teased knowingly. Evelyn laughed through her tears. Adam was like family to her, as was his secretary, Carol. She even found herself softening toward Joey in her loneliness.

Not long after she hung up, the phone rang again, disrupting her sleep. This time she ignored it, drifting into uneasy sleep. She dreamed of Deborah's house, overhearing men whispering about schemes to get rich, about a new drug they claimed would transform humanity's belief in God. Just as the dream turned darker, she woke to the phone ringing once more. It was Veronica.

"I've been trying to reach you for days," Veronica said. "I gave Adam your number—he might call you soon."

"He already has," Evelyn replied softly.

"Good. And listen—I've decided to come visit. I do need a holiday after all."

After she hung up from Veronica, Evelyn drifted back into sleep and soon found herself in a completely different place. A vast, grey structure rose before her, resembling an aircraft maintenance hangar. It was in the evening, nighttime. The surrounding area was dotted with smaller buildings, all illuminated by powerful security lights that cast an eerie glow across the compound. From above, it looked like a heavily guarded installation.

In the next instant, she was on the ground, standing at the entrance of a reinforced door that led inside. The building gave the impression of an aircraft hangar where jumbo jets might be serviced, and yet Evelyn felt an undeniable sense that she wasn't supposed to be there—that even imagining stepping inside was forbidden. But she did.

The interior stretched out like a massive warehouse. Pallets of shrink-wrapped boxes were stacked neatly in endless rows, prepared for shipment. Each pallet carried labels with strange words and numbers—*CEREUS–A10989*, *CEREUS–B21057*, and countless other variations. Each seemed assigned to a different destination, organized with methodical precision.

Suddenly Evelyn was above it all again, floating over the vast floor, the boxes stretching as far as she could see. Voices broke her concentration—male voices echoing near the entrance. She moved cautiously closer, trying not to be seen. Under the harsh white light stood three men: two in work overalls, clearly warehouse staff, and another in a dark suit who carried himself with authority. As Evelyn crept nearer, her heart nearly stopped in her chest—the suited man was Graham, Deborah's husband.

She jolted awake. Someone was tugging her arm. Looking around in confusion, she saw Deborah at her bedside.

Shocked and surprised, Evelyn sat up, defensive. "What are you doing here?"

"I came to check on you," Deborah said softly. "You didn't come to work, and you weren't answering your phone. I was worried something had happened."

Evelyn frowned, her mind scrambling. "But… how did you even get into my apartment?"

"Don't worry about that. I know the manager here." Deborah's expression was earnest, tinged with concern. "You usually come in twice a week, and when you didn't show, I got anxious about your whereabouts."

"What are you talking about?" Evelyn snapped, agitation rising. "How did you even know where I live?"

Deborah looked puzzled. Evelyn had filled out her address and phone details in the office paperwork. To Deborah, it was simple concern for a colleague who had no family nearby. "I'm sorry if I startled you. I did knock several times, but you didn't answer. They told me downstairs that you haven't left your room in days. I just… I thought something was wrong."

Evelyn struggled to sit up but found her body uncooperative. Her arms felt heavy, her legs weak. Panic flared. "What's happening? Why can't I move properly?"

"Evelyn, you haven't been at work for over a week," Deborah said carefully. "As I just said, you haven't left your apartment in days. Is everything okay? It looks like you have been sleeping a lot. Have you been sick, not feeling well?"

Evelyn's chest tightened. "A week?" Evelyn repeated. Then she felt faint, suddenly aware of her hunger and the stiffness in her body. Had she truly been asleep for days?

She looked at Deborah through narrowed eyes, paranoia creeping in. Was this concern of hers genuine—or was Deborah somehow part of it? Evelyn bit her tongue, deciding it was safer to say nothing. "I'm fine," she said finally. "I must have overslept, that's all."

Deborah hesitated, offering to call someone for her, but Evelyn refused. She thanked her for caring, assured her she'd return to work soon, and politely asked her to leave. Deborah suggested she spend the weekend at her place, but Evelyn declined. Before leaving, Deborah scribbled her number and urged her to call anytime.

Once alone, Evelyn phoned Veronica in South Africa, recounting both her strange dream and Deborah's uninvited visit. They switched partly into Afrikaans, cautious of eavesdropping, and even used code words when referring to Susan's death. Evelyn's paranoia grew. Were the people at the Royal Doze spying on her? Was Deborah in league with her husband? Who else might be involved?

Veronica urged Evelyn to come home—either to South Africa or Australia—and reminded her that Adam may call, who had been worried since learning about her late daughter. Evelyn vaguely recalled already having that conversation, as though caught in a loop of déjà vu.

Later that day, weak but determined, Evelyn made herself tea and decided to step outside for fresh air. Down in the lobby, she noticed the receptionist staring at her in alarm. Guests gawked, some even recoiling and hurrying away as though she were some kind of spectacle. Evelyn ignored them, bracing herself against the icy wind as she stood outside the main entrance. She shivered, considering whether it was time to leave London altogether.

Amid the chaos of the city—honking cars, rushing pedestrians—she heard a familiar accented voice. Turning, she saw the elegant woman from days earlier, the one in the fur coat and long nails. With genuine concern in her eyes, the woman quickly took off her tan leather coat and quickly wrapped it around Evelyn. "Darling, what are you doing? You'll catch your death out here."

The woman, dressed exquisitely in knee-high boots and a lime green crocheted top, guided Evelyn gently back into the building. In the mirrored elevator, Evelyn caught sight of her reflection—and froze. She was wearing only her bra and panties beneath the fur coat hanging over her bare shoulders. Her hair hung tangled and wild, making her look unhinged.

She allowed herself to be led back to her apartment, dazed and speechless. The woman fussed over her kindly, offering to stay or call someone. Evelyn, desperate for solitude, thanked her instead.

At the door, the woman introduced herself with a faint smile. "My name is Luciana Santos. I live just down the hall. But I'm leaving tomorrow. If you need me, I'll be here tonight."

When Santos left, Evelyn collapsed into bed, reeling from everything that had happened. She resolved not to tell Veronica—nor anyone about roaming downstairs in her underwear. Some things were too strange, too dangerous, to share.

The next day, Evelyn felt steadier, more composed. She checked her appearance carefully before leaving the apartment, then hurried through the foyer with her eyes downcast, hoping no one remembered her from the day before.

Stepping outside, the warmth of the English sun touched her face. The weather was improving, which lifted her mood. She wandered in the direction of her office—though it was quite a distance, she had no fixed plans. Part of her considered returning home, yet another part insisted she was on the right path and should remain. After all, Veronica had promised to visit. Lost in thought and time, she suddenly found herself near Jacob's cake shop and Deborah's rooms.

Then she noticed something that made her stop. Across the road, Cyril was leaving Deborah's office and climbing into an expensive car. What was he doing there?

Curious, Evelyn crossed the street to see Deborah. Inside, she found her speaking with Maryanne.

"Evelyn? You here! How are you feeling?" Deborah asked with excitement. Evelyn found her enthusiasm difficult to read—too forward, almost overfamiliar.

"I am fine. Just checking my mail," Evelyn replied, though she knew there would be none. Almost without thinking, she asked whether Deborah's invitation to spend an afternoon together still stood. She felt she was wasting time, and before leaving England she needed answers—about Deborah, her husband, and, most of all, about Susan and Lucy. This might be her only chance.

"Wonderful! Of course, you can visit!" Deborah exclaimed, her excitement unrestrained.

Evelyn went to her office, shuffled some papers to keep up appearances, then locked the door again. Deborah was waiting outside the elevator, eager to arrange a time. They settled on Sunday afternoon.

As they parted, Evelyn asked, "By the way—was that Cyril I saw leaving earlier?"

"Yes," Deborah replied. "He was just dropping some things off."

"I thought it was him. He left before I could say hello."

Deborah giggled. "Are you keen on him?"

"No!" Evelyn answered quickly. "I just thought it odd he was here at our offices, that's all."

Deborah only laughed again, as though she found Evelyn amusing.

Back at the Royal Doze, Evelyn discovered dinner waiting under silver lids on a trolley by the table. She hadn't realized it was already half past five—her preferred dining time. The meal was plain, even dull, but the dessert—a warm apricot pudding drenched in custard—made her smile.

The days slipped by, and soon it was Sunday morning. Evelyn woke early, listening to the familiar corridor cleaners polishing the floor, which was far too noisily for such an hour, especially on a Sunday. She reflected on the past days, uncertain whether she was making progress. Money was running out; her holiday would soon have to end. She still needed to speak with Veronica—was she truly coming to visit, or was it only talk? If not, Evelyn decided, she would head home the following week.

Her thoughts turned to Deborah's house near the big park. How would she get there? Public transport, perhaps a taxi—Jacob wouldn't be driving her this time. She considered phoning Deborah for directions but hesitated; she didn't want to seem a burden. She decided she would manage on her own.

As she gathered travel brochures and maps from the room, she noticed an envelope slipped under her door. It read:

Dear Evelyn,
Will pick you up at 1 pm downstairs if you need a lift to the
Middleton's. See you then.
Cyril.

Evelyn froze, rereading the note. How did Cyril know where she lived—or that she needed a ride? Maybe Deborah had told him. Still, the thought unsettled her. With no better option, she agreed silently to the offer.

At one o'clock, she met him in the basement carpark. She slipped into his sleek car, nerves tempered by his warm smile and gentle manner. He seemed attentive, even grateful for her company. They spoke lightly of Australia's tourist spots as he drove, though Evelyn, despite herself, couldn't help noticing his handsomeness.

Deborah was waiting at the door, waving with great enthusiasm as they arrived. Her boundless energy, though genuine, was beginning to exhaust Evelyn, whose own smile felt forced. Still, she reminded herself her time in England was running short. She needed answers—today could be her last chance.

She saw immediately that Deborah's husband wasn't home, and Cyril departed soon after dropping her off. Evelyn asked, "Did you send Cyril to pick me up?"

Deborah shook her head. "When I mentioned yesterday you were visiting, he offered. I thought it was kind of him."

"Yes. I just feel… special," Evelyn replied with a thin smile, then shifted the subject. "Do you often host parties, with Jacob's catering?"

"Absolutely!" Deborah beamed.

"For you—or for your husband's work?"

"Mostly for Graham. I just go along, as a good wife should."

In the lounge, Deborah offered Evelyn wine, which she declined. She then talked about a young tree, her prized star magnolia in her garden that was struggling, pointing it out through the wide window overlooking the fountain and manicured lawn.

After a while, she fetched herself a large glass of wine, curling back into her chair with one leg tucked beneath her. Evelyn tried to remain casual as she spoke. "So, what does your husband do again?"

"Oh, Evelyn, let's not talk about husbands," Deborah replied airily. "I'd rather hear about you. Actually, I was thinking—what if we went on a holiday together? Spain, France… just us two?"

Evelyn looked surprised. "A trip? I don't think so. Work... I have too much on." The suggestion had caught her completely off guard.

"At least think about it," Deborah pleaded. "I haven't had a holiday with a good female friend in years. Always just Graham."

Evelyn forced a polite smile, but her mind was already racing. If she could slip upstairs, perhaps she might uncover something. Susan had been here, catering with Jacob. But what Evelyn needed to know was far darker—whether Deborah and her husband had anything to do with Susan's death.

"I was thinking... can we go upstairs again and take another look from the rooftop? It's such a beautiful day, and I would like to see the view from up there without rain this time." Evelyn said with a guilty smile.

"What a splendid idea," Deborah replied, leaning forward and taking a long gulp from her oversized glass of wine before standing. "Follow me!" she declared playfully, grabbing the half-empty bottle from the cabinet. Glass and bottle in hand, she swayed her hips in an exaggerated dance as she led the way up.

On the first landing, Evelyn recognized Graham's floor—his office and workrooms were here, all doors shut and secured. Deborah didn't pause, continuing to the next level, which belonged to her and Graham. The red and gold décor gave the space a warm, soothing atmosphere. A hidden doorway opened onto a narrow rooftop balcony.

The air was sharper than Evelyn expected, cold gusts whipping their hair and stinging their cheeks. Deborah dropped into a chair, flushed and short of breath, while Evelyn settled beside her, feigning amusement. The city skyline stretched in the distance, lovely but blurred by the biting wind.

"I need the bathroom," Evelyn said suddenly, a little embarrassed.

"Alright, I'll show you—"

"No, no. Stay. Relax. Have another glass of wine," Evelyn insisted.

"Well, don't go all the way downstairs. There's one on the second floor, just through that door."

Evelyn excused herself and descended the stairs. She found the second-floor toilet easily but didn't enter; instead, she listened. Graham might have come home unnoticed. The house was silent. She looked back at the door leading upstairs, it was closed, just like she had left it. Seizing the chance, Evelyn hurried to Graham's floor. All doors were locked, just as she had suspected. Frustrated, she returned to the second floor, where their bedroom door stood ajar.

Inside, the spacious room revealed two distinct halves, each personalized. Evelyn gravitated toward Graham's dressing table, where scattered belongings caught her eye. A nearly hidden door in the wall led into a walk-in wardrobe—and beyond that, a bathroom. Nothing unusual there. But back at the dressing table, loose notepads drew her attention.

She suddenly gasped. Shocked. Scrawled across one page, in bold heading, was a single word: *Cereus.* Beneath it, notes, numbers, and—on another sheet—a list of countries, some marked with ticks, others with crosses or question marks. Evelyn's pulse raced. "What is this…?"

"Evelyn?" Deborah's voice echoed from upstairs.

Startled, Evelyn shoved the papers back into place just as Deborah appeared on the landing.

"Where have you been?" Deborah asked, puzzled.

"What a big house you have!" Evelyn replied, forcing a light laugh and catching her breath.

"Didn't you use the toilet right there?" Deborah pointed at the door nearby.

"No, I went downstairs—the one I used last time," Evelyn said quickly, brushing past her and back toward the rooftop.

They rejoined their chairs. Deborah, still cheerful, poured another glass. Evelyn, however, could think only of the word *Cereus*. What did it mean? Where did these people fit into it? Deborah looked so harmless—could she possibly be involved? Or was Evelyn losing her mind?

Trying to probe, Evelyn asked, "Have you ever been to Australia?"

"No, but I'd love to. Why do you ask?"

"You and your husband seem well-travelled."

"Yes, but never Australia. I hear there are beaches and sunshine everywhere," Deborah replied.

"Cape Town's similar," Evelyn said casually, testing. "I went years ago. Have you or your husband been?"

Deborah shrugged, distracted. "Let's go back downstairs—it's freezing here." She carried the empty wine bottle with her, Evelyn close behind, still strategizing how to bring up *Cereus*.

In the loungeroom, Evelyn resumed her seat. Deborah poured another glass of wine and swiftly joined her, slipping into the chair and placing one leg under the other for comfort, urging Evelyn to stay longer, perhaps even overnight. Evelyn felt cornered. Enough subtlety.

She asked, "Do you remember two girls—Susan and Lucy— who worked with Jacob? Catering, I think."

Deborah frowned. "Why are you asking about the help?"

"My daughter knew them and hoped I might find them here."

"You have a daughter?" Deborah's eyes widened.

"Yes. Didn't I tell you?"

"No! I thought you were childless, like me."

Evelyn forced a smile, masking her unease. "She spent some time here in London. She mentioned Susan and Lucy worked for Jacob."

Deborah studied her closely. "Oh my God, you have a daughter. How old is she?"

"Nearly thirty. So—those names don't ring a bell?"

"Lucy, and… what was the other?"

"Susan."

Deborah shook her head. "No, sorry. If they worked for Jacob, why not ask him."

"I already have. He barely remembers a Susan. Too many casuals, no records," Evelyn explained. Then, with nothing left to lose, she asked, "Do you know anything about the word *Cereus*?"

Deborah repeated the word softly, frowning. Evelyn nodded, looking on with anticipation.

"Where did you hear that?" Deborah asked, suddenly tense.

"My daughter mentioned it—connected to those girls." Evelyn watched her closely.

Deborah sat forward, pensive, glass in her hand. "That's strange. I'm sure my husband worked on something called *Cereus*. How would your daughter know about that?"

"So, you *have* heard of it?" Evelyn pressed, feeling way out of her depth, but managed to retain composure, even though her chest burned with panic.

"Yes. It is a top-secret project Graham, and his company have been working on for years. Nobody is supposed to know about it." Deborah's voice had sobered. Then, after a pause, she asked, "Wait—what were those girls' names again?"

"Susan and Lucy," Evelyn replied.

"I don't know those names," Deborah muttered. "But I will have to ask Graham. Goodness—he's going to hit the roof."

She rose from her chair and crossed to the corner cabinet, retrieving an already-opened bottle of wine. After pouring herself another glass, she settled beside Evelyn, tucking her leg beneath her again, as she often did.

"You don't need to mention this to your husband," Evelyn reassured gently, noticing the shift in Deborah's mood.

"I am just wondering how they even know about *Cereus*," Deborah said quietly, sipping her wine.

Evelyn felt the conversation dragging on. It was late, and she still had to work out how she would get back to her hotel. She decided to steer things forward. With a softened expression, she asked:

"So… what exactly is Cereus?"

"It is a drug. A kind of sleeping tablet. Big business—lots of money in it." Deborah sounded weary, almost defeated. She sighed. "I really shouldn't even be telling you this."

"A drug," Evelyn said softly to herself, recalling her dream—hundreds of boxes marked *Cereus*. Were they all pills? Sleeping tablets?

Deborah had gone silent, troubled, clearly worried that her husband's secret was slipping into the wrong hands.

Then suddenly she gasped. "Wait! Did you say they were young women—this Lucy person and the other one?"

"Yes. Why?" Evelyn asked, leaning forward as Deborah's energy shifted.

"Were they part of any drug trials here in London?"

Evelyn remembered: Susan had briefly joined a trial before dropping out. "Possibly. Why does that matter?" she asked cautiously.

"I recall Graham complaining about people leaving those early-stage trials. He was furious—worried the whole project might collapse with so many candidates dropping out."

"So, they *would* have known it was called Cereus?" Evelyn asked.

"*Project Cereus,* yes," Deborah admitted. "Participants would have known the name. They signed secrecy contracts."

That was enough for Evelyn. She sensed she should downplay things before Deborah grew suspicious of her motives. "I do recall one of the girls being in a trial," she conceded lightly. Deborah, visibly relieved, quickly agreed they should avoid discussing her husband's affairs any further.

It was late now. Evelyn stood to leave. Deborah urged her again to stay the night, but as always, Evelyn declined. She gathered her bag, said her goodbyes, and knew—perhaps with finality—that this might be the last time she saw Deborah. Despite mixed feelings, there was sadness too. Evelyn only hoped Deborah wasn't entangled in Susan's death.

Unsure of her route home, Evelyn decided to retrace the road Cyril had driven earlier. Surprisingly, she felt no anxiety about the walk. Somehow, she trusted she'd find her way back safely—it was still daylight after all.

The next day, Evelyn reflected on what to do next. She was certain *Project Cereus* mattered, but she still didn't know what it really was. Just a sleeping pill—or something more sinister? And how could it tie to Susan's death? Was she chasing shadows, wasting her time and money in London? Veronica's earlier scepticism gnawed at her; perhaps Veronica had been right all along, which was why she hadn't come.

But just as Evelyn resolved to tell Deborah she'd be leaving England and closing the office, an unexpected arrival lifted her spirits. Veronica swept in with a hug so big it made Evelyn's doubts melt away. The friends clung to each other, relieved. Veronica wanted to hear everything—but she warned she wouldn't stay long. She had responsibilities at home and wanted Evelyn to return with her. In truth, she had come to fetch Evelyn.

Veronica animatedly described her flight over: restless, she'd pulled out her Tarot cards mid-journey, attracting curious passengers. Soon a crowd had gathered for impromptu fortune-telling until the cabin crew dispersed them. Evelyn, amused, had forgotten about those cards—until the thought struck her: perhaps Veronica could use them to track down Lucy.

Veronica only grinned slyly and said "no" a little too loudly, bursting into laughter at Evelyn's silence. It was only a joke. Still giggling, she promised to consult her cards later and see what they revealed about Lucy. Then, she insisted, they should enjoy London before preparing to return to Cape Town.

Soon the two were back in familiar rhythm: Tarot, tea, and talk of the occult. Veronica demanded Evelyn make a proper pot of tea, and though Evelyn wished she had Jacob's rolls to serve, she settled for ordering cakes and buttered rolls from the hotel kitchen. Once the squeaky trolley with their food arrived, they began.

Veronica asked Evelyn to concentrate on Lucy—though she had never met her—and shuffle the cards. Evelyn did so, placing them face down. Veronica arranged them in three rows: past, present, future.

The past revealed that Evelyn had met foreigners, been challenged, and left her comfort zone—accurate enough, but nothing of Lucy.

The present spoke of an overseas visitor bringing happiness. Evelyn laughed; Veronica herself had just arrived. Still, no Lucy.

Then came the future. Veronica leaned forward, eyes bright. "These cards are interesting. They say you *will* meet Lucy. Something to do with the Ace of Wands and the Two of Cups. See—this card shows a woman holding a sword, the Justice card. It suggests truth, justice, fairness. Meaning you'll gain clarity and uncover the truth you are currently seeking."

"How do you know it is to do with Lucy?" Evelyn asked.

"Because you focused on her," Veronica replied firmly. "If not Lucy, then someone deeply connected to Susan and Lucy. And you haven't met this person yet."

Evelyn was struck by the accuracy so far but wondered if Veronica was confusing Lucy with another woman she had recently met. She told her about the Brazilian woman, but Veronica shook her head—no, this was someone new. Pointing to the final card, she added, "The old man with the lantern—he's showing you the way. That you need to look within, introspection. A sign your spiritual journey has already revealed hidden truths."

Evelyn pondered for a moment, intrigued, then a sudden inspiration struck, perhaps those names have some significance. She quickly scoured the phone book for hotels or motels with names like *Justice, Swords, Cups, Wands, Old Man,* or *Lantern,* but found nothing. Veronica initially thought this a foolish idea but then suggested trying the internet. What did they have to lose?

At reception downstairs, they asked to use a computer, but the clerk directed them to an internet café nearby. When they asked her to check for hotels with those names, the young woman grew impatient. After a futile search, she again urged them toward the café.

As Evelyn and Veronica turned to leave, the receptionist called out, "Pity your friend's gone—she could have lent you one of her computers."

She was referring to Ms. Santos. Evelyn soon learned Luciana Santos was a computer expert working on a project in the country. She owned three extraordinary laptops—machines capable of astonishing feats. A cleaner swore she'd seen Ms. Santos talking directly to one of her laptops, where an animated figure on the screen conversed back with eerie realism. Its eyes followed her around the room. When it suddenly turned toward the cleaner and asked, *'Who are you?'* the terrified cleaner fled the apartment.

When they returned to their room, Veronica asked what the receptionist had meant. Evelyn kept her explanation vague—she didn't want Veronica to know it had been Luciana Santos who'd helped her back upstairs after she was caught wandering the lobby in nothing but her bra and panties.

"Oh," Evelyn replied lightly, "she used to live down the corridor. We'd bump into each other in the hallway and foyer, so we started chatting."

Veronica's attention shifted to the tarot cards still spread across the table. "I doubt this has anything to do with her—you already know her. This row points to the future. We will go to the Internet café tomorrow and see what we will find."

The next morning, they did just that, trawling through listings for suburbs, towns, and names tied to those cards laid out by Veronica. After hours of fruitless searching, they gave up in frustration and went for lunch instead.

Later, back at the Royal Doze, they settled in Evelyn's room to plan their next move. Veronica wanted to arrange dinner, so Evelyn spread out some takeout menus. Pencil in hand, Veronica began circling options, until something on one of the flyers caught her eye. She leaned forward and picked up a brochure for an Indian restaurant that had fallen face down. On the back was a small street map to the restaurant.

One of the street names jumped out at her—Lantern.

'I've found a Lantern Street!' Veronica exclaimed. "Wasn't that one of the cards?"

Evelyn confirmed. Then she immediately grabbed the local maps she had collected since arriving in London—three or four in total—and passed one to Veronica. They scanned through the maps together until Evelyn gasped. Lantern Street intersected with another. She sank back into her chair, astonished.

Right there on the map, Lantern and Sword Streets crossed—just blocks from where they were.

Chapter Fifteen
The De-Stress Room

They wish to keep you powerless, unaware, drone like…

Carol reminded Adam when he arrived that morning that Julie was scheduled to visit at 4 p.m. Adam recalled Tom mentioning that Julie wanted to see his office as well as the De-Stress room, and that she hoped to discuss ways he might improve it.

Julie, eager not to be late, showed up a little early. She appeared cheerful, and Carol immediately noticed the large plastic shopping bag she carried. Adam welcomed her into his office, making sure she felt at ease. Julie admitted she hadn't expected his office to look so stylish—it was modern, sleek, and far nicer than she imagined. She added that its location was excellent, easy for her to find. Adam then asked what she knew about the DS room and why she was so curious to see it. To him, after all, it was just another space with some modifications.

Julie, however, was genuinely enthusiastic. She explained that she loved music and colour therapy, and believed such an environment was one of the best ways to find peace. She also felt that spaces like these could help people connect with their Other Self. Julie even had a similar room at home—though unnamed—and was eager to compare Adam's setup with her own.

As Adam led her into the DS room, he couldn't help but notice her carrying a shopping bag. He suggested she leave the bag in his office, but Julie preferred to keep it with her, lugging it along into the room.

The DS room was about the size of a large bedroom, entirely windowless. Two hidden cameras were mounted discreetly above the door, allowing Carol to observe those inside. The room could be set for either a daytime or nighttime atmosphere, and the heavy padding on the inside of the door further blocked out exterior noise.

Julie found the room's design calming. The colours and furnishings suited its purpose perfectly. The walls were painted in deep avocado green and navy blue at the edges, while the ceiling was a dark midnight shade fading into black. A large flat-screen TV was mounted on the wall opposite the door, positioned at mid-height. At the centre of the room stood a plush reclining chair, its futuristic design reminding Julie of something from a science fiction film. By using a keypad, the chair's motorized frame could shift smoothly from upright to fully reclined, or any position in between.

The ceiling was dotted with thirty or so tiny, recessed spotlights, while along one wall stretched a glossy black cabinet with a bare, gleaming surface that looked like it was waiting for decorative touches.

"Very nice," Julie finally remarked, scanning the room. "I like that there isn't too much clutter. So many people try to do something like this and then ruin it with too much furniture or distracting items." She paused, moving toward the black cabinet. "Is there something inside this?" she asked curiously.

"Yes," Adam replied, smiling. "Some clients bring their own spiritual or new-age music, sometimes small items to help them relax. We occasionally store their things in here, though we usually encourage them to take them home—space is limited. Some even ask to use oils or incense, but we don't allow that."

"Why not?" Julie asked, still pleased with what she saw.

"Strong scents can overwhelm the next client, especially if they have allergies," Adam explained.

Julie nodded firmly. "Exactly. People don't realize how much damage heavy perfumes and chemicals do to the nervous system and general health." She then asked Adam for a demonstration.

Adam showed her the control system, explaining that both light and sound were operated from two panels: one in the room itself and the other at reception. Carol could oversee and control things remotely if required. He opened the top lid, attached to a stylish black little cabinet, just near the door, against the wall. Julie didn't even notice it. Inside the cabinet were a colourful set of switches, a sound system, a DVD player, and a collection of CDs and DVDs.

Flipping a few switches, Adam dimmed the main light until the room was completely dark. Slowly, the space came alive with shifting colours—deep red, green, blue, and purple. The seamless blending of colours gave Julie the uncanny impression that the room had its own consciousness.

As Adam adjusted controls, music began to play. A CD of Native American meditative rhythms filled the air, the drumbeats reverberating through Julie's body. His collection ranged widely, from whale songs, ocean surf, and rainfall, to opera, instrumental pieces, chants, and tribal drumming.

The lights danced in harmony with the rhythms, their tempo changing with each colour shift. Then the TV screen lit up, displaying waterfalls in majestic detail. As the music softened, the natural sounds grew clearer—the roar of water, the rustle of rainforest life, birds with radiant plumage breaking the stillness with their ethereal calls.

Julie was entranced. Just as she adjusted to the tranquil scene, she caught sight of a flicker of crimson and blue—a butterfly perched on a bright yellow blossom. It suddenly took flight, the camera following its erratic path across meadows and valleys. For a moment, Julie felt she had become the butterfly, soaring freely.

Smiling, she turned to Adam. "I wasn't expecting that!" she said loudly, then blushed when she realized the music had stopped.

The room was quiet again. Still gripping her shopping bag, she asked, "What do your clients usually do in here to relax?"

"Some sit and watch scenes from nature, paired with music. Others recline and simply enjoy the lights with soft sounds in the background—blue and green are the most popular colours," Adam explained, again glancing at her bag.

"And this helps relieve their stress?"

"Yes. Most clients say they feel ten times better afterward."

"Do you guide them, or are they left on their own?"

"Carol usually helps with that," Adam said, retrieving a clipboard from the cabinet. He showed Julie a set of colour-coded sheets, each offering instructions for different goals—stress management, confidence building, quitting smoking, overcoming addiction. Clients could choose for themselves, or Adam would suggest an approach and Carol would pass it along.

Julie tilted her head with a knowing smile. "What about exploring their spiritual or psychic side? Maybe even connecting with their supernatural self?"

Adam caught her tone but wasn't sure what she was implying. "Well, some clients do describe spiritual experiences and leave feeling rejuvenated," he said carefully. He felt slightly uneasy but tried not to show it.

"That's good," Julie replied. "But I'm talking about something deeper—helping people embrace their paranormal nature and connect with their Other Self."

"Oh… I see," Adam answered, though he really didn't. He wanted to wrap up the meeting and get back to his busy routine.

Julie, however, wasn't finished. Hugging her shopping bag as if it contained something precious, she said, "This setup is wonderful, but it's a shame you only use it for stress relief."

Adam decided Carol should hear this directly. She was the one who managed client sessions in the room, since Adam's own schedule rarely allowed him to supervise. He called her in, and Carol entered with notepad and pencil in hand.

Julie then explained that certain colours and rhythmic sounds could shift people from the physical realm into a spiritual one. She personally used her musical instrument to clear her mind and reach such a state.

Finally, she revealed what she had been carrying: a large, colourful tambourine. Carol's eyes lit up. "I haven't seen one of these in years! Look at those shiny jingles," she exclaimed, stepping closer. Julie demonstrated, shaking the instrument and tapping the drumhead with ease, the sound rich and lively. Carol even began to sway to the rhythm.

"Are you in a band?" Adam joked, laughing.

Julie climbed into the reclining chair and fumbled with the controls, asking how to tilt it back into a semi-lying position. Carol helped position it until Julie was comfortable. Julie closed her eyes, resting the tambourine on her stomach. Every so often she tapped or shook it, producing gentle, harmonious sounds, before laying it back down again, synchronizing the rhythm with her heartbeat.

Adam and Carol exchanged looks, silently agreeing to let her continue in peace.

"The tambourine's beat helps me enter a deeper state quickly," Julie explained. "It's like a key that opens the door to a hidden realm inside me."

Carol wondered aloud whether a spiritual state could be compared to simply having a stress-free mind. Julie responded by saying she saw a clear distinction between the two—being free of stress and experiencing a spiritual state were entirely different conditions.

"If someone is under stress," Julie explained, "they can't reach an ideal balance of mind and body. And without entering a spiritual or blissful state, they'll never truly grow or evolve as they're meant to. They will remain shackled to external forces, never free to choose their own path."

She paused briefly before continuing. "In fact, they end up shutting away a significant part of their true self. Their real potential stays hidden, untouched, and so does their humanity. Honestly, they might as well join the FAUNA group out there."

Julie went on to explain that only certain people, those with the proper genetic structure, possess the ability to enter hidden and extraordinary dimensions where boundless wisdom about life and its true purpose can be found. Those who awaken to this truth also discover that they are inherently connected to the very core of nature itself. Yet, countless others remain excluded, unable to access the quantum and electromagnetic layers within their own being, nor attune themselves to the universal field that unites the past, present, and future. These individuals, she said, are missing vital elements within their DNA and simply do not contain the essential codes. Julie described them as FAUNA-types—beings destined to remain outside the quantum realm where unconscious energies and unseen waves exist in harmony. They will never possess the keys that unlock the gateways to the true kingdom or the rightful frequencies of existence.

Adam and Carol looked on in silence.

Carol, looking bewildered, finally asked, "So how do you know if you have the right stuff—the right kind of genetic material?"

Julie was ready with an answer. "You'll feel it. There's an inborn awareness; a natural understanding of how the world operates and a deeper knowing that there's something more to one's existence. From early childhood, you'll sense you're different—your thoughts move in ways your peers' don't. You'll find yourself at ease navigating both the visible and invisible layers of reality. Your knowledge won't come only from the physical world but also from that mysterious somewhere that is neither here nor there, yet is undeniably real. You will struggle with unnatural conformity." She paused to breathe deeply, then went on. "This special material is often carried by just one or two family members and passed down through generations. Depending on their DNA, some will have a sharp vision of the supernatural, others only a faint glimpse, and some none at all. That is why human beings are so varied and why true peace on Earth can never exist."

Carol's only response was a stunned 'Wow.' Still with pencil in hand and nothing written down so far, she seemed to want to say something but then didn't. Julie noticed and gently urged her to speak.

"I might be wrong, but it sounds like you're saying only the rich, educated, or healthy people have the right stuff?" Carol asked carefully.

Julie smiled knowingly. "I understand why you'd think that, but no. Many Indigenous or so-called primitive or very poor people, even those unwell or without formal education, can be born with the right wiring to sense the unseen. Wealth, health, or social standing mean nothing. What matters is perception—how you see the world, how you interpret its patterns. A humble, open mind is crucial for grasping the paranormal."

"So psychic ability is like any other family trait—passed down? Meaning you could be royalty in a castle or homeless living under a bridge and still have it?"

"Yes."

"And if the family line is particularly psychic, their children are more likely to inherit those gifts?"

"Yes."

"So those spiritually gifted people would be able to talk to the dead and deliver messages from the grave?"

Julie's expression hardened. She frowned as though Carol had crossed a line. "Absolutely not! No one can communicate with the dead," she said firmly, giving Carol a piercing look. "Once life ends, it ends. Anyone claiming otherwise is not being truthful." She exhaled sharply and straightened in her chair, her plump frame shifting awkwardly as she clutched her tambourine.

"When a person dies, their life force departs. The body becomes empty, stripped of memory or connection. That energy reverts to something primitive, guided only by instinct to move toward its destined place." With that, Julie hopped off the chair and slid her tambourine back into the oversized plastic bag she'd brought.

Adam and Carol continued standing there, frozen in silence. Realising she may have spoken too bluntly, Julie quickly softened her tone. "Sorry if I sounded harsh. I need to be gentler about these subjects. I usually don't talk about them, but with you two, I feel I can." She turned to Carol with concern and asked if she had recently lost someone close, assuming that must have been why Carol brought up the afterlife.

"Oh no, not at all—I was just making conversation!" Carol said hastily, now more confused than ever. "Still, most people won't believe what you're saying," she added uneasily.

"I know," Julie replied. "But that's their issue. When they die, they will see the truth."

"And what will they see?" Carol couldn't resist asking.

Julie chuckled. "Nothing. They'll see nothing—because they're dead!" She burst out laughing. Carol suddenly realised how foolish her question had sounded, though she had expected a more thoughtful reply.

They soon returned to the waiting area outside the office, shifting their discussion back to the De-Stress room, where Julie described how meditation and guided imagery could help people connect with their Other Selves. Julie's psychic talents were undeniable—she was known as a remote viewer, able to replay past events for evidence and insight. Yet Carol remained unsettled by her dismissal of life after death. How could someone with such extraordinary gifts reject the idea of an afterlife? Wasn't that the whole point of psychic phenomena? These contradictions lingered in Carol's mind long after, haunting her with questions she couldn't shake.

Julie settled comfortably in Adam's office, intent on discussing the process of contacting his Other Self. Adam accepted reluctantly, realising he had little choice since she had left him none. She wasted no time and launched into her explanation. She told him that once he understood the steps, the practice would be straightforward. The first requirement was to dig deep within, using guided meditation and other methods to calm his mind and body. He had to picture himself entering a state of blissful relaxation, an essential part of the journey.

Julie explained that the goal was to detach from the physical world and move into a passive mental state, much like meditation, where one becomes open to whatever might unfold. After his body and mind were fully relaxed, he would need to drift toward sleep— though not completely. He had to enter the twilight state, the thin borderland between waking and sleeping, where his body edged toward sleep, but his awareness remained active. This state, existing between reality and the dream world, was where he must direct his consciousness to leave the body. From there, he should imagine travelling into vast space—featureless, boundless, and empty of distraction. Only his awareness should remain, no longer tied to flesh and bones but existing as pure energy, surrounded by calm and serenity. The intention was for Adam to feel absorbed into this emptiness, to feel safe and fully at peace there. Then, he was to visualise another presence nearby and to draw that energy towards him—a current of energy moving through the dark. It did not come with shape or sound, nor with anything the eyes or ears could catch. It was known only through awareness, a recognition that stirred somewhere deep inside him. There was no fear, only the strange comfort of familiarity, as if he had always known it. Unseen, as he himself was unseen, they met—two currents of invisible force converging in the vast silence.

And yet, both would recognise each other. It would be felt, known, and trusted, as though bound to him by something ancient. The connection would be as strong as family, like a soul-long bond. In truth, the entity was part of Adam himself—a reflection of his own consciousness. Like a friend lost and rediscovered, it was his Other Self, the missing piece, a cosmic counterpart that most people have but never acknowledge.

Julie went on to explain that Adam's Other Self was constantly with him. At certain moments it might appear close at his side, while in the next it could be far off in another dimension, yet still connected to him in the way quantum entanglement binds particles. She added that some people think of it as their Soul Mate, others call it a Guardian Angel, and for Image Carriers it is known simply as the Other Self.

She continued, "That invisible aspect of us is an extension of our humanity, a divine gift. When we work with our Other Selves, we gain knowledge from both familiar and mysterious sources, elevating us beyond the ordinary. But like learning to walk or create with our hands, we must learn to engage with this force. Our Other Selves are aware of us, though we rarely understand them. They exist because of us, and we guide them with our thoughts, instincts, and actions. They are celestial extensions of our being that appear when we are born and continue with us throughout our lives."

Julie went on, "Every person has this ethereal twin. When it warns us through intuition, we dismiss it; when it seeks to reach out, we ignore it; when it manifests in front of us, we react with fear. The great irony is that we are the ones who summon it—through thoughts, impulses, quantum resonance, and connections not yet understood in this dimension. But caution is needed, for sinister entities may attempt to masquerade as your Other Self. If one is unprepared, it is easy to be deceived, manipulated, or even overtaken by an impostor."

She paused, letting Adam absorb her words, then added, "Our electromagnetic field, surrounding every living cell and encircling the entire body, is a vast information network. It is constantly communicating with others and with our Other Selves. These energies cannot exist without us—they are bound to our spirit until our final breath. Whether we realise it or not, we are always guiding them."

Julie's attention drifted to a plant by the window, and she walked over as she spoke again. "Image Carriers know how to call their Other Selves home. Most people, however, remain unaware they even have such a companion. Yet your cosmic double longs for your recognition. It seeks your attention, your trust, and your approval. It wishes to join you, to protect you, to restore your sense of completeness. Above all, it wants to come home. But forces exist that would prefer you never discover it. They wish to keep you powerless, unaware, drone like. Only those who embrace their Other Selves can step fully into their true strength and destiny."

Julie promised Adam that she would write down the process so he could share it with others who wished to meet their Other Selves. She spoke of the need to go within in order to reach outside, which puzzled Adam at first. But the more he reflected, the more it became clear. To disconnect from the outer world, he had to turn inward and find the inner doorway that opened to the greater spiritual landscape. It was not the physical body that could pass through the eye of a needle, but the subtle energy of the soul. To Adam, this meant releasing consciousness from the body and using imagination, energy, and focus to cross from matter into spirit.

When Julie finally departed, Adam felt an unexpected lightness. He could not help but wonder—was that thing he had seen in his bedroom years ago, struggling to take form, could it have been his Other Self? And if so, what message had it been trying to deliver?

Chapter Sixteen
Private Investigations

Evelyn noted her strange gait—it reminded her of a praying mantis…

Evelyn and Veronica reached their destination the following morning. The motel was called *The Bearded Man*. It stood at the corner of Lantern and Sword Streets. It was about ten o'clock, and the place seemed to have just opened its doors. The two women stepped inside. There were no patrons yet; the building felt empty. Veronica noticed a man scrubbing large metal trays behind the bar. Evelyn trailed her as she approached him.

When Veronica called out, the man jumped, nearly toppling into the tray since his back had been turned. He smiled awkwardly and asked if they wanted a room upstairs, clearly aware they weren't there to drink alcohol so early in the day. Evelyn asked about Lucy without hesitation—she had nothing to lose. To their surprise, the man pointed toward the stairway leading to the upper floor.

"Is she here?" Evelyn asked, her eyes wide.

"Yes, she came in just before you. Didn't see her leave, so she should still be up there," the sweaty bartender replied.

Evelyn and Veronica froze, stunned. They hadn't expected such an answer. Was it the same Lucy, or only coincidence? Evelyn's patience broke, and she tugged Veronica's arm, steering her away from the counter. They set their bags at a table near the staircase. The man behind the bar shrugged when they abruptly walked off, then returned to scrubbing trays.

Evelyn decided she would go upstairs alone, instructing Veronica to wait below. If Lucy—or any woman—came down, Veronica was to stall her until Evelyn returned. If anyone suspicious went up instead, Veronica was to follow and warn her.

Veronica retreated to a corner seat. The motel was dimly lit; the high windows let in only thin shafts of daylight. The air reeked of cleaning fluid mixed with old liquor and tobacco smoke, and the building itself seemed ancient, possibly centuries old.

Evelyn disappeared upstairs. A minute later, she reappeared, looking unsettled. Veronica watched her speak briefly to the bartender before Evelyn turned back toward the stairs and vanished again. He had told her Lucy was staying on the third floor in one of the executive suites—there were only two rooms up there.

Evelyn soon stood outside one such suite. The door was half open, and movement inside was audible. She pushed it open and saw a young, dark-skinned woman hurriedly packing. She looked in a rush, darting around the room. Evelyn instinctively felt she had found the right person and stepped inside, shutting the door quietly behind her.

"Lucy?" she called.

The girl jumped, startled, and spun to face the intruder. Shock flickered across her features.

"Can I help you?" she asked, her body shifting uneasily.

Evelyn noticed how alarmingly thin she was—gaunt, skeletal. She seemed no older than twenty-one or twenty-two, with flawless skin and striking, doll-like beauty. Her enormous blue eyes sparkled, commanding Evelyn's attention, though her fragile frame looked unhealthy.

Evelyn thought she resembled a miniature model, barely five feet tall.

"I'm looking for Lucy," Evelyn said gently, trying to appear friendly.

"Lucy?" the girl echoed, not confirming the name, but Evelyn was certain she was the one.

"I know you are Lucy. And I know you knew my daughter. I only need to ask a few questions, then I will leave."

The girl glanced at the shut door behind Evelyn, realising it blocked her escape.

"Your daughter?" she said, continuing to stuff colourful clothing into an orange and blue bag.

"Yes, my daughter Susan. I know you knew her." Evelyn's tone was firm. The young woman, though radiant in her youth, was clearly anxious and calculating her chances of slipping past the strange woman in her apartment. Evelyn tightened her hold on the room, snatching the keys from the side table. "Lucy, I'm not leaving until you tell me about my daughter. And neither are you."

Fear flashed in Lucy's eyes. Her bags were only half-packed, and a white satchel lay open on the floor, filled with wigs—black, blonde, brown, curly, straight, even pink. Disguises? Evelyn wondered what this girl was up to.

Weighing her options, Lucy realised the erratic intruder might be dangerous. She took the keys; she is blocking the door. She looks unhinged. The quickest way out was to comply. Then make a quick getaway.

"I can't talk about Susan," she blurted while continuing to pack, her thin limbs moving with insect-like precision. Evelyn noted her strange gait—it reminded her of a praying mantis.

"What do you mean you can't talk about Susan?" Evelyn asked, inching closer but still blocking the door.

Lucy's composure cracked. Tears spilled as she pleaded, begging Evelyn to leave before she got into trouble. Her luminous eyes seemed innocent, but Evelyn wasn't swayed.

"What are you talking about? What do you mean you can't talk about Susan?"

"I can't tell you!" Lucy sobbed. "Please, just leave!"

"I'm not going anywhere," Evelyn snapped. "Tell me what you know about my daughter's death."

Lucy sank onto the bed, wiping tears from her cheeks.

"Susan is… dead?" she whispered, stricken.

"Yes. Susan is dead, and Sabrena is in the hospital fighting for her life," Evelyn said sharply.

Lucy looked stunned. She sat in her vivid outfit—lime-green cotton top clinging to her thin bony shoulders, white shorts with a golden sash, and turquoise-studded gold earrings glittering from her ears. She was dazzling, yet fragile, and whether her grief was real or staged, Evelyn couldn't tell.

"What do you know, Lucy?" Evelyn asked softly, almost maternal.

"Nothing," Lucy muttered, eyes lowered. "I didn't know they would hurt her."

"They? Who are *they*?" Evelyn's voice rose, making Lucy squirm. She dabbed her tears with a bright yellow cloth.

"Those people," Lucy whispered. "I don't know who they are."

"Why would they want to kill Susan?"

"They thought she overheard their plans," Lucy came clean.

"Plans? What plans?" Evelyn folded her arms, taking a step back.

"They have awful secrets," Lucy explained shakily. "They feared Susan had heard too much. I swore she hadn't, I told them so!" Her voice grew sharp with impatience.

"Secrets…" Evelyn said, pacing the room, her mind spinning. Who were these people? Could they truly be responsible?

"They even tried to blame my parents," Lucy said suddenly, guilt clouding her face. "But my parents are just employees. They had nothing to do with it."

"Your parents? How are they involved?" Evelyn demanded, cheeks flushing red.

"They are not involved!" Lucy snapped. "They only did what they were told. They were paid for their work—it had nothing to do with Susan's death."

Evelyn struggled to process it. What about Sabrena's role?

"And Sabrena? What do you know of her?"

"I don't know anyone by that name," Lucy replied quickly, now clutching a fresh purple handkerchief.

"Then why blame your parents if they weren't involved?" Evelyn pressed.

"They're not my real parents. They were used by those powerful people. My parents knew nothing about Susan." Lucy stood, fetched a bright pink towel from the bathroom, and slowly folded it, avoiding Evelyn's eyes.

"So, you're adopted?" Evelyn asked. Lucy said nothing, staring down.

Finally, she grabbed her handbag, slipping away the handkerchief. "I can't escape those people. If I could, I would. If they knew I was talking to you, they would terminate me too." She straightened, hastily packing as though expecting someone's arrival at any moment.

"Did they tamper with my daughter's car to cause the accident?" Evelyn asked suddenly, her voice heavy with regret.

"I don't know much; all I heard was they arranged for someone in Hungary to deal with her," Lucy replied, her tone now clearer, shifting from helpless victim to a woman in control. The tears had stopped, and she no longer looked as fragile.

"Deal with her?"

"Yes, one of their assassins, the kind who makes problems disappear. That's what I overheard. They have these people everywhere!"

"What people?"

"You don't understand how vast and powerful they are. They could wipe out both of us right now, and no one would ever know!" Lucy's manner grew firm as she began gathering her bright belongings with surprising speed and determination.

"How did they kill Susan?" Evelyn asked reluctantly, unsure whether she was ready for the answer.

"The assassin was meant to stage a car accident. I thought they only wanted to frighten her…"

"So that assassin was in Cape Town, on the mountain, that day?" Evelyn asked.

"Yes, that is what I overheard, but the plan didn't go smoothly. I had to pretend I wasn't eavesdropping otherwise I may be next... I did hear them talk about some car going over the edge to make sure. I didn't know it was about Susan at that time."

"So, you already knew?" Evelyn shot back angrily.

"No!" Lucy's voice cracked as it rose, sharp enough to make Evelyn flinch. She locked eyes with her, unblinking. "I only heard about the accident afterward. Like I told you, they didn't even know I was listening. No one told me anything. I overheard them talking—by chance. I didn't even know it was Susan at first, though…" Her breath heavy; a flicker of guilt passed over her face. "Though I had my suspicions. But what could I do? For my own protection, I forced it out of my mind—until now."

Her bags now packed, Lucy stood taller, showing neither weakness nor fear. "I have told you all I know," she said firmly. "I have to go—I'm expected somewhere else." Evelyn, despite everything, felt sympathy for her. Lucy's fragile frame seemed too small for her large head, suggesting some medical condition, yet she was still strikingly attractive. Dressed in fine clothes, she gave the impression of someone wealthy or famous, someone who might travel the world modelling and mingling with the rich and famous.

Before Lucy left, Evelyn asked one last question. "Are Graham and Deborah Middleton involved in Susan's death?"

"I told you, I don't know who they are. I only heard the names online when my parents were talking. I never saw their faces—they were blurred by security filters."

Evelyn quickly produced her notepad and asked Lucy if they could exchange numbers in case she needed to speak again. She also felt a strange compulsion to protect Lucy, suspecting her adoptive parents had exploited her. Evelyn couldn't help but imagine Lucy had perhaps been abducted—or purchased—from a poor family in some third-world country.

Lucy recited her number, which Evelyn jotted down. Evelyn then gave her own, Veronica's mobile number, which Lucy entered on her orange-and-purple phone with astonishing speed, barely glancing at the screen.

Moving briskly, Lucy searched the apartment for final items, then asked Evelyn for the keys she carried. Evelyn handed them over, and Lucy instructed her to lock up when leaving. Moments later, Lucy was gone. Evelyn, still unsettled, decided to search the apartment for anything useful. Finding nothing, she left and hurried after Lucy to say goodbye and express her wish to remain in touch.

Downstairs, Evelyn saw Veronica sitting in a beam of sunlight near the window. The light from the street-facing window encircled her head and shoulders like a glowing halo, giving the moment a dreamlike quality. Lucy was already gone.

Veronica seemed relieved that Evelyn had tracked Lucy down, and she immediately asked what Lucy had revealed. When Evelyn shared that Lucy had confirmed her suspicions about Susan's death, Veronica was oddly calm, not nearly as shaken as Evelyn expected. Detached and aloof, she gave the impression her mind was elsewhere. Meeting Lucy didn't surprise her much. They agreed to return to the hotel.

As they were leaving, an attractive middle-aged man in a tailored grey suit entered. Evelyn was delighted to recognize Cyril. He paused when he saw them, his eyes locking on Evelyn. "We shouldn't keep running into each other like this," he said, sounding unconvincing, almost awkward.

"Cyril!" Evelyn exclaimed, giggling nervously. "What are you doing here?" Realizing she might have been too direct, she quickly added, "Sorry, none of my business." She smiled shyly, not knowing where to put her hands.

"That's all right," Cyril replied warmly. "This is like my home away from home. I've got a comfortable room upstairs." He beamed at her.

Veronica hesitated, unsure whether to introduce herself or slip away. Cyril, perhaps realizing how intently he had been focusing on Evelyn, shifted toward Veronica and offered an embarrassed nod.

"Hi," he said awkwardly. He went on to explain that he always stayed at the Bearded Man because he loved the food and atmosphere, which reminded him of home. Though he sometimes stayed with Graham and Deborah, he preferred privacy when in London. He added that he was returning to Germany at the weekend and warmly invited Evelyn and her friend to visit at any time.

On the way back to the Royal Doze, Veronica noticed a dramatic change in Evelyn. She was laughing more, cracking silly jokes, and even giggling loudly—behaviour that irritated Veronica, who wondered whether Evelyn was in love.

Back at their hotel room, the mood shifted. Veronica was quiet and subdued, as though something weighed on her. Despite their remarkable discoveries with Lucy, she acted as if the day had been ordinary. Evelyn, puzzled, asked her directly what was wrong. Veronica insisted everything was fine but confided she planned to return to South Africa as soon as possible—hopefully the next day if she could secure a flight. She wanted Evelyn to come with her.

Four days later, after Veronica had already left, Evelyn herself boarded a flight back to South Africa. She had settled her monthly bill with Deborah and cancelled her lease. Surprisingly, Deborah took the news well, almost encouraging Evelyn that returning home was the right decision. The pace of recent events left Evelyn dizzy. She longed for rest.

Darkness fell, then lifted. Evelyn thought she was in bed about to drift off, only to realize she was in a cramped, dim office. Papers, a half-empty bottle of whisky, a glass, and a filthy ashtray cluttered the desk. Dust coated everything. Male voices came from outside the door. Feeling she shouldn't be there, she frantically searched for a hiding place. Finding none, she pressed herself against the wall behind the door. Two men entered, their backs to her, allowing her to slip silently into the hallway. She now found herself in a vast warehouse.

The hallway opened onto endless rows of pallet-stacked boxes. Against one wall sat a desk with a small filing cabinet, tools, tape, jars, and a clipboard. Evelyn snatched the clipboard and saw invoices detailing shipments of boxes to different countries. Voices drew near again—she was trapped. Her only chance was to crouch behind a large crate near the desk.

From her hiding place, she heard one man bark, "We need to move the East side shipments immediately! Another four hundred thousand units arrive Tuesday—we need that space. I don't care how long it takes, just get it done!"

Her dream shattered when she awoke on the plane. A little girl, maybe eight years old, leaned precariously over the seat in front, staring at her. Evelyn realized she was still en route to Cape Town. The child chattered noisily with a woman beside her, disturbing Evelyn's sleep. Scowling, Evelyn sat up, irritated; she disliked children, especially ones who intruded like this.

Again, those boxes, she thought. What did they mean? Sleeping pills? Something worse? And always the voices—different accents, echoing in her mind. She pulled out her notepad and quickly scribbled down everything she remembered.

At last, the plane landed. Waiting at the airport was Veronica, looking weary and tense. Evelyn noticed but didn't comment. They drove silently, a long stretch, back to Veronica's country home.

There, Veronica busied herself with tasks while Evelyn napped to fight the jet lag. When she awoke, she found Veronica packing clothes for a trip. Evelyn didn't pry, sensing she needed space, and instead kept to herself. After an hour reading in her room, Evelyn went outside to her favourite chair on the back veranda, quietly observing as Veronica continued to rush about. Evelyn couldn't help but wonder—where was Veronica going?

After what felt like an eternity, Evelyn finally heard the phone ring loudly inside. She heard Veronica answering it, arranging to collect someone. Evelyn grew curious—who was Veronica going to pick up? Was it Sabrena? But then she realised Veronica hadn't once mentioned Sabrena. A troubling thought crossed her mind—was the girl even alive? Hopefully not dead. Evelyn felt she had to find out. Perhaps this explained Veronica's odd behaviour. Yet before she could think further, a harsh sound intruded. It resembled someone running an electric polisher. Strange…

Gradually, Evelyn became aware, surfacing into consciousness. That same irritating noise continued, the abrasive hum of an industrial floor polisher. Its shrill echo rattled inside her skull. Did the cleaner now enter her apartment, shouldn't he be outside in the hallway? She squinted and scanned her surroundings, yet nothing was familiar. She was no longer in her apartment in London. That's right, she thought, I am back in Cape Town. But to her horror, she was not back at Veronica's place either. She appeared to be in a hospital ward, lying flat in a bed. As her eyes focused, she noticed an elderly, stocky man in overalls working the polisher near her bedside. The early morning light streamed in through the blinds.

Confused, Evelyn looked around, still lost in bewilderment. Abruptly, the grating whine of the polisher stopped. Silence filled the room. The older man in overalls stood frozen, eyes fixed on her. He stared; she stared back. Then the polisher clattered to the floor as he let it go and bolted from the room in panic. Moments later, he returned with a nurse, followed closely by another nurse and then a doctor. In an instant, Evelyn became the centre of attention, surrounded by people firing questions at her—her name, the date, if she knew where she was. But Evelyn remained mute, frightened, and utterly disoriented.

It was then she noticed the machinery. Strange devices buzzed softly around her. Adhesive pads clung to her scalp, wires trailing down to monitors. Tubes fed into her arms, taped in place. Realising this, anxiety flared, and she panicked. She tried to rise from the bed, but nurses and the doctor pressed her down, urging her to stay still.

"You are safe here, calm down," one nurse said firmly. "How many fingers am I holding up?" asked the young male doctor, raising three thin bony fingers. His accent carried the tones of South Africa.

"Do you know the date?" he continued with his rapid-fire questions. More staff filed into the room, peering curiously at her.

Then a deep, commanding voice thundered from the doorway, startling everyone. The on-call matron barked at them to lower their voices and clear the room at once. She was a solidly built woman in her fifties, arms folded, radiating authority. The group dispersed quickly, subdued. She ordered a younger nurse to remain and closed the door. Approaching Evelyn, she introduced herself with a faint smile. "So, you've finally woken up. I'm Margaret."

Margaret was old-school—efficient, strict, no time for nonsense, but reliable. Order returned under her watch. Evelyn looked around: three empty beds stood unused; she was the sole patient in the ward. Her throat felt raw, her mouth dry, words difficult to form. Margaret gestured for the nurse to fetch water while she checked Evelyn's pulse and machines. As Evelyn sipped, she noticed Margaret jotting notes on a clipboard at the foot of the bed, pausing now and then to check her watch. Finally, Evelyn managed a faint whisper.

"Where am I?"

"You're in Cape Town's finest hospital, my dear," Margaret replied with crisp assurance, her accent distinct.

"Why?" Evelyn's voice strained.

"Because you had a breakdown," Margaret explained firmly. "But you're safe now—nothing to worry about."

"A breakdown?" Evelyn repeated in disbelief.

"Yes, but it's behind you now. You'll be fine," the nurse reassured her. The younger nurse echoed this gently, stroking Evelyn's arm. "You have been away for a long time. We are glad to see you awake again."

"Away? What do you mean, away?" Evelyn asked, fear creeping in.

"That's enough talking for today," Margaret cut in. "Rest now. I'll return later." She signalled the nurse to follow her out.

Evelyn lay back, dazed, still half-convinced she was dreaming. Yet the aches in her body proved otherwise. She scanned the strange ward, questions piling up. How had she ended up here? What did "breakdown" mean? Did it happen after London? Where was Veronica? Was Susan alive or was she dead? Anxiety nibbled at her chest.

Half-asleep, she heard voices. The doctor had returned, speaking with the young nurse. He leaned over, peering through dark-rimmed glasses. "Good morning," he said assertively. "Any pain? No? Colour's better. Good." He rattled off questions, barely pausing. Then with a quick smile, he promised to check in later and disappeared down the corridor.

The nurse offered Evelyn tea or biscuits, but she declined. Food was the last thing on her mind. Then Evelyn remembered.

"Yes, nurse? Do you know about my daughter? And how long have I been here?" But the nurse only smiled kindly, assuring her the doctors would explain later. Evelyn pressed on: "Then what about my friend? Veronica?" The nurse's smile widened. "She's on her way. We phoned her as soon as you woke."

By midday, Veronica arrived with the nurse. She hovered at the doorway, transfixed. For a full minute, the two women stared at each other silently. The nurse excused herself, whispering to Veronica, "Go ahead, talk." Alone, Veronica broke, rushing to Evelyn's side.

"Oh God, Evelyn, you terrified me!" she cried, scolding before bursting into tears.

"What's wrong with me? What happened?" Evelyn demanded, struggling to sit up. Veronica hurried to support her with pillows.

"You had a mental breakdown," Veronica said softly.

"A breakdown?" Evelyn gave a faint laugh, expecting it to be a joke. "Seriously?"

"Yes. Very serious. We had to bring you here."

Evelyn frowned. "I keep hearing hospital, but where am I?"

"You're in hospital. You've been here three months… in a sort of coma," Veronica explained gravely.

"Three months? A coma?" Evelyn gasped, disbelieving. Yet Veronica never lied. The truth showed in her weary face—she looked older, drained. Evelyn's thoughts spiralled, panic rising, breath shortening. The room spun. Veronica, alarmed, fled to fetch the nurse. Quickly, they calmed her, guiding her breathing until she settled. Still shaken, Evelyn noticed her friend's troubled expression—Veronica seemed burdened, hiding something.

As Veronica lingered at the foot of the bed, the nurse touched her arm comfortingly, then left them alone. Veronica spoke gently: Evelyn might be able to go home soon. "Home," Evelyn whispered with relief. "Yes, I want to go home." She leaned back and drifted into sleep.

The next morning Veronica returned, having booked a nearby hotel. Driving back and forth was too much. Entering the ward, she saw Evelyn spooning mushy cereal—banana-flavoured baby food. Evelyn disliked it but knew progress meant release, possibly by Friday. She longed to escape the hospital, haunted by memories of Australian mental wards.

Veronica was surprised to see her upright, colour restored. Evelyn looked far better than expected. Veronica forced a smile but couldn't mask her unease. Evelyn noticed—she knew her too well. After finishing her cereal, Evelyn asked what was wrong. Veronica dodged her question, promising they'd talk once home. But Evelyn persisted. Veronica left briefly, returning with the nurse. Evelyn stared at them both, baffled.

Finally, Veronica asked what Evelyn last remembered before hospital. Evelyn paused, her memory fractured. Was it after London, or when she first arrived at Veronica's house? She faltered, confused. Veronica exchanged a look with the nurse, then asked gently: did Evelyn know about Susan's death? Evelyn froze. Slowly, fragments of memory stirred. Susan was gone. After a pause, the nurse softly confirmed it: her daughter, Susan, had passed away. Did Evelyn remember that?

Evelyn was startled by what she was hearing and tried to make sense of why they were treating her like a child. She was equally unsettled by Veronica's odd behaviour. Why was Veronica acting this way? The nurse gave a quiet smile and stepped aside, subtly encouraging Veronica to keep speaking with Evelyn. But Evelyn quickly realised that if she wanted to be discharged by the end of the week, she had to play their game. She had to pretend she was normal. Evelyn was well-practised at these games, having spent much of her younger years in psychiatric wards, where she learned how to convince doctors and psychiatrists that she was ready to be released. She smiled warmly and said she already knew about Susan's death and would talk about it after leaving the hospital.

At first Evelyn thought Susan might still be alive, that perhaps her so-called breakdown had confused her, but she soon accepted that Susan really was dead. The nurse eventually left them alone, and Evelyn motioned Veronica closer, asking directly what was going on. Veronica admitted they were worried she might suffer another mental breakdown because of Susan's death.

Evelyn was stunned and reminded Veronica that she had known Susan was dead—that was the reason she had gone to London, to find out more. Veronica stepped back and gave her a frosty look. "What are you talking about, Evelyn?" she asked impatiently.

"That's why I went to London. Remember?" Evelyn whispered, not wanting the nurses outside to overhear.

"London?" Veronica sounded concerned. "You didn't go to London." She paused before repeating, "Evelyn, you didn't go to London. Why are you saying this?"

"Yes, I did. And you came with me, Veronica. We went looking for Lucy at that bar, don't you remember?"

Veronica fell silent, staring down, torn between correcting her or letting her believe it. In the end, her better judgement took over.

"Evelyn, you had a mental breakdown a few days after Susan was at my place. Remember when those men came and removed her body? That was three months ago," she said gently. "You lay in bed for days, barely conscious, not speaking or responding. They finally brought you here, and you've been in this hospital ever since."

"A breakdown?" Evelyn gave a short smile. "Veronica, now you're frightening me. What about Lucy, and London, and—?"

"Evelyn! Enough! You had a mental breakdown. Everyone says it's because of Susan's death. There was no London. And who is this Lucy you keep mentioning?"

"What are you saying, Veronica?"

"I'm saying you had a mental breakdown. There is no London, no Lucy. You came here three months ago after Susan's death. We cremated her near Cape Town, and the very next day you collapsed. You've been here ever since."

Evelyn felt a chill. Veronica's voice carried frustration, and Evelyn realised she had to be careful. She didn't want to be locked away again. Deciding she could no longer trust her closest friend, she quickly agreed with her. She said it had all been a dream, that there was no London or Lucy, and that she had simply had a nervous breakdown but was much better now. Veronica, relieved, believed her.

Over the next few days, Evelyn improved by saying only what people wanted to hear. Veronica, too, seemed to relax, her worried look fading as her usual self returned. By Friday morning, everyone was pleased with Evelyn's recovery, and the psychiatrist came to assess her for release.

What followed shook Evelyn deeply, and she instantly knew she must stay calm and rational, or risk being confined indefinitely.

That morning, after breakfast, Veronica and Evelyn were looking at photographs of Susan when a middle-aged woman entered the room. Her name was Deborah, a psychiatrist at the hospital. Evelyn's heart nearly stopped—Deborah Middleton from the UK stood smiling at her, asking how she was feeling.

For a moment Evelyn couldn't respond, wondering if she was still in some kind of coma. Veronica noticed the sudden change in her mood and stepped slightly closer but gave the psychiatrist space to speak directly to Evelyn while keeping a watchful eye on her.

"I'm fine," Evelyn forced out, trying to sound calm and collected.

"Do you remember any of our sessions together?"

"Sessions?" Evelyn repeated softly, confusion flashing across her features. Her heart hammered against her ribs, threatening to give her away. She inhaled deeply, steadying herself. She had to remember—this was all part of the game. Appear calm. Appear confident. Appear normal.

"Yes," Deborah said gently. "I came often to see you here. Sometimes, when you were well enough, you even came to my office. We spoke about many things." She talked to Evelyn with the ease of a longtime acquaintance, smiling reassuringly.

"When I was well enough? What do you mean by that?" Evelyn asked carefully.

"When you were more aware of your surroundings," Deborah explained warmly. "At times you lay silent for hours, unresponsive.

But there were moments when you stirred and were more aware, even if you didn't speak. I always felt that some of what I said reached you. I knew it was only a matter of time before you came back to us."

"What was wrong with me?" Evelyn asked quietly.

"That is still a mystery," Deborah admitted. "Perhaps a semi-coma, or a trance brought on by the trauma of losing your daughter. Some doctors suspect another condition altogether. We even tried contacting your doctors in Australia, but with little success."

"Who did you contact in Australia?"

"Don't worry about that for now," Deborah said. "What matters is whether you're ready to return home and live your life again."

She asked Evelyn a series of simple questions that felt like traps, but Evelyn answered smoothly. When the psychiatrist asked about Susan's death, Evelyn froze, unsure of the right response. Nothing seemed stable anymore; truth and illusion blurred. She glanced at Veronica, who looked at her with hope. Evelyn then calmly told Deborah that she knew how Susan died but preferred not to discuss it right now. Her subdued tone convinced Deborah.

"Alright, Evelyn," Deborah said kindly. "Just remember, no one is to blame here. It was a tragic accident. Those mountain roads are notorious." After a pause, she added, "Her friend has recovered well—lucky to be alive."

Evelyn stiffened, realising she meant Sabrena. She kept her composure, answering whatever came her way, determined to win her release so she could continue investigating Susan's death.

"Before I go," Deborah added with a smile, "you should know you have a loyal friend right here." She nodded to Veronica. "She's been by your side almost every day. And you've got good friends back in Australia too. Adam calls regularly for updates. I feel like I know him already. I'd better let him know you've woken up."

Deborah promised to return later and left. Evelyn, left alone with Veronica, wondered what her verdict would be—and if she'd ever get out.

Veronica finally sat next to her, looking hesitant. "I have some news," she began softly. "I was thinking of going back to Australia with you, for a holiday, if that's alright."

"Australia?" Evelyn repeated, confused. The last thing she wanted was to go back. "What do you mean, going back with me?"

"Well," Veronica explained, "Susan and I had planned to visit you there. Things changed, of course, but while you were in hospital I realised life's short. I want to do more adventurous things. So—Australia, here I come." She gave a small smile, but Evelyn showed no enthusiasm.

"We'll talk about that once I'm out of here," Evelyn said dismissively.

Later that day, Deborah returned as promised, bringing good news: Evelyn was cleared to leave, provided she returned the next week for follow-up tests. The psychiatrist even hinted that Evelyn will be fit to return to Australia soon, which confused Evelyn, but she played along. Why was Deborah so keen to have Evelyn return to Australia so quickly? That afternoon she was discharged.

Packing her belongings, Evelyn marvelled at how quickly her strength had returned. Only days ago, she could hardly move; now she was walking about, collecting clothes she barely recognised as hers. Veronica had bought her pyjamas, two gowns, and other necessities when she first arrived.

Soon Veronica returned, visibly upset; after visiting Sabera in another wing of the hospital, but Evelyn didn't ask questions. Her mind was on getting out of that hospital as soon as possible. Together they went down to the hospital's garden. Veronica told her to wait while she fetched the car from the hotel car park, about a fifteen minutes' walk away, but instead she flagged down a taxi that had just arrived.

Evelyn sat in the sunshine, admiring the neatly kept gardens, the budding spring flowers, and the warmth of the day. Before long, Veronica pulled up in her old but dependable four-wheel drive, and together they left the hospital, heading back to her remote home in the wilderness.

After they had driven a fair distance from the hospital, Evelyn cautiously asked Veronica for her version of Susan's death. She trusted Veronica, but in this fragile moment she needed reassurance that Veronica was still on her side. Evelyn knew that if she acted strangely or said something unusual, Veronica might just turn the car around and take her straight back. She wanted to check in with her friend before going any further, because she had to convince Veronica she wasn't losing her mind.

Veronica, in her usual manner, replied that her account of the incident was probably no different from Evelyn's own. Evelyn asked her to repeat it, anyway, explaining that parts of her memory were missing. She assured Veronica she was fine, reminding her that both the doctors and Deborah had said lapses were normal after a coma. Veronica then described the crash on the mountain: Susan's car skidded out of control, slammed into the mountainside, and then went over the edge. Sabrena was flung from the car and landed on a rock ledge ten feet below. Her injuries were so severe that, according to Veronica, it might have been kinder had she died in the accident.

Evelyn didn't respond to this version, still questioning whether she was dreaming. "So, no other car hit them and pushed them over?" she asked.

"No, that's what the report concluded."

"And when exactly did the accident happen?"

"In May."

"Was it daytime, or night?"

"Late afternoon, just before dusk." Veronica sounded irritated now. "Let's not go into this, Evelyn. The doctors want you to rest and focus on pleasant things."

"Yes, all right," Evelyn said quickly.

They pulled up at the corner store where Sabrena once worked with her father. Evelyn sat silently, taking in the familiar scene. She was stunned that three months had passed since she had last been there. Wildflowers and tall grasses lined the roadside, evidence of the changing season. Spring was clearly on its way. Veronica soon returned to the car with two reusable bags filled with groceries.

They continued on toward Veronica's house, only a short distance further. Veronica thought of mentioning how devastated Sabrena's family had been, but decided it wasn't the right time. She also noticed Evelyn never asked about Sabrena during her stay at the hospital.

When they arrived, Veronica's front garden overflowed with blossoms of every kind. It had burst into colour since Evelyn's last visit, as though spring had arrived early in Veronica's yard. Evelyn realised how much work her friend must have put into tending each plant. Watching Evelyn pause to study the vibrant flowers, Veronica thought of Susan, who too would linger in the garden, staring as though she saw something invisible to others.

After a light snack, Evelyn began searching for Susan's belongings, hoping to find proof for her suspicions. Veronica busied herself in the kitchen, preparing dinner. Later, Evelyn entered and asked if she could see the notebook containing Susan's writings that Veronica had saved.

"How do you know about my book?" Veronica asked, surprised. "Did I mention it to you before?" She couldn't recall if she had—Evelyn was never interested in such things.

"It's in my room. I will get it for you." Veronica wiped her hands on a tea towel and returned with the notebook. She found Evelyn seated in the dining room near the window for light. "When you're finished, please put it back in my room," Veronica said. Evelyn nodded absently, already lost in thought.

Evelyn leafed slowly through the journal, torn between continuing her search or moving on. The pages deepened her sadness. Soon she joined Veronica in the kitchen with a new question. She remembered seeing a prescription among Susan's things and asked if Susan had ever taken sleeping pills. Veronica confirmed she had—once or twice when she first arrived from London—but had stopped within a week or so after she arrived.

"Do you still have the prescription?" Evelyn asked.

Without giving it much thought, Veronica pointed to the hallway cabinet outside Susan's room. Evelyn headed toward the cabinet and opened the drawers and found a small bottle of tablets along with a worn notepad. Her heart quickened as she recognised Susan's handwriting—scribbles, symbols, and sketches of fruit and flowers. She carried the notes outside and sat on the veranda, poring over them.

The grapevine overhead had grown thick, forming a leafy canopy. The veranda now lay partly in shade, proof that months had slipped past her. Tall flowers crowded the backyard, and fruit trees thrived wildly. Evelyn marvelled at Veronica's ability to keep it all so lush.

That evening, after dinner, Evelyn shared her find. Veronica recalled Susan's habit of doodling and jotting down her thoughts, only to throw them away later. Veronica had often rescued the pages, either giving them back or keeping them. She remembered Susan always carrying the notepad when she first came from London, though she had stopped shortly before the accident. The memory made her smile faintly.

As the night wound down, Evelyn prepared for bed. She picked up the sleeping pills and went to Susan's room, with Veronica following out of concern. "Don't worry, I am not planning to harm myself," Evelyn reassured her, opening Susan's suitcase. She asked what Veronica knew about the medication. Veronica explained Susan had brought them from London and stopped taking them soon after, though she had once fallen ill with migraines and hallucinations. Susan believed it was the medication that made her sick. Evelyn checked the label on the bottle, noting the doctor's name and address in London.

The next day, Evelyn looked up the doctor and discovered he was a well-known physician and head of a drug-testing lab in London. She managed to reach his receptionist over the phone, who was cheerful and eager to help. The woman even encouraged Evelyn to donate or volunteer for trials, promising good pay and government backing.

Evelyn began to wonder if Susan had been involved with that same lab. She pressed Veronica for details. Veronica recalled a call from Susan, just before she left London, saying she had received money for joining a drug trial but quit because the medication made her ill. The drugs caused strange visions, including vivid images of her childhood dog, Whisky, long since dead. The hallucinations had spooked Susan deeply, though she and Veronica had later laughed about it. Veronica had urged her to abandon the trial and find normal work.

Evelyn suspected this might be the same trial Deborah once mentioned. She remembered the name Cereus and phoned London again, asking about it. The receptionist politely refused, explaining that drug trials were confidential.

That night, Veronica overheard Evelyn's call. Curious, she researched the word "Cereus" herself the next morning. She discovered it was a rare cactus flower, white and exotic, found in deserts across America and elsewhere. Beyond that, its meaning remained unclear, so she and Evelyn decided to set it aside for now.

Time passed quickly, and soon Evelyn was due for a hospital check-up. On arrival, Veronica explained she needed to visit Sabrena to deliver the things her family had sent. Evelyn said nothing, absorbed in her own thoughts. She longed to cut ties with the hospital for good.

While Veronica went one way, Evelyn attended her appointment. The doctor was running late, and the receptionist asked her to wait or return later. Instead, Evelyn went looking for Deborah. Though Deborah's office was locked, the hallway felt strangely familiar. Evelyn peered through the door's glass panel, spotting a potted plant in the corner, a painting of fighting zebras, and the odd sculpture of a two-headed giraffe. She was still staring when a staff member asked if she needed assistance.

"I have an appointment with Deborah," Evelyn declared with confidence.

"Yes, Evelyn, I'm aware of your appointment, but you should know by now that Deborah only sees her patients after lunch."

Evelyn was startled that the woman not only knew who she was but also knew her by name.

"How do you know my name?"

"Evelyn, you've been coming up here for weeks to see Doctor Middleton."

"Oh, of course," Evelyn said, quickly reminding herself to play along. *Keep up the act,* she thought. "Yes, I know. I just figured she might be catching up on paperwork, and since I'm free while waiting for my other appointment, I thought I'd try my luck and see if she could see me now."

The stranger smiled warmly and asked how Evelyn was managing. Evelyn replied that she was doing fantastically well. Soon she learned the woman's name—Maryanne, Deborah's receptionist.

Evelyn left the psychiatrist's office and went in search of Veronica. They had arranged to meet in the waiting area where Evelyn was to see her doctor. When she arrived, the waiting room was crowded and noisy, yet Veronica had not returned from her visit with Sabrena. Evelyn sat down, picked up a magazine, and waited. Moments later, the anxious-looking receptionist caught her eye and motioned her forward. Apparently, the doctor had just come back and, while preparing to call another patient, noticed Evelyn.

The doctor greeted her with delight at her progress. He told her she was doing well and wished to see her again in four weeks, though she could arrange an earlier appointment if needed. After the brief consultation in his cramped office, he quickly ushered her out. Evelyn returned to the bustling waiting room, but Veronica was still nowhere to be found. She stepped outside instead, choosing a seat in the shade to admire the well-kept lawns and flowerbeds. The place was alive with people: some smoking desperately, others weighed down by heavy burdens. Children scampered about in new clothes, squirming with discomfort, some sighing for home while others looked frightened.

Before long, the sun shifted and pierced beneath the veranda roof, beating down on Evelyn's arms and face as though mocking the people sitting against the wall. Just as she rose to move, she spotted Deborah walking up the path toward the entrance. Evelyn stood quickly and followed her inside. When she called out, Deborah stopped, greeted her warmly, and together they headed toward her office. Evelyn noticed, with some curiosity, that Deborah carried two bottles of wine in a bag.

In the office, Deborah asked Evelyn to recount Susan's accident. Evelyn repeated what Veronica had told her, keeping the story simple and consistent. She explained that she knew Susan had died and that Sabrena had been badly injured but had survived. Deborah then pressed for details about Evelyn herself—what had led to her breakdown, and what she remembered from before it. Evelyn could only say that she had felt constantly exhausted and wanted to sleep. She vaguely recalled the coffin at the cremation, fragments of the service, and returning home to bed. The days afterward were a blur, and she mostly remembered sleeping until she woke up in hospital.

Deborah probed further, asking if Evelyn could recall anything from their sessions. Evelyn, wanting to appear normal, admitted she remembered little, just that there had been talk of wine and England. She immediately wondered if she had revealed too much.

"Oh!" Deborah exclaimed with a wide smile. "You remembered that? Please, go on."

"That's all. Just scraps. I'm sure more will come back soon." Evelyn smiled back, now trying to reassure Deborah. "Can you fill in the blanks for me?"

"About what?" Deborah asked, puzzled, shifting in her chair to get comfortable.

"I'm just wondering why those two things stuck in my head—wine and England."

Deborah laughed softly. "Amazing, isn't it, what people hold onto? Here I am trying to be professional, and you remember the one thing I probably shouldn't have shared." She admitted she enjoyed a good glass of wine with dinner, adding the confession with slight embarrassment.

"And England?" Evelyn persisted.

"That's where I'm from," Deborah explained. Evelyn had noticed an English accent but hadn't given it much thought.

"Do you go back often?"

"Occasionally," Deborah replied firmly, sitting back in her chair, tucking her one leg under the other, her posture easing into a more relaxed state. "But my husband is the traveller, not me."

"What do you mean?"

"He does business across Europe, and we still keep our home there. I prefer staying here, only visiting when necessary."

Evelyn decided not to push further. The talk was becoming personal, and she sensed Deborah was studying her closely whenever she thought Evelyn wasn't looking. Still, Deborah's warmth was undeniable. She seemed genuinely fond of Evelyn, describing her as interesting and assuring her that they got along well—even if Evelyn could not remember their sessions. Evelyn tried to resist, but she couldn't help believing in her sincerity.

Finally, Deborah stood, scribbled something at her desk, and told Evelyn she would only need to see her once more before returning to Australia. Again, Evelyn wondered why everyone was so eager for her to go back home. Deborah scheduled the follow-up for the same day as her doctor's appointment.

Later, Evelyn found Veronica in the crowded waiting room, reading a magazine. Veronica was cheerful as she explained that Sabrena would soon be discharged, having finally been given the all-clear. For the first time, Evelyn asked how Sabrena was faring, and Veronica assured her that despite her injuries, she was recovering well. The women left the hospital together in better spirits than when they had arrived.

That evening over dinner, Veronica once again raised the idea of holidaying in Australia. She felt she deserved a break after the recent hardships and thought joining Evelyn in Sydney would be ideal. Evelyn, however, wasn't ready. Her mind kept circling Susan's death, Deborah and England, Lucy, and the strange events of the past three months. They had to be connected somehow. She only needed more time to piece it all together. She also couldn't ignore Veronica's recent aloofness and the fact that she had abandoned her Tarot cards.

After dinner, Evelyn confronted her. Veronica's behaviour had been troubling, and Evelyn wanted her friend back to her old self—especially if they were to travel together. She also noticed that Veronica seemed unusually eager to appease her, which was unlike her.

"What's with this sudden talk of Australia?" Evelyn said suddenly, catching Veronica off guard. "Since the hospital, it's all I hear from you. Why now? What's so urgent about going to Australia all of a sudden?"

Veronica faltered, then replied softly, as though trying to avoid a fight. "I just think it will do us good. I really feel that I need a break from all this, and going back with you seems right—not just for me but for both of us."

Evelyn, ignoring the calm tone, pressed further. "And what about your Tarot? What's happened to that?"

"What do you mean?" Veronica's body stiffened.

"You haven't mentioned the cards. I haven't seen you use them. Is everything all right?"

Veronica's expression darkened. She hesitated before answering. "Everything's fine, Evelyn. I'm just focused on helping you recover. You were in hospital for three months. You were very sick—I thought you'd never wake up. I only want to support you."

"Does that mean pretending Tarot and Susan don't exist?"

"No," Veronica answered quickly. "I just feel it is time we take a break from all that and focus on more positive, everyday things."

"Why?!" Evelyn snapped.

"Because I have had time to think," Veronica admitted. "We lost Susan, and you nearly died. I have been re-evaluating my life."

"That's nice for you," Evelyn shot back. "But I don't understand why you are acting so differently, re-evaluating your life or not, it is not you… Well, that's up to you, Veronica."

Veronica lowered her head in silence. After a brief pause, Evelyn continued. "So, you're telling me no more tarot, no more reading cards, no more talk of Susan?" Veronica's mournful look gave no answer.

"This is not you, Veronica. I don't get it!" Evelyn sighed heavily. "Okay, if this is what you want, then so be it."

Just when Evelyn was about to get up and leave, Veronica suddenly confessed. She told Evelyn that she had been struggling with her cards. Worse, she had been haunted by a sense of dread, convinced that Death itself lingered near. To protect herself, she had hidden the Tarot away, believing that avoiding them might keep the Grim Reaper at bay.

Evelyn was taken aback and remarked, "I remember we spoke about this years ago, when you felt the same way about negative entities. But you eventually overcame it." Veronica didn't respond. She just lowered her head again in silence.

That night, Evelyn struggled to settle, but after hours of shifting about, she eventually slipped into deep sleep. Once again, she drifted into the strange yet familiar warehouse. Rows of pallets were stacked with boxes, tightly bound in plastic wrap to keep them secure. Everything was neatly arranged, filling the space in an orderly fashion. This time, she could make out more of the labels. *Cereus Sleep: Experience Deep Sleep with a Difference.* As she moved closer, a familiar male voice caught her attention near the entrance. She followed the sound toward the exit door and saw Graham, Deborah's husband, talking on his phone just outside. Evelyn couldn't catch everything he was saying, but she heard him mention that most of the cargo had been delivered and was ready for distribution.

Just then, the rumble of machinery echoed across the warehouse. A man in overalls drove a forklift, carrying large pallets toward the exit. Evelyn saw several large trucks parked outside the open doors, waiting to be loaded. She then woke up. Hot and bothered, Evelyn questioned why she continued to have these bizarre dreams. They must mean something, surely. Or was she still trapped in a coma?

Evelyn lay awake for over an hour, turning over the thought that she might be losing her grip on reality. Finally, she rose and prepared breakfast. Veronica remained withdrawn, quiet, and heavy with thought. Evelyn carried her tea outside and sat on the back veranda, letting the morning sun wash over her. She reflected on the dream, trying once more to piece the fragments together. Soon, she returned inside, collected Susan's notes along with a notepad and pen, and began jotting down the dream's details. She studied Susan's writings, along with Veronica's notes about her card readings. A memory resurfaced. Evelyn went looking for Veronica and found her in the kitchen.

"Veronica, do you remember that night in the lounge room, when I tried to connect with what happened to Susan and you had your cards out?" But Veronica's expression made it clear she didn't want to revisit that evening. In fact, she didn't seem to want to talk at all.

"It was when I tried using my psychic skills," Evelyn said, with a smile.

Veronica finally responded, her voice cool. "Yes, Evelyn. But why are you bringing that up?" She busied herself, moving around the kitchen.

"You were upset that night. You said something about the clock not working," Evelyn added, following behind her.

Veronica turned sharply. "Evelyn, that was the beginning of your breakdown. You started falling ill, sleeping endlessly. That's when it began."

Evelyn froze, stunned. "Was that when I lost it?"

"Yes!" Veronica answered quickly. "It was awful. I didn't know how to help." She drifted toward the sink, wiping it down.

As Evelyn turned to leave, Veronica suddenly asked, "How do you even know about the clock?"

"The clock?" Evelyn repeated. "Oh, yes. You said it stopped after nine o'clock, but later discovered it was working again?"

"Do you remember the exact time?" Veronica questioned, her face pale.

"I'm not sure... maybe 9:07 p.m.?"

Veronica stared, speechless, her expression softening. "Evelyn, how could you know that? I never told anyone. That night you were already falling into unconsciousness." She turned back to the sink, splashing in the water as she washed cups.

Evelyn continued gently. "You were in the lounge with the lamps covered in fabric, candles lit. You'd pushed the table and chairs aside, laid those bean bags with the animal print on the floor—the ones from the shop down the street. You wore your traditional clothes. Remember, I said you looked like an Egyptian Queen, full of secrets."

Veronica often rearranged furniture and lit candles, so that much wasn't unusual. But the clock—she had told no one about how it had stopped at 9:07 p.m. and then mysteriously resumed working.

"I felt a presence in the house that night," Veronica admitted at last, her tone softening.

"A presence... and the time? That has to mean something," Evelyn said, frowning.

"I don't know," Veronica replied. "But it must be important. The clock was perfectly fine afterwards."

Evelyn said nothing, only smiled faintly before stepping outside again. She sank into her chair, now shaded beneath the heavy loquat tree and thick grapevine that blocked the sun.

For a time, things between the two women grew easier—until one morning Veronica left early, not returning until late in the day. Evelyn, arranging flowers from the garden, saw her friend come in looking sad and tearful. She asked what was wrong.

Veronica explained she had gone to collect Sabrena's father first, then both had driven to Cape Town to bring Sabrena home from the hospital. The girl had been there over three months. Veronica had known Sabrena for years, admired her strength and ambition, her independence, her plans to study and travel the world. She had always supported her with clothes or small gifts and had even funded the trip to Cape Town that ended in tragedy.

Now Sabrena's dreams lay in ruins. Veronica described watching her father, a proud man, break down in tears at the sight of his daughter. She sat there unrecognisable, with her packed bag beside her—the very one Veronica herself had bought. Again and again, he left the room to compose himself, unwilling to let his daughter see his tears and grief.

Sabrena's injuries were devastating: deep scars across her head, her face disfigured, both ears gone. She was paralysed in one limb, the other gravely damaged. Toes and part of her foot had been amputated, along with the fingers of her left hand, barely held together when she was first admitted.

Veronica had helped wheel her out, joined by a nurse who apologised for not being there earlier. Her father returned, his tears held back, his smile forced for Sabrena's sake. But the extent of her injuries meant a lifetime of care.

Tears streamed down Veronica's face as she shared this with Evelyn. It was the first time Evelyn had ever seen her cry as an adult. Suddenly, Veronica's strange behaviour made sense: she had been in mourning all along, burdened with guilt over helping fund the trip. She believed that if she hadn't, Susan might still be alive and Sabrena unscathed.

Veronica confessed her fears for Sabrena's family, crushed by poverty, and admitted she was drowning in despair. Evelyn, shocked, apologised for not realising sooner. She invited Veronica to talk more about her feelings, but Veronica explained she preferred silence when she was low. That was how she coped.

Soon after, Evelyn faced her final appointment with the doctor, along with a visit to Deborah. She reminded herself she needed to appear sane, normal, and ready to leave hospital life behind.

The two women drove through the rain and wind to Cape Town's largest hospital. The car seemed to know the road by heart after months of travel. Once inside, Veronica waited while Evelyn met the doctor. Moments later she emerged, smiling brightly as the doctor shook her hand and wished her well, having cleared her to return to Australia.

Next, they went to see Deborah. After reviewing Evelyn's notes, Deborah asked about her health—any dizziness or symptoms she should know of—but Evelyn reported feeling well. Deborah then went outside to get Veronica, inviting her to join them.

"Do you recall any sessions with Veronica present?" Deborah suddenly asked. Evelyn hesitated, not wanting to seem vague or insane.

"Could you remind me of one session in particular?" she asked.

"Of course," Deborah said. "Remember when Veronica told you to snap out of it and wake up?"

Evelyn had no memory of that. Thinking fast, she replied, "No... anything else?"

Deborah pressed gently. "Try to think of something yourself. What comes to mind?"

Evelyn considered Sabrena, knowing how much Veronica worried over her recovery. She decided that must have been discussed. "Well, I think you spoke about Sabrena—about how she was doing, maybe?" she suggested, glancing at Veronica.

Deborah smiled warmly and said, "Yes, exactly. See? Your memory is coming back." Veronica, however, looked uncertain and remained silent.

Evelyn could not recall much more about their past sessions, but she presented herself calmly and with confidence, telling Deborah that she had made a full recovery and that her prognosis was positive. Deborah agreed, confirming that Evelyn was cleared to travel to Australia and that, despite her long stay in hospital, her progress had been remarkable.

On the drive home, Veronica barely spoke, responding only with the occasional nod as Evelyn tried to make conversation. She did not appear pleased that this visit marked the end of Evelyn's hospitalisation. Now Evelyn was free to do as she wished. Once they arrived home, Veronica disappeared into the kitchen while Evelyn wandered about idly, growing restless with her friend's shifting moods. Later in the day, after a short nap born out of boredom, Evelyn went looking for her. She found Veronica in the lounge room with the television on so low it was almost inaudible.

"You've been awfully quiet today," Evelyn remarked. Veronica gave a faint smile but said nothing. "Are you feeling all right?" Evelyn asked.

"Yes. Just a little tired, that's all."

"Veronica, you are never tired—and even if you are, you're still talkative. What's going on?" Evelyn asked, her frustration showing. After a pause, Veronica weighed whether to speak or dismiss the matter again. Finally, she said, "Evelyn, I don't know what you're doing. I know you. You're putting on a performance for those doctors." She trailed off midway, her voice heavy with resignation, as though she no longer had the energy to argue.

"I won't deny that, Veronica. But I am well. I just don't want this dragging on forever. You know how these people like to stretch things out. I feel fine, considering…" Evelyn faltered.

"Considering what?" Veronica straightened, expecting some revelation.

"Considering Susan's death." Evelyn continued quietly, "I lost a daughter too. I'm doing my best to live one day at a time, but I can't shake the sense that there's unfinished business."

Veronica hadn't expected such an answer. She stood in silence for a moment before walking out of the room. She didn't ask what Evelyn meant; she knew better than to invite an argument. Besides, she recognised that Evelyn was grieving just as much as she was.

By the following day, Veronica's mood had shifted completely. Evelyn noticed and even wondered if it was now Veronica's turn to suffer a breakdown and end up in hospital. But that night Veronica resolved to change course. She realised she had to support Evelyn rather than wallow in guilt and despair. Strange as Evelyn could be, her intentions were not harmful. There was no benefit in lingering in sorrow any longer. It was time to begin anew. Reluctantly, Veronica acknowledged that Evelyn had been striving to do this from the beginning. Whether Evelyn's "mission" was grounded in reality or not, at least she had purpose and direction. Now it was Veronica's turn to reclaim her own life.

Evelyn noticed that as the day went on, Veronica began to resemble her old self, the anguish gradually lifting. Veronica had loved Susan deeply, especially since her return from England, and she also carried a heavy sorrow for Sabrena, though she knew she could do nothing for her. The events of the past three months had been beyond her control, devastating and unexpected.

That afternoon, Evelyn gave Veronica space indoors while she sat outside in her usual chair, leafing through Susan's notes as she often did when bored, all while keeping an eye on a spotted eagle-owl nesting in the corner pine tree.

The back door creaked open, and Veronica appeared with her Tarot cards in hand. Evelyn noticed but said nothing, pretending not to see them. Veronica sat down heavily, smiling broadly at Evelyn, clearly expecting her to comment. Evelyn remained silent, waiting for Veronica to speak first.

Eventually, Veronica confessed that she had been thinking only of herself, overlooking the fact that Evelyn was grieving too. She admitted that she had been consumed by visits to the hospital, Sabrena's struggles, and the endless cycle of death, illness, and travel, all while trying to hold together a semblance of normal life. Her own needs had gone unnoticed. She explained that Susan's presence had made her feel valued and needed again, something she hadn't experienced in years. In Susan, she had rediscovered her worth, only to lose it once more. But she also realised that it was no longer right to remain trapped in mourning; she had to reclaim her life.

Evelyn, touched, thanked Veronica for everything she had done and assured her that she would always be her closest friend and ally. With tears in her eyes, Evelyn apologised for taking her for granted. Both women then broke down crying together.

That evening, Veronica suggested doing a card reading after dinner. Evelyn was relieved; it had been a long time since Veronica had shown enthusiasm for her craft. Leaning forward, Evelyn watched eagerly as the cards were placed on the table. Yet Veronica seemed cautious, struggling to interpret them, which surprised Evelyn given her lifelong experience. After reviewing them carefully, Veronica began to explain their meanings while Evelyn took notes.

Veronica then admitted that before Evelyn's breakdown, her readings had always carried the same ominous themes—loss, mass death, endings, catastrophe. It had frightened her so much that she stopped using the cards, afraid she was cursed or attracting death into her home. Now the same messages were resurfacing. Was the Grim Reaper still hovering near, or was something even greater unfolding?

Evelyn reassured her that Susan's death might be clouding her perception, and that the cards reflected their grief rather than a looming disaster. But Veronica was unconvinced, troubled by the sense that something dreadful was about to happen—perhaps even affecting many lives, like a great calamity. Evelyn tried to soothe her, reminding her that disasters like earthquakes or tsunamis do happen, and that such events were part of life. Reluctantly, Veronica accepted Evelyn's reasoning and considered setting the cards aside once more.

As night fell, a cool wind swept across the yard, scattering Evelyn's papers to the ground. They decided to go inside. Veronica made tea, while Evelyn opted for a small whisky she had been sneaking from the bottle on top of the fridge—something she later discovered Susan had bought when she first arrived in Cape Town.

Settling in, Evelyn asked about her time in the so-called quasi-coma, wanting to know what Veronica had been doing while she lay in hospital. Veronica admitted she had been in shock for weeks, uncertain if Evelyn would survive. She had worried constantly about Sabrena and been overwhelmed by questions from doctors about Evelyn's medical and psychiatric history—questions she often couldn't answer, or chose not to, for fear of saying too much or saying the wrong thing.

Evelyn then attempted to test Veronica about her time in England, recounting part of her dream that she believed to be real. Veronica, however, changed the subject, shifting instead to Evelyn's appointments with Deborah, where she had seen Evelyn undergoing psychometric assessments and similar tests, something she found disturbing. She admitted to Evelyn that she struggled with her unpredictable moods—one moment showing improvement, waking up, and the next sliding backward, deteriorating again. The constant shifts were agonizing for her to watch, and so Veronica finally chose not to attend any more of Evelyn's meetings with Deborah.

"Deborah nearly invited you to dinner at her home," Veronica said out of nowhere, "and she even asked me to come along. But her superiors discouraged her. She honestly believed that sharing a meal at her place, outside the hospital, might bring you back to reality. But of course, it never took place." Veronica went on, explaining that Deborah was convinced Evelyn was making headway, which was why she had decided to continue the twice-weekly sessions. Evelyn was left speechless, overwhelmed by the extent of everyone's determination to help her, and by Veronica's steadfast loyalty.

She then asked Veronica whether the name Lucy meant anything, but Veronica regretfully admitted it did not. Deflated, Evelyn began to wonder whether the whole thing had been nothing more than a cruel dream. Perhaps it was simply her mind's way of coping with the crushing truth of losing a child. Had her brain shut down, weaving a story about Susan's death so she wouldn't collapse completely? Was this how memory and grief played tricks? Was it all no more than an illusion, a desperate fabrication of the mind? Evelyn began to wonder if her whole time in London had been nothing more than a dream—some lingering thread of that coma she had been tangled in. Perhaps everyone had been right all along. Maybe it was time to go back to Australia, to let the ghosts fade behind her. And Veronica—yes, Veronica deserved a holiday. After everything she had endured, Evelyn was not going to stand in her way any longer.

The following morning, over breakfast, Evelyn announced to Veronica that she would be going back to Australia and dearly wished for Veronica to come with her. Veronica's face lit up instantly, as if she had been waiting for this moment all along. She told Evelyn that her bags were already packed, and she was ready to leave.

Chapter Seventeen
The BBQ

The three men, each from a different generation, stepped into the backyard…

Joey was restless. He wanted to visit Tom again, but Adam suggested they wait. Afterward, Joey considered inviting Tom for dinner or perhaps a weekend barbeque. Adam also thought that sounded like a good idea. Maybe a small gathering with Evelyn, her visiting friend Veronica, and Carol could work, but Joey wasn't enthusiastic about that idea. In truth, he wasn't very interested in Evelyn. What he wanted was Tom's undivided attention, since Joey had his own agenda. Adam also sensed that Evelyn would likely decline anyway, as she disliked being in large groups.

When Adam phoned Tom, Tom was cheerful and instantly agreed to come over for a Sunday barbeque. He seemed genuinely thrilled, his enthusiasm obvious in his voice. Adam found himself surprised by Tom's excitement over something so ordinary as a weekend barbeque.

That Sunday morning, Adam and Joey rushed to tidy up the house. Common sense said they should have taken care of it the day before. Yet men, as Joey often proved, had a habit of leaving things until the very last moment—shoving dirt under the rug or tucking it into corners where no visitor would ever think to look. Unfortunately for him, Adam walked in just as Joey was mid-swipe, trying to disguise the mess. Without a word, Adam thrust the dustpan and brush into his hands and stood over him until Joey crouched down, dragged the dirt back out, and swept it away properly.

Tom arrived exactly on time. Later, he told Adam he had come early but parked down the street for a few minutes before approaching. Adam scolded him, reminding him that the time was not set in concrete. Tom, however, had different views: arriving too early felt rude, while being late was equally disrespectful. Old-fashioned in his ways, he had dressed impeccably, polished shoes, and neatly clipped silver hair. His sports jacket appeared to have many interesting stories to tell. Meanwhile, Joey was nearly bouncing on the spot, like a child awaiting a gift, and Tom was the gift-giver.

The three men, each from a different generation, stepped into the backyard. Flames licked at wood in the brick-built barbecue by the fence. Joey started scraping the hotplate with a large metal utensil, making loud scraping sounds.

Adam invited Tom to sit, guiding him to a chair brought out especially for him. Tom leaned back, taking in the scene, at ease in their untidy yard. Oddly enough, he seemed more comfortable there than in his own lavish gardens at home.

Once finished at the hotplate, Joey rejoined them under the covered patio near the kitchen door. He noticed Tom didn't have a drink and quickly darted inside and returned with beer bottles. Adam reminded him to fetch soft drinks and water instead, recalling that Tom usually drank only tea or water. Tom chuckled at Joey's disappointed face when Adam corrected him. Begrudgingly, Joey went back inside and reappeared with Tom's orange juice in a rather tall champagne glass, which made Adam roll his eyes again.

As drinks were served, Joey began describing his dreams and UFO theories, hoping Tom might interpret them. Tom remained quiet, giving the impression he wanted the day to be light-hearted rather than professional. Adam noticed that Tom seemed different—gentle, even grandfatherly—content to let them lead the conversation. At times he looked inward, smiling faintly, as though lost in thought. He seemed happy just to be there.

Joey soon excused himself to prepare the gourmet sausages, tomatoes, and onions. The sausages hissed on the plate, filling the air with rich aromas. Adam joined him, and together they tended the barbecue while Tom, delighted by the smell, sat watching. When Joey dropped a sausage, quickly scooping it up when he thought no one noticed, Tom laughed quietly. But Adam had seen it and tried to take the sausage away, sparking another spat. Joey then shouted over to Tom, asking if he owned a dog.

Adam returned to Tom, who observed Adam's irritation with Joey. Tom knew exactly what he was witnessing, and it was what he had hoped to confirm. Before the day ended, Tom would make his decision, and it would be final.

When the food was served, Adam and Joey made sure Tom got the best-cooked sausages while they took the burnt ones. Adam's salads and bread were excellent, and the cold sliced beetroot completed the meal. The afternoon was shaping up as a success.

Out of the blue, Tom asked Joey about his future. Joey eagerly took the chance to discuss his psychic abilities, while Adam slipped inside to clean dishes and prepare tea. When he returned with a tray of rolls and jam—Tom's favourite—he overheard Joey and Tom animatedly debating life after death.

Joey had asked if Tom was ever married. Tom revealed he had been, but his wife had died years ago from a hospital allergy after minor surgery. He admitted he had never recovered, insisting that true love comes only once, and Patricia had been his.

Since Tom worked with Image Carriers, Joey asked if he could contact her spirit. Tom's answer shocked him. He explained that after years of study, he concluded there is no afterlife. When a person dies, their soul departs to an unknown realm, severed from all memory and feeling. Love, anger, joy—everything vanishes when the body dies.

Stunned, Joey asked about reincarnation, but Tom dismissed it as myth. His research suggested humans survive only through procreation—passing on genes, not spirits. Evolution, not rebirth, explained humanity's continuity.

Tom elaborated further: one's emotions and memories exist in the body, not in some spiritual dimension. Death erases them, but through genes, fragments can be inherited. People recalling past-life visions may simply be experiencing ancestral memory passed down through biology.

Adam recalled Julie once saying something similar. He encouraged Tom to have a roll. Tom quickly accepted the offer, smiling as devoured one, butter and jam spilling onto his fingers.

"I heard Joey ask about reincarnation," Adam said. "Many people believe in it. Are you saying it's not true?"

"Yes, my friend. It does not exist."

"Really?"

"Sadly, yes. I wish it were true, but evidence says otherwise."

Adam then shared personal stories of strange encounters he had kept secret. That strange entity appearing in his room all those years ago, his out-of-body experience, and everything that followed—he finally felt ready to share it with them.

Tom suggested those were likely supernatural but harmless, perhaps glimpses of unseen realms. He advised Adam not to dwell on them but to embrace them as part of a rich life. He explained that one's "Other Self" might appear through symbols—animals, voices, or faces—but it was not truly the dead speaking.

Joey turned wide-eyed to Adam. "Why didn't you tell me about those things?" He sounded hurt.

Adam shrugged his shoulders and now wished he had not said anything, as Tom didn't really give a suitable answer. Now Joey was unhappy with him for not sharing earlier.

After an uneasy pause, as the three men sat not knowing how to continue, Joey was the first to speak, breaking the silence.

"But what about all the ghosts people say they seen..." He paused, searching for another thought, but Tom was already ready with his own question.

"Joey, have you ever seen one?"

'No, not yet," Joey replied with a grin.

"Well, people see many things that aren't really there. Just because something is witnessed doesn't make it a ghost. People tend to see what they want to see, and that includes psychics too." Tom took a breath, wiping his mouth, eyeing the plate of jam rolls. Then he added, "In some cases, young man, what they are seeing is their Other Self reaching out to them."

"All right then," Adam cut in, thoughtful, "what about those who claim to have lived before, or say they have seen or heard their dead relatives? Are they deceiving themselves, or just imagining things?"

"Yes, in most cases it's self-delusion, though sometimes it is indeed their Other Self," Tom answered, smiling as he took another roll spread with jam. "People insisting they've been to places they've never visited in this lifetime may simply be recalling coincidences, or else memories inherited through their genes from ancestors. And when it comes to seeing or hearing the voices of dead relatives, yes, it's possible—but what they're experiencing is only memory, not the actual presence of the deceased."

"So, if I believe I've lived a past life..." Joey leaned back in his chair, watching Tom chew on his roll. "You're saying it's actually memories from my relatives who lived then?"

"Exactly," Tom replied in a sing-song tone, licking his fingers while eyeing the last roll.

Adam joined in, bolstered by what Julie had already taught him. "It is the same as being artistic, or left-handed. These traits are inherited, just like some illnesses travel down family lines. I'm starting to think memories work the same way. Sometimes we dream or flash back to what our ancestors once endured."

Tom studied Adam for a moment, then glanced at Joey, both of them attentive to his every word. Then, looking toward the garden, he gathered his thoughts before speaking.

"You're right, Adam. I've often heard people describe strong recollections or familiarity with certain time periods, like the 1800s or 1300s. They assume this means they have lived before, but it doesn't. It simply reflects experiences their ancestors went through. There's nothing mysterious about it!"

Joey piped up, realising something. "So just like diseases get handed down, distant memories can too?"

Tom nodded, reclining in his chair.

"And what about people who say they speak with the dead, or even help police solve murders and find bodies?" Joey pressed.

"Image Carriers can do such things, but their skills are unpredictable, fleeting. And remember this—Image Carriers only pick up on the living. Once someone dies, their soul or consciousness have already left this reality. Even if it could be traced, or made itself known, it would not remember its life, its identity, or its death."

"So, anyone claiming to talk with the dead isn't really doing so. They're probably reading the living relative," Tom continued. "Real psychics can tune into people's minds, catching memories and impressions of the deceased, then relay them back."

"And what about those psychics who help the police with details of a crime or victim?" Joey asked again.

"As I said, they can only draw from the living. They may be picking up from the killer, the witnesses, or even the detectives who already hold details of the case. Psychics often read what investigators already suspect, and their accuracy can be unsettling. What they're really doing is linking into the minds of living people for knowledge."

"There's also something else," Tom added. "An unseen layer just beyond our senses that clings to past events and emotions. Some psychics tap into that. Image Carriers do it too. But we still don't know if that field exists right here in our physical world, or in some other realm or dimension entirely."

By now Adam and Joey were drained—whether from food or the intensity of the subject, they weren't sure. None of them had expected such a heavy discussion.

Silence followed. Joey wandered over to the barbeque, while Tom looked perfectly at ease, as though long accustomed to these topics. He was endlessly knowledgeable and talkative, though on arrival he had been quieter and more reserved. Adam's reflections were broken when he noticed Tom had eaten nearly all the jam rolls. Neither he nor Joey had touched them, too absorbed in Tom's words to notice.

"Do many people know about this?" Joey asked as he returned to his chair.

"About the fact that there's no life after death?" Tom said as he polished off the last roll. He wiped his sticky hands on a paper serviette Adam had set out.

"It makes no sense," Joey insisted. "So, there's really no such thing as life after death?"

"Sadly, no. That's why you must enjoy life while you are alive."

Adam, redirecting slightly, asked, "What about psychics, including your Image Carriers? Do they all work from the same place, or believe the same things about death?"

"A fine question, Adam," Tom said, smiling. 'Everyone is different, shaped by personal circumstances. One Image Carrier might reach similar outcomes as another, but will probably use vastly different methods to reach the same or similar conclusion.

"I even know some who believe the soul continues after death—but not in the way most people imagine," he concluded.

Adam and Joey sat stiffly, clearly struggling to follow.

"So psychic powers are inherited, but shaped by upbringing, and must be trained over time?" Adam asked, now leaning back with pride in his deduction.

"Yes. Like any skill, they must practice. Image Carriers learn to connect with other dimensions, interact with their Other Selves, even attempt astral travel if their genetics allow it. It is part of who we are. Humans are extraordinary—we can heal ourselves, sense things beyond the five senses, receive warnings through premonitions. Each of us has an electromagnetic field brimming with information, linked to a limitless collective field. Some can sense other dimensions. All we need is to learn how to access it, and trust our instincts."

"But it feels meaningless," Joey blurted out. "We're born, we achieve, then we die—and that's it?"

"That's the truth in simple terms, my friend. Whatever happens to the soul after death is unknown. If it returns, it has no memory. All that matters to us is contained within the physical body—the pleasures, the experiences, the relationships. When the body dies, those things end. The soul departs, but stripped of identity, it becomes nothing we can relate to. It's no longer alive to us."

Adam, thinking quickly, countered. "What about people who claim to meet other beings in other dimensions and get messages from them?"

"That has nothing to do with life after death," Tom replied. "Yes, there are many realms. Some people, like Image Carriers, can cross into them while alive. What they find may be others doing the same, or energies existing in their own right. But it is not proof of an afterlife."

"Could they be our dead relatives?" Joey asked again, leaning forward.

"Unlikely. Even if they were, they would have no memory of us or themselves. It makes no sense they'd be wandering around for no reason."

"So all of it is within the body. Once the body dies, everything ends? And the soul goes somewhere unknown, never recalling its earthly life?' Adam asked quietly, still processing.

"That's more or less correct," Tom nodded. "Many Image Carriers and Overseers accept this. Even religious leaders and the Owners know the reality—once we die, physical memory ends. So, discussing life after death is pointless."

Adam and Joey slumped, defeated. Then Adam leaned in with one final question. "So, what purpose does the soul have if it means nothing?"

"As I said earlier, you're partly right. At birth, the soul—or consciousness, becomes activated through our unique biology. It is part of the physical body, yet it is also tied to our Other Self, its spiritual half, which acts as a gateway between the physical world and hidden dimensions and greater realities. Many describe it as an essential element of the human journey. When the two works together, that is when you become whole, complete. That is when you become supernatural, as they say. Over time, brilliant minds have come to recognise this and learned how to tap into that spiritual self. But when we die, the life force, or soul, detaches from the physical body and returns to the energy field. But on its way there, a battle unfolds— shrouded in uncertainty, its details lost in time. All that is known is this: as it moves forward, there are non-human forces trying to subdue, to capture and trap the unsuspecting soul, while it struggles toward freedom, desperate to break away and leave the shackles behind. However, if one's Other Self is there upon death, and joins with your soul, becoming whole again, that is when you will be able to avoid the traps set for you, as it is your other self that is your protector during this journey. It is your Other Self that has the knowledge and holds *memory* of who you really are. Without awareness of your Other Self, you remain unguarded—both during physical life and on that crucial passage beyond death. And that, my friends," he said, lowering his voice to a conspiratorial hush, "is why they erased Image Carriers from history. They want your Other Self to remain hidden forever, a secret they never want you to discover."

Adam listened carefully but leaned forward, waiting for more. Tom, however, had stopped, leaving the air heavy with unfinished thoughts.

Finally, Joey broke the silence. "Who are the Owners?"

Tom looked uncertain, not sure if Joey was addressing him, especially since Joey also glanced at Adam.

"Oh, you mean me?" Tom asked with a faint smile, curious how Joey even knew that name.

Before Adam could step in, Joey replied, "You mentioned the Owners a moment ago?"

Tom thought back and realised he had. Though he didn't want to continue along that path, but the words kept coming out anyway. "Let me put it this way," he said. "At the very top of the elite ladder, the ruling classes scheme to shape and control both society and the planet itself. They are like wolves hungry for dominance. Yet above them sit the Owners, concealed from sight, shaping the course of events so that the shadowed figures below move only according to their will. Ordinary people are the sheep, and what lies within is being prepared for harvesting."

The mood shifted. Adam hesitated, unsure how to respond. He was still wrestling with Tom's strange description of life after death and the Other Self, more detailed than anything Julie had explained.

Joey, meanwhile, tried to keep composed, testing Tom's logic and returning to an easier topic, if one could call it that. "So, you're saying those haunted houses people talk about aren't really haunted? The strange noises and moving objects are caused by people themselves, using psychic energy without knowing it?"

"Exactly! Well said, my young friend. Now you are catching on." Tom gave him a proud smile. "Most of the time, people are scaring themselves by unknowingly moving objects or triggering sounds. Of course, sometimes it's just the wind." He chuckled softly.

"But these Owners," Joey changing track again. "Who are they? Are they really in control, manipulating us?" He slumped back in his chair.

"That is a tale for another day, young man. I think we've had enough heavy talk for one day." Tom now changing the conversation, as he smiled warmly, his eyes dropping to the empty plate before him.

Adam, still lost in thought, recalled one of his clients, Harry, once paralysed by anxiety. Harry had made real progress, eventually booking a trip to the UK to confront his fear of flying. He was fascinated by the crop circles of Wiltshire. When he returned, he was captivated, collecting books and studies on the intricate patterns. Somehow, his anxiety had vanished, replaced with determination to decode the mysterious symbols and uncover their source.

"Do you know anything about the crop circles in England?" Adam asked, testing Tom further.

Tom gave a measured reply. "All I'll say is that they reflect the human connection, the Other Self and what's ahead. Some say knowledge, others say solutions, and some believe they're warnings. Interpret as you will."

"What does that even mean?" Adam frowned, more bewildered than before.

"The whole picture isn't always in front of you. Sometimes you must look elsewhere to understand," Tom explained. "Some theories tie them to the quantum field, others to gateways or ancient designs. A few even suggest biological codes, hidden signals... Dimensions."

Tom refused to elaborate, clearly enjoying Adam's puzzled expression. "Maybe you can ponder that for yourself," he chuckled, glimpsing again at the empty dish. "I won't make it easy for you. But here's a hint—why not ask your Other Self?"

'Harvesting what?' Joey suddenly blurted out.

Adam and Tom both turned to him. Tom grinned broadly. "Well, well. Joey is smarter than I realised."

Joey had picked up on Tom's earlier words about people being sheep—ready for harvesting.

Tom explained that Image Carriers believe humans hold an electromagnetic, quantum essence, a unique energy form, many call the soul. Certain entities, he said, seek to exploit this unique and unproduceable essence for sinister ends. Rather than the soul moving into the genuine light after death, and before merging with its other self, there lies the danger of being drawn toward a false light, carefully crafted to trap and imprison the trusting soul. However, if the soul unites with its other self upon death, as I mentioned earlier, together, they become untouchable—both weaponised and shielded—protected from the false path, the manufactured light of doom, and from those evil forces awaiting their capture.

The two men sat frozen. Adam looked like he might slide right off his chair. Joey, however, smiled faintly, offering Tom a steady glance.

Outside, the wind stirred, and Tom shivered, as if chilled. He stretched out his legs, yawned loudly, and the others followed suit. Stroking his stomach with satisfaction, he declared his contentment.

Rising to leave, he thanked them warmly, saying he would never forget the day.

They watched as his car disappeared down the road. Walking back inside, Adam and Joey shared mixed feelings about the day. But they agreed that Tom was indeed a nice man—strange, but nice.

Chapter Eighteen
The Update

Unexplained energies can manifest physically, and their origins may very well be hidden from our everyday senses…

At 6:30 a.m. the next morning, Adam's alarm rang. Sydney greeted him with a crisp, clear morning. He showered quickly, ate a rushed breakfast, and stepped outside into the damp spring air.

At work, Adam unlocked his office, pulled files from the cabinet, and got straight into them. Before long, he heard Carol arrive. She carried flowers as usual, her way of brightening the waiting area, and she was as cheerful as ever. Carol always seemed to radiate joy. She asked if Adam wanted a coffee, mentioning she was heading to her favourite café up the road. Adam declined. She reminded him that Evelyn would be coming in, remarking on her illness in South Africa. Carol couldn't grasp how someone could be deathly ill, bedridden for months, and then recover so suddenly. And the revelation that Evelyn had a daughter struck both Carol and Adam as a complete mystery.

Later that morning, Evelyn arrived with Veronica. Adam was relieved to see her safely back and intrigued to finally meet the woman Evelyn called a friend—since he and Carol had always assumed Evelyn had none. He'd only spoken briefly with Veronica on the phone while Evelyn was unwell, and she struck him as peculiar, much like Evelyn.

Carol attempted polite conversation with Evelyn as they waited, but Evelyn gave her the cold shoulder. Carol wasn't surprised;

Evelyn's prolonged illness had done little to change her personality. She was still the same distant, unsociable woman.

When Adam emerged from his office, he welcomed them warmly and motioned for them to enter. He smiled at the two unusual women, though he couldn't help doubting his earlier assumptions about Evelyn. He never imagined her boarding a plane and flying across the world alone, nor could he easily accept that she had a grown daughter. Evelyn remained an enigma—appearing simple at times yet clearly far more complex. Sensing Adam's energy, Evelyn quickly asked about his well-being. Adam reassured her that everything was fine.

Their conversation turned briefly to Evelyn's worries, and she reminded him not to treat her as a client. Adam did so out of habit, given her constant tendency to anticipate catastrophe.

Turning to Veronica, Adam introduced himself, but Evelyn jumped in, introducing her friend with a sly grin, calling Veronica her best friend and insisting Adam make her feel welcome. Veronica laughed, flashing a wide smile. To her, Adam and Evelyn seemed like an old married couple, bickering yet familiar, and she immediately warmed to him. When she had first spoken to him on the phone, she thought him odd, but now she found him likeable.

Evelyn asked Adam if he had thought much about her ordeal in Cape Town. He dodged the question and encouraged her to tell him more instead. In truth, he hadn't given it much thought; work had piled up, and he had even forgotten some of the arrangements he'd made with her before she left South Africa.

Excited that Adam was listening, Evelyn recounted her time abroad. She spoke of her coma and the lingering struggle to process it, then pressed on to her travels in England—tracking down Lucy, who, along with her parents, she claimed was linked to Susan's death. She described meeting Deborah, her husband, and their circle, placing special weight on Cyril. At Cyril's name, Evelyn stumbled, then paused, studying Adam and Veronica's reactions before continuing.

After a heavy silence, Adam asked Veronica what she made of it all. Veronica admitted she didn't know; as far as she knew, Evelyn had been in hospital in Cape Town during the time she claimed to be in London. She insisted she'd never heard of Lucy, and neither had Sabrena—though Sabrena hadn't spoken much about the accident, and likely never would.

But something Veronica said caught Adam's attention. She explained that her intuition told her something significant was coming, though she wasn't sure it related to Evelyn or Susan. Lately, her extrasensory abilities had felt blocked, leaving her unable to read Tarot or tune in as she normally did. In her experience, whenever such blocks appeared, something major always followed. This time, the feeling lingered stubbornly, refusing to let her return to her normal life. Adam asked her for more about this 'something big,' but she couldn't say. He turned to Evelyn, asking if she sensed anything similar, but she seemed fixated on England, insisting Susan's death was no accident. Even Veronica suggested Evelyn wasn't making much sense, leaving Adam puzzled.

"Evelyn?" Adam asked. "What do you mean Susan's death was not an accident? Wasn't it a car crash?"

"I can't explain. I just know it wasn't an accident. They staged it. I saw it in a vision beside Sabrena's hospital bed."

"They?" Adam asked, confused. "Who are you talking about?"

"The people connected to Lucy. Susan knew something, and they wanted her silenced. I've always believed it, and Lucy confirmed it."

"Who is Lucy?" Adam questioned, looking to Veronica for clarity. But she stayed quiet. She had promised Evelyn she would be more supportive after her release from hospital, even if her words sounded incoherent. Veronica trusted her friend's gift, believing that if Evelyn didn't make sense now, she eventually would. Patience had always been her approach.

Evelyn smiled at Adam with satisfaction before looking over at Veronica. Adam, though baffled, recalled Tom's advice about being an Overseer: to record stories without judgment, to connect details that others might overlook, and to wait until meaning revealed itself.

His curious, analytical mind was an asset, but his training as a mental health professional urged him toward evidence and logic. Yet he knew he needed to step back and accept the unseen as well. He recalled a training seminar years ago, led by a peculiar elderly woman with a shrill but clear voice, who had insisted on a bio-psycho-social-spiritual approach. Her words still echoed in his mind.

She had paced the room, stressing that treatment must address the whole person—body, mind, relationships, and spirit. "If someone struggles with obesity, look at physical health, then emotional issues like stress or grief, then their social world—relationships, hobbies, community. And don't forget their higher self, their sixth sense, their spirituality, whatever that means for them."

Remembering her words, Adam resolved to give Evelyn's story the space it needed. He also saw it as practice for becoming an Overseer himself. He liked the thought of stepping into Tom's role, and he felt comfortable in that position. After all, Joey was an Image Carrier, and Adam had already been caring for him for years.

"Tell me more about your story, Evelyn," Adam prompted. "What about Lucy… Tell me more about her?"

Evelyn sank back into her chair, finally lowering her guard. Veronica remained watchful. Evelyn continued, "Lucy is like their stepdaughter, at least that's what I gathered—it was never made clear. But she also told me they hired an assassin to kill Susan."

"An assassin?" Adam's concern deepened; the tale was becoming more troubling.

"Yes, that's what Lucy confided. She was terrified, desperate to get away from them. I think she feared for her own life," Evelyn explained, speaking quickly.

"How did you meet Lucy?"

"In my dreams—or coma, whatever it was. She appeared vividly, like she was right there. Even before I saw her, I kept sensing her name. It just came to me at random times."

"Where is Lucy now?" Adam asked, watching her reaction.

"I'm not sure. Probably in England. That's where I last saw her, running away from those people."

"Which people?"

"I don't know. But I do sense that Deborah's husband is involved somehow. I'm still piecing it together."

Adam turned toward Veronica and asked about Evelyn's illness and what led to her hospital admission.

Veronica gave a clear, measured account. She explained that Evelyn was fine one day, then behaving oddly the next, and she assumed it was Evelyn's way of coping with Susan's death. She noted Evelyn's state worsened after Susan's body was cremated in Cape Town. On returning home, Evelyn had been silent, then suddenly began recalling moments from her childhood and Susan's first steps. She was reliving happier memories from their past. "Then she became domineering," Veronica added. "She ordered me to walk with her in the garden, down the road, across to the field. She wanted to cook, bake, pour tea, and drink alcohol—all at once. She went into this hyper state, and that's when I thought she was losing her mind."

Veronica explained that she tried calming her, encouraging rest, though Evelyn often insisted on staying up all night.

"I recall one night," Veronica said softly, "I checked in on her and she was finally asleep. But the next morning, I couldn't wake her. I tried again at eleven, still nothing. I phoned the doctor, but he couldn't come and sent an ambulance instead. They took her to the local clinic, then transferred her to Cape Town that evening."

Adam asked whether Evelyn had shown progress in hospital. Veronica replied that at first, she was in a coma, unresponsive. Weeks later, her eyes opened but she still didn't interact. They eventually sat her up and wheeled her outside, yet she only stared blankly. A psychiatrist visited repeatedly, assuring Veronica she would recover.

"And one day while cleaning, my phone rang. My knees nearly gave way when I answered the phone, the nurse from the hospital told me the news—Evelyn had woken up. I will never forget that call," Veronica finished, leaning back with relief.

Adam looked at Evelyn, asking if she recalled any of this. Evelyn frowned in confusion, saying she remembered bits and pieces—Deborah's fondness for wine, their home in England, her husband's business trips across Europe.

"Then why are you so sure Susan was killed and not in an accident?" Adam asked again, leaning forward, puzzled.

"Because I know it wasn't an accident. Lucy is at the heart of this. She's from England, and Susan was there too. They must have been connected, somehow, I think. Lucy knows the truth, and she was terrified when I ran into her at the hotel. She was trying to get away."

Adam recognised two overlapping stories but resolved to examine them both. He asked the women to write their accounts separately, including any impressions or intuitions that surfaced. Both agreed. Evelyn seemed comforted now that Adam was listening to her and taking her story seriously.

As they left, Adam thanked them and advised arranging another session with Carol. The two women departed cheerfully, chatting as they walked out. Adam leaned back in his chair, a faint grin on his lips. Reflecting on his first mission, he realised he was, like Tom, on the path toward becoming an Overseer. Spinning in his chair, pen pressed to his lips, he pondered his next step.

Chapter Nineteen
Overseer in the Making

Was this truly the work of an Overseer...

Adam found himself driving into his office on a Saturday afternoon, just as he had reluctantly agreed to three weeks earlier. The city felt oddly quiet, as though the weekend had drained it of its usual energy, leaving only the occasional hum of passing cars and the faint chatter of pedestrians wandering along the footpaths. He hadn't been in the mood for work, yet Evelyn's persistence over the past few weeks had finally worn him down. She had been calling repeatedly, leaving polite but insistent messages, reminding him of the details she had written down for him during their first encounter. Adam couldn't quite believe that more than three weeks had slipped by since his initial meeting with Evelyn and Veronica in his office. Time had moved swiftly, but the memory of that strange first encounter still lingered in his mind like an unfinished chapter.

The day itself matched his mood. The sky was overcast, heavy with the promise of rain that never quite fell, and a restless wind stirred scraps of paper and dry leaves along the road. As he pulled up outside his building, Adam spotted the two women waiting patiently in a small rental car they had taken from the hotel where they were staying. Their expressions brightened when they saw him, and after a brief exchange of greetings in the car park, they followed him inside. Evelyn carried herself with a sense of urgency, while Veronica, quieter by nature, trailed a step behind, watchful and reserved.

Unlocking the front door, Adam hesitated for a moment before flicking on the lights. It was the first time he had set foot in his office on a weekend for a long time, and the change of atmosphere was unsettling. The building was silent, almost unnaturally so, and the familiar corridors carried an echo that made the place feel less like a workplace and more like a mausoleum. The shadows seemed thicker, the stillness heavier. He couldn't help but question, just for a moment, why they had chosen a Saturday afternoon for their meeting. Then he recalled Evelyn's earlier complaints—that their last conversation had been too rushed, interrupted by phone calls and appointments, with Adam distracted by other clients. She had wanted a meeting free from interruptions, a time when he could focus entirely on what she had to say.

They settled into the chairs of his office, and it was immediately clear that Evelyn had come prepared. She clutched a large folder, bulging with papers, and a curious handbag that looked out of place, almost antique in style. Veronica, as usual, was more understated but carried her own folder as well, though she kept it close without making a show of it. Adam, deciding to ease into things, began by asking them their views on life after death—a topic that had been troubling him more and more, and one he was eager to hear their perspective on.

"No such thing," Evelyn replied instantly, without much thought. Her tone was sharp, almost dismissive, and it surprised Adam. He had expected a longer explanation, or at least some thoughtful preamble, not such a blunt response.

"Why do you say that?" Adam asked carefully, hiding his facial expression so as not to betray his surprise look.

Evelyn leaned forward, her eyes steady. "Do you think I'd be sitting here with you if I could talk to Susan from the other side?"

"So why can't you?" Adam asked, his curiosity outweighing his restraint.

"Because she's dead," Evelyn answered plainly. "She's gone. Nobody can reach her now."

Her certainty carried the same strange finality that Julie and Tom had spoken with, yet Adam noticed Evelyn didn't seem to fully grasp the reasoning behind her own conviction. When he pressed her further—asking where Susan's soul might be now—Evelyn couldn't provide an explanation that satisfied him. Instead, Veronica spoke up for the first time, supporting Evelyn's view. She recounted something her grandmother had often told her: *you don't cry for the dead, because the dead don't cry for you—they no longer know who you are.*

The words struck Adam with their stark simplicity. Oddly enough, they echoed what Tom had once said: that when a person dies, they lose all memories of their previous existence.

Evelyn, however, added a more personal layer. She confessed that she had dreamt of Susan often, and at times, especially when she stayed overnight in Susan's old room at Veronica's house, she could almost feel her presence there.

"Isn't that proof that her spirit lingers?" Adam asked, leaning forward, hopeful that this might contradict her earlier dismissal.

"Yes," Evelyn admitted softly. "But it isn't her. It's me. Those dreams are nothing more than my own memories of her—fragments of what we shared, replaying themselves in my mind."

Veronica, emboldened by the conversation, shared her own experiences. After her grandmother's death, she often imagined seeing her still seated in her favourite chair, serene and familiar, as though nothing had changed. But with time, Veronica had come to realise those visions weren't glimpses of another world. They were the mind's tricks, memories surfacing unbidden, shaped by grief and longing. Sometimes she even saw her grandmother in strange, unfamiliar places—settings that made no sense—and wondered if those moments held meaning. For a time, she had convinced herself that her grandmother was trying to communicate from beyond the grave. Yet as the years passed, she grew to understand that what she saw was her own anxiety projected outward, given form through the comforting image of her grandmother.

"If life after death were real," Veronica said at last, her voice heavy with resignation, "then why haven't I heard from her? If anyone would have reached me, it would have been my grandmother."

The room fell quiet. Then Evelyn broke the silence by producing Susan's notebook. She laid it gently on Adam's desk, opening the pages to reveal neat handwriting, strange symbols, and peculiar drawings that carried an unsettling energy. Their stories and explanations were not much different from what they had shared during their first visit, yet the tangible presence of Susan's belongings gave the discussion a more personal weight.

By the time they finished, nearly three hours had slipped away unnoticed. Evelyn and Veronica finally rose to leave, each placing their folders into Adam's hands before heading out. He assured them he would review everything carefully and get back to them soon, though inwardly he knew his schedule was already packed tight. He avoided making promises he couldn't keep.

When the women had gone, Adam sat for a moment in the empty office, exhausted and ravenous. He secured the door, locked up behind him, and stepped back into the cool evening air. Driving home, he decided to grab a bite to eat at the local drive through burger place. His thoughts churned. How could he possibly find the time to wade through their mountains of notes, arrange further meetings, and manage all the details they insisted on sharing? Was this truly the work of an Overseer—shouldering the weight of other people's burdens with no compensation, no support, and no clear end in sight? How had Tom managed all of this? Adam could only hope that the answers he sought would eventually reveal themselves, as the path ahead loomed like a vast, uncharted territory—mysterious, unpredictable, and heavy with consequences he could neither see nor measure. If clarity did not come soon, he knew he would be forced to walk blindly into a journey shrouded in uncertainty, a journey that promised no way of turning back once begun.

Chapter Twenty
FAUNA

What does the word FAUNA really mean…

Adam found himself once again hurrying over to Tom's house, this time because Tom had a special visitor—Ethel, one of the most advanced Image Carriers, who had surprisingly agreed to meet with him. According to Tom, Ethel rarely met with anyone, let alone strangers. On the phone, Tom had sounded insistent, telling Adam that this was a once-in-a-lifetime opportunity and that if he didn't come right away, he would likely never see her. Luckily, Adam had no clients booked that morning, so as soon as he hung up the phone, he headed straight over.

Tom was visibly relieved when Adam arrived so quickly. In the corner of the room sat the elderly woman, quietly sipping from a teacup. Tom introduced them, and Ethel smiled faintly while studying Adam in silence. The men sat down, and Tom explained that he and Ethel had been discussing some of the same subjects that came up at Adam's recent barbeque, and that Adam was welcome to join the conversation and ask her questions if he wished.

Adam felt once more as though Tom had thrown him into a situation without warning. The woman seemed detached, sitting back as though she might drift off at any moment. When Tom gestured for him to approach her, Adam hesitated, not wanting to disturb her peace. Then, without warning, Ethel set her cup down, stood, and crossed the room toward them.

"So, you must be Adam," she said in a sharp, high-pitched voice.

Ethel was a small, solidly built woman who looked as though she might be in her sixties, though Adam would later learn she was eighty-two. Her speech was clear, loud, and cutting. She reminded him of a trainer he once knew who spoke about the bio-psycho-social-spiritual dimensions of life, and for a moment Adam wondered if they could be related. She wore an old grey cardigan that draped over a plain, dark skirt that reached her ankles—clothing rarely seen anymore. Everything about her felt as though it belonged to another era, even down to the small brown square shoes that caught Adam's eye, which he imagined had been crafted by a rustic woodland cobbler.

Adam smiled politely, telling her it was a pleasure to meet her. She immediately asked what he knew about her, but Adam found himself at a loss—he knew nothing at all. Tom quickly stepped in, explaining that Adam was considering becoming an Overseer and that he currently lived with an image carrier. Ethel's gaze did not move from Adam as she asked what level this image carrier ranked. Adam once again had no answer.

Turning away, Ethel drifted over to the window. With her back to them, she traced her fingers slowly down the heavy drapes.

"I will be leaving soon Tom. If your friend has any questions for me, now is the time."

"Yes, yes," Tom said, clearing his throat. He nodded at Adam to encourage him.

"About what?" Adam whispered, but Tom didn't reply. Leaning closer, Adam said softly, "It doesn't matter, Tom. Just let her go home."

But Ethel interrupted, her voice carrying from across the room. "The brighter your light, the longer you hold onto your memories," she declared, pausing before adding, "and the darker your light, the faster those memories fade." She turned back and walked over with her hands clasped behind her, stopping near Adam but refusing to sit. Standing over him, her piercing gaze fixed on his, she asked, "Do you understand what I mean, Mr. Adam?" Her tone was that of a strict teacher, and Adam felt like a reprimanded student.

He found himself recoiling. To him, she seemed blunt and unfriendly, with little sense of social courtesy. Unsure what to say, he simply shrugged, not wanting Tom to think less of him but equally unwilling to answer. It had been a long time since Adam had felt this tongue-tied.

Ethel let out a long, heavy sigh, still looming just a few feet from his chair.

"What about FAUNA?" she suddenly asked. "Surely you know FAUNA?" she added with sharp sarcasm.

Adam, flustered and wanting the questioning to stop, repeated back, 'FAUNA?'

"Yes, my boy, FAUNA!" she shot back without hesitation.

Adam looked over at Tom, suspecting some trick. But Tom looked down at his hands, unwilling to intervene.

"Do you mean Fauna as in Flora and Fauna?" Adam finally offered.

Ethel burst into a loud laugh that seemed to rattle the room. As she wobbled back toward the window, she mocked, "As in Flora and Fauna, he says! My God, Tom, this man knows nothing!" Tom sat frozen, saying nothing. To Adam's dismay, Tom seemed cowed by the old woman, unwilling to defend him. Adam felt his respect for his friend slipping, and a growing desire to leave took hold. It had been years since anyone had made him feel this small, this belittled.

"Are you FAUNA, my boy?" Ethel suddenly barked, raising her voice so it echoed through the room. She rubbed the curtain fabric between her fingers again, staring out at nothing. "Yes," she whispered, almost to herself. "I think you are FAUNA."

Adam looked over at Tom, silently conveying his displeasure, but Tom only gave him a weak smile before looking away again.

After a moment, Ethel wandered to a nearby cabinet, sliding her fingers down its glass door, before turning back toward Tom.

"I think you should train this Mr. Adam of yours," she announced. "He is terribly naïve about us." Then she returned to her seat, lifted her teacup, and sipped calmly, as though nothing had happened.

Tom scrambled for a response. "Adam is well-balanced," he insisted. "He knows much about people like us. We just haven't spoken yet about FAUNA." He tried to reassure Adam with a faint smile, though he hardly seemed convincing.

Adam sat in confusion, half hoping the cantankerous old woman might fly away on her broomstick. She asked about his work, then pressed him with more personal questions, which he answered tersely, disliking her more with every exchange. When she asked if he possessed psychic abilities and he admitted he did not, she broke into ear-piercing laughter that reminded him of the squawking cackle of the Australian kookaburra bird.

Once again, she set her cup down and drifted back to the window, her fingers finding the curtains as before. Adam couldn't help wondering what strange pull the window held for her.

After some very awkward moments, she finally explained more to Adam. FAUNA, she said, was not about animals or plants, but an acronym used among Image Carriers. It described those who lacked psychic sensitivity, insight, or mystical awareness—people bound by limitation, unable to access their Other Selves. These were the ones controlled by shadowy forces; blind followers used as pawns. Some posed as experts in corrupt positions, way out of their depth, and as always, these gullible people continue to miss the greater truth, blinded to the bigger and righteous picture. Such people, she said, were Useful Idiots—unwitting tools of hidden powers. Spiritually hollow, their inner spark dimmed, they blundered from one mistake to the next, disconnected from their true selves. Their physical lives carried on, but their Other Selves were lost and adrift, reducing them to mere FAUNA, empty shells in need of the hive just to survive.

Non-FAUNA, by contrast, were those who embraced their full being—body, mind, spirit, and electromagnetic field. They possessed common sense, clarity, and freedom, envied by the FAUNA groups who remained enslaved by manipulation and neuro-hacking. According to Ethel, many of these awakened individuals now sought one another out, living in hidden communities where they could support and protect each other from the controlled and sometimes violent FAUNA masses.

By this point, the tension in the room had shifted. Ethel's tone had softened, losing its earlier harshness.

Adam finally felt comfortable to speak. "I've never heard FAUNA described that way before," he admitted, "but I can see what you mean."

"I certainly hope so!" Ethel snapped, forcing Adam to shrink back into himself once more. "I explained everything to you in baby language!" she shrieked. He was baffled by how coarse she was and why she seemed determined to be unpleasant toward him. Without another word, Ethel turned back toward the chair in the corner, snatched up her shoulder bag, and announced to Tom that she was leaving. Tom made no attempt to persuade her otherwise, already aware that the meeting had run its course. "If you dislike someone, Adam, there's no need to harbour nasty thoughts about them," Ethel added as they exchanged farewells. She gave him the faintest of smiles before glancing at Tom. Adam was utterly bewildered by her remark.

As Tom opened the front door, Ethel paused, turned toward Adam, and lifted her dress slightly above her ankles, revealing a pair of square brown shoes. She peered down at them, shook her head, then laughed loudly as she walked out. What a strange and discourteous woman, Adam thought, and he wondered if she had somehow known about the cobbler remark he had kept to himself earlier.

Adam followed Tom back into the lounge. Once he was certain the old woman had truly gone, he quickly turned on Tom, demanding to know why he had been forced into meeting her. He also questioned Ethel's behaviour outright, asking Tom if she might suffer from some kind of mental illness. Tom apologised for putting him in such an awkward position, explaining that it was important for them to meet. He added that many in their circle were eccentric or had their peculiarities, but he had grown used to it. Image Carriers, he reminded Adam, came in all forms, as he had just witnessed.

"What was she even going on about—the brighter your light and the darker your light?" Adam asked, still looking perplexed. "And FAUNA—where the hell did that nonsense come from?"

"Settle down, Adam," Tom chuckled in his familiar manner. "She isn't that terrible; just blunt, old-fashioned, and different. But her heart's in the right place. She's also getting on now in her years."

Adam felt sheepish hearing Tom defend the woman, though he wasn't about to let his guard down.

"I think I've heard Julie use that word before," Adam admitted, taking a seat, clearly relieved that Ethel had left. "But I thought it was about wildlife or bushland. What does the word FAUNA really mean?"

"Let me think… I always have to stop and really think with these damned acronyms," Tom said, pausing. "That's it. F *is for Fake*, A *for Antagonist*, U *for Useless*, N *for Naïve*, and A *for Apathetic*."

"So fake, useless, and naïve people can't be psychic, and never will be?" Adam asked, more confused than ever.

"Don't take it too literally," Tom advised. "People burdened with those traits will struggle to set their psychic houses in order. To be truly intuitive, you need alignment with your real self, free of those qualities. FAUNA is just our shorthand for recognising such obstacles."

Adam sank comfortably into his chair, reflecting on Tom's words. He could understand the reasoning, but he also thought it wasn't something you could announce publicly without backlash. After all, even the fake and naïve have rights, he mused. And what of the useless and antagonistic? Surely, they did too. He giggled quietly to himself, recalling the earlier thought about Ethel's shoes, before pressing on with more questions, aware that time was running short.

"What about the levels Ethel mentioned?" Adam asked.

"Image Carriers are ranked on different levels—some more advanced than others," Tom explained.

"Like measuring their psychic powers?" Adam asked.

"Yes, though it's more complex than that. Some Image Carriers excel in one area but lack in another. Joey, for instance, shows incredible strength in certain abilities but not across the board. That's why the rating system exists, though some Image Carriers reject it and will not be a part of any rating system."

"But Madam Ethel is a special case," Adam said sarcastically, laughing to ease his tension. "I suppose she ranks highly?"

"She is one of the most gifted. She's seen much, guided us with countless predictions, and driven our group forward."

"So what would her rating be—compared to Joey, for example?"

"I couldn't say about Joey, but Ethel usually hovers around eight, sometimes nine. Most others in our circle sit around seven."

Adam then asked if Ethel could read minds, recalling her comment about the shoes. Tom laughed knowingly. "Ethel can do remarkable things, though she rarely explains them. She will just drop a line, and you will know she knows.”

Adam pressed further, asking why Tom insisted he meet her. Tom revealed that one of Ethel’s talents was reading electromagnetic fields, which allowed her to gauge a person’s self-awareness and their connection with their Other Self. Tom also wanted Adam to hear firsthand their knowledge about life after death, especially since it had been a hot topic at Adam’s barbecue a few weeks earlier.

“So that’s what she meant by the brighter your light, the longer you remember?” Adam asked.

“Exactly,” Tom said, though with a trace of embarrassment. He had expected the meeting to go far better than it had, though he also had unspoken motives for inviting her.

“So what does Ethel know about the after-death thing that you don’t?” Adam asked cautiously.

“Much of our information comes from her and others like her. Image Carriers often agree on the larger picture but vary on the details. I’ve got her records downstairs, along with accounts on the soul’s journey and life after death.”

“So, there really is a soul that moves on?” Adam leaned forward.

“Yes—a light force, consciousness, whatever you want to call it. After death, it leaves the body, retaining memory only briefly,” Tom explained. “Ethel, and other gifted people like her told us that the soul must remain bright with light. Anything that hinders its growth or betrays its purpose dims it, and once light is lost, it can’t be replaced.”

“Meaning bad things you do make your soul dimmer?”

“Not dimmer exactly. Think of it as patches in a puzzle—parts of the soul darkening while others still glow.”

"Isn't this in the Bible—sin darkens the soul?" Adam teased.

"Something like that," Tom sighed. "Most religions once held the truth, but over time their teachings were twisted and diluted, losing sight of the original story."

"Let me get this straight. The soul lives on briefly after death, either glowing bright or marked with dark patches?"

"Yes. The brighter the soul, the longer its memory after death, and the closer it draws to its Other Self. If it holds enough light, the soul can swiftly unite with its Other Self, escaping those traps I spoke about earlier and ascending toward a higher plane before reaching its ultimate destination. But those steeped in darkness, cut off from their Other Self, stumble through that realm in blind confusion. Even if they slip past the traps awaiting them, they will eventually be claimed by the lower levels."

Adam leaned back silently, taking it all in. It echoed religious tales from his childhood, though he still struggled with Tom's claim that there was no true life after death.

"I'm confused," Adam admitted. "You're saying there's no life after death, yet you're also saying the soul continues on. Isn't that proof we do live after we die?"

Tom slouched, awkward in his chair. "It doesn't matter. Once the soul leaves the dead body, it's over. We're gone. It will have no memory of us—it might as well be alien. That's not life after death."

"So, when you said the brighter the soul after death, the more it remembers, you meant just for a short while?"

"Yes. Seconds, maybe minutes—never hours or days."

"Okay. So, within those fleeting moments, the soul is aware of what's happening?" Adam asked, fiddling with his car keys.

"Exactly right. But don't forget—time here is not the same elsewhere. Once the soul joins its Other Self, all physical memory dissolves.

Adam now felt drained. He wondered if he would ever succeed as an Overseer, already having stumbled in his first meeting with a highly rated Image Carrier. He still had to read Evelyn and Veronica's accounts from South Africa, and now this heavy truth about death weighed on him. He couldn't help but think how the world would react if Tom's words were ever made public. So many still believed in Heaven, Hell, or some promise of existence beyond the grave.

It seemed that one's Other Self played a crucial role in preparing the soul for the passage into the afterlife.

Adam's mind stirred with yet another question for Tom, though he couldn't understand why he continued to torment himself with such thoughts.

"Doesn't this suggest that there must be memory, intelligence, or some higher plan at work—if souls' journey to such a place and seem to arrange themselves into levels? Like the bright ones rising to the higher realms while the dimmer, darker ones descend to the lower levels?"

"It could suggest that," Tom admitted, "but it's irrelevant. What we do know is that brighter, more advanced souls progress more quickly and ultimately end up in a higher place than the darker ones. Beyond that, we cannot know, for no memory remains and nothing exists that our Image Carriers can connect to. One of them once described it like a seed—falling, sprouting, growing, bearing fruit, and continuing the cycle. There is nothing spiritual about the process; it simply unfolds. Nature drives it. The same principle applies to what happens to our souls once we pass on."

The weight of the discussion gave Adam a dull headache, the intensity of the morning beginning to wear him down. Before departing, he shifted the subject.

"You have a beautiful home, Tom," Adam remarked. "Maintaining this property, travelling abroad, and meeting regularly with Image Carriers—it must require a great deal of money to keep such a life going?"

"I am an old man, Adam," Tom replied with a smile, as though anticipating the question. "I have worked all my life, and I have done well for myself. I also invested wisely."

Adam held back, certain that Tom had more to say. He was right.

"Besides," Tom added with a mischievous grin, "never forget that we have the privilege of having Image Carriers around us."

Feeling the pull of duty, Adam decided it was time to return to his office. The mystery of Ethel still baffled him, but he admitted she was important in some way, and he expressed regret to Tom for holding unkind thoughts about her earlier. He also mentioned his ongoing work with Evelyn and Veronica. Tom seemed delighted by this and assured Adam with confidence that he would one day make an excellent Overseer.

Adam left Tom's home feeling overwhelmed by unanswered questions. Back at his office, Carol briefed him on his clients' upcoming appointments and mentioned that the DS room was fully booked for the next three months. It was clear that another DS room would soon be necessary.

Meanwhile, Evelyn and Veronica continued exploring Sydney. Veronica was captivated by the Blue Mountains, that vast wilderness of steep ridges and valleys only a couple of hours from the city. She also fell in love with Sydney's coastlines and the striking beauty of its harbour. The idea of returning home felt unbearable, and she began considering staying on for another month or two.

That evening, Adam returned home and prepared dinner as was his habit. Joey, his young friend with the once-wild hair, had finally cleaned up his look, his hair neatly cropped short. He looked more handsome than ever, and his wide grin greeted Adam warmly as they slipped into their familiar evening routine. Joey, as always, had plenty to say.

Far away, in a large house nestled in Sydney's wealthy, leafy suburbs, an old man sat alone, looking silently at a black-and-white photograph of a woman named Patricia. She had been gone for many years. His fingers traced the glass frame as a tear welled and slipped down his cheek. Tom could feel it in his bones—something momentous was coming. Calls from Jennifer, Amanda, and other members of the group blinked across his answering machine, but he ignored them all. They, too, sensed what was drawing near. The only call he had taken earlier was from Ethel. She had cast her vote in Adam's favour, declaring him the right person for the monumental task ahead, and that the long search had finally ended. Tom smiled knowingly as he looked over the remaining secret ballots. Their responses satisfied him.

Yet Tom still wondered—was there any time left to stop this catastrophe? The release was close, a deception dressed as salvation, ready to ignite a chain of events no one could resist. Once unleashed, it would not simply spread; it would devour, sweeping across the globe with a force unlike anything humanity had ever seen before, dragging billions of unsuspecting souls into a place of no return.

Chapter Twenty-One
The United Show Begins

A sleeping experience like no other.

After decades of guarded experiments, researchers in Europe and America announced a revelation that rattled the foundations of belief itself. They had developed a medication that awakened a dormant region of the brain, one that allowed sleepers to glimpse their deceased relatives. The revelation ignited headlines across the globe, leaving many religious communities triumphant.

The breakthrough had been hidden behind layers of secrecy, perfected in shadowy laboratories, tested endlessly on volunteers sworn to silence. The patent was valued in the trillions, and for years the project was guarded as if it were a weapon. Now, at last, the long-guarded secret could be unveiled, and the exhausted scientists and financiers exhaled with relief.

The discovery had been accidental—an offshoot of attempts to treat depression, trauma, and sleep disorders. But a particular blend of compounds produced effects no one anticipated: it seemed to release something from the brain, perhaps the soul, some hidden spark, permitting it to wander into realms where the dead resided.

After countless trials, the drug was deemed ready, and within a year governments began authorising its release. Marketed as a sleeping aid, it was soon whispered about as something far greater: a passage into the afterlife. The tablet was branded *Cereus Sleeping*, named after the rare white flower that blooms only at night, its packaging declaring simply: *A sleeping experience like no other.*

The pill spread like wildfire. Some sought sleep, others sought reunion with their dead, and all found themselves drawn in. Advertising was scarcely necessary—yet opposition quickly arose. Critics warned of unnatural interference, of a trespass against the boundaries of life and death. To drown out their critics, the corporation unleashed a dazzling global campaign, astonishing audiences everywhere with its elegance, its reach, and its startling effectiveness.

The corporation behind Cereus Sleeping deliberately timed the unveiling of its extravagant, multi-million-dollar campaign for exactly 9 p.m., English time, using the moment as both a publicity stunt and a way to maximize attention. In the weeks leading up to the launch, they promised eager viewers that what they were about to witness would shatter every existing benchmark and deliver a spectacle unlike anything ever seen before.

But on the much-anticipated evening, not everything unfolded as smoothly as planned. A small but determined group of protesters, outraged at the pharmaceutical corporation behind the sleeping tablet, tried to sabotage the carefully orchestrated launch of Cereus Sleeping. Their chants and banners disrupted the glamorous atmosphere for only a brief moment before they were swiftly overpowered and escorted away by imposing security guards dressed in black. The disruption barely left a mark, and the spectacle pressed on. At precisely 9:07 p.m.—a mere seven minutes behind schedule—the screens of households across England lit up, making the country the first to witness the extravagant advertising campaign tailored exclusively for Cereus Sleeping. They were introduced to a dazzling computer-generated woman, an animation so sophisticated she appeared almost alive. She captivated audiences with her flawless, luminous dark-brown skin, striking sky-blue eyes that seemed to pierce through the glass, and a chic hairstyle that transformed subtly depending on her mood, or even on the cultural backdrop of whichever country's broadcast she appeared in. Viewers sat spellbound, entranced by her presence, as if some new kind of icon had just been born.

They named her Lucy. And soon, Lucy was worshipped. Children begged for dolls in her likeness, young people inked her name into their skin, and her face became a global icon. Songs, prayers, and fashions revolved around her image. For billions, Lucy was more than a marketing creation—she was proof that the gateway to heaven was real.

But soon cracks appeared. Users found they could not truly converse with their dead; they could only watch, as if through a glass wall. Scientists insisted they were not gods—that the living could not enter the afterlife, only witness it. For many, the thrill of reunion curdled into frustration. They demanded more than sight—they wanted voices, answers, touch.

Then something remarkable occurred: rumours began circulating that certain individuals had crossed over and managed to come back with accounts of their journeys. These people insisted they had passed through a spiritual doorway during sleep, stepping into the sacred dwelling of the departed and engaged face-to-face with lost relatives, companions and even their pets. No longer were they confined to looking in from a distance; instead, they were entering fully and meeting the dead directly.

Suddenly media outlets began parading guests who swore they embraced lost lovers, spoke with deceased parents, or shared secret knowledge. One woman in particular electrified millions by declaring she had reunited with her late husband and mother, while on a popular day time television show, describing it as more vivid than waking life. The audience wept and cheered, clutching free boxes of sleeping tablets handed out on stage.

Yet the sense of hope and joy was short-lived. Disturbingly, those same media outlets soon began reporting on a surge of overdoses linked to Cereus Sleeping tablets. Then more people were found dead, with lengthy suicide letters apologising to their live loved ones; a month later, many more people were discovered dead in their apartments and homes. Soon, an epidemic erupted, with hundreds of thousands of people committing prescription suicide. Many people left notes stating that it was much better on the other side. Many more placed messages on their webpages and online, claiming that they were better off with their deceased loved ones. Life had become too difficult, too ugly for them; they were better off in the afterlife. The living were abandoning life for dreamlike death in numbers no system could contain.

The most recent estimates claim that nearly four billion souls have already chosen to cross over, vanishing willingly into the unknown. Cities grow hollow, nations crumble, the earth itself feels abandoned. The question still lingers, tormenting those left behind: have the departed genuinely found their lost loved ones, or have they succumbed to the greatest deception in human history, ending their own lives for a mirage of the afterlife that Image Carriers have long dismissed as nothing more than fiction?

Thank you for reading this book.

A few Image Carriers wanted me to include a final Chapter about Common Sense.

See next page for details.

Chapter Twenty-Two
Common Sense

What happens when an expert's field becomes obsolete or irrelevant...

What is an Expert?

As the old adage goes, 'experts' don't always seem to have much common sense. But is this truly accurate? In contemporary thinking, it is often suggested that to become an expert, one must surrender common sense and intuition, as if the two cannot coexist. The implication is clear: the more knowledge you accumulate in a specialized field, the further you drift from practical judgment. If this is the case, then gaining authority in any subject may require forfeiting one of humanity's most basic survival tools: common sense.

But what of the origins of expertise? Is an expert made or born? Nature versus nurture—can mastery be cultivated through training and experience, or does it require preexisting physiological and psychological wiring? In other words, do those who lack common sense by birth tend to gravitate toward technical or intellectual fields, ultimately producing lives constrained by a narrow focus, devoid of philosophical reflection, mystical insight, or the rich tapestry of other human experiences?

Human development has always hinged on the principle of survival of the fittest. This natural law has governed life for millions of years, if not longer. Were experts present in ancient times? If expertise were a genetic phenomenon, handed down to a few gifted individuals, would these 'experts' have survived in early human communities? Likely not—without practical instincts and the fundamental common sense essential for daily survival, they would have perished. Common sense, in this view, is not merely practical; it is evolutionary.

Are modern humans perhaps moving in the wrong direction? Have we overemphasized the value of hyper-specialization, elevating narrow expertise over holistic understanding? Being an authority in a single area does not equip one with survival skills or a broad perspective. Common sense functions as a kind of cognitive glue, integrating numerous facets of thought, emotion, and experience. Human beings are complex, multifaceted creatures. Focusing entirely on a single discipline risks alienating us from the diverse qualities and natural inclinations that define our lives. In some ways, each person carries within them an esoteric state, a connection to the larger collective field of consciousness. Sacrificing these essential qualities to become an expert is not merely self-limiting—it diminishes the full expression of one's being. Narrow-minded expertise can capture only a fragment of life's totality, leaving the so-called expert perpetually behind, always chasing the richness of reality that they have forsaken.

And keep in mind, the role of an expert is usually transient, short term. What happens when an expert's field becomes obsolete or irrelevant? In such cases, it is often those grounded in common sense—family members, friends, or community—who provide support and continuity for the displaced expert. Expertise, it seems, cannot thrive in isolation from practical wisdom and human connection. You will often find someone with commonsense behind the scenes guiding, if not protecting the so-called expert.

I have been particularly disturbed when reviewing the backgrounds of some self-proclaimed experts: the lives they have led and the destruction they have sometimes left in their wake. Many operate in a narrow, self-contained worldview, oblivious to opposing perspectives. Investigations reveal a recurring pattern: some were born with flawed genetic predispositions, which they may pass down through generations. The result is often a cohort of individuals limited in creativity, adaptability, and emotional depth. Such people can inadvertently—or deliberately—damage their communities, mismanage resources, and exploit others, all while clinging to a false sense of authority or superiority. At their worst, these individuals appear emotionally sterile, lacking empathy, self-absorbed, deceptive, and disjointed from the multidimensional reality of human life. Those attuned to common sense can often perceive this conflicted energy, and it is far from a comforting experience.

Could it be, then, that the modern expert is a relic of a bygone era, ill-suited for the dynamic and interconnected world we now inhabit? When true adversity arises, it is often the overly specialized, narrowly focused expert who falters first, unable to navigate the demands of real life.

In conclusion, while knowledge and specialization have their place, the wisdom of common sense remains indispensable. Expertise without grounding is fragile, incomplete, and, ultimately, destructive. Those who ignore this, risk losing not only their relevance but the essence of what it means to be fully human.